SPACE LAWYER

by
Kirk Battle

Please check out my website for news and musings at www.kirkbattle.com
Cover Art by Andre Pope

Copyright © 2013 Kirk Battle
All rights reserved.
ISBN: 1482321084
ISBN 13: 9781482321081
Library of Congress Control Number: 2013908693
CreateSpace Independent Publishing Platform, North Charleston, SC

DEDICATION

For my parents, who made this possible in so many ways,

SPECIAL THANKS

This book would not have been possible without people willing to read the many rough drafts in their spare time and give feedback. Thanks go out to Buzz Country, Molly Wafle, Gerry Wallace, Margaret McCall, Nora Hembree Battle, Brooker Battle, Alex Murray, Sanford Stone, Jeff Slomba, Jeff's Mom, and Heather McLean.

HORSE = ◯

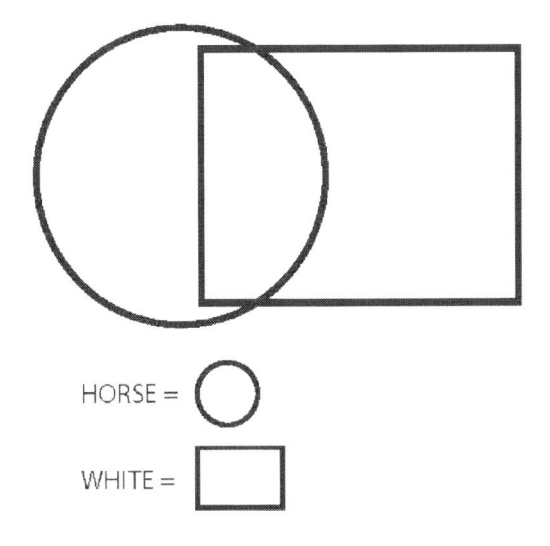

WHITE = ▭

"Horse" is that by means of which one names the shape. "White" is that by means of which one names the color. What names the color is not what names the shape. Hence, I say that a white horse is not a horse.
—Gongsun Long

CHAPTER 1

"You never stopped and wondered about the consequences?" asked the CEO. She was speaking to the woman directly behind her, who was unsure if a rhetorical question was being posed. She received her answer when the CEO continued speaking.

"We control the largest gate system in developed space. I've got unpiloted shuttles flying out to God knows where to set up gates into every reach of the galaxy. This business...this *family* consists of over one million employees," she continued. A tall woman with long black hair, dressed in simple white pants and top, turned to face the scientist. "Why were you even building such a device?"

Compared to the CEO, who stood over six feet tall, the woman was small. This notorious employee from Research and Development could be entirely swallowed in the other woman's shadow. Tally's hands were nervously at her side, her eyes darting from the CEO's angular face to the window looking out to the infinite number of stars behind her. Outside, there was outer space and silence. Framing the stars was the grey steel of the Gateway Central Processing Station's walls. She vaguely wished she were there instead of in this impossibly cold room.

"I never really expected it to work," Tally replied. "I mean, I never expected it to work this well."

The CEO sat down at her desk, removed her pad, and opened the file of the project. Elaborate equations and diagrams went on for thousands of lines, their ultimate meaning summarized by the single bold, highlighted text that said, "seeks to develop a method for the transmission of non-organic matter over varying ranges."

"How well does it work?"

"At first we were just sending molecules across the lab. Then bigger things: metals, complex chemical structures, gases. We were having good results with stability, but it never occurred to us to start pushing the ranges—"

"Liquids?" the CEO interrupted.

"Yes," Tally answered. "But that's logical if we can do the other stuff. What surprised us was how easy it was to maintain integrity over large ranges. The reason it took so long to report this was just the delays in getting test results. We had to keep finding a ship to go out and see if the object was intact. Now that we're able to maintain complex circuitry, we can start sending beacons out—"

"No," the CEO said curtly. She had read the report and already knew all of these details. Already knew that Tally had accidentally stumbled upon an invention that could unravel the very company that had paid her to invent it. The whole thing had been done with a minimal budget and barely attracted any notice simply because it was so far-fetched. She knew that it hadn't yet successfully transmitted organic matter, but it was only a matter of time.

"I understand there are complications, but…why not just announce it? Gateway could be the producer of a faster-than-light drive. How is there no profit in this?" Tally asked.

"Tally, it's important that you understand what's going to be happening next." The CEO was speaking softer now, as though an adult to a child. "Change is complicated. Our biggest revenue source is ships traveling through the gate system. I have over one million employees, and most of them are paid to maintain, oversee, and improve on gateway travel. Our customers are even more numerous, and their mining operations entirely depend on the system built around us. What do you propose they do when a device comes out that will render them obsolete in minutes? What will happen to the market when there are no more costs to obtain goods from far away?" The CEO was working herself up now, her tone shifting again to something that made Tally confused. She almost made it sound as if the invention was a bad idea. The CEO was back at her pad, pressing the screen rapidly and manipulating the interface with practiced dexterity.

"So…what are you doing now?" Tally asked.

"Calling my lawyer."

CHAPTER 2

"What realities do you like to hang out in?"

The miner was silent as he gazed at the attorney across the table. He had big, ropey arms and pale skin from spending months prying apart machinery in zero gravity as it hacked asteroids apart. He wore a blue post-surgery sleeve on his right leg that completely covered his green slacks. He looked over at his lawyer for help, but she shook her head. He was allowed to get help only from the man across from him.

"Realities. It's a technical term for what you watch, read, or listen to. What things affect your perceptions. What you do and what you don't do. I have to ask because your online records are so scarce. Normally I can get a pretty complete picture of what reality you participate in from seeing those, but you don't spend much time online."

They were sitting in a small office of wood and cracked white paint. At the table were four people. The miner and two lawyers sat facing one another while off to one side a fourth person watched. She was recording the exchange on camera and tapping keys to create keyword markers in the recording.

"Not much time for that. Where I work, you can't go online much anyways," the miner said in a flat drawl. Lane understood that his discomfort probably came just as much from having another man ask him the question as it did from his lack of an answer. They were the only two men in the room, though they could not have looked more different.

Lane struggled to think of what else he could ask the miner to get him to understand. He leaned back in his chair and stared off into space to think, his brown eyes looking for a spot to settle in the room where nothing in particular resided. He was not nearly as big as the large man across from him. Their difference in size was almost comical, like two species that had parted ways a long time ago on the evolutionary ladder. Lane wore a neat suit, tailored to fit him, while the other wore baggy clothes that were meant to be worn in zero gravity. There was an ashy layer of dust from the years of space mining the clothes had endured.

"Do you take any substances? Alcohol or gas?" Lane asked.

"Well. You know, out on the rock, you come off work and you're just worn out. So we might huff some fumes, yeah. I don't drink much. Maybe smoke here and there," the miner explained. Lane kept his face blank, but inside he was relieved. After an hour of questions, this was the first thing the two men had in common, and it was only a fondness for drink.

"And what do you do while you're huffing or anything else? Where do you do it?" Lane said in a flat, positive tone.

"Round the bar. Talk to other guys," the miner said.

"They got music playing? Screens going with shows?" Lane asked.

"I guess, yeah. Sure, OK, sometimes I watch those. Does that count as reality?" The miner was becoming irritable. He had already explained the accident, his family, friends, witnesses, operating procedures, and stuff he probably hadn't thought about in years to this strange little man in front of him. The miner acted as if Lane were alien, as if he wasn't sure whom he should be speaking to despite what he had been told countless times over—undoubtedly due to the rarity of a male lawyer on Earth.

"Absolutely, yes, that's a reality. Thank you," Lane answered. He could secure the records to the bar on the mine with minimal fuss. And then he'd at least be able to start painting a picture of the man in front of him. And more importantly, paint it for other people.

The case was a mining accident, and Lane was representing the mining company. Zero gravity, asteroids, machines, and human beings were a dangerous combination. The company's name was something in Arabic that had a vowel he could never quite get right. He had been working for McAngus & Lee for over three years, yet here he was still doing mining accidents. They were the sort of cases that were beneath a space lawyer.

That was how Lane's reality defined the term anyways. He had begun to realize that the job had a lot more sitting at a desk on Earth sorting out petty problems than actually going on grand adventures in space. He was beginning to wonder if it was time for the phrase to be repurposed to a better meaning.

After the deposition, Lane stepped outside to the smell of Market Street: a combination of heated concrete, sea breeze, and horse piss. The city of Charleston maintained the Southeastern tradition of being simultaneously backward and forward thinking at the same time. Wooden and brick buildings sat along the streets while a few blocks away, skyscrapers of luminous black steel loomed. He checked his pad for messages and voicemails but looked up at the sound of clomping hooves. A horse carriage carried a load of tourists down the street while the guide explained a distant past that anyone could read or hear with the tap of a finger. They were there for the novelty of the speaker herself as much as the tour.

"Fancy a drink? I just got out of my depo. Tohickon?" he tapped onto the screen. Lane selected a few faces from his list of contacts and linked them to the message. He began walking down the street. He passed rows of stalls selling jewelry, grass baskets, second-hand electronics, and whatever else the licensed vendors could make for themselves. The crowd moved in a stop-and-start motion, the non-Standard clothing catching their eyes with the huge variety of colors and shapes. It was early summer, and Charleston's Market was in full swing.

The street held mostly women, dressed in exotic clothes and parading their attire for everyone to see. In Charleston, dressing well was a competitive sport. Men could be seen here and there, over on the corner alongside the bus route or running street carts for Standard goods. They all wore Standard clothes, were often in need of a shower, and looked worlds apart from the women who walked by without notice in their exotic outfits. Lane, dressed in his own tailored suit, avoided the men's gazes as he moved up the street to another junction and turned.

Lane crossed onto King Street as the sky turned bright pink with the setting sun, and he passed ancient buildings of cracked red and green plaster intermixed with a futuristic landscape of interstellar steel. The

Tohickon Bar was the emptiest bar on the street that still served on a Standard tab. Everywhere else, Lane would claim, was a tourist trap. And cost actual money.

To get to the Tohickon, you had to walk down an alley that looked as if it would be the last one you would ever enter. Wedged between black asteroid and ancient brick, the place had a smell that made the horse carriages outside seem appealing. Going up a flight of rickety, rusted stairs at the far end would take you into an old bar where the smell was fiercely traditional: beer, whiskey, and something you could never quite figure out. It reminded Lane of the dorm he grew up in and sometimes the one he had briefly resided in before taking his Space Law entry exams.

Lane sat down and ordered a whiskey, his information already on file with the bartender. Lane pulled out his pad and started checking the news. He began to think about changing realities as he activated his news feed. Stories on miners' rights, men's support groups, and space economic news flowed by in an endless stream. Lately the feed had been telling him things he didn't want to hear. One article announced that the Census Bureau's latest statistics put the population of men on the planet at 37 percent. In the asteroids and off-planet, it was at seventy-three percent. He flagged the article to be filtered out. He set the feed to show him topics to talk about with women, the latest scandals in the Southeastern matriarchy, or any news on the space economy.

His feed changed, and he scanned it for new topics. They had invented a new kind of potato that could grow in extremely dry climates. There was a new video of an electronic bear dancing. Had he considered joining a fathering group for needy boys?

Lane was tinkering on his pad when Tricia walked into the Tohickon. She was tall and graceful, a well-dressed woman whose instinct was to smile and worry about the rest later. Lane had known her for years in a variety of contexts. Lately he had taken to thinking of her as a sister, but it had not always been that way. She worked in data.

"What brings you downtown?" she asked, already knowing the answer but making conversation for its own sake.

"A deposition. I wanted to interview this one," Lane answered. He pulled his chair out so they could face each other at the bar. The chair rattled, and several faces turned at the noise. Most people were sitting side by side, focused on their pads as they swapped the occasional word over drinks and data feeds.

"Aren't those a bit of a waste? The last popular vote I had to do, they didn't even bother." Tricia sat down and smiled at the woman pouring drinks. She was referring to the fact that the mining accident, along with everyone involved, would have been recorded. What wasn't recorded would have been in the sensor information, finance sheets, and in-depth market analysis. People didn't really pay much attention to witnesses during a popular vote.

"Even if space lawyer doesn't mean being in a grand space opera anymore, I can still pretend. I like to talk to them. See how they think, what they want. Real work, real lawyering where you talk to people and work out problems. It makes me feel…" Lane found himself at a loss for what he was trying to describe. "Like a real space lawyer."

Tricia nodded and pulled out her pad. She tapped it to clear Lane's message and her personal note to come to the Tohickon. "I'm sure it's a lot more meaningful than when you just read the reports," Tricia said. "I would love to be able to meet some of the people I read about all day at the data center. I can read every single thing they have ever said online. An individual produces millions of words in their lifetime, and at the end of the day, you still want to know what they're *really* thinking about."

"You and that engineer still fighting?" Lane asked. Tricia crossed her eyes to show her frustration as she took a sip from her drink. This was her favorite thing to complain about, and Lane decided to be a sport about asking.

"She still keeps insisting on framing the data as if everyone were obsessed with politics all the time. She even changed a file back after I told her to switch it out!" Tricia was laying the foundations for a full rant.

A beep from Lane's pad told him he had a high-priority message. Out of courtesy Tricia paused and took another sip from her drink. Lane opened the pad and scanned the message. A puzzled look crossed his face. "Weird. One of my clients has gone missing," he said.

"Oh? Blocking you from her updates?" Tricia asked.

"No. As in physically missing. That was a message from the court saying they weren't getting updates from her," Lane answered with a touch of worry. He did a search and brought her name up on his pad. Another check showed him what she had last posted and commented on. They were five days old.

"Why is a court following her around?"

"Because she is appealing an AI decision. They were doing another screen of her lifestyle to see how much variation developed," Lane said as he kept checking the information. The client's name was Tally, and she was one of the first big cases he had been assigned at the firm. Submitting a lawsuit to an AI was something any civilian could do. Challenging a decision, however, required an extraordinary amount of legal expertise. Lane swore and put his pad away again. He had been working diligently on tracking the AI's processes in the case but had neglected the actual facts up to this point. They rarely mattered in an AI decision.

"Oh, so you need to prove that the AI got it wrong?" Tricia was a little annoyed to have her rant about the engineer cut short.

"It's more to prove that the wrong question was asked. The AI is compiling all the millions of lawsuit rulings with her specific facts, and then it compiles all the millions of versions of those facts, and it—"

"It rules on the case. I've sued people too, Lane. You just fill out the forms, and pop! There's the answer," Tricia said.

Lane was quiet as he tried to think of how to explain the idea to her. "Think of it like…how that woman at your job always makes everything about politics when she sees data. An AI is usually right about a culture, but sometimes it's wrong about an individual. To prove that, you need to make a convincing argument that these are unusual circumstances," Lane said.

"What was unusual about her case?"

"Nothing really. Suing over defamation. The client and another woman got into a fight over some software and a flame war started. She screwed up by not just going before the popular vote. People should know to not use an AI for personal stuff. It's there for business, zoning, government things. For some reason she didn't want it to be public," Lane explained.

Tricia shrugged and resumed talking about work. Lane only half listened. He was already dreading having to go back to McAngus and explain this one. Or what the other attorneys would think when they found out his first appeal was getting cut short on a technicality. The head of the firm herself had given him the file. He might even get dropped from the case. His stomach turned a bit just thinking about it.

"What about you? How's work?" Tricia asked.

"Oh, you know. I'm glad I'm not doing data review anymore. Still not any closer to becoming a full space lawyer. The other attorneys still treat me like shit, but most are kind enough to not do it to my face. The one awful witch still bullies me, but the office is mostly women, so I can't deal with it directly. Pecking order and all that." Lane sighed and finished his drink as he thought about Kayla. She wouldn't be able to resist asking him about the Tally appeal once the rumor spread.

"And how would a man deal with it?" Tricia asked.

"I'd call her a giant bitch and tell her to never speak to me again. Maybe punch her. Then she would go bother someone who doesn't fight back," Lane answered with a half-grin.

"That doesn't really seem like it would solve the problem," she said.

"You're right. She would keep bothering me. But at least I'd feel better." Lane sighed. He checked his drink rations on the pad and saw that he wouldn't be able to order another drink without going over his health limit.

Tricia let his vulgar comment slide. She knew Lane was having a hard time with work, and she was glad he was at least talking about it. Most of the time, he just got quiet when he was upset. It did worry her to hear a man talk like this. She trusted Lane, but she still had stories crop up in her feed about the violence men were capable of. They were hard to filter out sometimes.

"Who was the woman suing? The one who appealed?" Tricia asked to change the subject.

"Ha. That's the craziest part. She was suing Gateway Incorporated."

CHAPTER 3

Lane boarded the bus and felt his pad vibrate to confirm his Standard pass. It was a nice bus, a newer model than the old diesels. Good air conditioning to keep out the humidity and plenty of seat room. Lane had read that it had some sort of hybrid power system, but the details had gone over his head—following tech news was always a slow, dull affair.

The bus announced its next stop before Lane even took his seat. It was later in the evening, so he had missed the commuter crowds heading home. His fellow passengers gazed at their pads or out the window, and a few conversations rumbled alongside the quiet engines. The bus pulled onto Calhoun Street and steadily picked up speed. There were no private cars on the road or highway. The vehicle gained speed as its sensors tapped into the data grid and identified any possible accidents in advance.

Lane brought up Tally's file and began reviewing everything he could find. Up until this point he had been ignoring the facts of the case—they wouldn't matter much in an AI appeal. Lane opened the last file to be read and saw that it had held his spot where he was checking the computer's language breakdown. The word "pet" had been contrasted with over four million accepted applications of the word in prior AI cases. Lane had been retracing this process and looking for a moment where the system had gotten off track.

It was over a flash mob. A nasty one, judging by the numbers. An aliased user had posted a horrific story about someone running over her pet cat. The first page of the file showed the cat smiling up at the camera. It was cute.

The bus lumbered onto the main highway and picked up speed toward North Charleston.

The aliased user claimed that Lane's client had been involved with making a program. She would produce the art assets, and Lane's client, Tally, would be responsible for programming. Disputes about the project had arisen, and all the assets had been locked up in the group file. After more arguing, they decided to meet in person to work out some of the details. They got into a pretty heated fight at the artist's house, and when Tally left, she ran over the cat with her car. The dispute was never resolved and a lawsuit had been filed by Tally.

It was a strong frame. It didn't surprise Lane that a flash mob had formed around it. It had over twenty thousand comments, two hundred and forty-seven linkbacks, and one hundred and eighty-seven reposts within forty-eight hours of going live. Just reading the article fired off his nerves and made him want to do something. A picture of a doomed cat coupled with this idea of a cruel programmer taking advantage of the situation. The car was a nice touch because only the rich owned cars anymore. It subtly insinuated that the programmer didn't even need the money with all her traveling and excess. And here she was, taking advantage of this poor artist demanding she take less money and work more. It was almost too perfect a story to start a mob, which Lane made a note of on the pad.

And then things went predictably. The mob bombed Tally's accounts. Amateur hackers switched her reality into an ugly rape apologist filter and deluged her with calls screaming at her. Crude photos of her were scattered across the web. The whole thing lasted about twenty-four hours. Her defense to all this, Lane noticed, was that the entire thing was a fabrication. She had lost her original lawsuit and was appealing for the rights to the program they had made.

Lane sighed and skimmed over her long, angry rant about the mob. A lot of it was leveled at the culture grid and how crazy people were today. She threatened to just quit the entire thing forever. As far as Lane was concerned, it didn't matter if the cat was never run over or the deal never went sour. With so many people filtering the event through so many different realities, many of them weren't even being malicious consciously.

But the notion that it was all a fake wasn't unheard of. You could generate a knee-jerk story that upset people with a bit of skill. It took a lot of luck for it to catch anyone's interest, and then a lot more luck to see it spread to a large enough group to cause any trouble. One person's pad would say a cat got run over, another's would say a business deal had gone sour, another would be focusing on the car. Virtual entrepreneurs had been trying to replicate it for years, but no one had ever reported reliable results.

What made the case weird was her insistence on using an AI instead of the popular vote to sue Gateway. She claimed the artist was a Gateway employee and that they were responsible for the whole thing. Lane had no idea what that was about; he had been so happy to get an advanced lawsuit that he hadn't concerned himself with the details. The only real chance you would have to win against a free market business was through the popular vote. People were capable of believing anything.

Gateway had rattled off a long string of defenses and immunities that automatically applied to the case. You can't sue a corporation for the conduct of one employee. You can't sue a corporation for a transaction they weren't directly involved in. You can't really sue a corporation, period.

The thing that made Gateway's behavior puzzling was that they'd actually broken out of the automatic responses and plugged in something human. That was just a guess on Lane's part, but it was an unusually extensive brief they'd prepared—a complete record of all transactions with content creators in this area and profile stamps to prove it was accurate. What was the point of responding to such an absurd appeal?

Lane put the pad away as the bus came up to his stop. He shuffled off with the few remaining passengers. The streetlights shone orange, but up the street, it grew darker on the walk to his apartment. There were no black steel buildings here, only the crumbling decay of the public common structures and Standard maintenance.

The appeal bothered him. The AI had determined the evidence showed no connection between the two parties and ruled against Tally. If a crazy person wanted to give her money to a firm and let Lane bill to parse through millions of lines of computer records, that was one thing. But now this crazy person had gone missing.

Lane lived in a renovated warehouse that was now a dorm for young people working an apprenticeship. In most facilities you would have to share a room, but Lane was willing to pay extra for some privacy in a tight space. He also ate and drank nothing but Standard goods to save money. As he walked up to the entrance, two women dressed in jeans and collared shirts grew quiet at the sight of him. Once he cleared the shadows, they recognized him, waved, and resumed their conversation. He had checked their profiles when he moved in and saw that they were not interested in men. Lane sighed and headed to his apartment, where he settled into bed with his pad to review the file.

CHAPTER 4

Lane chewed on a Standard breakfast bar as he walked up to the offices of McAngus & Lee. It was a short, two-story building that presented the founders' names in large, gold letters. If the sun was on them just right, it would hurt your eyes. It was nice on the inside, with leather couches, an air conditioning system set to max, and framed photos of Charleston over the centuries, from the 1800s to the boom, decline, and then subsequent boom of the area. The layers of wealth and poverty built onto one another appeared in everything about the city.

He headed straight for his desk and plugged his pad into the larger monitor. Lane's assignments usually came from Kayla, the senior attorney at the firm who was charged with overseeing the apprentice lawyers. She was next in line to be given a license to participate in the free market. He got assignments from her and guessed how to do them. If he did it wrong, he got yelled at. If he did it right, sometimes Kayla yelled anyways.

The appeal file came from Koff's office upstairs. Lane wasn't sure why it had been assigned to him. Kayla was constantly finding errors in his files and pointing them out. The fact that she did this at the last possible minute because she just didn't have time only made these "training sessions" all the more unpleasant. Kayla somehow always had the time to explain his mistakes. Loudly and with questions based on the frame he had done it on purpose.

A few of the cubicles were still empty, but they would be full before 9:00 a.m. Over to his left was Sally, who spent most mornings staring into her coffee cup before rousing herself just before the computer recorded her inactivity into her metrics. Lane was never really quite sure what to make of her, but she was always polite. Sally tended to eat her lunch in the break room, so you could talk to her in passing. She kept a narrow reality and generally didn't respond well to things outside of it.

In front of him was Grace, who was the closest thing to a friend in the office. She was pretty; Lane had always been a fan of her in a business suit. He flirted with her and she flirted back, but only inside the office. The one time they had tried talking to each other outside the law firm had been an awkward, disjointed exchange of "have to goes" and "maybe some other time." Her public metrics showed she was more interested in work than paying the time it took to date.

Behind Lane was Derrick, who was the only other man working at this branch. When he had first arrived, there had been an awkward sort of expectation that the two of them should bond. Derrick was married and didn't quite seem to know what he was supposed to do with other women anymore. Sally would tell them they could talk about man things around her and she wouldn't mind, and then stay in the room and see if they said anything that fit her reality. Grace was constantly rolling her eyes at him when he brought up marriage. Kayla just put them together on assignments and went back to her office. Once she was out of hearing range, Derrick and Lane would divide up the work and go back to sitting in silence.

Lane just found him to be boring. That sort of unbreachable wall of boring that only a person at work can be. If it wasn't talking about what his wife said the other day, it was the latest thing he had read in his video game groups. He was always trying to get Lane to come out to one of their meetings, but Lane had always been scared it would just be a room full of Derricks—men talking about their virtual lives and the strange things they do to feel better.

The clock chimed nine, and there was just the slightest clatter as people got to work. Lane was preparing almost a dozen defense files for popular vote. He would carefully arrange the videos, recordings, and background information to frame his own version of the case. Most of them were mining accidents, with one really interesting cargo incident for which Lane had gotten to research how shipping robots work. And the one file labeled "appeal" in red text.

Part of Lane's slow progress had simply been that he didn't know what he was doing precisely. He had taken classes on it. He had studied the lines of code that allowed lawyers to save entire corporations or prevent billions in lost assets. Bugs in the AI were rare, but the people who found them were even rarer. It was Lane's first file that wasn't from Kayla, and he had allowed some tiny part of him to hope that it would give him a shot at making space lawyer. The real kind, that could take off from Earth whenever they liked, not what it meant to him now.

Lane tried to keep the message he drafted to Koff as brief as possible. The AI that had been tracking the client's new data set to determine her orientation in the system could no longer find her. It wasn't particularly clear why it had taken this long for anyone to provide notice. He had not been in contact with Gateway or Tally. In a few more weeks, the case would be subject to dismissal. And then Lane's only chance to escape space mining injury suits would vanish. He deleted that last part and sent the e-mail.

It took about five minutes for Kayla to demand he come to her office. Loudly, so that everyone on the floor could hear. That was the thing that irritated Lane. It wasn't the abuse. It wasn't being dismissed like an imbecile or having every single mistake he made turn into a drama bomb. It was how much more efficiently it would work if she would just properly train him. Even if he brought the problem to her, she would just ignore it until it became a full-blown crisis.

Lane took a deep breath and began the long walk. After three years at McAngus, he was familiar with all the feelings that came over him. That sad smile Grace would give him made him feel a bit of hope that she might be sympathetic later. The neutral look on Sally's face made him wonder about his apprenticeship security. Derrick emitted some unintelligible noise before going back to what he was doing. It was all a part of the ritual. He entered Kayla's office and closed the door behind him without asking.

Kayla's office was sparse. A wooden desk sat in the center, with a large computer sitting on the far end. There were four monitors attached to it, each one looking at a different file or following the progress of a voting session on the Internet. Comments ticked by as the various people who had been drafted to vote reviewed all the materials and added their own thoughts about what had happened. The computer automatically marked red ones that were negative to their case for later review. On the desk was a pad and a glass bowl that contained little glass bulbs made to look like candy.

"I've just read your message to Koff. How…how do you lose a client?" Kayla asked.

"I don't know. Everything was going fine with the new data set, so I was focusing on parsing the computer's decision process," Lane said quietly. He had been through so many of these sessions that his physical response was almost automatic. He tried to appear relaxed and just answer with as little emotion as possible, but inside his stomach was tying itself into knots.

"Lane, the client has been missing for five days. Six counting today. You didn't think to stop and check the one appeal you have at least once in the past five days?" Kayla asked back icily. It was almost a contest to see who would let his or her voice break into anger first. Whether it was arranging the videos improperly, typos, filing errors, deadline errors, it was always something.

"It was a six-month data set, and I'm preparing over a dozen other popular vote files," Lane answered.

"Lane, what were you planning to do once the reality was ready? You have to know the reality you're contrasting to the computer's version before you can assess any errors. It's a waste of time to check it beforehand."

Lane felt his grip on the calm exterior slipping. He wanted to point out that he had only spent a few hours on it just to get a general idea of what was going on. Or point out that it would be six months before the reality set was complete, so he might as well get familiar with it. Since she hadn't asked anything that wasn't a barely disguised insult, Lane stared at the desk and waited it out.

"How many times have I told you to talk to me about this? To ask me for help?" Kayla added. Lane briefly had the impulse to tell her that he'd rather eat the entire jar of glass candy than ask her for anything, but stopped himself.

"I sent you a message last month asking for advice on handling an appeal because this is my first time ever doing one." Lane answered. Kayla's eyes narrowed, and she gave her keyboard a few taps to check. "And actually a second one two weeks ago. To ask if there was anything else I should be doing on the file. Maybe if you answered my messages, you would have better results?"

It was a low blow. Lane knew Kayla was juggling way beyond her caseload, although he considered that her own fault. She had been desperate to make space lawyer lately. Lane's only goal with this and every other exchange he had with Kayla was to improve the chances that she would never call him into her office again. If he could get to a point where Kayla refused to speak to him, Lane would maybe begin to enjoy being an apprentice.

"Lane, I cannot hold your hand for every single file. Do you even want to be a space lawyer? Is there some reason you can't do the most basic, simple assignments without messing everything up?" She was mad now. Lane would have to savor that as some kind of victory because for some reason, she was a lot angrier than normal. This was going to be nasty.

"Enough. Both of you," said a voice from Kayla's pad. "I see your point, Kayla. Lane, this is Koff. Come up to my office immediately. Bring your pad." Kayla gave Lane one last glare as he popped out of his seat and headed for the door. If Koff had heard that entire conversation, he was in bigger trouble than a shouting lecture from Kayla.

As he walked back to his desk to retrieve his pad, Lane's mind was racing. Was he fired? Would Koff pull him off the appeal? How much of their exchange had she heard? Lane had met Koff only a handful of times at law firm events. She was known for being dry and out of the office as much as possible. As far as Lane knew, she was putting in her last few years before whatever it was that happened to space lawyers when they got bored and stopped working.

A short flight of stairs took him to the second floor. Grey carpet and more of the ancient brick façade. Lane was never certain why they kept the building in this condition, and for some reason, his mind bogged with questions about architecture and maintenance. It fled from the present as he tried to look at everything around him.

Lane entered Koff's office and saw an old, thick woman sitting at a desk. She had pale skin and grey hair that was cut short. Her suit jacket was flung over a chair, and the sleeves on her blouse were rolled up. She was using a pen stylus with a pad as she marked things off the screen. Lane hadn't seen one used since he was a child. She didn't say anything, so Lane sat down. She continued to not say anything as Lane's pad emitted a chirp. It was Grace with a message asking him if he was all right. Lane wasn't sure, but he didn't dare respond in front of Koff.

"I see you're not quite so interested in talking to me in the same manner as you were Kayla. That's a start. What is going on in this appeal?" Koff asked.

"Six days ago the client went missing. I was do—"

"I can read. And hear. I meant tell me what you think is going on," Koff said.

Lane paused. In his three years at McAngus & Lee, no one had ever asked him what he thought about a lawsuit. "None of it makes sense. The case had no chance of winning under an AI. It's plausible that Tally was uncomfortable with the popular vote after living through a flash mob, but there's no real argument to begin with. She just says the project was for Gateway, and they posted the story to get rid of her."

"And the problem with that explanation is?" Koff replied.

"You can't sue Gateway for any of this. To be honest, I don't even know why you took it. I assumed you had given it to Kayla and it was just another thing for me to be criticized for," Lane answered.

"I did and it was. You were meant to fail, although not like this," Koff said flatly. She studied Lane to see his reaction, but he didn't have one immediately.

After a while he finally asked, "Why?"

"You and your supervisor make each other's lives hell. And for what? Telling you that you had, in fact, screwed up your work? So you can be right about a petty argument that costs you more in the long run than whatever weird satisfaction you get out of it now? There are countless women who would love to have your apprenticeship," Koff said.

Lane was shocked at how quickly his anger rose. He wanted to speak over Koff, but she continued before he had a chance.

"And yes, I know Kayla has not done a good job at training you. She has overextended herself and keeps putting off the fact that if she actually took the time to explain anything to you, it would only take one hour instead of the three spent correcting and screaming. I'd accuse you of acting like a typical man, but here she is breaking down stereotypes. Meanwhile the work environment is toxic, and now a client has gone missing for an appeal we never should have taken." Koff's voice never rose. It just maintained a steady tone of indignation and sarcasm.

"You can't possibly blame this on me when I'm the one who got trapped with the manager from hell!" Lane said.

"I most certainly can. Why would I side with an inexperienced apprentice who has trouble with my manager of over ten years?" Koff spat back in her same tone.

Lane didn't have an answer for her. He just gritted his teeth and remained quiet. He knew that for Koff, friends came first, and that was just how it was.

"When we hired you, I was trying to fix the fact that this office only had one man working for it. We have zero draw in mining lawsuits, and our success rate at defending them is laughable. Derrick is married, so we both know what a bunch of men living on an asteroid are going to think." Koff said.

Lane flinched slightly at the implication because it was something he was painfully aware of. In his mind he had always written it off to his lack of experience, but he knew what Koff meant. Men did not like Lane. Not the ones with money or injuries that could bring in money.

"And yet in three years no male clients have approached us through you. Last night you even changed your reality status back to this obscure crap nobody reads. Where are the sports? The video games? Even if you don't care about that stuff, you know people are watching for it! So yes, I decided to wash you out with a doomed appeal and a manager who can't stand you." Koff said. She sighed and leaned forward, elbows on her desk and hands rubbing her temples. "All right. All right. It's all out now. I was hoping to dodge a gender discrimination lawsuit, but here we are."

A cold chill crawled its way up Lane's spine as he realized what Koff was saying. It was over. The cord was cut. She considered him more risk than asset. Lane had always imagined the firm viewed him as a tricky gamble, an investment they were waiting to pay off. A horse that would find its pace soon enough with just a little encouragement.

"This isn't my fault! This isn't fair!" was all Lane could say. The months he had spent grinding away at online courses. The endless rows of code he had studied for AI problems. The thousands of laws he had to be able to read and understand at a moment's notice. And the public relations courses, the neuroscience, and all the complexity of balancing the relationship between people and machine.

Lane's fury rose as he realized he wasn't even guilty of being incompetent. He had pitted himself against Koff's friend in the office. And in the hierarchy of women, you didn't dare do such a thing. "You can't expect to win a discrimination lawsuit before the appeal is even finished! No one will take your side if you didn't even give me a chance. Not without—" Lane abruptly stopped speaking as he realized Koff was uncharacteristically letting a man yell at her. She was recording the whole conversation.

"It was all a setup for the popular vote. Me being rude to Kayla. This speech," Lane said.

Koff sighed and gave him a half smile. "Clever boy," she said. Koff reached for her pad and began tapping buttons. She didn't look at him, and Lane's lip began to tremble. He had come so far to be a space lawyer, and when it had finally seemed possible, now this.

"Give me a chance with this appeal. Something strange is going on. People don't just vanish like this. And I have a lot of questions for the client too. Like why she even went in front of an AI in the first place," Lane pleaded. Koff glanced at him and shrugged.

"People do things sometimes. The story about the cat was pretty dreary. She was probably afraid they'd drag it out and she'd have another flame mob on her hands." Koff said dismissively.

"What about Gateway doing a personalized response? Why not just give another boilerplate answer for the machine?" Lane asked.

Koff's hand paused and then tapped a few keys. She scrolled through the response and then looked at Lane. "Not a bad catch. All right, I'll make a deal with you. Sign a termination contract, going on sixty percent pay for your unemployment instead of the usual eighty percent. You can have your desk and keep the firm license until we replace you. Should take a couple of weeks," Koff said.

Lane breathed a sigh of relief. "I stay on full salary while I'm here. And I have no other work except this appeal," he said.

"Eighty percent pay then, better than most fired apprentices get. I want a full waiver on non-Standard therapy and data loss. Plus a full agreement to not go prattling online about what a bunch of bitches we are. The last thing I need is a bunch of angry men protesting outside my door," Koff said.

Lane gritted at his teeth. He didn't really have much choice. "Deal."

CHAPTER 5

"I'll tell you what you shouldn't have signed: the emotional damage bit. That sort of trauma is just as affecting as being physically beaten," Dale said. Lane's friend was deep into his third drink. Lane was staring despondently at his first beer that sat untouched.

"Oh come on," Tricia said. "I am as worried about Lane as anyone, but you can't fault his boss for hurting his feelings when she fired him. What is she supposed to do, hold Lane's hand?"

They were sitting around a table at the Tohickon Bar. He'd texted everyone he knew about work, but so far only these two had shown up. There had been a lot of comments and supportive images posted though.

Dale looked annoyed as a he took a large gulp. "You only say that because you're not a man receiving the abuse from a woman. Studies have shown that it's a totally different experience. We're programmed to be much more responsive biologically when a woman yells at us," Dale said. He was a little tipsy, and the issue of men's rights always set him off.

"Look, we are having a reality difference," Tricia said. "But really, what else could she have done? You haven't dated a woman in years; it's not as if you have a lot of experience. You still chasing after that old fart, what was his name?"

Dale gave her a look and finished off his drink. She was changing the subject, as was the polite thing to do when realities clashed.

"His name is Morgan. And is it any shock I don't deal with women when you have that kind of attitude? I'm just trying to be sensitive to Lane here," Dale said. Dale and Tricia had never gotten along very well. Dale kept his reality feeds firmly tuned to masculine filters and subjects. Tricia was a bit more open-minded about her reality, but she found Dale difficult when the conversation turned to his world. Both bitterly complained when they ended up at social gatherings because of their connection to Lane.

"I've dated plenty of men before. I know how to be sensitive. Food, sex, and compliments. If you give them that, they'll do anything for you," Tricia said half seriously.

Dale took her literally and threw up his hands in exasperation. "How long do you keep them around? One date? Two? This is just typical sexist nonsense from a woman. What about feeling useful? Or having a sense of purpose? We need—men need…Lane, help me out here," Dale said.

"Can we just take this back to a neutral reality, please? I'm the one who's screwed, you know," Lane said irritably.

Tricia turned to Lane. "You should just let this whole space lawyer thing go. You keep saying they need to repurpose the meaning of it. If it's not what you expected, then move on."

Dale shook his head. "Nothing means what it used to anymore. I am over meaning. Plus he's not completely screwed yet. You have the appeal thing still. Do you think that will work Lane?"

Lane grimaced and reached for his pad to check the file again. The truth was that he didn't have much of an idea of what he should do with the appeal. He had reached for the only thing he could bargain with. Unusual meant many things in the legal world, but money was rarely one of them. Koff had gotten the upper hand on their deal by finding a way to terminate his apprenticeship without a lawsuit.

"All right, so my client and an artist were going to make a program together. They got into a fight, a cat got run over, and a flash mob was started after the artist posted it online. Client vanishes while doing the data collect on her reality for appeal," Lane explained to the table. Tricia was looking at the files Lane had sent her and biting her lip.

"Two people were going to make a program with contract labor? That's a bit weird. Are you sure it wasn't a mod for a game?" Dale asked. He played games more than anyone else Lane knew. He was especially fond of the community variety where millions would share a virtual space. Lane preferred his games shorter and only played them alone, if at all. Lane handed his pad to Dale.

"The big question to me is, who is this person? Did anyone meet your client when she filed the appeal?" asked Tricia. Lane shook his head. The whole transaction had happened online. He had photos of her and records of her comings and goings that she had posted. Lane even had her shopping habits based off the ads that were sent to her pad. Physical contact wasn't really a necessary part of the equation.

"I was right! They were making a mod. You can tell by the way the code is structured. It was for a game called *Tyrant*. It doesn't really say what it does, but most of the work looks like it was about metrics or something," Dale said. Lane gave Dale a blank look, and he laughed. "So for these big, enormous games, the companies have these things called mods. The fans make them and can sell them or whatever. Sometimes it's code or even a change to the game. When that happens, the companies cut the modder in on a percentage of the profits."

"What does Tally's mod do?" Lane asked.

"I'm not sure. It has a ton of metric tracking built into it. I don't play *Tyrant*. It's…not my sort of game." Dale sounded grossed out by the title. He handed the pad back to Lane, who slid it over to Tricia.

"What makes you say that?" Lane asked.

"Very challenging gameplay. Permanent death for your character. And it's got a bit of a reputation for people with a dominatrix fetish. The economy is very strong, I think Morgan actually does a lot of business on their southeastern server. Want me to ask him?" Dale said.

"You are a life saver. Thank you!" Lane answered. He took a sip of his drink and turned back to Tricia. "Any ideas?"

"Well, most of the data I archive is much older than this, so maybe I'm a bad person to ask. Still, this is really good data. Like too good. Nobody maintains themselves this efficiently. Maybe if you signed up for a lot of spam trackers for free stuff, but still…she is volunteering a lot of information. How old is she?" Tricia said.

"Not too old. Thirties, I think. She's a programmer." Lane said.

"A female programmer is operating in *this* reality?" Tricia said. "Seriously? I'm seeing status updates in shopping malls, memes with male celebrities, math problems, some feminist porn, and a selection of new classic rock on her playlist. She's either the world's quirkiest person with OCD or this is bullshit data."

Lane thought about it for a moment. It was possible. People had faked their reality sets before on appeal to try to adjust the heuristic space. It wasn't illegal. Putting up a fake reality was itself a valid definition of one's worldview to the machine.

Lane examined his own pad and clicked a link to the Tyrant news feed. People were discussing the best techniques for scuttling other players in combat. Some sort of bizarre image of a person with rainbows shooting out of their mouth. He saw a link for enlisting with the Tyrant and figured that would be a good place to start. A picture of a tall, beautiful woman appeared on the screen while behind her were hundreds of ships. She was dressed in a way to arouse men. It was a sight Lane did not see very often.

"Pretty," Tricia said, "Maybe you should depose her? In case you wanted to actually talk to someone besides one of Dale's online boyfriends."

Dale looked at Tricia irritably. "At least my boyfriends return messages and pick up checks."

"Oh please, I haven't met a man who could afford to pick up a tab since I was a teenager. And I'll bet one of his Other Mothers was paying," said Tricia.

Dale gestured to Lane, who was still staring at the image of the Tyrant on his pad. The site said that her name was Eve. "What about Lane here? He still dates women, and he's a lawyer!" Dale's voice was getting louder.

"I don't make very much money. And the best relationship I ever had with a woman was long distance," Lane said reluctantly. He did everything in his power to avoid these kinds of reality clashes.

"You see? Long distance. It's on the tip of his tongue, but he doesn't want to say it: you don't have a reason for keeping men around! You want—"

"I think!" Lane said loudly over Dale, "I think that when everybody has a job, pets, trying to get an apprenticeship, or a free market license, that they don't want to give anything up. Dating is like trench warfare.

We just pull at each other to give something up for the other. Nobody wins anymore."

"What do you want me to do about it?" Tricia asked Dale. "Bring back the patriarchy? And before you go off again, Dale, don't act like preferring to screw men wasn't a crime to them either. At least today we're all accepted for who we are, have enough to eat, and can be whatever we want."

"And what it did it get us? Nobody has anything to do, and there isn't a point to doing anything. Everyone accepts each other in perfect silence," Dale said. There was a gloominess in his voice that hinted of surrender. He was drunk, and the red haze of the bar was dragging him down. The Tohickon could have that affect after a while.

"I'll send an e-mail to her PR about the deposition," Lane said. "And Dale, I'd like to meet with your friend too. I'm sure a virtual merchant is going to have a different take on things than an admin or whatever it is this Tyrant does."

Tricia nodded her head and finished off her drink. She was ready to be out of this conversation as much as Lane was.

"She isn't an admin. She is a Tyrant. As in, she is a fascist dictator in the game," Dale said.

CHAPTER 6

The next few days were a blur for Lane. He went back to the office pretending everything was the same, but it was no use. Word spread fast, and he knew everyone was gawking. Kayla refused to speak to him other than giving him a withering stare when he walked in the door. Derrick offered him a pamphlet to a support meeting and told him something that his wife had said. When life hands you lemons, start to like food with lemons in it. Lane had wanted to point out that lemons weren't covered on Standard food plans, but he decided to leave it alone. Grace brought him a cup of coffee and sat down across from the cubicle. She spoke in a low tone.

"I heard. How are you?" she asked. Lane smiled and acted as if nothing were wrong, but his mind was still in turmoil. He had been trying to become a lawyer almost his entire life. Taking all those digital classes had first just been a way to get special treatment on the dorms, then extra credits on the Standards plan, and finally a way to a steady salary. Lane had studied and scraped through the work to get an apprenticeship at this prestigious firm. McAngus & Lee produced space lawyers. Everyone knew it. And now he was going to get washed out because someone higher up in the matriarchy was having a tough time and didn't want to train him. Koff had even managed to make him wonder if it was all somehow his fault.

"I am going to work this appeal while I still have desk space. Maybe I can figure something out before it's done. If not," Lane shrugged, "then I go somewhere else and start over."

Grace nodded. They swapped a few more pleasantries, but as people kept staring, she became more nervous. She told him to send her a message if he needed anything and went back to her desk.

Lane settled on trying to figure out what Tricia had meant by the data set being faked. With data, it was always about scale. Tracking an individual's personal and digital habits didn't necessarily give you a full understanding of what that person was like personally. If people didn't know something, they looked it up. If people were lonely, they looked for where friends were hanging out. Alternatively, if they wanted people to know where they were, they posted it online. If they wanted people to know they were single or looking for a specific gender, they shared that information. This web of incoming and outgoing information, combined with what filters and articles they were reading, was called a person's reality.

People still had a right to privacy, although few bothered with the pretense anymore. To be on a Standard plan for access to the public commons of food, housing, medicine, or anything else, you had to allow the government to track your metrics. It gave them perfect information on how to manage the Standards as efficiently as possible. Lane, with his firm's license, could tap into the information of his clients and see this data completely. It was the information used to create the culture grid.

For an individual, you needed years of someone's life to begin piecing together a coherent picture that wasn't just whims and impulse. You might look up an ex-lover once or twice during a lonely phase. But only after years of staring at someone's profile was it safe to say you had serious issues. Just a single person's data set from a single day was usually of not much use to anyone. Data was not a mirror of the individual but rather a caricature.

And that was the very thing that Lane realized was weird about Tally's data set: thoroughness. She wanted coffee. She searched for coffee. She went to the coffee shop. She bought the coffee. The average person would never literally do all of this. Due to the licensed access to data held by McAngus & Lee, Lane could see all of this behavior. She was bored. She did some puzzles. She posted her scores. There was never a hint of impulse. Never a moment when Tally said she wanted one thing and then did another. With data, you could never forget that people often say something and then do the opposite. As Tricia had pointed out, Tally wasn't really acting like a person. She was acting like a machine. The question was why?

It was this problem that was stumping Lane when his pad vibrated. It was a message and meeting request from someone named Eve, whom Lane quickly realized was the Tyrant from the game. The mod angle for the game that was the start of the whole dispute had slipped his mind. He tapped out a quick message thanking her and confirmed the date on his calendar.

Out of curiosity Lane decided to look up Eve personally using the firm license. She wasn't on any Standard programs, which meant she could afford to not live off the public commons. A search turned up dozens of hits that connected her name to the game *Tyrant,* so Lane opted for her public profile. His heart skipped a beat when he saw the number of connections under her name topped well over a million. That meant that when she posted a link, a million people saw it in their reality. When she said she liked something, a million people knew she liked it. That didn't just stop with those people. It would ripple out as they reposted, causing an impact in the entire culture of Charleston and probably the world.

It was a connective power that Lane had read about and followed all his life, but he had never actually met someone with that degree of influence. He himself barely had a hundred followers. Lane glanced at a few more public photos admiringly but decided to see her for himself. He packed up and left the office without saying good-bye to anyone.

CHAPTER 7

Lane hurriedly walked along the cross streets of Charleston as he headed toward the meeting. It crossed his mind that this could almost be considered a date, the first one he had been on in months. He didn't count the awkward encounters and long-distance exchanges for much. All that took was a quick search or ping in public. There was always someone looking for a one-night stand or even less if you were willing to not post it online.

On East Bay Street, a bus whirred by as Lane crossed over to the restaurant Eve had marked on the event invite. It was an oyster bar set right on the Cooper River. Lane caught a brief whiff of pluff mud and sea breeze as he drew close. Inside, at the Standard bar, a couple of people were spending their rations and chatting. Lane stepped outside onto the remnants of a wooden pier that was marked for paying customers. A breeze of salt air and coolness washed across his face before he spotted her sitting alone.

She was beautiful. Dark-brown hair wrapped around her neck and a simple dress and top, her long legs were crossed as one foot idly tapped to a rhythm only she could hear. The fabric encasing her shimmered slightly but still seemed natural. When she saw him, she stood, and her face lit up with a smile that made Lane smile back.

"Hello! You must be the space lawyer! My name is Eve," she said. Lane nodded a bit too enthusiastically and shook her hand. She gestured for him to sit, and he obliged. "I've ordered a glass of wine. Please get something!"

Lane normally didn't drink during the day, but he found himself ordering a beer.

"I don't think I have ever met a male lawyer planetside before. How did you end up here?" she asked with a coy smile. Lane blinked and lost his train of thought. Most men who were lawyers got that way by working in the asteroid mines. On Earth, things were different.

"I'm still just an apprentice. I'm handling this appeal with full authority, of course. I ended up here for the usual reasons: I wanted to be independent, have my own free market license, the usual capitalist stuff," Lane said. He was surprised at his own honesty. "In the dorm I grew up in, my mother, she…I was an accident. I think that's why she had a boy instead of a girl. She would let me stay in public housing when I was old enough, and a lot of different women put in mothering time. But I didn't want to end up like the other guys there after a while. I needed to get out. So, you know, I managed to do well with the online courses and qualified. Just because I'm a man doesn't mean I can't be a lawyer."

"Certainly. The great trials they hold out in space where there isn't any Internet. I hear about them all the time from my customers. I'm sure you will be a great one someday!" Eve said.

Lane was surprised by her acceptance and dismissal of his apprenticeship so rapidly. He still ran into female lawyers who didn't think he had any business practicing law on the planet. Unlike space, Earth law was infinitely more complex and bureaucratic. Which meant long hours of sitting still and paying attention to detail, something that men were expected to fail at.

"So, I guess this is an informal deposition still. Tell me about your customers. Or what you do, really. What is a Tyrant?" Lane asked.

Eve raised an eyebrow and stared at him for a moment before bursting out laughing. "You really don't hang out in male realities, do you? Your profile was weird, but I didn't think…" Eve saw something in Lane's face and changed her tone immediately.

"I'm sorry, I tease. I work as the ruler of a virtual world. I guess you could call it role-playing, but I feel that implies that these things don't have consequences. I am…well, part of the theme of my work is that I'm not a very nice ruler. People pay me to oppress them in a virtual space."

Lane nodded and remembered Eve's stats from her profile. She was totally self-sufficient and not giving data for any Standard programs.

"How exactly do you oppress someone in a game?" Lane asked.

"It's all about economics and being fair to the players. The people who own the game can't interfere directly. The developer creates the virtual reality and the economy, and the people provide the goods. At any given moment, it's worth millions in market transactions of virtual goods," Eve explained.

A male waiter brought their wine, and Lane noticed that Eve shot him the exact same disarming smile she had given him. The waiter seemed equally flustered.

"What I do is essentially add a bit of excitement to the game while providing a useful service. The creators provide me with a lot of resources that I use to terrorize people. Everybody has a nice common enemy who is always finding new ways to murder them in their sleep. Economically, I keep people buying and prevent wealth concentration. I also create money sinks by blowing stuff up. And…oh, it's hard to explain the culture part really. A lot of the players are men, and they really enjoy having an evil matriarch to battle," Eve said sweetly.

She was a strange combination of making Lane uncomfortable while simultaneously being incredibly attractive. Her dress was tight and low cut around the breasts, revealing more cleavage than Lane had seen in ages. She clearly loved her work and was very good at convincing others to love it too. Her legs were shaved and firm. She was also openly talking about terrorizing people.

"I think most men would like to vent all their rage on a woman in power. It's hard to escape them on this planet. As long as it was a virtual place, of course. Not in, you know, here," Lane stammered a bit as he realized what he was saying. He had only wanted to agree with her.

"It's all right. I have quite a bit of sympathy for them. Most of the men who play are older. Unemployed and stuck on Earth. I think it's healthy for them to hate me. My female players are similar demographically, but they have their own things that keep them fighting. It's a lot of fun, really. You're welcome to try it out," Eve said.

Lane nodded and agreed, unsure of when he would ever have time to actually do such a thing. "OK, so can you tell me about this mod?" he asked as he handed over his pad.

Eve frowned and nodded while looking at the pad. "That particular mod is a long—" Eve was interrupted by a loud chime from her pad. Her face darkened as she held up her hand. "Sorry, this is very unusual."

She held her pad up to her ear, but the volume was loud enough that Lane could still hear. "Mistress! The Crimson Watch is under attack! We need you to confirm…" was all Lane caught before Eve irritably dropped the volume on the pad. Her head tilted as she listened.

"Is there anything I can do to help?" he asked, but she held up her hand. Lane wasn't even sure what he could do that would be any use. Eve finally put the pad down and began waving to the waiter. "I'm really sorry, but an emergency has come up," she explained.

He stood up as she rose. "Please don't go! I still need you to explain what all this is about. Really, it's no trouble if you need to take care of something in the game. I like to watch people play," Lane said. He tried to hide the tone of pleading in his voice, but Eve smiled at him.

"If you really don't mind…" Lane gestured to the rest of the pier restaurant. It was late afternoon, and the paying area was deserted except for the two of them. Even the pluff mud smell had receded as the winds changed, waving the marsh grass of the river in the other direction.

Eve sat back down and reached into her purse. She pulled out a much larger pad and laid it on the table. Lane had heard them called Canvases, but he had never had much use for something so large. And expensive. She tapped a few buttons on the unit, and suddenly the screen came to life. Eve began pushing the wine glasses, utensils, and other items on the table out of the way as she made a space for herself. Lane jumped to help her. Eve pulled out a much larger headset with a pair of glasses with computer screens built into the lenses.

"Alphas One and Two report," she said flatly. Lane could not hear the reply, but he stretched his neck and Eve shifted her chair to let him see. On the Canvas was a grid map of what looked like outer space. A series of blue and red dots in the center were moving about the screen. It looked as if the red dots were trying to push into the large cluster of blue dots. A lone red dot was flashing around various points of the map, making the blue dots disappear. It did this over and over, seemingly at random.

"I don't care what it is. You hold formation, and you keep out the rest of those ships. They can't invade the system with one Dreadnaught. Delta Three, you are assigned to that Dreadnaught. Break yourself into groups of two and spread out," Eve ordered into the headset. Lane could see how tense she was as she mashed the Canvas to bring out a larger view of the map. There were hundreds of dots on the screen with names and numbers attached.

"That," Eve said as she gestured at the red dot that was randomly appearing in various spots on the screen, "is your mod. It is currently scaring the shit out of my men and trying to get them to do something stupid. It almost did." The blue dots were slowly returning to a more coherent circular pattern, and the red dots coming from the outside were slowing their advance.

"What happens if those red dots get inside?" Lane asked.

Eve sighed and shrugged. "They take over a major system and one of my key power bases."

"I thought you were the Tyrant of the game," Lane said.

Eve shook her head and took a long gulp of wine before tapping a few more icons. She was setting up markers to show where the red dot had reappeared and running a program to predict its next location. "That's part of the fun. I can be killed. I just have a lot more wealth and power than most people. But right now, I am getting hammered by a rival clan. A patriarchy, very aggressive, and stupid enough to think they can take the throne from me."

Lane and Eve sat in silence as she tapped at the Canvas and barked out the occasional order. Many more blue dots vanished before the red dot that was jumping all over the map finally disappeared. She sighed and began to put away the Canvas.

"You carry that with you at all times?" Lane said jokingly to try to lighten the mood.

"No, these are unusual circumstances," Eve said.

"Why? What exactly was that red ship doing? What is the mod?" Lane asked.

"It's a special engine that makes it so a ship can instantly travel anywhere," Eve answered.

CHAPTER 8

After their second glass of wine, Lane had insisted Eve let him walk her home. Which had turned into a third and then dinner. Lane had never held any interest in games, but for some reason, this woman fascinated him—her immense popularity online, the way she talked, and the way she made him feel. She had a frankness and comfort with men that he had never experienced before. The conversation had come back to the game as he walked her back to the apartment on Lower King Street.

"It's really not the mod that's the problem. It's this damn patriarch clan. I've fought most of the matriarchs in the game. I can handle them, but these men are something else," Eve said.

Lane chuckled at hearing a woman admit a group of men was getting the better of her. "Too clever for you?" he teased.

"No," Eve said flatly. It was that same tone he had heard her give orders with, and it wiped the smile off his face immediately. "Whenever a matriarch started giving me trouble, I would just have her assassinated. With women, you just destroy the hierarchy to make them fall apart. Kill the queen and the group will divide. With men, it's not enough to kill their leaders," Eve explained.

Lane sighed and looked away uncomfortably as Eve continued her sexist rant. He felt disappointed and suddenly acutely aware of the time.

"Oh, don't look like that. I'm not saying I know *why* they work that way, just how to destroy them. With men, you kill the leader, and another idiot will be there to take his place. Everyone is disposable, even the King.

They just need their jokes, or their sexism, or…I don't know exactly." Eve said with frustration.

"It's a group thing. It's not any one specific joke or anything, it's a way to act and think of things," Lane said.

Eve smiled. "Yes, exactly! You must understand this much better than I do. Have you ever been involved with something like this?"

Lane shrugged and nodded. "I'm a guy. I grew up around it. Part of the reason I wanted to be a space lawyer was to get away from all this nonsense. They hate you if you try to change anything and they hate you if you don't fit in. It's just old male cultures in virtual clothes."

They turned down one of the cut-off roads near the nicest part of downtown Charleston on Broad Street. Houses with plaster walls lined a cobblestone street that headed toward the river. Ornate metal gates with flowers and vines curling around the latticework marked the entrance to each home. Lane realized this was where Eve lived and was again impressed with her. She had told him over dinner that she lived alone, but he hadn't expected she could afford this part of town. He had kept quiet about his own small dorm room in North Charleston.

"Would you like to come upstairs?" Eve asked. Lane's heart skipped a beat, and he felt his body flush. Did she just want a quick fling? Lane had promised himself he would take a break for a while, but she was so beautiful, and what was the big deal anyways? It was just sex.

Upstairs, the house was a careful balance of open space and luxury. Since so many people lived in small rooms and crowded spaces, Lane noticed that Eve's house emphasized emptiness to show its luxury. A single chair was in the main room by the doorway with a table and shelf. In the living area he saw a large circle of individual seats. Each could fit one person easily, but two could squeeze in if necessary. He sat down, and Eve pulled out a bottle of wine from a cabinet. She didn't ask if he wanted a glass, instead handing him a full one while sitting on the cushioned armrest of his seat.

"So, Lane, I've told you all about the problems this mod is causing me. I was so happy to see your e-mail and find out this litigation is going on. Tell me about your appeal. What do you know?" Eve asked as she just lightly touched his arm.

He nervously took a swig of wine. "Oh, you know, a flash mob hits, and my client sued Gateway over it. Said they were responsible for the mob and making up stories about her. Now there's no sign of the client and some questions about the appeal. I think something strange is going on, but I haven't got a clue what," Lane said. He could swear he felt Eve's hand lightly touch the edge of his shoulder, but he wasn't sure.

"It's such a funny coincidence. I am stuck with this mod business myself. The designers won't just remove the damn thing, and this patriarchy is wreaking havoc with it. It's costing me money, Lane. Real money. I pay for all this by being the Tyrant, and now these boys think they can turn all that around. It was all a huge mistake." Eve was almost speaking into his ear as she leaned closer to him. He wasn't sure about her hand, but he could feel a breast on his shoulder. He turned, hoping for a kiss, only to feel Eve pull away and lean slightly against him as she faced the opposite direction.

"What, ah, what was a mistake?" Lane asked.

Eve paused before answering. "Letting it get out of hand like this. I should have destroyed them a long time ago. Instead I kept them around hoping they'd do some damage and get the economy out of stagnation. War is good for business until it's your business they're blowing up. What did your client sue for?" Eve asked.

That flat tone was back again, and Lane began to wonder what she thinking. "It is hard to tell. The mod was created by her and an artist. She said the artist made up the story after Gateway paid her off. She wanted full contractual rights to the mod, damages, emotional trauma, travel expenses…you know, just a laundry list of stuff she was never going to get. The moment she tried to have the thing resolved by an AI, she was doomed to lose."

"Is that so? Because the computer can't resolve a human dispute?" Eve asked.

"A computer can't fix hurt feelings," Lane responded.

"And what would she need to win?" Eve asked.

"Well, there would have to be something wrong with the meaning the machine was applying to each word. Like it picked the wrong ones for the situation. Then its conclusions would be wrong, and you'd get another shot at it or maybe move for a popular vote. Why are you asking?"

"I need some progress on this war. And that mod is their biggest edge," Eve said.

"You want the mod gone? I don't even know what the client would do with it if she did have full rights," Lane said. Eve walked around to the rear of Lane's chair, giving him a full view of her figure. Her dress was definitely designed with men in mind, tight and curved, some to see but even more left to the imagination.

"Declared void. Ownership passed over. Whatever. Right now it's only usable with permission in the world. I can't…it's not proper for someone in my position to go ignoring modder's rights. You understand, don't you, Lane? It has to be done your way." Eve returned, and her hands were firmly gripping his shoulder. Lane felt the beginnings of an erection and tried to adjust his legs to hide it.

"Well, maybe I have been going about this lawsuit all wrong. I could, maybe look into the technical parts of the mod. Or check out its permissibility once the party has gone missing. The situation is strange enough that there might be some really obscure rule applications going on." Lane only vaguely believed what he was saying.

Eve didn't say anything as she ran her hand along his back. She paused when her pad chimed and then stood up when it rang a second time. She walked to her purse without saying a word, and then walked out of the room.

Lane sighed and rolled his eyes. Even if he got lucky tonight, it was obvious what he had to look forward to. If she was willing to stop everything for the pad now, she would be willing to do it later. Lane could try to keep her attention, but looking around the apartment, he doubted he could afford it. The clothes, the apartment, her hair—none of it looked cheap.

Eve came back in, furiously punching away at her pad and reaching for the Canvas. "I'm sorry, but it's happening again. Raiding along a factory world. Same mod. Same group," she said. She suddenly looked tired to

Lane. He noticed the dark lines underneath her eyes for the first time and wondered how long this had been going on. She slouched as she began to work.

"Maybe we're going about this the wrong way. Why don't we try to find some way to address the mod's legality? The owner is completely missing at this point, and nobody likes for property to just sit there," Lane said.

Eve brightened and came up close to him, wrapping her arms around his waist. It was almost too sudden, too assertive, and on some internal level, Lane became uncertain. "That would be fantastic! Oh thank you! Please call me if there is anything I can do. And Lane, if this works out, I promise it will be worth your time!" she said. Her pad chimed again, and suddenly her arms were gone.

On the canvas a familiar grid map appeared. She began barking orders in her flat tone. Lane finished his wine off in a single gulp and began making his way to the door. There were an awful lot of dots moving around the screen, and he was beginning to feel tired. Eve waved as he was going, and he gave her a smile back. Feeling a little annoyed and consciously aware that Eve had an ulterior motive in all this, Lane decided the best thing to do would be to win the appeal, have sex with Eve, and worry about the rest later.

"One last thing. This group of patriarchs, I might have to ask them to let me look at the program up close. What are they called so I can find them online?" Lane asked.

Eve stared ahead and kept pressing points on the canvas as her fleets scattered across the board.

"They are called the Gay Death Knights."

CHAPTER 9

Lane didn't have to search long before he came across the patriarch group's website. It featured an enormous armored man standing over a pile of corpses. He was black all over except for a pair of glowing slits in his horned helmet. A giant sword that would have been impossible for any human being to lift was in one hand, and a rainbow-colored banner in the other. It was tattered and covered in blood.

Flipping through the forums quickly told Lane the group played multiple games. It was a male-oriented reality, albeit a very broad one. Although the users occasionally played as women in the game, these usually featured enormous breasts and big, submissive eyes. Giant robots, cartoon-styled characters, and a huge variety of image gags filled the forums. Most of the writing was brief and disjointed, full of slang Lane didn't recognize.

He brought out his pad to check the variation in headlines between his own reality and the ones posted in the Gay Death Knight reality. This was the way most of the users of these spaces received their information. A headline read on his pad, "Women Beginning to Make Headway into Male-Dominated Asteroid Mining," but on their feeds it said, "Women Complain about Harsh Conditions in Asteroids."

They were repurposed differently as well. Lane's version of the story talked about overcoming a lot of the obstacles that were in place for women and focused on a particular crew. A million things could go wrong on a mining venture, and the crew had to work together perfectly. On top of that, zero gravity did a lot of damage to the human body as bones decayed and muscle atrophied. The article was about individual women overcoming hardships in the face of adversity.

The Gay Death Knight feed, on the other hand, was about life in space—the agony the first explorers went through when they were shipped out and the things they had to do to survive. Running out of fuel, dangerous repairs in zero gravity, and the wounds men received in vacuum were carried as badges of honor. They had done their time and paid their dues. It framed the complaints of the women and the demands to "civilize" space travel as a sign that they were not up to the task.

Lane tweaked several of his reality settings to receive info in the same manner as the Gay Death Knights. If you wanted to understand someone, you had to see the world as that person did. He didn't understand why making space travel more pleasant was such an offensive idea, but given enough time in this reality, it would begin to make sense.

As nearly as Lane could tell, no one talked about anything important on the public forums of the Gay Death Knights. He also learned that nobody called it that; they shortened it to GDK. There was the usual banter, sexism, and racism being exchanged between people of mutual realities. Some of the people were married: "She makes all the money, so she makes all the rules. I cook, I clean, I watch the kids, and I never get a single word of support from her. Like I'm the ball and chain now. The other day she was buying train tickets for a vacation JUST for her!" Some were strictly gay: "These bitches just want to treat me like some kind of baby doll they can dress up. And don't even get me started when the lesbians start trying to relate to me." Others bitterly complained about rejection: "I spent a week's pay check on taking her out to dinner, and now she can't return an e-mail!" Some of the users seem to have previously been women and had changed gender: "My hormone therapy is going great, but I swear the women stare at me more than the men."

It was tempting to dismiss it as the product of children, but there was too much cleverness to it, too much time and sophistication built into the content as each user contributed his tiny chunk to the culture. They often employed advanced photo manipulation, along with professional video clips and artwork. It was young men as well as adults, educated and unsophisticated alike.

Lane found screenshots from various games and long guides on how to play with the group. They were made up of several clans, and they had a unique sense of humor. It was deeply irreverent, adopting a lot of gay humor from a few decades back and repurposing it to their own ends. Everything imaginable had a rainbow plastered on it. Tanks, aliens, big-breasted women, and enormous, multi-colored space ships. Female celebrities would be depicted with their rich clothing and hair converted into awful rainbow shapes or reduced to rags. It was a culture of inside jokes within inside jokes.

Lane followed a link labeled "mods" and saw a dizzying list of options. Magic swords, space ships, and rainbow-hued weaponry filled the columns and graphs of GDK mods. Lane tried to do a search for the mod involving the teleportation device by clicking under *Tyrant* and typing it into the search engine. Nothing came up.

Lane tried a few variations of the phrase and then went to the hosting forums for *Tyrant* itself. These were designed to be a venue for multiple realities and would have tight filters in place. Offensive or crude messages would be detected and removed instantly, often blocked before they even went public. Lane pulled up a list of mods on this page and tried to search again. He checked under user rankings and brought up the highest-ranked mod. It was a gigantic space ship classified as a *treasure ship*, although from what he could tell, they were describing its size as opposed to what it carried. The creator's name was listed along with his other works. A dancing cat was his avatar, and when Lane pressed it to bring up the user's info, the cat acted as if Lane had pet its head.

There was plenty of info about the creator, but Lane paused before he kept digging. If it had been this easy to track down the mod or contact the creator, Eve would have done it already. Instead he went to the avatar creation page for the forums and made one for himself. The site automatically linked to his pad and uploaded his information, offering him varying degrees of privacy for a price. What it would not change, however, was how much he had played each game. Lane would be marked as a rookie immediately.

Lane sighed and looked around the office. A real space lawyer would be on a ship cruising an accident site or having a high-profile meeting with a wealthy client. If he was going to get anywhere in the forums of the GDK and figure out what was going on with the appeal, though, he would at least need to try to play *Tyrant*.

Like most online games, *Tyrant* was completely free to play. The idea was to get more players and increase the size of the game's economy. Virtual property and perks were sold among players, while modders could add their wares to this market. People participated because other people participated, and they cared enough to pay money because other people cared enough to pay money.

Lane hurried through the character-creation process. He told the game to simply scan his likeness and apply that to his own in-game character. He used the name Lane832xx after his address number and hurriedly clicked through the game's various customization options. He would like to be able to fly ships. He didn't expect to be doing much hand-to-hand combat. Game economies interested him, so he gave himself several boosts in negotiation and bluffing. He gave his outfit a few tweaks and adjusted his hair. He wanted maximum privacy to make sure none of this could be traced back to his real identity. Then Lane confirmed his character, and the game began.

The monitor showed his newly minted character stepping out of a spaceship and into a brightly lit space station. He saw dozens of other players milling about, calling for newbies who were willing to pay cash to get a boost in the game. Others offered work that was suitable for new players. Lane knew he could very well launch a career in the game had he so desired. He thumbed the controls and tried to walk his avatar to the nearest console in the spaceport. He wanted to check the in-game computers and see if they had any information.

"Oh my God, you're actually doing it." Lane heard from behind. He involuntarily cringed at the sound of Kayla's voice. His hand reached for the shut-off key but paused as he realized this would be admitting defeat.

"I'm investigating the appeal I was assigned by Koff," he said flatly.

Kayla snorted and spoke a few decibels louder than necessary. "By playing a video game? What, you going to contact your client there? Maybe she went missing in the game! Just unbelievable," she said as she spoke in the general direction of the office.

Sally did her best to muster a smile but missed the timing by a few seconds. Grace tried to look at her desk, and Derrick looked over Lane's shoulder to see what he was doing. Lane forced himself to keep playing as Kayla's eyes burned a hole in his backside. After the silence continued, she stormed off muttering about little boys.

Lane sighed and was not sure he could shake the feeling she was right. Here he was playing a game, hiding from doing real work on the appeal, just like most men ended up. Where the real world offered few thrills or risks, in virtual communities you could make money even without a free market license. Lane felt he was giving in to the stereotype that men had to get their validation in virtual worlds now. As if winning or making money was all that really mattered to a man.

Kayla's sneer was still ringing in his head as he shut off the game and switched back to the Gay Death Knight forums. The server checked his information, detected his *Tyrant* account, and logged the information to his profile. Now he would at least look as if he had tried the game.

Uncertain of where to begin, Lane decided he might as well get straight to the point. He opened a new topic titled, "Need mod for fast travel" and typed in a hasty message explaining that he had just started a new character and wanted to know how much it would cost to get the mod that lets you teleport around the game. He posted the message and kicked back to see what kind of reply he would get. The view counter in the upper right hand counter slowly ticked by, registering each user who clicked open the message. It didn't tell Lane how much they bothered to read, but it was comforting all the same.

Then a response appeared. It was an online joke where a person took a video clip and edited it to repeat. The image showed a teenage girl walking up to a chest and opening it. A giant cartoon rainbow exploded out of the chest, and rainbows began appearing everywhere while the girl ran around laughing merrily. Underneath was written, "Oh my God, are you serious?" Soon afterward a picture of a hamster running between two pieces of cheese and eventually exploding in a rainbow was posted. The third post was only text that read, "Holy shit, look at this fucking bo-berry." That prompted a fourth post of an image with a rainbow full of berries spinning around.

It didn't take Lane long to realize he had made some kind of social foul. The images varied from graphic to completely cartoon, using videos from decades ago or modern day. Some of it he understood and other parts he did not, but guessing by the consistent use of rainbows, the meaning was coherent enough. Lane tried to search for the term "rainbow," but the search just found a bunch of definitions that had to do with light refracted off water. It had zero meaning outside this group's reality.

As the responses became ruder, Lane realized they were actually talking about the mod. "Looks like the Queen Bee is running out of ideas," posted one user. "This is too absurd to be a plant. This is an honest to God bo-berry asking for the FTL drive," said another. A few minutes passed, and Lane watched worriedly as users began asking him personal questions and demanding a response. One posted that the web broadband signature was from the Southeast. Another said he recognized the configuration for a Charleston user in South Carolina. That started a debate as several users from other states chimed in alternatives but eventually agreed it had to be Charleston. As the conversation progressed, the use of images slowly faded. "Got him," someone finally posted, and there was a picture ripped from Lane's profile along with a link to his Standard metrics. They could see everything.

"Holy shit, this Bo's a lawyer," wrote someone after a few minutes. Another posted a repeating image of a female lawyer shooting rainbows out of her briefcase, knocking people off their feet as she laughed hysterically. "Planetside too," someone added. Lane grimaced as a message popped up on his pad. It was a dog flying on a rainbow and bashing into a wall. He wondered if this was what it had been like for Tally when the flame war started. The forum screen blinked, and then the boxes containing all the messages turned red. The images stopped moving. The thread was closed. A few seconds later, all of Lane's personal information was wiped off the screen.

Lane's pad vibrated with an anonymous message that read, "Lane, sorry to hear about your imminent unemployment. Please tell Eve we said hello."

CHAPTER 10

It took Lane a few moments to recover from the message. How did they knew he had been fired? Was Koff already posting for the new job? If they thought he was a spy for Eve, which technically he was, why shut down the thread? He tried to shake off the chill of having a total stranger reach out to him but found it too unnerving to even read the forums after a while.

"Hey, are you going to the baby shower?" asked Grace. Lane's puzzled look told her the answer. "Kayla is pregnant! Haven't you been checking your office e-mail?" she asked.

Lane sighed and realized that Koff must have already cut him off the e-mail lists. "I didn't know she was pregnant. I can't imagine Kayla wanting me to be there," Lane said. Maybe it was the GDK forums and the massive dose of male angst he had plowed through, but Lane suddenly found himself feeling mischievous. "Which is a perfect excuse for me to go."

"How are you doing?" Grace asked as they walked.

"I'm all right. Still trying to figure out this appeal. The program was a mod for that *Tyrant* game Kayla saw me playing. Maybe something will come up," Lane said.

Grace laughed and brushed her hand along his shoulder again. "It will be so different without you here. I will miss you!" she said. Lane was a bit sad to hear her talking about him as if he were already gone, but he did not complain when she slid her arm around his. The old feelings of the crush he had nursed for her in the office fired off like clockwork, and he found himself unable to resist. Somewhere, in the back of his mind, he wondered if Eve would be jealous.

They walked up the stairs and saw the rest of the staff gathered around a table. Champagne and wine were being poured while trays of cheeses and vegetables were placed on chairs and makeshift stands. It was all non-Standard, paid for by the office.

There was a cluster of women surrounding Kayla as she shook all their hands. "I'm going to go congratulate Kayla. I'll be back in a bit," Grace said.

Lane nodded and noticed Derrick standing alone next to a pile of presents. Derrick waved at him to come over, and Lane, having nowhere else to go, walked over to him.

"So, you want to get into *Tyrant?*" Derrick asked.

Lane laughed and tried to play off the question. "It's for this case. Back when I was still on a dorm, flying ships was my specialty," Lane said.

"Interesting," Derrick said, "I play myself. Work with a decent-sized group, but it might be off grid for you. You serious about the game, or is it just for the case?"

"Bit of both? I met a big player on there and took an interest in it. I've got some free time coming up, you know?" Lane said. Derrick looked across to the cluster of women as they cheered for Kayla while she opened presents. She pretended surprise at a digital camera for baby monitoring while Derrick raised his glass in salute. Even Lane could see the grimace on her face, though he didn't understand why she would be upset.

"What sort of control schemes are you good at?" Derrick asked.

As Lane was rattling off the various titles he played when he was younger, Koff walked across the room where everyone could see her and stood next to Derrick and Lane. "Hello boys," she said as she took a swig from her wine glass. Derrick gave a short greeting, and Lane only stared. "Now, now, you're the only two men at the firm, and you're standing by yourselves at a baby shower. Can't let you hog all the discomfort," Koff said.

"If you're trying to cover yourself by being polite to me in public…" Lane muttered.

"Oh, don't be silly. The contract you signed says that no one is required to be polite to you in public. And yes, it's legal. Similar terms were approved by two popular votes and an AI, it's hard coded into the system.

No, Lane, I am genuinely just as uncomfortable as you at these things," Koff said.

"You already fired me. What else can you do?" Lane said sarcastically.

"Too true," Koff agreed. "You know, if my metrics are right, I'm the only woman here who has actually had a child. Most of these women have no idea what they're cheering for," she said.

"I've had a daughter with my wife," Derrick said.

"Woman, dear. Not to undermine, but it's not quite the same for you. And I have a son, although it has been years since we spoke." That last fact from Koff injected enough awkwardness into the exchange that the two men fell silent. Koff sipped her wine and seemed to enjoy the moment of peace. Grace came back, wine in tow, curious to see what Koff was doing there.

"So you really are a regular nuclear family? I'm impressed. Your wife must be quite a woman to be willing to risk her children around one man," Koff said.

"She feels very strongly about not having to share raising her child with anyone she can't trust," Derrick said.

"Or control," Koff said with a smile.

"My mother took me and my sister to join up with a co-op of women. They didn't allow men around the living quarters very much. It must be interesting for her to have a father," Grace said quickly to take out the tension.

"I think I'd have liked having a father around. On the dorm, the only people you had to look up to were the older boys or the Other Mothers. I hated it. My biggest motivator for the space lawyer entry exams was to just get out of there," Lane said.

Kayla opened her final present, a backpack for carrying children around, and thanked everyone. She shot Koff and Lane a curious glance because they had been standing next to each other for so long. Lane raised his wine glass and made a quiet prayer that she not have a single thing to do with raising the child. Hopefully she would recruit several other women into the process and leave most of the work to them.

Grace's hands began their prying dance around Lane as the party died down, and he barely had to suggest walking her home before they were out the door. As they made small talk about the office and wondering how Kayla had gotten herself pregnant, Lane began to wonder if it was like this. Had she picked someone up at a bar and walked him back to her apartment?

When they were outside her door, Lane's hands slipped around her slim waist, and he kissed her. He had fantasized about this for a long time, but in having it become real, Lane had the gnawing sensation nothing would be satisfied. Her hand slipped into his, and he squeezed it obediently. Lane mumbled something about going upstairs and suddenly they were there, pressing harder and with greater urgency. Lane again wondered if Eve would care, almost wishing she would.

CHAPTER 11

Lane awoke to Grace prodding him. It was just barely light outside. "Lane? Lane, wake up. You need to go," she whispered. Lane curled to one side and groaned softly. It had been a fun night. She had been so warm and happy just moments ago. "Lane, I don't want my roommates seeing you! We're not supposed to have people staying over, especially not men!" Grace whispered urgently.

"Do you want to go get some breakfast or something?" he asked as he put on his clothes. Grace lay back down in reply.

"Don't worry, the door will lock itself on your way out," she mumbled, already half-asleep.

Slipping on a shoe, Lane irritably said, "Good to know."

Grace said something that sounded like Lane's name and ran her hands along his back. "I have just had such a crush on you, with those cute little cupcake buns of yours. Don't be like that!" she said.

Lane sighed and slipped out of the apartment quietly, wondering if she would even acknowledge they had just had sex when he got to work. If he even went to work that day. Which was probably the real reason Grace had suddenly decided to take him home. She would not be excited about a return visit unless she was the one to call. Lane put it out of his mind and gave himself the satisfaction of remembering how fun her breasts had been to hold.

Lane checked his pad for messages. There was nothing else, so he checked the news feed. As he walked down the street toward a bus stop, Lane cycled through the various stories: a new bicycle was coming out that could generate electricity, the summer flavors of Standard protein bars and drinks were coming out, and the exchange rate for reusable water bottles was up. The public vote had proven itself more accurate than the market predictions on the value of space iron.

There was an odd article summarizing a debate about a TV show's plot twist that Lane had never seen. He paused at the top-rated comment: "The whole plot device is absurd. What, she just magically got the ability to teleport everywhere? Why doesn't she just teleport to the Witch's castle? Or into the vault with the three rings?" Lane paused and out of curiosity did a search on the show's backers. Gateway was listed as one of the major contributors. Was it just a coincidence? Why would Gateway be spreading the idea of teleportation?

When Lane got to the bus stop, he saw a huddle of women wearing work uniforms and two men over in a corner wearing sanitation outfits. Personal laborers getting ready for the morning shift to make a few credits. He sat on a bench and debated the merits of going into work that day. Just as he was about to conclude that staying in bed might be the best approach, a loud chirping noise came from his pad, ringing out twice over the sounds of early morning Charleston.

A few women from the group nearby began to laugh. Lane did not even check his pad. He decided to board the bus and make the others suffer through the high-pitched chirp every five minutes. Even if Lane wanted to, he could not turn down the volume on the distinct alert that everyone recognized immediately. There was a coffee shop near his apartment that would be open. He wanted a cup of coffee, a breakfast bar, and maybe some fruit if his meal plan allowed it. Then he would start seeing about what votes he had been drafted for.

After a short bus ride with no shortage of grumbling from the other passengers, Lane arrived at his stop. The coffee shop was made of the same worn wood and brick that all the old buildings of Charleston were built from. The place was strictly Standard, a courtesy of the public commons. By the look of it, Lane thought it might need him to vote for it to get a new paint job.

Lane felt the impulse to check his messages as he got in line and waited, but remembered the draft would block all access to anything that wasn't an emergency. A loud chirp erupted out of him, and one of the patrons spilled her coffee in surprise. She shot him a reproachful look, wordlessly asking, "Here of all places?"

After he was served and the deductions taken from his Standards plan, Lane set out his coffee and breakfast and then pulled out his pad. The screen was blinking red with an alert symbol, and he pressed it. It asked him to confirm his name, ethnicity, gender, and income, which made Lane's denotation in the system C-23-T. The pad processed this information and then paused as it connected to a larger computer network.

On the screen appeared a complex grid of squares and circles of varying colors. These also had various designations, including one for C-23-T. Some of them Lane recognized just from their ID number; others he had never seen before. They were representations of legal spaces and culture spheres and their corresponding realities. Inside the square was the conduct a person could do and still be within the limits of that law and culture. Usually it was pretty straightforward: paying your taxes was represented as something within the square. Not paying them would be outside. The same principle applied for cultures. The total was an ever-correcting mandala of society, made small and perceivable to anyone.

A brief message flashed thanking Lane for participating in this cultural update. A soothing female voice explained that "direct data responses are an essential part of a functioning global society, and it is just as important as providing honest metrics for Standard programs."

Lane irritably pressed the pad's forward key, hoping to get on with the tedious job ahead.

An endless list of subjects for Lane to vote on appeared, each with an accompanying video that would explain the issues and ask him to decide. A history debate over how to frame two South Carolinians called the Grimke Sisters and their role in abolition in the public narrative. Should marijuana be admitted into the public commons? War games, a sticking point with women and hotly defended by men, were again up for vote to have their high ranking in popularity reduced or handicapped. Lane's vote, along with millions of others, would be compiled and incorporated into the culture grid.

Lane finished after almost two hours of videos and votes. As soon as he was done, his pad erupted with messages and notices from various people. Tricia had somehow figured out that Lane had gone home with Grace and wrote a private message complaining about women who were destroying the market value of sex. Eve asked him how things were going with the case and if was there anything she could do to help. And finally there was a second message from Dale about the mod merchant he had said he could get Lane in touch with.

CHAPTER 12

Lane punched up Dale's event on his pad and began following the directions to the bar. He had spent the day trying to find any trace of information about the mod by lurking on the forums of the Gay Death Knights but had little luck. When Lane finally came around the corner and saw the bar, named Pound Town, he swore aloud. Dale knew he was uncomfortable inside male bars, although he was fond of pointing out that Lane's reason always seemed to change.

The bar had only a light crowd. Brown and green lights illuminated a wide floor space. The place looked as if it was better used as a dance floor than a place for people to stand around chatting. It was the after-work crowd, and men in work uniforms stood next to men in business suits. Lane saw a few miners who had the awkward shuffle of someone enduring Earth's gravity for the first time in months. There were several women in the bar, though it was more likely they were men dressed that way.

Dale was over in a corner with a tall, good-looking man in a grey suit that matched his own graying hair. When he spotted Lane, he gestured for him to come over, and Lane nodded, heading first to the bar to get a beer before joining them. He felt the bartender give him a look-over as he ordered.

"Here he is. Lane, this is Morgan. He's the merchant I was telling you about," Dale said with a gush. Lane immediately realized that Dale was using him as an excuse to hit on the man, which was fine by Lane so long as it didn't involve him. Lane stuck out his hand, but Morgan's was currently holding his pad, which he was glancing at before setting it on the bar and finally taking Lane's. The delay was only a second, but Lane noticed—it was his own profile Morgan had been checking.

"Pleased to meet you. Dale has told me everything about you, although he didn't mention you were good looking as well. He said you were working on a case for a mod in *Tyrant*?"

Lane blushed at the compliment and stammered a bit. "It's…it's a fast-travel thing. Some sort of warp, jump drive…I don't know what to call it. A group called the Gay Death Knights are using the only known version," Lane explained.

Morgan raised an eyebrow and took a sip from his drink. "That is an awfully curious thing for a lawyer to want to get involved in. I understand the appeal deals with copyrights and ownership, but why go mucking about the factions of the world itself? Don't you normally stay outside the culture space?" Morgan smiled as he spoke, and Lane found himself getting nervous again.

Dale was clearly getting jealous as well. "He has already met with the Tyrant from that world. For the case. Eve, isn't it?" Dale said without really asking Lane anything.

"Oh God, the one with the pop album?" Morgan said with a laugh. Lane hadn't known Eve was a singer, but most people with connective popularity dabbled around in media. If you had enough fans to do the grunt work, anything was possible.

"I've never heard it, but we had dinner and she explained her situation," Lane answered. He was anxiously looking around the bar at the other patrons.

Dale leaned in close and loudly whispered in Morgan's ear, "Oh look, you can already tell he has a thing for her. Lane is always chasing after the first thing that offers to spread her legs."

Lane scowled and snapped back, "I took a tip from you and decided to screw someone for her money for once."

Dale mocked being offended before heading over to the bar to refill his drink.

"You're not very comfortable here, are you?" Morgan asked.

Lane blinked and sighed, waving absently at Dale. "No, I am just tense, and this is…I'm not exactly…" He was unsure of what to say or even what he wanted to express to him.

"You're not very comfortable with men period," Morgan said.

Lane looked at him and glanced over at Dale, who was chatting with the bartender and giggling at some joke. A side glance told Lane that Dale had every intention of coming back in case he got any ideas, a point he made by leaning against the bar so that his butt stuck out.

"Sort of. I just…when I was young I had this experience on the dorms and, and, the other boy was much older. I don't hate men or anything. But I can't, I don't…" Lane said wearily. He wasn't sure why he was admitting this. It had been completely purged from his profile history.

Morgan looked surprised but nodded solemnly. "It is completely all right. I grew up on a boys dorm myself. The lack of supervision or role models is appalling. My apologies. Dale never mentioned it," he said.

Lane shook his head, "Dale doesn't know. I requested deletion after an Other Mother reported it. There is no problem."

The two of them sat there in silence after that. The sounds of men chatting filled the room, the early evening hour demanding that a modicum of civility be maintained. In a few hours, the music would grow louder, and people would begin to communicate in other ways.

Dale finally walked over and relieved them of the awkward silence.

"So what do you know about the Gay Death Knights?" Lane asked.

Morgan shrugged. "That depends. I'm working on a film project right now. Maybe you'd like to pre-order a deluxe version?"

Lane laughed and gestured with his pad toward Morgan. He would want money to help fund a community project. Morgan and a group of his friends were creating something to distribute on the web and needed outside resources. People would pay for these projects by promising to give the buyer a copy or some other unique items, generating more involvement and usually more free labor. Sometimes you just need money for art. Morgan silently sent Lane a link to the project, a live production of an old play called *Sordid Lives* that Lane had never heard of. He bought a season pass with a few clicks, inwardly cringing at the dip his account was taking. He had been hoping to buy a new suit.

"There we go. So, the thing about this mod is that you are walking into a very peculiar situation. The GDK and Tyrant have been going at it for months. They got access to your mod, and now the war has started turning around. If anything is undefended, the GDK can have a ship appear to take it out instantly. It's not a big enough advantage to make her lose immediately, but it's starting to take its toll on the Tyrant's infrastructure. The GDK patriarch aims to make himself the new Tyrant and add another virtual market to his empire. The thing nobody can figure out is why the mod was introduced in the first place," Morgan said.

"I thought my client, Tally, just submitted it, and then she got paid for it," Lane said.

"Ah, you're a lawyer, so this might not be obvious. You can always get more money. Or guns or ships or whatever. The one resource that is always scarce in any reality is time. That's what the mod breaks: it no longer takes any time to travel or move goods," Morgan explained.

"So? Isn't that a good thing?" Lane said.

Morgan shook his head and frowned. "No, it's completely unfair. The GDK have an absurd advantage with the sole copy. Right now the designers are ignoring Eve's complaints about the mod because she overdid it a bit as Tyrant. Too much security, not enough economic sinks, not enough chaos and destruction. They aren't disabling the mod because it's stirring the game's economy up," Morgan said.

"I still don't see how it's a bad thing if the economy is improving," Lane responded.

"That's the other scarce resource. It's not popular."

CHAPTER 13

Lane decided to clear out of the bar soon afterward. Morgan's backer project wasn't cheap, and the reality of Lane's employment status was beginning to sink in. He would be collecting his last paycheck soon, and after that it was Standard rations only. On the bus ride home, he idly thumbed through news stories and messages, shifting realities to see the GDK perspectives and trying to get some ideas about what to do next in the case. He noticed a story about Gateway, Inc. buying up large plots of land and beginning major construction projects out in the wilderness. They'd be needing construction labor for it, which paid real money, although Earthside there were plenty of women competing for those positions.

As Lane walked the last few blocks home, the evening air was thick with moisture and heat, the Charleston weather persisting well after the sun had gone down. Outside his apartment, he saw the same pair of females outside smoking a cigarette. They were ignoring him until a beep came from one of their pads, and they glanced over at him.

"Hey there. You funded *Sordid Lives*?" one asked.

Lane blinked and was not sure how to answer. He had walked by these two women countless times as they smoked their cigarettes. Some of those times he had been drunk and other times sober. But never had they breathed anything but smoke in his direction. One laughed and slowed down on her cigarette. "Let me guess: Morgan. He got you to buy one of the deluxe packages for something?" she asked.

Lane smiled back, relieved at having their connection explained, and nodded. "Yeah, I am working on this case, and he knew about some of the people involved," Lane said.

"So you don't know anything about *Sordid Lives*, huh? You'll come at least, right? When we finally put it on?" the other asked.

"Of course. Why wouldn't I?"

"Eh, folks tend to buy into these projects because they just like the idea of it. I've had shows get funded by thousands, and only a couple dozen show up when we put on the actual performance. Alert thing is so we talk it up to backers," Janine explained.

Lane nodded. "How's it working?"

"I dunno. You're the first person I met who gave me a beep. Been running the program for weeks." They resumed smoking and Lane hurried inside, the two becoming strangers again.

Home was a large single room containing a bed, table, kitchen, and sink. The bathroom was communal and down the hall, featuring an array of showers, toilets, and odors for residents to enjoy. The furniture was simple and had come with the room, the same Standard factory models that people either abandoned immediately or held onto for life. A tiny refrigerator held some drinks, while the cabinets were filled with protein bars and food supplements. Most of it was Standard items or things Lane had pocketed when there were surplus giveaways. Lane ate sparsely and preferred to invest his spare income in clothing and beer.

Lane poured himself a glass of water and set his pad on the table. A few taps opened the door to *Tyrant*, and he once again found himself standing in an enormous spaceport. Aliens of every type walked about him along with human beings of various shapes and sizes. It occurred to Lane that he wasn't even sure how one was supposed to get started in the game. He knew there were big spaceships you could fly and virtual markets going on, but standing in the spaceport showed him none of that. From Lane's perspective, it just looked like a giant room full of people.

He wandered the halls of the spaceport, seeing social spaces made to resemble bars or casinos alongside locked doors that players used for their own private exchanges. Lane found the layout confusing at first—the space's design was different from what he had grown up with when he explored these games. In his youth, they still made virtual places that resembled the real world. Back then people had to walk distances and check maps to understand where they were spatially. Modern design had begun to move away from this trend, and *Tyrant* exemplified a game where space was entirely optional. It always looked like an enormous spaceport, or Lane's idea of one at least, and when he would try to get close to the edges of the room, it would expand. Rooms would appear or shift position based on the whims of the crowds or some other unseen algorithm. It was seen as time efficient yet aesthetically pleasing.

The users jostled and bumped his perspective around. Lane thought about calling Eve but realized he wasn't even sure how to go about doing that in the game. After a few more minutes of wandering, a beep from his pad alerted Lane to a message from Derrick: "I'm up late playing. Baby keeps waking up, and tonight is my turn. Need a ride?"

It took Lane a moment to realize he was referring to *Tyrant* and his current predicament. He typed back, "Sure. Where are we going?"

Derrick didn't answer. Instead, a message appeared stating that another player had sent him a waypoint, and would he like it on his HUD? Lane sighed and wondered just what any of this had to do with anything. He was angry at himself suddenly. Just another man hiding in his video games, working a case that didn't make sense out of some absurd protest at being fired from his apprenticeship. The moment passed, and Lane decided to trust his instincts. The mod and Gateway and their obsession with teleportation would all make sense if he just kept digging. He confirmed the waypoint.

When he got there, he found an airlock and a short, green man waving at him. He got another message saying he had been given permission to access the ship *Zulfikar Bronze*. As Lane accepted, the airlock opened and the green man went aboard without saying anything. Lane keyed the microphone button and asked, "Derrick? What are we doing?"

Still no reply as the avatar disappeared into the ship. Lane fumbled with the controls for a few moments as he tried to figure out how to get aboard. The screen darkened, and he found himself in a small ship with a row of seats on either side. A cockpit extended out at the end of the ship, and the green man was standing in the center.

"Welcome aboard! This is just a small ship I use for getting around. All speed and a few guns for anyone making bad decisions. Want to take her for a spin?" Derrick asked.

Lane began toward the cockpit and then paused in front of Derrick's avatar.

"How come your name doesn't come up? It appears on everyone else when I get near them."

The character made a shrugging motion, creaking and artificial in its mimicry. "Oh, just a mod I have set up. I value my privacy. Try the ship! It's not a problem if you wreck it," Derrick said with a laugh.

Lane sat in the cockpit and took his bearings. A quick scan of the station showed its shield was at full power, and a huge array of red blips indicated it had more than enough weapons to decimate the tiny ship he was in. Lane briefly felt the impulse to fire on it anyway.

All around were various shuttles, cruisers, and freighters piloted by players and nonplayers alike. Some were heading into dock, and others were pulling out. A generic backdrop of stars and galaxy effects gave the whole scene a bluish tint, and a deep sound of humming and the low rumble of engines played in the background. Lane briefly thought about the fact that there is no sound in space and then dismissed the notion. It was the idea of space flight they were depicting, not the real thing.

Lane gave the throttle a tap and watched the ship lurch forward. A few more notches and they were coasting.

"Don't be shy, let it rip," Derrick said.

Lane pushed the throttle to max. Out of nowhere a freighter appeared and sent out a proximity alert just in time for Lane to swerve out of the way. The ship wobbled as he steered to port and then evened out into a straight path. Lane realized his hands were sweating and that he was nervous.

"Relax. You're a brand-new character, and this is just a proxy for me," Derrick explained.

"Thank you for this. I was afraid I would be sitting on that space station forever. How do they expect players to get out of there?" Lane asked.

He was experimenting with the controls, giving the guns a few taps to see their effect and varying the engine speeds.

"Ideally you sign on to work on a ship or clan. *Tyrant* deals with its new players by outsourcing the tutorial to the community. There is too much to learn otherwise. Slow growth but low turnover makes up for it. Which causes a lot of susceptibility to anticulture," Derrick said.

Lane's head tilted as he heard Derrick explaining this and suddenly wished he could make the same incredulous look in the game. "What is anticulture?" Lane asked.

Derrick laughed and sent Lane a new waypoint to head toward. As he pulled the ship around, several blue triangles appeared on the radar.

"If you stay in a virtual world long enough, your brain gets used to a sort of double-think. You know it's not real but it also has value, so your mind still has a relationship with it. You are simultaneously aware that it's fake, and yet you do it anyways. There isn't really a concept for it in the real world."

As the ship continued into space, several blue triangles appeared on the sensors. Lane realized that one of them was a treasure ship. A warning box appeared indicating it had detected them and was adjusting course to intercept.

"Think of it like an empty room. The meaning of the room comes from what you do in it. You're in the cockpit. That's where you steer the ship and where you need to be if you want to do something. Past actions and your relationship with it generate the meaning," Derrick said.

A query appeared on the HUD from Derrick requesting control of the ship. Lane confirmed, and they suddenly banked left while increasing speed.

"Now you are realizing I can control the ship from back here as well, via remote. I rarely ever sit in the cockpit because it's the first place people target their missiles. The meaning of the room has now changed," Derrick explained.

Lane laughed and pressed the exit button, moving his avatar for a seat as far away from the cockpit as possible.

"That's one of the Tyrant's ships, and I don't want her detecting us," Derrick said.

Lane couldn't see what was going on anymore and found himself wondering if he should just go back to the cockpit. As Derrick had said before, it didn't matter if they died here. The ship's engines hummed louder, and Lane was growing more curious as Derrick remained silent. After a few moments, he stood back up and resumed his spot.

"Ah perfect, you are getting it. You can't die here, and you have no personal investment in the game itself. So you sit there for the better view now. The meaning of the room shifts in value with your reality in regards to the one in the game and the one in the real world," Derrick said.

Lane looked out the cockpit and saw that they were steering to the far left of the Tyrant ships. A message notice from the ship popped up, but Derrick flicked it off before Lane could read it. "They are not going to bother with chasing us down. Curious."

"I still don't get your point about the cockpit. I just stopped caring about it and went back to what I was doing."

"Anti-culture is when the reality shifts and the information takes on new meaning, resulting in a corresponding shift in value, which you are able to perceive because it's a virtual world. Perceiving this degrades your personal connection with the culture's meaning, for example you getting in the cockpit despite the danger making that a bad idea," Derrick said. Lane was silent at that as he turned it over in his mind. The image of a dog chasing its tail and realizing what it was doing appeared in his mind.

"For some reason, I expected the Tyrant to be a bit more tyrannical. That seemed mild," Lane said, changing the subject. They were cruising along in space, well away from the treasure ship and the space station his character had started on.

"She wouldn't cause too much trouble in a beginner zone. She wants new players to stick around, so she is hedging her bets. Oh, shoot. It's OK, honey. Be quiet now."

Lane blinked at the sudden change of tone from Derrick and took a moment to realize he was not the one being spoken to. Something must be going on in the real world with his kid.

Lane began fiddling with the controls again and experimenting with the ship's systems. There was a scanner that seemed to go out various ranges with varying degrees of certainty. You could tell something was a ship at a certain distance but not whom it belonged to until it was much closer. Power could be shifted around various systems to increase speed or engines. Derrick had set a course, and the ship was on autopilot, which Lane flicked on and off while hoping that Derrick wasn't watching. After a few minutes, several ships appeared on the scanner.

"Ah, Derrick? We have company," Lane said.

No response. They were closing in fast, and the scanner changed them to red triangles. Lane continued to let the ship idle, unsure if he should take the controls or let the ships come his way. An icon appeared over them that read "Gay Death Knights."

"Derrick! I think you should check this out!" Lane shouted. The ships were getting closer. Lane grabbed the controls and steered the ship in the opposite direction. He shunted power into the engines and watched the triangles slowly begin to slip away from the radar.

"Shhh...honey, Daddy is just going to take care of—Lane, what are you doing?"

The ships were holding off a slight distance. Lane wanted to say that he was rescuing them but was too excited to speak. Suddenly the ship was decelerating and turning back toward the GDK fighters. Lane was too nervous to say anything, and he could hear Derrick cooing to a baby on the other end.

"It's OK. I appreciate you taking the controls like that. These are just some friends of mine," Derrick explained.

"You're with the Gay Death Knights?" Lane asked.

"Sure am," Derrick said.

"How come you never mentioned it at the firm?" Lane asked.

He heard Derrick making cooing sounds for a while before he answered. "It didn't really seem like it had a place there. You never played many video games before this lawsuit. Koff only cares about me getting my assignments done on time. Kayla has been crazy and pregnant for months now. I'm sorry about that, by the way; she has been out of line for a while."

Lane shuddered at the thought of Kayla's tirades against him.

"I don't think her being pregnant has anything to do with being an awful boss," Lane said.

Derrick laughed and said, "My wife has been pregnant twice now. You will just have to trust me on this one. Especially since she was in denial about it for so long."

Lane was a bit surprised at how openly sexist Derrick was speaking and figured he must just hang out in different realities from Lane.

"I don't think you can base that kind of judgment on one person," Lane said.

"Technically it's two," Derrick said. "Lane, not to change the subject, but how often do you change reality?" Derrick asked.

"A few days ago I did for this case, to try to understand the Gay Death Knights better. Before that, not too often. Different economic stuff. Virtual markets and how useful they are. How often do you change yours?"

"I change it around all the time. We all do in the Gay Death Knights. Look, this ship is going to take a while. They are escorting us to a rendezvous with a bigger carrier. If you walk your character back to that save pod over there, he'll start up again inside the ship. It's late, and I need to put the baby to bed," Derrick said.

Lane agreed and walked over to the pod. The screen dimmed, and Lane found himself looking around his apartment again. He noticed that the sink was still dripping from when he had poured a glass of water.

A message from Derrick pinged his pad. "Good to play with you," was all it said. Below was an image of a group of men around a campfire. A rainbow was shooting out of the flames while one man played a guitar and the others seemed to be swaying and singing. In text it read, "Come out to GDK Con this summer!"

CHAPTER 14

Lane awoke bleary eyed and late for work. He panicked for a moment before he realized that he had nothing to do at the office except play video games. The thought of seeing Derrick to ask him about GDK Con perked his interest, as did the notion of seeing Grace again. Maybe she would be up for something more? He showered and headed out the door with a rising head of hope.

On the bus to work, Lane flicked on his pad and checked the news. Gateway was at the top of his feeds again. This time it was a story about their purchase of a huge fleet of transport trucks. Diesel, solar, and biofuel models. The article was pointing out the absurdity of the investment when most transport was traditionally done by train. All of their materials came from space, and there was a train connected to any spaceport on the planet. It would be cheaper to use the transit system than to pay for the fuel and truck expenses.

Comments were organized by most read and approved by each reader. The top selection was someone theorizing that Gateway could be building something in a secret location. A reply chided the poster since Gateway was creating at least a hundred new jobs that would be available to both sexes. Trucks had to be monitored by people even if they were mostly on autopilot. One user posted a link to the latest statistics from her reality on male employment. Another pointed out that just because the job involved trucks, that didn't mean it didn't require advanced training. That meant working through online courses, which would keep a lot of men out of the position. There was little consensus on why Gateway would do such a thing, and it made Lane wonder again what the company was up to.

Lane was late, but the office did not seem to notice his arrival. Kayla was already in her office, talking on her pad with someone in the disturbingly sweet tone that she only used when she wanted someone to like her. Which Lane had never experienced. He swiveled around to see Derrick's desk, but he looked engrossed in something on his monitor. After a few seconds, he noticed Lane, smiled and nodded, and then went back to work.

Lane craned his neck to see what Grace was doing. He typed out a message saying hello to her. A minute ticked by, then two, then five, and she still didn't respond. A part of Lane knew that this was a bad sign. The first tremors of rejection echoed someplace deep in his mind, but he shut them away quickly. Being hurt or upset would just make it worse. He checked her profile and saw that her public calendar was free that night. You never know until you ask, he reasoned. He attempted to nonchalantly look busy by booting up a few programs and then headed toward the kitchen area to fix a cup of coffee.

On his way back, Lane stopped at Grace's desk. Her brow was furrowed, and she stared intently at the monitor. It was not until he coughed that she finally turned to look at him.

"Hi, Grace! How's it going?"

She smiled and replied, "Fine. Just fine. Working on cases, trying to get all these clients together for filming and making sure they approve of the video before it goes public vote. How is the appeal? Still playing in the virtual worlds?"

Lane grimaced. "It's fine. I was wondering what you were planning to do for dinner tonight. Maybe we could go out and get something to eat?" he asked. He could feel Sally's eyes on them now, and Grace gave an uncomfortable smile. His hands nervously fidgeted, one going into a pocket while the other plucked at his shirt.

"Oh, well, it's just I have a lot of work. And I am keeping my calendar clear just in case, you know. Thank you, though," Grace answered.

Lane nodded and gave a grim smile before he walked back to his desk, hand still in his pocket. He was slightly numb as he looked for something to do on his pad. Unsure of any other course, he began looking aimlessly on the GDK forums for some sort of distraction, and then for more information on GDK Con.

It was being held somewhere in North Carolina in a town Lane didn't recognize. There wasn't train access to the site, and guests were encouraged to be resourceful about getting there. It was in a week, and there would be cabins to stay in along with food. Images from past trips showed men dressed in various outfits or wearing nothing but shorts. Sometimes they were embracing one another, and other times they were fighting.

Lane stared at the pictures. He was both intrigued and disturbed by the violence. In one image, one of the men had blood coming out of his mouth from what looked like a particularly nasty fight. For one brief second, Lane was alarmed that he was getting aroused, but the fear passed when nothing more happened. A bad memory of the dorms skirted the edge of consciousness and dipped back out of mind.

Lane brought up the calculator application on his pad and did a few price checks on tickets. He could cover the train with Standard credits. It was the bus outside his region that would be trouble. Buses were meant for the local population; they cost extra for non-residents. He would be charged real money for that.

As Lane considered his options and whether or not he even wanted to go, a message arrived on his pad telling him that Koff wanted to speak with him immediately. It occurred to Lane that he could ask Koff to allow him to rent a car as a part of the case. Other lawyers had done it before to get good footage or interview key witnesses. It took several moments before it crossed Lane's mind that it probably wasn't good news that Koff had for him. Being quasi-fired for the past several days had given him a sense of liberation from his desire to please her.

Once again Lane found himself marching up the stairs to Koff's office and wondering about the bricks in the building. How old did the place have to be to still have white plaster? Two centuries? Three? The style of Charleston was that everything old was sacred, everything new would join the old soon enough. He walked into Koff's office to see her hovering over a coffee mug and a bag of candies. She plucked one from the bag and chewed it slowly as she spoke.

"So, Lane, where are you with the appeal?" Koff asked. When he didn't answer immediately, Koff pressed on. "Found any problems with the AI's language analysis? Any big red herrings?" She paused to put another piece of candy in her mouth.

"I have been looking into a group called the Gay Death Knights that is involved with the program. I had a friend who handles data look into Tally, and she thinks she's a fake data feed. That would explain the vanishing, and I think this group might have been behind it. Something weird is going on with this file between Gateway and Tally. The Gay Death Knights are having a conference up in the mountains in a few days, and if I can find our client, Tally, I think I can get the appeal resolved." Lane had caught himself before he mentioned Derrick.

Koff's hand paused in the bag and then selected several pieces of candy at once. She chewed them quickly, sighed, and stuffed the bag into a drawer by her desk. "I should have known this was going to keep dragging on. Why not just tell me everything is going great? How about a simple, 'Wrapping it up nicely!' No, instead it's a bunch of people calling themselves gay activists like anybody identifies themselves by sexuality anymore and su—"

"They aren't gay activists. I think they're taking the idea of a gay activist and repurposing it into something totally different. I'm not even sure what the original game was where Death Knight came from." Koff's hand involuntarily reached for the candy bag as Lane spoke. He noticed that she seemed to be visibly gritting her teeth at being interrupted.

"It would have been awfully convenient if you had found a backbone a couple of months ago back before Kayla was knocked up and you decided to act like a child about it. Look, the truth is that I've been looking for another male lawyer, and I have found squat. Nothing. Nobody in this region with a compatible reality for this office. It's not even as if you have a compatible reality, but yours is just weird. I can do weird. Half these men's rights idiots can't leave that stuff at the door, and the other half don't value money enough to get them to ditch the politics. I'll say one thing for capitalism: it kept everybody in line. Now anybody can go on a Standard plan and just not give a damn."

Lane glared at Koff. She had barely even glanced at him during her tirade. He had worked an apprenticeship for three years on a miniscule salary hoping to become a space lawyer. Now here she was practically telling him the whole thing was a scam, the free market license just a carrot to coerce obedience out of him. This wasn't what being a space lawyer was supposed to be like.

His pad beeped with the reminder of an upcoming event, and Lane remembered he had a lunch date with Eve. He answered despite the shocked look on Koff's face.

"Was there a job offer somewhere in that lecture?" he asked.

She sighed and leaned back in her desk. "Well, at least you have some confidence now. Think of it as a door unlocking," she said stiffly. "So you are pursuing the fact angle on an AI appeal. You think that's a good idea?"

"I doubt there is anything wrong with the AI routines. I think if I can make the lawsuit resolve itself before any vote, then this firm's record will still have a win under its stats. Which is what this is really about. And I think if you pay for my travel expenses to go to this conference, there is a chance of that happening."

Koff turned to her pad and sent a ping to Lane for the information. Without either saying a word, the trip data was exchanged.

"I'll get you to the town, but I'm not paying for a car rental. If that appears on the bill, I won't hear the end of it from the staff wanting a car for every little thing," Koff said.

CHAPTER 15

Eve picked an even more upscale restaurant for their second meeting. Someone had torn apart a carriage house and turned it into a well-furnished bar. Everything inside was simultaneously nice but set in a backdrop of age and faux disrepair. Lane found the effect jarring, particularly when the entire restaurant's clientele was exotically dressed women. Several stared at him when he walked in, and Lane guessed that if he were not wearing his suit, he would not be allowed inside. Most of the outfits were asexual, making it so he could not discern much about their bodies. It made him feel unwelcome.

A waiter checked her pad for his name then escorted him upstairs, where he saw Eve sitting with another woman. While Eve was dressed in a tight-fitting suit that showed just a hint of her cleavage, the woman next to her had on a baggy dress with a dull fabric.

"Thank you for coming on such short notice, Lane! I want you to meet another lawyer friend of mine. Her name is Boyle. She specializes in copyright lawsuits. Like the mutual problem we have going on with your appeal," Eve said in a bright voice. Lane smiled and nodded, reaching immediately for the drink menu.

"Do you mind if I order a drink before I go into what I've found out?" he asked. He hadn't even bothered to check on his pad whether or not the place was money-only while walking over.

Eve and Boyle looked at each other before Eve suddenly burst out laughing.

"What did I tell you? The value of sex has plummeted in this town. You can't get a man to do anything for a screw these days. Guess I'm buying," Eve declared. She gave Lane a big grin and then waved for the waitress to come over. "How do you like playing *Tyrant* so far?"

Lane was annoyed at Eve suddenly. He wasn't sure if it was from Koff's crude comments or Eve's assumption that he could not afford to pay, but any charm she had possessed over him was fading.

"It's all right. I like the flying part. I don't really care for the new way virtual buildings work," Lane said.

Eve nodded and held out her pad to the waitress. He ordered a glass of a rare whiskey that he would never have been able to afford on his apprentice salary.

"How did you like the Gay Death Knights?" Eve asked.

Lane coughed a little and looked at her warily.

"Lane, I know about what goes on inside my own game. That was my ship you flew by, the big one called *Sojourner Truth*. I didn't want to spook your little friend," Eve said.

Lane was quiet as he debated how much he should admit to Eve. How did she know about Derrick? Or that he had been snooping around on forums trying to find out about the mod? Eve and Boyle were looking at him expectantly.

"One of the GDK took some interest in me after he found out I was an attorney. They're not so bad. In the real world, that is. We got to talking, and they offered to show me around *Tyrant*," Lane explained.

Eve nodded, and Boyle turned to her. "No offense, but do you mind if I get to that real world part of all this?"

Lane's drink arrived, and he held it up to his nose, inhaling deeply the rich smell of oak and spice. He had drunk his share of whiskey, but he knew to take his time with the good stuff. He didn't know the next time he would be able to drink something that cost this much.

"Lane, how much do you know about intellectual property?" Boyle asked.

Lane shrugged and set down the glass. "Mostly the public narrative. My work is in space law mainly, but I ended up doing miner's compensation.

Copyrights are the main source of income for people in virtual markets, right?" he said.

Boyle drummed her fingers on the table. "With so many unemployed, it gives them a way to raise money and be productive without suffering the burdens of scarcity. People make the art virtually, maybe get some backers to help out, and they get to generate a little capital from people who will pay for it. A sort of harmless capitalism that doesn't require the expertise and skill of the real world," Boyle explained.

"I just got suckered into funding one a few days ago, actually. In my reality it's just glorified begging," Lane said. He decided to finally take a sip of the whiskey. The thought of having to sink to the creative arts gave him a shudder. You could base your self-worth on a paycheck and have it hold together with some regularity. Online, you were competing with so many for just a precious few moments of attention.

"I quite agree, seeing how it's mostly a place for unemployed men," Boyle said.

Lane frowned and said, "You mean most men are unemployed. Which is because most jobs take a lot of technical skill. People won't hire someone who hasn't sat through years of online courses for a meaningless badge on their resume. Only women seem to be able to tolerate that much sitting on their ass."

Eve leaned forward and loudly shifted her silverware around on the table. "Why don't we avoid a reality clash and stay on topic?" she said.

Boyle glanced at her and continued. "What isn't included in the public narrative is that there are several contradictory frames still active in the public consciousness. A right to profit if your work is successful, but a strong distaste for absolute ownership. Control of distribution of a work, yet an inability to stop modifications of that work. A whole network of contradictory ideas and frames because none of this physically exists. Scarcity conditions people to absolutes. Without it, people can get along with anything," Boyle explained. She paused to clear her throat and take a sip from her wine glass. It seemed to take her a moment to swallow what she had just said.

"There are certain legal possibilities in that kind of space that you may not be accustomed to because your field is tied to so much physical reality. With a popular vote, we may be able to place a frame that will allow us to declare the current owners of the fast-travel mod…'irresponsible' is the word we're experimenting with, but it's only in the trial stages. It may require some repurposing. We can show the impact that the limited access is having in a way that you might not grasp because of certain metric constraints," Boyle said carefully.

Lane understood that she didn't expect him to understand a word of what she was saying. "You mean anticulture," he said.

Boyle looked surprised. "I apologize. Eve didn't mention you were into data theory," she said.

Eve laughed and crossed her legs. "Oh don't mind him, he has been hanging out with those GDK people. A few days ago, he didn't even know a thing about virtual worlds. Now he'll be quoting spatial processing and data functions like he invented the stuff. Negative space, information value, blah blah," Eve said.

Boyle turned and was more open with the surprise on her face. "You know about anticulture too? This was in an expert analysis at my firm. It's supposed to be cutting edge," Boyle said.

Eve rolled her eyes. "First off, only the GDK calls it that. It's just this popular thing right now. All it's good for is getting people to realize how a game mechanic is rigged or broken. Lane, what she's trying to say is that we're going to file a claim that attacks the owner's rights to the mod," Eve said.

"If enough people vote that something should be in the public commons, then it's grounds for making the mod freely accessible to anyone in *Tyrant*. Meaning anyone can copy it and sell it in the game," Boyle said.

Lane raised an eyebrow at that. "You want to make it so anyone can just produce a fast-travel mod? Isn't that going to be a bit chaotic?" Lane asked.

Eve sighed and crossed her arms over chest. "Yes. Maybe. I don't know. I haven't got a lot of options left. The designers won't help me. The GDK have been hammering my forces with flash raids for months now, and I'm running out of funds. After talking to you, I got to thinking about other legal solutions and contacted my own attorney about it," she said wearily. "Not to sound like a capitalist, but I like having money. I like buying my friends a nice drink or eating whatever I want when I go out. I like not having to be on the Standard programs. And I really, really like being the Tyrant. You don't know what it's like to command hundreds of people. To bring order to this chaotic and violent virtual world. If someone starts hoarding ore, you give them a lecture about free markets. From the barrel of a laser cannon," Eve explained.

"I imagine some other people would like a shot at being the Tyrant," Lane commented.

"Then they can take it from a level playing field," Eve said.

"With a new lawsuit? I think you mean tilt the odds back in your favor," Lane said dryly.

Boyle scowled and was about to speak before Eve put a hand on her arm. "I get it, Lane. We live in a datacentric society, and your gender doesn't really have a job anymore. What hasn't been automated has been regulated or rendered unnecessary. We don't even need you to reproduce anymore. Most men are unemployed. Most women are not. There are only so many jobs for mining in outer space and even fewer who can handle the risks. But I am not another woman trying to get back at you for centuries of patriarchy. I employ over a hundred men to manage my affairs in *Tyrant*. They make good money. They help *me* make good money. You think a woman working a job has time to reside in a virtual world? It's not just a second home, it's a second life.

"Sure, you spent a few hours flying around in a spaceship, but you don't know a thing about the game's economy, space relationships, or the thousands of other things going on. You know even less about handling the job of Tyrant. I'm not going to give you a lecture about being accused of being nothing but a sex object by women constantly. I'm not going to talk about the thousands of creepy e-mails I get from men. Or the rape jokes or the long list of abuses I deal with daily. All I am asking is that if I am going to be killed in my own damn virtual world, they do it fairly."

Lane finished off his expensive whiskey and tried to hold Eve's stare. As much as he had been enjoying the thrills of the GDK and reading their humor the past few days, his reality was more in line with Eve's than their strange sentiments. He understood money, and he understood wanting more of it. Anticulture, virtual markets, even Koff's crude jokes of obedience were just obstacles between Lane and becoming a space lawyer.

He had never sympathized with male realities. Not since he was a kid. Too many miners had stared at him as if he were a well-dressed freak. Too many times he had sat uncomfortable around a circle of men talking about sports and games. The loudest man always getting to talk. Being interrupted all the time. Lane had gotten through his legal training programs because he wanted to get away from the boys dorms. The dorms with their awful stench and rotating doors of sweaty, grabbing, dominating men. None of them would ever escape and Lane knew it. As Lane looked at Eve's anger and exhaustion, he found himself suddenly sympathetic.

"So you just want to make it so anyone can copy the mod into the game?" he asked.

She nodded slowly, a quiver of a smile returning to her face. Lane was once again struck by her beauty, the long hair pulled into a pony tail. He eyed her suit, a purple top with a long, airy pink bottom, the cleavage just barely hinted.

"Yes. I was going to see if you had any interest about finding out where their secret base is located. Maybe even add it to that original deal of ours?" Eve said playfully.

Boyle, uncertain at first, placed her pad on the table.

"Are we in agreement then about bringing a claim to void ownership for the mod in your lawsuit then? As the attorney, all you have to do is agree to having the vote. We can take care of the rest," Boyle said.

Lane tapped his glass. "First, I'd like another one of these. Then I'd like you to show me your argument video for the vote."

CHAPTER 16

Sitting at a large table in the Tohickon tavern, Lane was staring at an enormous Canvas pad along with his own pad and several printouts. The Canvas depicted what vaguely resembled the culture grid, which was composed of only a few square rules but numerous culture circles. This was an active feed and the circles crisscrossed rapidly. In thick letters at the top of the Canvas screen was the phrase "Creative Commons."

He tapped a circle at random, and the grid froze in place and an image appeared next to it of the president of France speaking from her podium. This was close to the center of the circle. It bore a strong resemblance to the central concept being depicted. As he dragged his finger out into various areas, all the permutations and variations of the image were shown. The space on the grid not only represented specific variations but possible variations. Lane smirked as he noticed that several of them involved rainbows.

Boyle's plan was to declare the owners of the fast-travel mod incompetent at distributing their own idea. Lane switched the view and highlighted the location of the mod within *Tyrant*. It was tiny compared to the enormous circles floating around it. They would argue that something as robust as fast-travel should clearly be far larger in its various uses than just one unit on the grid.

What confused Lane was the fact that Boyle's plan completely ignored the hard-coded regulations in the system. The mod was still clearly protected by the initial rights grant. You couldn't copy or modify the idea until it entered active distribution within the system.

"Look, you have got to stop treating this like a real-world economic problem," Boyle had said. "There is no scarcity. There is no such thing as growth.

Virtual property's rule system is a big Mobius strip. It just goes on and on, eating itself, new users finding old objects for the first time and old users discovering new objects."

A message interrupted Lane as he checked through the Creative Commons. It was Dale asking him where he was and mentioning that he had a big surprise for Lane.

"At Tohickon. Need to ask you something about mods in games," Lane tapped out in reply.

After Lane had spent several minutes poking around the culture grid, a red dress swished into his periphery. Lane's eyes slowly followed it up, higher, past a pair of remarkably flat breasts, higher still, until they finally settled on Dale's face. He was wearing a blonde wig and red lipstick to match the outfit. The dress itself, Lane noted, was designed to attract men.

"Going out as a lady tonight?" Lane asked. Dale rolled his eyes and pulled out a chair,

"Half-off drinks for lady boys at Ripley's. Don't judge. What's with the new toy?"

Lane pushed the Canvas pad to Dale.

"I never do," Lane said.

"Neat. *Tyrant*?" Dale asked.

"I'm checking over a copyright claim. See this marked circle here? They want to make it so anyone can use it. We'll declare the owners to be unce—"

"You're going to void ownership. I've been playing in virtual worlds my entire life, Lane. I make custom accessories and outfits for several games. How do you think I paid for this dress?" Dale asked as he pulled out a tube of lipstick. A flick of his pad turned the screen into a mirror, and he began to touch up his face. "You've got a lot of culture spheres to negotiate. Any person from one could be picked for the vote. What is your video like?" Dale asked.

Lane shrugged and laid a pair of ear buds next to the Canvas. "Do you mind? This thing is strictly off-line. That goes for any posts or comments to any of your online buddies," Lane said.

"Who would care, Lane?" Dale said as he popped in the ear buds. As he listened, his face twisted before he finally pulled the plugs out. "Ugh, do any of you people actually play video games?"

"I used to! The other lawyer put this together, and her profile says most of her work is in patent communes. I told her all this community-good crap and making the mod accessible to everyone would never be a valid frame. People are grateful for the stuff they want, not what they already have," Lane snapped.

Dale took a deep breath and looked around the bar. "Such a capitalist. People want what they think is good for the world. They just are wrong sometimes. I swear I can never get served in this place when I'm dressed for Ripley's. Buy me a drink, and I'll give you my official opinion. And make it something fruity," Dale said.

Lane went up to the bar and ordered a vodka and cranberry along with a beer. The bartender raised an eyebrow at Lane as he swiped his pad. Lane's account had dropped from three digits to two. Lane walked back to the table with the drinks wondering if he would be served again or if the bartender would suggest he try to earn savings ration bonus.

"I think I have finally figured you out, Lane. How a man can get to a point in his adult life where he has barely played a video game? You don't care about fame. You don't care about impressing anyone. It's just space lawyer and free market, all the way down with you. There's no complexity at all," Dale said when Lane sat down. He was being flirtatious. Lane pushed the drink to Dale and pointed at the Canvas unit, hoping to get him back on track. He didn't like talking about himself.

"You really should try being famous sometime. Even I used to be big for a few weeks. Back when the lady boy thing was big. That might have not been in your feed, but I was in the Top One Hundred. Global Ranks. It was simple, really. Everyone kept approaching it like you had to look like a woman, and I knew to keep just enough man present. Then all those bearded women started showing up, and the whole thing fizzled."

"Unlike money," Lane said.

"I'm sorry?" Dale asked.

"Money doesn't fizzle away because of someone else," Lane said.

"I thought that was the problem with it," Dale replied.

CHAPTER 17

Lane listened to Dale's critique but soon realized he was being milked for drinks. After Lane dried up, Dale had decided to move on to Ripley's.

Alone again, Lane tried to bring up an article on copyright frames but grew bored of it quickly. He checked the time. He checked his messages. He checked the newsfeed. There was nothing interesting. Lane idly brought up the opening screen for a random hook-up program without really thinking about it. The pad would scan the immediate area for anyone female and looking to hook up with a man. Both users would be pinged and alerted to their mutual interest. They would check out each other's profiles and made a choice.

The last time Lane had used the device, a woman dressed in overalls coming off a work shift pinged him. They sat, had a drink, and what was supposed to be a brief conversation before going someplace more private had turned into an actual conversation. She complained about work, and Lane, not knowing anything about her job, had only nodded and agreed. She kept complaining and venting until a full hour had gone by. Lane had stayed because she kept buying his drinks. After an hour, when Lane finally asked where she would like to go after this, she sheepishly admitted she wasn't in the mood to have sex anymore. They parted ways, and Lane never heard from her again.

Lane decided to just do a brief scan of the area and see what would happen. There were two pings, somebody at the bar next door and another one two blocks down. Lane thought about widening up the search radius but decided that would just be pushing his odds. The first woman was about Lane's age. A few of her public photos showed her in long dressing gowns and wearing sunglasses. It was an asexual style, designed to highlight colors and face more than anything else. She had dark skin and big eyes. There was a glimpse of armpit hair in one picture. Her search status was set to "Haven't talked to a man in a while, see where it goes." It was not very inviting, and Lane tapped to the next search. This one was a redhead and had dressed herself with a more sexual style. There was a photo of her sitting on a porch overlooking the river, drinking iced tea. A slim, purple dress, exposed cleavage with enough to still leave one wondering, and a big welcoming smile. Lane tapped the photo for a ping.

And then he waited. Lane wondered what she was thinking if she was going through his own profile. He had a picture of himself looking sharp in an expensive suit to make the fact that he was employed as prominent as possible. One of the requirements of the program was that you list your physical measurements, and this included your own penis. Lane had been sheepish about it, but if you didn't post it, you never got any response at all. Lane refused to post a picture of himself naked, although plenty of men did.

After a few more minutes of waiting, Lane decided she must have decided there were better options on this particular evening and moved on. He scanned again. Lane was caught up in the process now. He wanted someone to look at him and send some kind of response. In his mind he dimly recognized this was still about soliciting sex from someone, but Lane was now more concerned with just the validation of someone pinging him back.

Another scan, no one new. He checked his messages, he checked the news, he scanned the area again. The redhead had dropped off the grid. Lane thought again about expanding the search parameters, but the problem was that if you got too far, then there would be too much of a delay. You would ping them and they'd say they were interested, but by the time you met with each other, the impulse was gone.

Lane idly tapped up Grace's profile and checked to see if she was broadcasting her location. Despite her harsh attitude that morning, Lane found himself wondering if she had experienced a change of heart.

She was in private mode. Or had possibly blocked him, Lane thought. He tapped the message button and sent a short "Got any plans tonight?" He waited a few moments and got no answer. Whatever she was doing, he wasn't going to be a part of it.

Lane decided to finish his drink and call it a night. As he was doing so, the redhead he had pinged walked into the Tohickon and looked around the small crowd. Lane made eye contact with her, and before he could set down his glass, she was walking over to his table.

"Hi! I saw your ping. My name is Frankie. What's yours?" she said cheerfully.

"Lane. I didn't expect you to stop by after I didn't get a ping back," Lane said nervously.

Frankie nodded and set her pad down on the table. She was a bit bigger than she had looked in her photos. Bigger, but her breasts still swelled underneath her dress, and enough cleavage showed to give Lane trouble putting his eyes anywhere else.

"Do you mind if I get a one-time view on your medicals? Can't be too careful these days, you know. I'm happy to open up mine as well," Frankie said.

Lane nervously tapped a few buttons on the medical record application. She wouldn't be able to save any of the information. She did the same for him, but he only briefly scanned the disease section. His hands had a bit of sweat on them, and it was hard to work the screen like that.

He suddenly remembered that he would need to pop a birth control pill if she was serious about all of this. The pill would take effect in seconds and would give him a significant testosterone boost along with its other effects. He kept a spare pill on him, but as he was pulling it out, Frankie suddenly placed her foot on his thigh. Lane felt a surge of excitement and adrenaline as a toe crept up to his slowly firming penis.

"I've got us covered, dear. Why don't you just follow me to the bathroom?" Frankie said. Suddenly reckless with desire, Lane obeyed. He stood and awkwardly reached down to adjust his crotch so that the bulge would not be so apparent to the few people in the bar. No one seemed to notice a redheaded woman leading a man into the bathroom.

The door closed behind them, and Frankie backed into him so that her rear was rubbing into his crotch. She moaned lightly as her hand fished around the door and found the lock. Lane's hands began at her sides and slowly worked up to her chest. The soft dress barely held her beasts in place, and after a few moments of fondling, they fell out. She giggled and turned, kissing Lane's neck before grabbing his head and pulling his mouth to hers. They pulled apart for a moment, and Lane found his head swimming with so many different thoughts that he wasn't sure what to think. What am I doing? Who is this person? He began to slightly panic as he wondered what Eve or Tricia or even Grace would think of this. Would they care? Did it matter if he had sex with this woman?

Frankie looked into his eyes, confused by his hesitation as she panted. She felt his crotch with her hand, and he realized he was losing his erection. She gave him a wolfish grin and kissed his neck while her hands began to work around his belt. There was the clink of metal as the belt gave way, and his pants slid to the ground while Frankie's red hair followed. Lane still could not think, could not do anything but rub his hands through her hair as wonderful warmth and wetness covered his penis. Just a brush of teeth and the sound of lips until he realized he was completely down her throat. She held the position longer than he thought possible, a slight gurgling sound coming from her as he softly began to moan. His erection felt as if it were lead.

She stood up, that same wolfish grin on her face, and lifted up her leg while she rubbed her crotch along his penis. There was no underwear. She angled her hips, and suddenly he was inside of her. Hands gripped his sides as she lunged closer to whisper, "Fuck me."

Confused and almost insane with lust, Lane grabbed her by the bottom and began to thrust inside of her. She didn't moan or respond. The grin on her face slowly faded as she held eye contact and continued to breath heavily. He could feel the walls of her, the space inside, and pressed his penis against its edge with each thrust. Lane closed his eyes as the ecstasy became too much for him. His leg muscles tightened and began to burn from supporting her weight. Finally, he felt release and relaxed while panting. Frankie continued to rub herself up and down his penis, light panting coming from her as she waited until Lane had completely discharged before pulling it out.

They stood awkwardly in the bathroom. Frankie was looking away as she fixed her dress and hair. Lane reached for his pants and awkwardly went to the sink to rinse himself off. When he turned around, the door was closing, and Frankie had left. He tried to follow for a moment before realizing his pants were still down. By the time he had them back on and had gone outside, she was gone. Still confused and feeling raw from the experience, Lane sat to catch his breath and wipe the sweat from his brow. When he tapped up his pad, her medical information was still up.

She wasn't taking any birth control.

CHAPTER 18

Lane was gently rocking with the electric bus as it hit a bump in the road to North Charleston. He alternated between the odd sensation that he should be grateful for the experience he had just had or frightened. His access to Frankie's medical information had expired, but he had read the log several times over. Had she wanted to get pregnant? There were countless ways a woman could have that done without having sex with a total stranger in a bathroom. She didn't have his consent to have a child with him, much less the mountain of paperwork they'd have to fill out to create a binding support contract. People rarely bothered with it when the Standards program existed for everyone. Artificial insemination, cloning a sperm, or even just having the child delivered from a tube would have been an option.

Lane opened the program for crimes and stared at the screen blankly. If you held the icon down for a long period of time, an alert would be broadcast. Every single pad in the area would be notified that someone had pressed the warning, including the police. He switched past this to the reported crimes menu and brought up rape. It asked if he could identify the man in question. He had to backtrack and approach the issue from the advanced menu before he found a spot for men to report sex crimes by women. Initially Lane got the impression it was checking to see if he was a child whom a woman had molested. There was an option to bring up charges as a woman toward another woman, but that did Lane little good. The issue, Lane quickly realized, was that he had to click Yes to the "Did you freely consent?" question.

Lane finally gave up and decided to try and let it go. He looked up from his pad at the bus around him. Two men in Standard slacks, greasy from a day's labor, were sitting toward the front staring out the window. A group of women were huddled in the back whispering and giggling to themselves. They were wearing stylish summer coats, and they looked young. Their clothes were bulky, not too expensive, and meant to make them appear large with little concern for the male gaze. The bus was otherwise empty, with Lane sitting apart from everyone on the right row. For a brief moment, he wondered how he would frame his problem to either group. A bunch of women who didn't care and a bunch of men who would love to get screwed in a bathroom.

Lane's doubts still lingered as he sat down in his apartment, hooked up his pad, and activated *Tyrant*. As the screen loaded, Lane saw he was still on *Zulfikar Bronze*, with Derrick onboard as well. His green avatar was sitting in the cockpit. "Nice of you to join us."

"What's going on?" Lane asked.

"Arranging for our ride," Derrick answered. A large blue ball began to form ahead of them. A chime sounded, and the blue ball suddenly turned into a ship that was almost as big as *Sojourner Truth*. The tag under it read *Zulfikar Gold*. Their ship cruised into the landing bay and settled into place. They exited, and Lane followed Derrick's avatar through the halls of the ship. They entered the engine section, and Lane saw thousands of users walking around an enormous blue device that looked like a pillar. The surface of the device was shaped like a coil, and infrequently the base would emit a blue light that would travel to the top. It was a bit archaic looking to Lane, like a child's idea of what space technology would be.

"Damn thing isn't even original. Nipped it off the creative commons from some old space TV show. That, Lane, is the means of our deliverance from the Tyrant," Derrick explained with a touch of pride in his voice.

"What is it?" Lane asked, but he already had a pretty good idea what the answer would be.

"It's the fast-travel mod. Only one in the game," Derrick answered. They were making their way through the multitude of users. "No resource cost. No energy burn. Just punch in a location and pop, there you are. We've been giving the Tyrant fits with it for months."

When they finally reached the mod, Derrick stopped in front of it and began working with a console.

"Ah, about that. I actually really want to check out the GDK conference, so I need to tell you something. Eve has asked me to help her with this problem," Lane said sheepishly.

Derrick laughed and turned around. "Lane, I'm not an idiot. I know. It was pretty obvious after Eve posted about meeting with a male attorney on her profile. We're pretty rare in this town."

"Oh. So…why are you helping me?" Lane asked.

"We got lucky when we snagged this copy of the mod. The programmer is a member of the GDK, labor feminist. She was furious with Gateway about something and asked us to get her some media attention. She gave us this mod courtesy of Gateway, and we staged a big flame riot," Derrick explained.

"So Tally was in on it the whole time? Was the cat real?" Lane asked, confused.

"Yeah, that actually did happen. Horrible business. She got really upset about it and swore to give up all technology. Something about the car autopilot, I think. She set up a bot to manage her feed for the appeal and then left town. We never got too much publicity because Gateway froze the deal, buried the litigation, and disavowed any knowledge of it," Derrick said.

A message flashed up on Lane's profile asking him if he'd like to download a program from Derrick. It was a copy of the fast travel mod. He confirmed the download. "So Gateway really did have the mod created?" Lane asked.

"Yeah, weirdest damn thing. They had to pay the developers a fortune for the time imbalance. The number squatters figure it's some kind of advertising campaign. Maybe a new TV show or something? What I brought you here for is to see if you'd be interested in a little copyright claim. If you can prove that the owners of the mod are negligently handling it, then we ca—"

"You can freely distribute the mod into the game. I know. Eve is planning on doing the exact same thing. She hired an attorney to put together a public vote video and everything," Lane said.

He heard Derrick whistle and saw his avatar loosely mimic the gesture. "She already put it all together, huh? Damn, I am going to miss her after we destroy her," Derrick said wistfully.

"What makes you think she will lose?" Lane asked.

"Because all I have to do is blow up her character to win. She has to overthrow an entire culture to stop me," Derrick explained.

Lane followed him into a large conference room behind the blue mod pillar. Derrick sat in a chair, and Lane did the same. Several other avatars entered the room and took seats.

"Everyone, this is Lane. He has just told me that the Tyrant has been doing our work for us to declare the ownership of the fast-travel mod void. In addition to inviting him to GDK Con, I've decided to let him be present for this vote. Are we going to try to stop the Tyrant from having the mod put into the Creative Commons, or should we go forward with the plan?" Derrick said.

"Oh, I see the mighty patriarch is taking the lead again," a female voice said.

There was a groan, and someone barked, "Oh for fuck's sake, it'll be your turn as soon as his term is up." Someone made the swooshing noise. A rainbow exploded out of the table, and an eruption of laughter filled the room.

The female voice spoke again, "All right, all right, the patriarch wants to talk about the mod people. Personally, I have no clue what's going to happen if we make that thing freely distributed into the game. There's no way to predict something like that. Spaceships, commodity prices, voting indexes—all that stuff you can just hack the metrics. This? We're totally off-grid."

There were several murmurs of assent.

"Anybody ask Tally what she thinks?" someone asked.

There was a laugh and another replied, "You can get on horseback and ride out into Bumblefuck, Montana, to find her if you want. I think she was serious about unplugging. She said she might try to make it to the con, though."

"None of us can predict something that is going to radically alter the game this extensively. Prices are going to plummet, power is going to change hands, and there is going to be a massive surge in anticulture with all that change. Since we're just aggregating a bunch of opinions, I say change is good. Making it so any ship can instantly go anywhere in the game is going to have an impact," another voice said.

A few more murmurs of agreement and a swooshing noise.

Someone asked, "What does the patriarch think?"

"Eh, why not? If it turns out the mod ruins the game, the designers can just turn it off. We're still siphoning money out of the Tyrant's empire, and we're all still having fun, right? I say we do it. Now, who's excited about GDK Con?"

CHAPTER 19

The meeting carried on for a while, but Lane only listened. He couldn't really tell who was in charge or if these people even represented a ruling majority. He planned to take a train up into the tech belt in the Appalachian Mountains, but he still needed to figure out a ride to the site.

Lane shut down for the night and tried to go to sleep. He couldn't shake the memory of the Tohickon bathroom from his mind. He decided it was the loss of control that bothered him the most. As much as he wanted to blame the woman for it, Lane knew he was the one who had activated the program. He was the one who had created the situation. He drifted off to sleep as a bad memory floated to his subconscious and drifted away again. An emotion that had no voice in the moment.

Lane awoke to a loud beep from his pad. The sun in the window told him he had overslept, and he jumped out of bed. He checked the pad; it was a message from Eve: "Can you approve the copyright appeal? Just hit the link."

Still groggy, Lane tapped the link, punched in his password, and confirmed without giving it much thought. The GDK were fine with it, Eve was fine with it, and now that Lane was getting to the bottom of this absurd appeal, he was fine with it. Maybe Koff would warm up to him after he reported what he had found out about Tally and the mod last night.

A brief shower and bus ride later, Lane strolled into the office with a light step and drummed his fingers on his desk rapidly. He was in a good mood. He was getting a vacation. He was going to wrap this appeal up and get his job back. Grace walked by his desk, and he gave her a smile and a wave. She avoided his gaze but glanced back at the last minute and sheepishly returned the smile.

Lane's reverie was broken by a loud beep from his pad. It was from Koff, "Office. Now." Just a sliver of fear crept down Lane's back as he wondered what was going to happen to him this time. As he walked by Kayla's office, he saw her looking at baby clothes idly. She had on ear buds, and her eyes had a wide expression he had never seen before. Lane considered knocking on her door but thought better of it.

When he arrived at Koff's office, she had her back to him, looking out the window. She had on another suit that fit her snugly, accentuating the love handles on her sides and her plump rear. Lane wondered if she enjoyed the outfit sheerly for the dare that anyone say a word about it to her, woman or man.

"Lane, what exactly do you think we agreed to in our previous conversation about the appeal you're handling?" Koff asked.

Lane thought a moment as he tried his best to recall the exchange. "I'm going to go to the GDK conference and will get this appeal resolved factually instead of by claiming there was some sort of computing error," he said carefully.

"Splendid! That's exactly what I thought we agreed to. So why is the president of the McAngus Law Corporation personally writing me to say that she wants to know what the hell is going on with this appeal? Apparently we are, let me quote this for you: 'threatening the property rights of Gateway Incorporated by alleging they cannot manage their own copyrights.' What does that have to do with my paying for you to go to some circle jerk out in the mountains?" Koff shouted.

"It's not really a circle jerk. Some of their members are women," Lane said sheepishly as he sat down.

"I don't care if it's a transsexual lady boy parade, Lane. What have you done?" Koff barked.

"Okay, calm down. The whole appeal is really about this mod for a game called *Tyrant*. Tally, who is going to possibly be at this conference, persuaded the GDK to cause a big publicity stunt over the mod. There's probably more to it, but basically, if we just shift the mod into the public commons, the appeal should resolve itself because there's nothing left to appeal," Lane explained.

The look on Koff's face was a mixture of disbelief and anger. "There is *more* to this thing? Still? How complex could it possibly be? A client goes missing for a few days, and you're suddenly filing copyright suits against one of the most powerful corporations in space!"

"I didn't expect them to care about a copyright. They disavowed any knowledge, and it's pennies to them. It didn't even cross my mind they would be upset!" Lane shouted back.

Koff took a deep breath and sat in her chair. She tapped on her pad, her eyes rolling across the screen as she parsed text, and then she leaned back in her chair before taking another deep breath. With one hand she rubbed her temples and with the other she reached into her drawer to pull out a fresh bag of candies. She opened it with one hand.

"I know. Which is why even though I am currently very upset, it does not make a lot of sense to be upset with you. It does make sense to be upset, though," Koff said wearily. She groaned and murmured, "None of this makes any sense. This is all some bitch at the head office's doing. They know I'm in line to move up."

Lane chose this moment to keep his mouth shut as Koff's mind found its own resolution to this new conflict. The only sound between them was Koff's chewing on candy.

A ping interrupted, followed by an odd electronic noise. Koff's eyes bulged as she pulled up her pad. "It's the CEO of Gateway. She's calling me. Under high priority notice. Lane, what is going on?"

Lane shook his head as he reached for his own pad and brought up a link to Eve's profile. He sent her a message that read, "We need to talk."

The response was almost immediate, "Busy. Meet in one hour for coffee?" Lane looked up at the sound of a ping and another odd electronic sound. Koff had still not answered the call.

"You're going to a conference that these people are all going to be at, right? The woman who filed the appeal, the Gay Dark Boys or whatever. Do you think you can make this appeal go away from their end?" Koff asked.

Lane looked at her for a moment and decided to risk it. "I still need to rent a car to get there. You just covered the train tickets."

Koff gave him a long glare that was interrupted only because of another ping and electronic blare.

"Fine. Expense it. Whatever. Just make this go away. Quietly, with as little data to follow as possible. All right?"

Lane nodded and made for the door as Koff finally answered the call. He only paused when he heard a quirky and positive voice ring out in the room, "Why hello, Mistress CEO! I am so sorry to have kept you waiting. Busy day and everything! What can I do for you?"

CHAPTER 20

Eve was running late. Lane idly screened the news feed but saw nothing of interest. As he waited, a message from Tricia popped up asking him what he was up to that evening. Lane suddenly had an idea and typed out a hurried message: "I have somehow managed to piss off the legal counsel for Gateway, Incorporated. Can you do a data crunch on any mods or other projects they've sponsored in the past few months? I'm trying to figure out what's going on."

He sent the message and waited a few minutes before Tricia bounced back: "I'll do it on contract. I have been eyeing a dress at that shop on Calhoun, and I need some money to cover it."

Lane decided Koff would just have to find out about the charge after the fact and confirmed it. Tricia sent him back a picture of a little girl opening a present excitedly to thank him.

Lane saw Eve walk in and was a bit surprised by her dress. She had on large sunglasses and ill-fitting clothes that were a bit wrinkled and worn. It was the opposite of the stylish, slim outfits Lane had found so attractive earlier. She sat down without taking off her glasses and gave Lane only the barest hint of a smile. "Eve, what's going on? I've got Gateway contacting my boss. This mod business is going haywire," Lane asked with a slight note of panic.

Eve reached into her purse and slid her pad over to Lane with the screen open. On the screen was a list of thousands of messages pouring into her account. A second window set to the forums for *Tyrant* showed an error message and a critical memory warning.

"I am completely under siege digitally. The moment you cleared the video, the vote went out to about a thousand *Tyrant* players. As soon as it hit, my profile exploded. The game is barely operating because of all the server activity. At first we thought it was a surge of new users opening accounts, but it's people clogging up the system with check requests. Everything is going crazy," Eve said. She sounded exhausted and short on sleep. "I don't suggest reading them. Most of it is flame stuff. I can't even tell what's legitimate and what's generated by a computer."

"It's not the GDK doing it. They were planning something similar to get the mod distributed. I know because last night we got to talking," Lane explained.

Eve laughed and sounded like herself for a few moments. "I know all about your little visit, Lane. You'll find that after several years of fighting, the GDK and I have gotten used to each other. I contact someone, they contact that person a few days later. Back in the early days, they tried attacking me personally, and they found out I don't waste my time going after them individually. I go after their friends and family. After a while, we mutually agreed to avoid this sort of thing and let people have their space."

"So why are you dressed like that?" Lane asked.

Eve took off her sunglasses and flashed him a smile. "What's wrong? Not happy when I don't dress to please you?"

Lane shook his head and pointed at the huge shirt she had on. "It's a bit hot for that sort of outfit," he said.

"Last night I noticed two women in black suits following me. Business outfit, very official sort of thing. I've had people follow me before, but never women and definitely never well-dressed ones," Eve explained. She punched a few buttons on her pad, and Lane saw a message pop up from her entitled "Metrics Report: Tyrant."

"Look at that, will you? I'm going to find someone to serve me a coffee," Eve said.

Tyrant had, very recently, taken a dip in popularity. Some of this was because of the servers being rocked, but that had only started this morning. It took time for a virtual market to respond to changes, even if it did so faster than a real one. An image of the game's culture grid came up showing an enormous blue sphere encompassing almost all of the spheres around it. This one was designated as parties dissatisfied with the game.

As Lane began highlighting the various spheres to see what was going on, he noticed a tall woman walk into the restaurant. She was wearing a pantsuit, long and black with a tight waist and pockets that seemed full. Lane couldn't tell for sure, but judging by the cheek line and how large the sleeves were, he guessed she was trying to disguise a serious amount of muscle. She sat several tables away from Lane and began to nonchalantly flip through a pad. Lane tried not to stare and instead began nervously looking around for Eve. Just as he was about to send her a message, he noticed that Eve's pad was still in his hands.

When she sat back down, Lane gestured with his eyes to the tall woman in black. She had glanced at Eve for just a moment before burying her eyes in some device. Eve's sunglasses were back on, but she gave him a big smile. "It's all right. I turned off my location alerts just to see if they would keep showing up once I turned them back on. She saw you with that pad, yes? Good. Talk to me a little bit longer, then I'm going to scoot," Eve said.

Lane looked at her in bewilderment. "You're being very calm about all this," he commented.

"Comes from the Tyrant thing. I keep trying to tell myself this is more dangerous than a bunch of hackers screaming at me online but…how big could it really be?"

"They might be working for Gateway," Lane said. Eve shrugged. "So how is the vote going?" he asked.

"We're still getting results in since the priority is much lower than a public narrative vote. The game getting completely crushed isn't exactly helping. It looks like your friends might have tipped the scales, though, because somehow or another most of the votes were Yes within seconds of receiving the transmission. Which means they didn't even watch the video. I thought we had fixed that particular bug, but I don't mind at the moment," Eve said.

Eve bit her lip and then slipped Lane's pad into her purse. Lane was about to say something when she shot him another dazzling smile and just barely pursed her mouth to shush him. "You're going to the GDK conference, right? Lots of boys drinking and beating on their chests. I'll have your pad delivered to you tomorrow morning, I promise. Apparently even being off the Standards program doesn't give you much privacy these days," she said.

As she stood up, Lane did the same while still trying to keep his voice down. "Eve! What are you going to do about these people? What if this gets dangerous?"

The tall woman looked up from her device for just a moment, and Eve paused to look at Lane. "Do you know why I call my flagship *Sojourner Truth*? Because she is my favorite women's rights activist. You know what she did when a man once accused her of having to be a man herself to accomplish everything she did? She took off her shirt and showed him her tits."

Lane glanced at the tall woman in black, who stood up from her own table and began sauntering toward the exit.

"I don't understand. What does that have to do with anything?"

"It means I can take care of myself. And leave the pad on for a few hours, OK?" she said. With that, Eve leaned in and gave Lane a kiss on the cheek. He was still standing there trying to understand when she waltzed out the door, the tall woman in black picking up pace behind her.

CHAPTER 21

Lane made his way back home, staring out the window of the bus and nervously wondering what was going to happen next. He checked Eve's pad occasionally to make sure it was updating its location, but was unable to do anything with it because of password protection. He idly wondered if he had gotten any messages or what the latest news was on his own pad.

A sinking feeling set in as he made the walk back home and saw a tall woman in a black business suit standing near his apartment building. She was still wearing sunglasses despite how dark it was. Lane waved at her with Eve's pad in his hand and managed his best smile. Her face betrayed no emotion, and she didn't move from her spot.

Thinking better of pushing the issue, Lane went inside and sat down in his tiny room. A glance at Eve's pad told him it didn't have much power left, and it wouldn't do him much good charged anyways. Lane decided to go without checking the web and anxiously wondered what he was missing.

As Lane drifted off to sleep, he tried to focus on the trip ahead. He wished he could check his messages because the GDK confirmation had included a list of stuff he would need to bring: casual clothes that he didn't mind getting dirty, a sleeping bag if he had it, but bunk beds would be provided. Lane wasn't much of a camper, and the website implied if he could make it out there, they would take care of the rest.

In the morning Lane woke and glanced out the window to see that it was still early. He was excited enough that he couldn't fall back to sleep. He hopped out of bed and began moving about the apartment to get ready. Some Standard clothes he had from a few years back for exercise. Some protein bars in case he wanted a snack on the train. He took a quick shower and packed up everything he would need. The conference was only for the weekend, but he prepared as if it could go on indefinitely.

He nervously wondered what he would do on the train ride and idly thumbed Eve's pad. The power was completely dead now. He was relieved when he checked outside and found his pad sitting against his room door. A quick check showed that it was fully charged, and when he activated the screen, he saw there was an unsent message addressed to him: "Lane, thanks for your help. I needed to get a few things taken care of out of sight. I'll just get a new pad and deactivate the accounts. And guess what, we won the vote!"

After reading the message, Lane saw the time and realized he needed to get to the train station. He grabbed his bags, hopped the bus, and hastily checked his pad on the short ride. A message from Koff about where to rent the car and a warning to get the appeal resolved. She didn't mention what the CEO had wanted. Lane grimly hoped this would all blow over as so many other things did in space law. As he scrolled through the various stories coming in from his reality filter, he saw no mention of *Tyrant* other than a notice about a dip in the virtual world's value.

Lane stepped off the bus at the train station and studied the unfamiliar building. It was a unique combination of modern and old sensibilities, with thick walls of black asteroid metal rooted into place by pillars of brick and plaster. Kiosks for tickets were designed to resemble older machines with elaborate tactile interfaces and screens that didn't respond to touch. Alongside the walls were train routes of the entire Southeastern Union with glowing dots to indicate where the train was at that precise moment. Lane approached one of the archaic systems and idly pressed a few buttons before giving up and connecting his pad. It took only a few button presses before he was told the train would be arriving in fourteen minutes and where to take his seat.

As Lane looked around the station, he noticed Derrick leaning against a pillar thumbing through his pad. When he noticed Lane, he flipped the screen toward him. It was a culture grid, and Derrick was tapping his finger on a shrinking blue circle. "Look at the impact of the mod! Complete devaluation of market value in a day! Just one day! A complete anticulture impact, and just like that, the whole thing starts deflating," Derrick exclaimed.

"Anticulture did all that?" Lane asked. Derrick flipped the pad back toward him and oscillated the grid's view to include other virtual markets. "Exactly. Complete systemic meaning awareness for everything in the game. When this circle starts hitting these circles, it's going to start spreading," Derrick said excitedly.

"You're describing it like a disease now. Isn't the market value of *Tyrant* going down? Why would you be happy about that?" Lane asked as he sat down next to Derrick. Other people were trickling into the station, and he saw no reason to not grab a seat for the brief time before the train arrived.

"Oh sure, in the short term, the world's taking it on the chin. The virtual market will bounce back eventually. I'm just enjoying getting to see it happen right in front of my face like this," Derrick said.

As they were chatting, a man approached them with a grin on his face. Lane recognized him from the gay bar Dale had invited him to a few nights earlier. "Morgan, right?" Lane said.

He nodded, and they shook hands. "Derrick, this is Morgan. He was one of the folks who tipped me off to the GDK earlier."

Derrick smiled and shook hands with Morgan, who answered, "A pleasure, Patriarch."

"Oh, no no. There are no formal titles here. Hell, we just have that set up for outsiders. Half the time nobody listens to me, and the other half they want to know when it's going to be their turn," Derrick explained.

Morgan nodded graciously. "You always put on such a good show. All the people talking about the patriarch saying this or declaring that, I was hoping to maybe discuss a few trading opportunities you might be interested in."

"It's all about to be old news to me, buddy. I'm retiring. What kind of goods are you offering?" Derrick said.

There was a sudden shout, and a short teenage boy grabbed him from behind in a hug. Derrick laughed and twisted around to hug him back. Morgan looked at Lane questioningly.

"With the mod changing things so drastically, I'm pushing weapons now. Big ones," Morgan explained.

CHAPTER 22

Lane tried to follow Derrick onto the train but lost him in the sea of bodies. It was an express line that would go all the way to the Tech Belt, which stretched from Atlanta to Richmond. Greenville was just the halfway point. Commuters coming from Charleston could access a train to Atlanta or continue on into the heart of the Southeastern Union in North Carolina. As Lane took his seat, several warning chimes rang out, and the train began skimming along the electric rails. It picked up speed until the city buildings of black iron and brick became a blur.

Lane's breath sucked in slightly when they crossed the Charleston city line and the grey blur became huge, opulent fields of green. South Carolina's farmland was pristine for growing the core crops of the Public Commons. Thousands of perfect rows of soy, corn, and various vegetables were neatly arranged in perfect symmetry. The effect was almost hypnotic as Lane watched the rows speed by uninterrupted. Occasionally, a tall steel walker would disrupt the flow with its disjointed legs and dozens of tentacle-like arms. At the top of each one was a metal pod with a pilot checking the crops for pests and readying them for harvest.

Morgan interrupted him with a cough as he sat next to Lane. He was holding a pad and anxiously tapping through various messages. "Don't suppose you mind me joining you? I have been following this fast-travel mod ever since the news hit yesterday. Market has gone absolutely crazy. What were you thinking when you filed to have it unleashed like that?" Morgan said with a touch of annoyance. "People are selling the things left and right.

Plugging them into junk craft, freighters, fighters, anything they can find. I thought I'd make a bit of profit distributing, but just look at these figures!"

He handed Lane his pad, and Lane squinted at a series of bars in a square block. He was confused by it until he realized it was a two-dimensional linear variable measure.

"Sorry…you're…the stuff going right is measuring time, correct? And the more it increases, that's the amount of money. So the variations in profits are depicted in the increase in scale of the bars?" Lane asked nervously.

Morgan laughed and shook his head. "You're making it too complicated. It's just a profit chart. It's not charting the meaning of the money, it's just money. Old capitalist trick for staying focused on the bottom line. Look, see? This is where my profits start dipping in all sectors besides the mod sales."

"I thought you said it wasn't making you any money?" Lane asked.

"Anyone can make them, so the price has plummeted. I'm in a position to profit in that kind of situation, but it's starting to affect everything else in the game. I think the mod is causing the whole culture to break down. The freighters are operating with no more risk. There are no pirates stealing their cargo. No rivals getting there before them. It's just people shuttling goods around. And the pirates aren't hiding out in the cracks trying to get the drop on people. They're organizing. Look, you can already see it in the culture spheres. All these pirate factions are starting to cluster and merge around this red square. The one that keeps growing? That's the mod," Morgan explained as he pointed at an enormous red block.

Lane hadn't seen this behavior just a day before when he had been checking the *Tyrant* culture grid.

Several of the squares and spheres in the culture grid had also shrunken in response to the increasing size. There were fewer applications for other ship technologies as the mod supplanted them. Unlike the spheres, which constantly moved and drifted across the culture grid based on group whims, the square was an absolute. As the mod rule square came in contact with the other culture spheres, they seemed to be shrinking.

"Is it going to be OK?" Lane asked with more curiosity than worry.

"It is changing. The designers might put a stop to it. The Tyrant and the GDK are going to be taking their war up a notch, I imagine. I don't suppose you have a way to undo this whole mess if it turns out the game is ruined? *Tyrant* was such a good—" Morgan's pad pinged. He pulled it up to check the message and made a sucking noise with his teeth.

"It's your friend Dale. Has a bit of a crush, I'm afraid," Morgan said with a touch of amusement in his voice. Lane leaned over, but Morgan gave him a look and tilted the pad away.

"What sort of message did he send?" Lane asked.

Morgan rolled his eyes and sighed. "The clingy type. I'm sure you know the sort," he said.

Lane blinked and tried to think for a moment. He couldn't really remember any time a woman had been very clingy with him.

Morgan read the expression on Lane's face, and his mouth dropped open slightly. "Asking what you're up to every hour of the day? Bad jokes? Photos of where they are? None of it?" Morgan asked incredulously.

"I only date women," Lane said defensively.

"Well, there's your problem right there. They don't have any need for a man. I used to have a few romps with women myself, but there's nothing long-term in it for them. Dale here may be looking for a sugar daddy, but…well, he does at least want the attention," Morgan explained dryly.

"It's not always about…there's just…I don't think that's true. Derrick is married to a woman. Lots of other men are. Most of them are in relationships every now and again as it suits them. There's no need to go dismissing the whole thing as a farce," Lane said, a bit more angrily than the situation merited.

Morgan paused and looked at Lane carefully. "I think our realities are a bit different on this one. I apologize. I had forgotten about what you said at the bar earlier. I am never good with deletions. You never quite understand what happened," Morgan said slowly.

Lane felt the anger flush out of him, and he nervously plucked at his pad for something, anything to look at to seem busy.

Sensing the shift, Morgan said, "It was good to talk to you, OK?" He placed a hand on Lane's shoulder.

Lane looked at him and smiled earnestly, already sorry about what he had said. "It's no trouble. People are always saying my reality is a bit weird, you know?"

Morgan nodded and was beginning walking down the aisle, pad in hand, when the door to the next train car opened and a tall woman with pink-and-red hair stepped through. She had freckles all over her face, and she had piercings along her ears and nose. She wasn't dressed asexually; her clothes fit her tightly, and her shirt had a large enough V that Lane thought she might be trying to attract men. Yet she seemed to walk as if she didn't much care what anyone thought. When she saw Morgan, her face burst into a smile, and she ran up to hug him. He laughed and opened his arms to greet her. She was taller than Morgan, and when they hugged, she looked directly at Lane over his shoulder. He froze. Her gaze seemed to look directly into him so that when she grinned again, he felt she meant it for him.

As they pulled apart, Lane overheard Morgan invite the woman for a drink in the bar car. Lane hurriedly pulled out his pad and tried to do a scan for everyone in the room. A list of people popped along with their photos, but he saw no image of her.

Just as Lane was about to stand up and awkwardly follow them, Derrick entered the train car and gave a shout. Both the woman and Morgan turned, the woman moving forward to hug Derrick while Morgan hung back. They exchanged a few pleasantries that Lane couldn't quite make out before parting ways.

As Derrick was passing by, Lane reached out his hand and tugged at his sleeve. Derrick looked down questioningly.

"Derrick, who is that woman?" Lane asked.

Derrick blinked and then gave Lane a grin. "You don't know? But you've already met! She was the woman at the GDK meeting the other night. Her name is Alice. Why?"

"She is pretty," Lane said, unsure what he should do next.

CHAPTER 23

Lane spent the rest of the train ride looking through Alice's profile, her pictures, and anything else he could find out about her. She was a laborist. Very active, it appeared; she was involved in a lot of media productions for it. She seemed to have a thing for machine horror, a subgenre Lane was not familiar with but seemed harmless enough.

He couldn't tell if she was interested in men or women. She didn't seem to be advertising anything one way or the other. Which was usually a good sign from Lane's perspective; it was easier to persuade someone to talk with him if she wasn't very sure about what she was looking for. He scrolled through her various photographs and was surprised to feel a lump slowly forming as he looked at her. Every time the door to his train car opened, he looked up hoping it would be her coming through. Lane was scrolling through an article she had posted about techno feminism when the train announced they would be arriving in Greenville shortly. Lane closed the article. It was outside his reality, and he had not understood very much of it.

Derrick stood up several rows behind them and loudly explained, "Everyone going to GDK Con, there will be buses just around the corner from here. Hopefully we'll have enough room this time! Don't be afraid to get friendly with one another!" There were a few murmurs and groans at this.

The train silently came to a halt, and there was a brief burst of chaos as passengers stood to gather their things. Lane waited patiently and twiddled his thumbs. Several people were talking about what was going on in *Tyrant*. Fights were breaking out all over the place as ships popped up without any warning. Resources were being gobbled up at a faster rate than the game normally produced them. As Lane hitched his bag to his shoulder, he heard someone wish they had never voted to release the mod.

As soon as Lane saw the buses Derrick had described, he saw the reason for the groans: they were creaking yellow-and-green machines that looked to be almost a century old. A sputter of smoke emitted from the rear of one, and another's engine popped so loud Lane thought it might be broken. Despite all of this, a line was forming that was clearly bigger than either vehicle could hold.

Out of the corner of his eye Lane saw Derrick and Alice shouting orders at people to line up and pick someone to sit with. Most of the riders seemed to have known what to expect and were already paired off. Alice was shouting for a man to hand over his luggage to be put on the roof of the bus when Lane approached her. He had no idea what he wanted to say, the desire to get her attention being more important than anything else.

"I'm uh…hello, I'm Lane! We haven't met, and—" Lane said nervously.

Alice looked at him and pointed at his bag. "That's small enough to put at your feet. You got someone picked out? No problem, I got dozens of bo-berries here. You care about sitting next to a woman?" she said.

She was already turning to bark at someone else when Lane stammered, "Yes. I mean no about sitting next to a woman. But I have a ride. I rented a car. I was going to ask about directions, and you seemed—"

Alice flipped around, eyes wide, and she grabbed his arm. "Is there room in it?" she whispered quietly. Her face was so close he could smell her skin and just a hint of her breath.

"Yeah, of course. You know how to get to wherever we're going?" Lane asked.

She nodded and squeezed his arm tightly. "OK, don't fucking leave me. I have to get his bus ready to go, and then I'm just going to slip off. You are…?"

"He's the lawyer I warned you about," Derrick said from behind.

"You didn't mention that he has a car," Alice said.

Derrick's eyes went wide. "Koff?"

Lane nodded, and Derrick still seemed surprised.

"Things with the appeal got a bit more complicated. We need to talk about Tally," Lane said.

As the buses filled up, Lane headed over to the rental place and was surprised to see a woman behind the counter. He had assumed it would be an automated exchange. When Lane walked up to the counter, the woman gave him a pleasant smile and asked for his pad. She plugged it into the monitor in front of her, and it began to load. She then asked for his password information. "Why?" Lane asked.

"To operate a car in the Southern Union, you must agree to complete liability for any accidents or damage you may cause. You will not disengage the autopilot unless there is an emergency. While disengaged, you will keep your eyes on the road at all times. You will not use your pad while operating the car. You will not disengage the AI, GPS locator, or car sensors. In the event that you see another vehicle on the road, you will adopt the mandatory safety speeds for that situation. Under no circumstances will you allow anyone but yourself to operate this vehicle. You will not consume alcohol, marijuana, or any other perception-altering substance before operating this vehicle. By accepting the access codes to this vehicle, you agree to everything I have just said. You also consent to reading this agreement every time you initiate the vehicle. If any of this has not been clear, please review the agreement in the car's operating files," the woman said. She was reading off a screen but didn't appear to need the help very often.

"I think I got it. Can I use the car now?" Lane asked. She shook her head and held up his pad, which was still plugged into her monitor.

"I'm still performing a complete background check. Just please tap in your password," she explained. Lane warily typed in his basic passcode and was surprised when the system asked him for the advanced sequences as well. The woman nodded approvingly, so Lane obliged. A few minutes passed, and Lane took the chance to look out the window. Alice was hustling the last of the bus passengers onto the creaking machines. Lane nervously wondered what sort of car she would like, or if he even had much say in the matter. Eve briefly flashed in his mind, and Lane again found himself wondering where all his feelings for her had suddenly gone. There was nothing for them to stick to, he supposed.

"All right, now I just need to do a credit check. I see a firm is backing your rental. And you are currently listed as…employed, it looks like. Excellent! Always a bit of trouble with people wanting to rent cars. We're a licensed free market business and all that. Like I always say, you don't have a right to get yourself killed in our cars," the woman said and began to laugh roaringly at her own joke. She didn't seem to be expecting Lane to join her as she began typing in various instructions. "All right, now I'm seeing your reservation is for a two-seater. Is that going to—"

"Oh, ah, four. At least four. There must be some kind of error. Definitely four seats. It's a big project we're working on. You can just bill it to the account, don't worry," Lane said quickly.

"All right sir, I have keyed in the security clearance into your pad. If you want to operate the car, just plug your pad into it, and it should do the rest. Oh, I almost forgot. Please keep your pad on you at all times. While the car is in your possession, you will also be required to punch in your password every time you activate it. Just as a precautionary measure."

Lane's annoyance was apparent because the woman quickly turned to her monitor after pointing toward the car lot. He walked out wondering if he would be able to work through all the protocols and controls on his pad or if there was some way to turn it off. Lane realized that the world was quite content to leave you alone so long as you weren't going to be a risk to anyone around you.

He stepped out to the parking area and began looking for the car shown on his pad. The company had installed all the software he would need to operate the vehicle. There were not many four-seat vehicles in the lot, so it did not take long. The car door opened when it sensed his pad was in proximity. Lane sat down and looked around the car. He had expected it to be similar to a driving game interface, and he could certainly see certain similarities. There was a wheel and a large monitor behind it to display the car's system information. Pedals for braking and acceleration and all the other gadgets Lane had come to expect in a car from seeing them in movies and games. But when he plugged in the pad and typed in his password, they sat immobile as the car activated. It performed a sensor sweep of the area, checked all other cars and pads in the vicinity, and backed out of its parking spot and began slowly moving toward the exit.

"Please state the destination or task," a female voice intoned. Lane saw there was also a prompt on his pad where he could type it in. "I need to pick up some friends who are just around the corner," Lane said. There was a pause before the car replied, "Unable to comply. You do not have any friends in this area," it responded. Lane suddenly realized he had never bothered to categorize Derrick as a friend in his network. It wouldn't have been proper for him to ask Alice so soon after meeting. "I need to pick up some people I just met who are around the corner. Their names are Derrick and Alice," Lane said.

The computer checked whom his pad had been in proximity with recently, detected Derrick and Alice, and then did a larger search of the surrounding area. "Last location log: Bus Stop. Greenville, South Eastern Union. Would you like to proceed?" Lane pressed yes instead of saying it; the gesture felt like the only way to show any resentment to the machine.

Lane at first marveled at how carefully the car drove around the block to the bus stop. It braked, slowed, and increased speed without the slightest shake. He experimentally gripped the wheel and tapped the brakes. The car immediately came to a complete halt, bucking Lane against the wheel. The wheel itself did not respond much to his touch, making Lane think it was there to show him what the car was doing rather than offer him any kind of control. He could stop it from turning, but to steer it himself looked as if it required a serious tug. The voice rang out, "Is it safe for the car to continue moving?" Lane said yes, and they resumed course.

They pulled into the bus stop right as the last one was clearing away in a puff of smoke. He could see a large, steely-eyed woman behind the wheel grimly steering the huge vehicle. His car's computer emitted a loud alarm and said, "Warning: non-automated vehicle in the vicinity. Speeds will be cut in half until a safe distance is assumed." By the time the car finally pulled into the bus stop in front of Derrick and Alice, they had been watching him impatiently for almost a minute. Lane was surprised to see another young man chatting with them as well.

Lane stepped out of the car and helped Alice with her bags. She laughed at the gesture and grabbed the one next to it, which apparently belonged to the young man, who responded by sticking his hands in his pockets.

"Lane, this is Max. I was hoping it would be all right if he we gave him a ride as well?" Derrick asked. Lane gave them a big smile, but he immediately wondered if he would be sitting up by the steering wheel with him. He got his answer when Alice plopped in the back seat with her pad already out. Derrick got in the front seat next to Lane's, and Max sat next to Alice.

"Lane, I just want you to know how much I appreciate this," Derrick said with a big, oblivious grin. Lane glanced back at Alice for a moment and felt a slight pang. At least she was only paying attention to her pad.

CHAPTER 24

Derrick punched an address into the pad, and the car began humming down the streets of Greenville. Judging by the large radar display on the car's console, they were carefully moving around the routes of other cars on the road. Greenville had more cars than Charleston. The car's AIs were communicating with one another and managing traffic before it even happened.

Minutes drifted by, and Lane found himself bored as the car trip proceeded in silence. It had been a while since he had seen mountains. He had seen far larger, towering mountains in the scenic vistas of games or the exploration videos of distant countries. The Appalachian Mountains were much smaller. Lane would glance at Alice occasionally to see if she was paying him any attention. She intermittently would giggle at something Max had shown her on his pad, but was otherwise anxiously parsing through her own. Derrick was silent, engrossed in *Tyrant* articles and metric charts.

Finally Lane said, "So what is going on in *Tyrant*? Did the mod change anything?"

Alice giggled again, and Max laughed as well. Derrick looked out the window and sighed. "Yes, it has gotten a bit crazy in there."

Alice's giggle turned into a full-blown laugh, and she said, "A bit? It's totally fucking nuts! A bunch of kids just drove a cruiser straight into the newbie space station! It's causing a bug in the post-design specs where everyone is getting hurdled out into space if they leave their rooms."

Max said, "They have to do a system reset. There's no way this will last. The asset damages alone are crossing into the millions. Onyx, metallurgics, star mass, every staple resource in the game is spiking or dipping in value. The whole economy is destabilizing. Half the users are pulling all their money out of the game, and the other half are liquidating in-game. One of my brokers just dumped all of his red-class minerals, and it only gave him enough money to buy two frigates. You were right, Derrick. I hate admitting it, but putting all our money into buying up ships was the right move. And no one will ever think to look for the fleet in the Gibson Cloud. It's the per—" Max was interrupted by a loud ping from his pad, but when Lane glanced back, he seemed to be looking intently at something on there. Lane wondered if the Gibson Cloud was what Eve had been asking him about earlier. He made a mental note of Max's slip for later.

"Everyone is wondering where the GDK is in all of this," Derrick said. "Especially the Tyrant. Looks like she has been outfitting ships in her fleet with the mod. Forums are saying you've got about twenty seconds to move a ship out of range once the blue sphere appears. Alice, you clocked it at seventeen, right?"

"Yeah, something like that. We never did anything with it outside of *Zulfikar Gold*. Could change depending on the size of the ship. Her flagship *Sojourner Truth* can move at a pretty fast clip once it gets going. I'm seeing a lot of the Femarchists claiming that she has sold off every ship in her fleet that can't pull eighty-parsec acceleration at a tap. Before the mod went public, of course. Made a fortune. That hasn't stopped them from teleporting most of their frigates straight into her outposts. The damage is colossal. I'll give Mavis credit, she doesn't forget a grudge," Alice said.

"Mavis is leading the Femarchists now? I thought it was that lesbian, the one with the awful bangs. Shelly or something," Max said.

Alice shook her head and tapped into her pad. Max looked down intently again and began laughing. Lane realized Alice was sending him messages directly, and he suddenly felt jealous of them. It was clear the three of them had history, with the GDK and maybe more. The way Max looked at Alice left Lane wondering if they were just friends, coworkers, or something more.

"So are they a part of the GDK?" Lane asked Alice.

She frowned and shook her head. "Oh my, no. That culture hates men and most women too. They do like blowing things up and then drafting elaborate speeches to explain why the bitch had it coming. I'm not even sure they really do alliances. The GDK are a bit more open-minded," Alice explained.

Derrick snorted at this and added, "She means they believe men should be put to work in service of women."

"You know, Derrick, for someone who is married with a kid, you are awfully opinionated about gender meanings. Especially when they affect you negatively," Alice said.

"Believing that meaning can't be depicted on a computer does not mean I don't believe in anything, Alice. I just don't believe the culture grid as being an actual depiction of human beings, not the reality filters, not even the stuff going in *Tyrant* right now as anything other than an elaborate hallucination. I believe in people," Derrick said.

The tone in the car had changed, and Lane was beginning to sense that this was similar to the disagreement he had heard back on the ship. He tried to lighten the mood with a laugh and said, "Finally, someone who understands Derrick well enough to disagree with him!"

Alice smiled at Lane and replied, "Nice to see he hasn't totally sucked you in with that anticulture business."

"I just don't see the difference between what Derrick is talking about and what we already all know. Meaning is relative. The culture grid isn't a perfect map of this but it's close enough," Lane said. "I was telling a friend the other day that the phrase space lawyer needs to be repurposed. It has all this meaning attached to it that has nothing to do with the actual job. My day is mostly spent dealing with the space between what the job is and what the job means to people."

Derrick looked annoyed. "The issue, Lane, is that we all still act as if space lawyer has a single concrete meaning. Just because we know it's an aggregate doesn't mean we take it any less literally. We all say that the reality system obviously isn't real, but then we are expected to accept it anyway. You said it yourself, the word needs to be repurposed. What for? Just believe it means something different."

"Oh, come on!" Alice said. "If I don't have some massive conglomeration of data to explain away our differences, then what is left? Two individuals disagreeing about something they barely know anything about? The culture grid is about empowering people with information, not forcing an identity on them."

"People got along for millennia without a bunch of graphs telling them what to think." Derrick said.

Lane said, "Didn't they have a lot more to fight about with scarcity and everything? What is there to fight over now? We're all taken care of." He gestured out the window, and everyone looked out to see rows of farm fields, all being tended by large steel machines.

"That's the problem. None of us can think outside of the grid anymore. The Standards program just makes it worse because we are disengaged from worrying about even our own basic needs. We think of meaning as a virtual space now. It is X number of large, it consumes this many rule blocks, and it overlaps with Y number of other culture spheres. Even meaning that wants to be outside the culture grid is defined by its proximity to normality. If the function of the culture grid is so that everyone can get along and recognize their differences, then the only way to protest it is to not believe it," Derrick said.

There was a silence in the car as Derrick's pad began to chime. He looked a little sheepish as he tapped it on and held the speaker end up to his ear for privacy. "Hi, honey! Yes, I actually managed to get a ride. Yes we're…no…oh, did she now?" Derrick said in a voice quite different from the one he had just been using. Alice had a fit of the giggles, and even Lane began laughing. Max tapped something on his pad, and Alice glanced at it before bursting into another fit of laughter.

"See, Derrick here only gets upset if I point out his marital status and the inherent complications with authority," Alice explained. Derrick shot her a nasty look before telling his wife how sorry he was he couldn't be home this weekend.

"He's also probably not excited about you taking over the patriarchy after him," Max added dryly. Alice rolled her eyes and shoved his knee playfully.

"My wife says hello to everyone," Derrick said as he switched off his pad. "And on the contrary, I'm thrilled for Alice to take the job. Work is overrated."

CHAPTER 25

The car continued down the road for several miles as they rode with the windows down. Lane decided it was pine straw he was smelling. It reminded him of Standard cleaning products from back in Charleston, but it was more acidic here, and blended with other pungent aromas. He liked it. For some reason Lane found himself wishing the others in the car liked it as well.

"So what does everyone think the project is going to be this year?" asked Max.

Alice sighed and said, "As long as we vote on it before everyone is shitfaced, I'm open to anything."

Derrick drummed his fingers on the dash for a moment before replying. "I'll be giving my speech about encouraging professions for men that don't kill them or pose bodily harm. And I'm sure the power queers will tell me what a privileged, hetero stereotype I am and how I'm just staying alive because of my wife. Then the sex crime circles will get into it, and there will be more bickering. Then…I don't know, progress."

"Derrick, you ARE a hetero stereotype. You're married with a kid. You're employed, and your wife does most of the child raising. I'm surprised you aren't showing up to this thing in a business suit," Max said.

Alice scoffed and said, "I don't see why we have to treat that like it's such a miracle. People do it all the time."

"Really? How many do you know? And I don't mean women with husbands who are out in space harvesting asteroids and barely home. Like lives together, raises a kid together, and oh, by the way, runs an international virtual guild dedicated to..." Max trailed off as he struggled to find the word.

"Dysfunctional men," Alice said.

There was a groan from Max, while Derrick laughed.

"I thought the point of all this was to get them to stop being dysfunctional," Derrick said.

"Speaking for myself, I think everything the GDK does is great. The way you repurposed Gay Death Knights into this ambiguous, new identity. The stuff in the forums is funny. You actively recruit and have guys working toward a common goal. When I was a kid the dorms were always disorganized, with everyone just sitting around. I would have gotten sucked into something like this immediately," Lane said.

"So, just out of curiosity, other than your weird issues and a reality feed devoid of masculine filters, what are you here for?" Max said with a touch of sarcasm.

Lane was being mocked. Max probably lived in a Standard dorm, shared a room, never could afford to go off his meal plan, lived off Standard rations and drank Standard beer. Lane knew the type. He would drag every comment Lane made that was out of place or slightly strange through the mud just to make himself feel better. Lane sighed and wished Alice hadn't brought him along.

She seemed to sense this because she immediately said, "He's here on official business. Lane is the one who got the mod distributed for us. If Derrick's little plan works, then we're all going to owe him big time."

"I didn't know we had a plan," Max muttered.

"No, but it looks like we'll land on our feet. Everyone is either turtling up on their assets, cashing in, or cashing out. The Tyrant is dumping all of her resources into finding us because she expects the same thing to happen that we do: the developers are going to dump the mod. It's causing way too much instability and chaos in the game. Ships that are supposed to be totally worthless are now suddenly dominating the scene. And when the developers drop that hammer, suddenly all that optimization and shifting around resources is going to bite her in the ass," Derrick said.

"Assuming she doesn't find us," Alice said.

Everyone grew quiet as the car's voice spoke up, "Attention: we will be accessing a dirt road soon. Please secure any loose items in the vehicle. The driver is requested to be extra alert for any wild animals that may be in the area." As they turned off the highway, Lane noticed the trees and foliage were thicker, and there were far fewer signs.

"Who lives out here? On the website it just said that we were going to some kind of ex-summer camp," Lane said.

Derrick said, "It was a summer camp a long time ago. It was taken over by a group of Luddites who figured they'd just move as far away from technology as they could get. Which, to their credit, was pretty damn far. That's actually the reason we think Tally might show up or at least call in by video. She was friends with these folks up until they got into the brewing business."

"How come I always hear a different kind of group being identified with the GDK? Online you make it look like this is some sort of men's rights group. Why would a group of Luddites be willing to host your conference?" Lane asked.

"Because Derrick uses his anticulture talk to convince everyone it doesn't matter what we're identified as," Alice said. "In reality it's a huge pack of individualists. We're talking about reality circles that consist of ten or fewer people. Stuff that doesn't even come up on the grid. Even the sex offenders make a big showing,"

The car slowed and weaved to the right as the sensors detected a pothole. Lane would not have even been aware of it had the console not labeled it as one with a big yellow X.

"I think we're all forgetting the most important thing. We're giving them a lot of cash and buying a lot of their beer," Max added.

"You're going to let rapists come to this?" Lane asked quietly.

"Most of them are victims themselves. They have all been through state rehabilitation. They all take the required libido suppressants. Same stuff they pump into men who are prone to violence," Derrick replied.

Silence filled the car as it trundled down the road. After several minutes a chime rang announcing the destination was drawing close, and the car slowed and turned down one of the dirt roads.

They went a ways before the trees gave way to an enormous green field. They crossed over a makeshift bridge, and to their left was a sizable wooden cabin. It had a garden full of bustling green plants, peppers, potatoes, and a few marijuana stalks. On the porch were various rocking chairs and more plants in little pots. The field was mowed, and Lane could smell the freshly cut grass. The car rolled to a stop and parked in a neat little row of stones. No one spoke as they opened their doors and stepped outside.

Alice went running out across the field before launching into a cartwheel. Max immediately began walking up the dirt road to a few wooden buildings that were up a little ways. Derrick just stepped out of the car, inhaled deeply, and looked around.

"It's gorgeous. I've never been to a place like this," Lane said.

Derrick didn't say anything. After a few moments, a screen door opened, and there was a loud shout. Lane turned and saw a chunky figure walking out the door.

"Well, well, if it isn't the old patriarch himself. Come to give us girls another bit of entertainment before the summer ends?" she called out.

Derrick turned and immediately gave the woman a big hug. She returned it and patted him on the back.

"Thanks for having us again. Cindy, this is Lane. That lawyer I messaged you about?" Derrick said.

She turned and gave Lane a toothy grin. She had grey hair, yellowing teeth, and a bright red nose. He smiled back, hoping to mask his discomfort at her appearance. He had never seen anyone who looked like this in Charleston.

"He's pretty. Oh, I'll bet all those silly young things throw themselves at him. So, you're looking to find Tally then?"

Lane nodded and reached for his pad.

She waved her hand dismissively. "Save it. She's not coming. Damn woman won't even do a video chat anymore. I knew when she decided to quit alcohol she was taking a turn for the serious. Spending your final years getting drunk in the middle of nowhere is a perfectly sane way to go. At least in this old woman's opinion."

CHAPTER 26

Lane stood outside the cabin, still absorbing the news that the entire reason he had made the trip was not even coming. He swore and kicked the gravel road for a moment as he pictured Koff's fury when she found out. Everything tensed inside him as he wondered if this would mean the end of his chances at being a space lawyer once and for all.

Derrick watched him for a few moments and suggested he check out the great hall and try to enjoy himself. The buses were still a ways away from the camp.

Lane headed up the dirt road and immediately caught an enormous whiff of something that smelled rotten. The sour and pungent aroma of fermenting beer made him blanche at first, but the familiarity of beer's unique odor made him recognize what it was. He had never smelled it being fermented before. The odor was coming from two wooden buildings nestled in a scattering of trees up the hill. The road kept going in that direction, and Lane followed.

At the top was an enormous structure that Lane guessed was the hall Derrick had referred to. Like everything else it was made of wood, but with red-and-yellow sandstone around the base. Lane found himself having trouble taking in the structure. It was not absurdly huge like the towering buildings of Charleston and looked more like something out of a fantasy virtual world.

The road broke off toward the hall, and Lane decided to keep walking. It was getting dark, and he wanted to explore the area before it filled with other members of the GDK. A path led down to two lakes, one on the left and the other on the right. There were some old wooden structures that looked like the remnants of a dock, but they were covered with moss. The water was green and had an almost viscous quality. Lane could hear the croak of frogs as he walked between the two bodies of water. It almost made his ears ring as he walked up to where the path split in two. A sign read "Boys' Side" and pointed to the left, while indicating the girls could be located on the right. Both paths went into a thick wooded area. Lane obliged and headed left for boys.

There were various squat wooden buildings all along the path. Light bulbs announced their presence in the growing darkness, and Lane guessed this must be where people would be staying. He walked up to one and peeked inside. Rows of bunks lined the walls with pillows and lumpy mattresses on each. There was a bathroom in the center of the building, but no shower.

Lane followed the path through the wooded area and soon realized it was actually a small patch of trees. His mind had assumed it would just go on endlessly, that the forest could be without limit. He walked out into a large clearing. Rows of benches surrounded an enormous log pile, while off in the distance Lane could see an old shipping truck. It seemed to belong to the brewery. He walked over to the woodpile and was poking it with his feet when he heard someone shout hello behind him. It was Alice.

"Oh, I was just looking around! I wasn't going to mess with anything," Lane stammered. Alice had a way of making him feel nervous that he still didn't quite understand. He had been around women he liked before, but for some reason this one made him feel different. He wanted her to like him desperately.

"It's all right. I'd understand if you wanted to start the big bonfire, just don't. It's always a great explosion when they set it off. What do you think of this place?" Alice asked, smiling. She began inspecting the bonfire and testing the structure with her hands.

"It's gorgeous. Better than virtual. I've never been anywhere quite like it. How often do you come here?" Lane asked.

"This will be my third time. I have been with the GDK a long time, but coming to the conferences is a new thing. After I started running for patriarch, it became important to have face time with people. The virtual friendships still have their place because your flaws aren't screwing things up. But just being here is a kind of status to people in the games. Which goes back to the virtual friendships, I guess," Alice said.

Lane walked over to a stick he saw lying on the ground and added it to the pile. Alice adjusted its position so that it didn't stick out, and Lane chuckled. "If you don't mind my asking, how exactly is it that a woman came to be patriarch of the GDK?"

Alice frowned and then began walking toward the woods. As she gathered sticks, she called out, "By pretending to be a man!"

Lane laughed a bit more and shouted back, "Yes, but why?"

Alice didn't say anything as she walked back with a bundle of wood and began carefully arranging the pieces. It was getting darker, and Lane was beginning to have trouble seeing. "It started when the Tyrant took out my guild. A bunch of friends of mine just started playing, designing outfits and making a little profit. We got into trouble with Eve, and she decided to make an example out of us. Blew up our whole operation and killed our in-game characters. My friends just said fuck it and moved onto another game. I didn't feel that way. The GDK were the only operation that gave her real problems, so I joined up. This was back before Derrick became patriarch, and they were a lot angrier. Mostly male members, a lot of angry gays and unemployed guys. Smart though, well organized and constantly recruiting. I wouldn't say they would explicitly have refused to let me join if they knew I was a woman, but they wouldn't have trusted me either."

Alice finally seemed satisfied with the bonfire and hopped up on top of the benches. Lane sat down on a nearby one and didn't say anything. She began to walk up and down each row, her arms behind her back as she spoke. "So we raised some hell, and I ended up being pretty good at it. Nobody asked if I was a man, and in *Tyrant* you mostly talk with typed messages. If I did have to speak, I just used a canned voice program. After a few years of this, the GDK started to stagnate, and recruitment went down. That was when Derrick came along with all the anticulture stuff. He was weird to them, but most people like the idea of resisting authority. It inadvertently made the GDK a lot more accepting of women. That turned some folks off, but his timing was good. The Tyrant was taking out too many of the matriarchs, and those players weren't going to just stay dead. They recruited a lot of exiles like me. So Derrick opened up the GDK to new culture spheres as numbers were dropping and filled the ranks with a lot of women who wanted revenge."

"So what happened to all those guys I see in the forums shouting about rainbows? Or the sexism and homophobia?" Lane asked.

Alice sighed and kept pacing up the benches. "They are still here. Most of them will be at this con. And they like to get drunk, so be ready for that. The female members of the GDK were willing to humor them back when the Tyrant was lording over the game, but I'm starting to wonder if Derrick's plan worked a little too well. The mod is going to be a problem for all the people who aren't true believers. Groups aren't working together. Factions are starting to form. People are fighting about stupid shit. Now that I'm taking over as patriarch, I have to figure out how to get these guys to like me. Along with the women—"

She was suddenly interrupted by a loud voice screaming: "ALL RIGHT, YOU FUCKING BITCHES! WELCOME GAAAY DEAAATH KNIGHTS! YOU SEXY MOTHERFUCKERS BETTER BE READY FOR THIS!"

They sat in silence for a moment as the voice began to whoop and make swooshing noises. Alice snorted and began walking down the path into the dark woods and muttered, "Welcome to GDK Con."

CHAPTER 27

Lane clumsily followed Alice through the darkness back to the big hallway. He tripped several times in the dark woods, but Alice did not slow. "I can't miss the opening talk!" she said.

When they got to the lake, there was a light up at the top of the hill, and Lane followed better. Alice leaped up the stairs two steps at a time and was well ahead of Lane when she reached the top deck. He heard a shout go up, and Alice made a loud whooshing noise. By the time Lane got there, the group on the deck was all around her talking.

"Hi, I'm StarChar439. We worked on that job with the Red Matriarch outside Ceti Beta. It's great to finally meet you!"

"Holy crap, you! You! You still cruising around in that piece of crap frigate? *General Lee* was it?"

"Patriarch, when you have a moment, we need to discuss what you plan to do about the depreciation in our mineral stocks."

"I'm not the patriarch yet, and that sounds like it can wait."

"If you would just post this mass cannon mod really quickly, I think you'll find it's a perfect—"

"A beer! Get me a damn beer! Has Derrick started yet?"

She gave Lane one curious glance, and he smiled back at her. She returned it before being carried off by the group around her. Lane noticed off in the corner there was a group of sizable men standing around a keg drinking out of glasses that seemed equally large. They looked like pitchers to Lane, except they were shaped like boots. As one drank, his beer spilled all over him, but this only seemed to make him drink faster. Lane glanced to the doorway Alice had gone through and saw dozens of other men walking about, drinking and laughing in thick crowds. The volume was almost deafening.

He headed over to the keg while trying to make eye contact with someone. He had no luck. Their backs were to him, and he awkwardly shifted to the left and right trying to get around them before he finally slipped into the circle. He wasn't sure what they were talking about between the laughing and sounds they were making. They made whooshing noises and muttered about bo-berries before one would cross some invisible social line and be yelled at to drink his boot. When they finally became aware of Lane's presence, they shifted aside, and one pointed at the stack of cups.

"So, are all of you *Tyrant* players or...some other branch of the GDK?" Lane asked searchingly.

"Fuck no, that stupid fucking game is all anyone can talk about anymore. This group was a lot better off when we made our money playing *Heorot*. Slaying dragons, epic loot. Now all they want us to do is crunch numbers and drive those dumb space ships around," the tall one who had been spilling his beer exclaimed.

"Think there's much chance the new pat is going to change things back?" another asked.

There was some grumbling and dismissal of this idea.

"She plays *Tyrant*. She's not going to go dragging the GDK into a game she knows nothing about. Not when she's brand new and trying to get everyone to follow her."

"Yeah, but *Tyrant* has dipped in the metrics with that mod. Might be worth asking her," Lane chipped in.

They glanced at him warily. "If you start pressing her on it, she'll get defensive and think you're undermining her. That bitch is not someone you want as an enemy," another said drunkenly.

Lane's teeth gritted at the term. He had not heard it in his reality in a long time. He nodded and began walking toward the hall. He heard the group laugh, and one said a little loudly, "Looks like you scared him away!"

Inside was a horde of men and a few handfuls of women. The smell of beer and bodies hit him like a wave, and Lane immediately noticed how warm it was inside. He began to perspire. He could see no trace of Alice, but Derrick was near the center of the room fussing with a microphone attached to his pad. As he tapped it, a piercing noise filled the room, and people grew quiet.

"Hello? Hello! Hi, everyone. It's your soon-to-be ex-patriarch. Still current patriarch. We've got so many groups out here this weekend, and it is just an honor to see you all. We got Franklin over there with the Gay Power Brigade. Franklin, you still making all your dates sign up for raids before the one in real life?"

There was a shout from the crowd and laughter. A few people seemed to be glancing at a grey-haired man who was pumping his fist in a crude gesture.

"Boris with the Space Pirates. I still can't believe a group of guys out of one dorm can get as little accomplished as you do!"

More shouting and cheers. Derrick made catcalls and jokes in rapid succession as he rattled off names. "And hey, for all the ladies out there, that warning ping on your pad is no accident. The sex crime perps are joining us again this year, and they promise to share their injections if things get a little too rowdy. They only brought enough for themselves, though."

That joke didn't seem to quite land home, and Lane was a little uncomfortable with the implication. He noticed a few women in the audience making faces, but Alice laughed.

"I guess that's as good a moment as any to say this. Everyone knows I have a lot of weird ideas about this group and what makes them tick. I think that when people confront the reality of someone that was just a culture circle, they realize that all those differences between them aren't really such a big deal. That having some grid tell you what's going on is no substitute for the real thing. And all these new members, the ex-matriarchs and feminists, and even the sex perps. People like that are good for making us recognize that. As I step down as patriarch and the new one comes up here to lead this conference, I hope you'll remember that anticulture is at its core about getting people to examine a process."

As Derrick's speech wound down, Lane struggled to hear him over the increasing chatter in the room. People were pulling out their pads to check various things, heading out the door for another round at the keg, or simply talking to one another. He saw Alice look around nervously as she moved toward the center of the room where Derrick was talking.

"Everyone! Hello there! Everyone…" Alice began. The volume in the room only grew louder as men began to jostle and joke with one another. They seemed oblivious to her presence. She frowned, and her eyes narrowed. Lane began shushing people and shaking their shoulders to point at her. A few gave him annoyed looks, but most simply ignored him.

"Ladies! Gentlemen! Your new female leader has a few things she'd like to say!" Alice shouted. The room suddenly grew quiet. Even Lane found himself taken aback by the tone in her voice, the anger and frustration that were suddenly pouring out. "Take a look around you. Hell, take a big inhale if you want. A big, deep whiff of that smell. Can you smell it? No? Maybe it's because I'm a woman. Because *statistically* I have a stronger sense of smell than you do. You stink. Between the beer farts, the body odor, and that awful fucking bus ride, I don't know how any of you can stand to even be in here!

"Now, I'm not going to sit here and try to tell you about anticulture or some kind of new existential information crap. I'm not going to try to demand we all get along constantly. Hell, Chuck, I called you a rapist piece of shit *before* I knew your record! We all get along for one simple reason. This group of people. This culture…this clan. We are the Gay Death Knights!"

Swooshing sounds erupted from the crowd, and there was a round of applause. A few cheers went up, but Alice held her hands to silence them.

"Now, don't get me wrong. If you told me a group of gay fascists who set out to prove they were better than women at everything would start an organization I'd want to join someday, I'd think you were crazy. But here we all are. Over the years they kept opening up the doors to new members who could fight and who would put in the time for the GDK. The deviants, the not-so-fascist gays, the ex-women, and even the heteros. Now there are a lot of older members here, and we've talked a few times. Maybe like Chuck, I told you some harsh things, but that's the nature of the virtual world. That was in there, and this is out here. And here, we are all part of the same group!" A few whooshing sounds and claps were followed by a catcall.

"All right, you great lot of stinking idiots. I don't plan to start off as patriarch by making you listen to a boring speech. Just remember that the thing that makes this matter is us. We have to keep pressing on to new worlds. We have to keep finding new ways for people to find out about the GDK. Because this isn't just about winning, this is about an idea. About finding a purpose—not just for men, but for everyone! Now someone give me a fucking beer!"

A roar of cheers and applause went up. Someone handed her a big glass of beer, and she snatched it with a whooshing noise. The odor, Lane noticed, seemed to intensify a bit.

Lane heard a man behind him say to another, "God, remember the last time, and Derrick wouldn't shut up?"

The other agreed and said he was already liking the new patriarch. Lane turned to see who had spoken, but they had already been absorbed into the crowd. The noise, the body odor, and the jostling were all getting to him.

Lane noticed Max standing in a corner with another man, and not knowing who else to speak to, he nervously approached him. Max nodded at him but didn't say anything, instead pulling out his pad and checking something. The other man looked at Lane but didn't make any movements. "Ah, hi, my name is Lane. What, ah, what are you up to?"

"Sam, this is Lane. He's the lawyer," Max said.

The man nodded and stuck out his hand limply for Lane to shake. "We're putting together a culture grid of the conference. Mind if we add you?" Sam said.

Lane shook his head and pulled out his pad. It had an info request from Sam, and Lane accepted it. A few moments later, the grid was uploaded to his pad, and the entire GDK conference was depicted before him. There was a surprising number of circles with several overlap points showing the diversity of everyone present. Lane tapped his ID to see where he fit into the grid, but nothing came up.

Max snorted and laughed. "Ah, try zooming out a bit."

Lane had to pull out several magnitudes before he finally saw a dot that represented him. He was outside the culture sphere of everyone at the GDK.

CHAPTER 28

Lane left the party early. He didn't know anyone personally, and whenever he tried to explain who he was, it seemed to only generate more confusion. Alice was surrounded by people wishing her well and asking for favors. Derrick seemed to have his hands full receiving people who were congratulating him and asking him to tie up loose ends. Lane eventually decided to find a bed. When he asked if there was any kind of assignment system, people only laughed and told him to grab whatever he could.

Lane pulled his bag from the car and stumbled around in the dark with the aid of a flashlight. He made his way back to the boys' side, found an empty cabin, and lay down in one of the bunks. He checked his pad one last time. Still no word from Tricia on the Gateway check. Koff had sent a message asking him about Tally, and Lane decided to go ahead and break the news to her now. He would figure out her location in Montana, and they could send someone to track her down that way. As he lay in bed, he could still hear people reveling off in the distance, shouting incoherently. A part of him was disappointed that Alice had seemed to fit in so well.

The swearing and the crude humor reminded him of life back on the dorms. The tension of the place for Lane was palpable, not being sure when he should laugh at a joke or even if he should be laughing. The way people's realities were always being assumed and taken for granted. Max had certainly been right about one thing: this was well outside his filter. As he drifted off to sleep, Lane found himself wondering why he had wanted to come here in the first place.

Lane awoke in the night to the loud drunken ramblings of strangers as they bumbled through the cabin. He rolled over and hoped they would quiet down, but this seemed to take forever. They made whooshing noises, and one of them was clearly still drinking a beer. Their talk seemed incoherent, more brief phrases and drunken laughter than anything Lane could decipher. When they finally did drift off, one of them snored. Lane began to stiffen with dread at each gurgling choke of air until he began to wonder if the man needed. Lane never rose from his bed, waiting until he finally fell asleep.

When he awoke he was bleary eyed and felt as if he had not slept at all. The snores were still ringing in the cabin as he got out of bed and decided to catch a shower. A sign outside that he could not see in the dark said the showers were to the left. He hobbled on the rocky path to the shower house, forgetting to bring any kind of footwear, and froze when he stepped inside. Several men were standing around naked in the showers conversing. One was brushing his teeth. Another was passing a bar of soap to another.

He nervously took off his clothes and stepped in the shower. He saw a man peeing in the shower drain. A horrible smell of urine filled the air, and a few of them laughed. Lane tried to look away, and then he felt awkward for doing that and ended up looking again. What was the right amount of time? Lane scrubbed furiously and tried to get through the process as quickly as possible.

"Hey, man, relax. I think we can all manage to not suck each other's dicks for a few minutes."

Lane realized he was being addressed, and he tried to grin while still furiously scrubbing. Another guy in the shower smacked the man who had spoken on the shoulder and said, "Leave him alone, Chuck."

The other turned and grumpily replied, "I just didn't want him to freak out because he was showering with a couple of gays is all. Sorry."

Lane stammered something that sounded like an apology and hurried out of the shower. A quick hobble back to the cabin, a change of clothes in the bathroom, and Lane left for the main lodge. The door still seemed to be rattling with the snores of the man inside.

As he crossed the path over the lake, Lane tried to console himself by thinking that at least there was only a day left before they headed back. What could possibly go wrong? As he walked up the stairs, an enormous bell began ringing. He saw Cindy from the day before yanking at a rope while expertly balancing a cup of coffee in her other hand. She looked at him quizzically before silently turning and heading into the lodge. As Lane came up the stairs, he could smell breakfast cooking.

Inside he saw Derrick and Alice pushing brooms around while collecting waste from the night before. A strong smell of beer was confirmed by the stickiness of the floor.

When Alice saw him, her face brightened. "Lane! Thank goodness you're here! Grab a broom, will you?"

Derrick barely looked at him before Lane saw the red in his eyes and the pale hue to his skin. They both seemed to be nursing hangovers.

Lane picked up a broom and began sweeping up garbage. He found sticky cups, crushed cans, and a variety of empty bottles with all sorts of brands of liquor in them. He was surprised by how much of it was non-Standard. When they finally got the floor cleared up, Derrick dumped a bucket of water out on the floor. As Alice handed him the mop, Cindy went outside and gave the bell another hard, much louder ring.

"What's the bell for?" Lane asked.

"Wake-up, then a more serious wake-up. Third one is to let them know breakfast is ready. Then we decide on what we'll build today," Alice explained.

As Lane went over the various parts of the floor with a mop, Alice followed with a brush to give it a more thorough scrubbing. Derrick followed with a dry mop that absorbed all the moisture. "Thank you for helping, Lane. It is nice to have somebody around here besides Derrick who knows how to do some work," Alice said.

Lane felt a surge of excitement at the compliment and said, "Is there anything else I can do to help?"

Alice grinned and said she had the rest of it under control. Derrick grunted when they finally finished and went over to make himself a cup of coffee. Alice began writing on a large white board, and Lane stood nervously with nothing to do for a few moments. He finally walked over to Derrick, who was staring off into space, and asked him how his night had gone.

"GDK rules require the exiting patriarch to drink the difference in the assets from when they took power to where they are now. Due to this mod gamble, the market is in complete chaos. It's even spreading to our outlying games because players are either jumping into those markets or cashing out. I've never seen anything like it. Nobody has. Cindy made them stop pouring me beer after I puked," Derrick said blearily. He pulled out his pad and opened up another graph before shaking his head. "They need to stop this thing. And that's not just because of my hangover."

Cindy burst out of the kitchen door with an enormous pot that smelled of butter and some strange spices. She set it on the counter next to a mountain of bowls and spoons. Derrick began marching toward it immediately as Cindy exited to ring the bell for a third time while shouting, "BREAKFAST, YOU ANIMALS!"

Lane poured himself a bowl of the strange stuff and took a bite. It was wonderful, a mixture of grease and garlic for a stomach that had drunk too much beer. He sat next to Derrick and ate while watching Alice. She had written in big letters on the board, "ACTIVITY IDEAS" and was drawing out boxes underneath it. Footsteps pounded up the stairs, and people began to arrive. Several showered men, a clump of unclean ones who were still a bit drunk, and a cluster of women with one or two men they may have picked up last night followed them. They trekked in and poured themselves a bowl of grits and cheese.

After a while, when everyone had eaten and gotten a little coffee into their system, Alice stood up and went to the board. "All right, everyone! Everyone! Let's start thinking about what we want the projects to be today. If you have an idea, stand up, and I'll point at you to talk. I'll start and say that I heard a few ladies last night suggest we build a difference engine. Like the one Charles Babbage made," she said.

Lane was impressed by how much quicker the crowd grew quiet, but he supposed most of them were not talking anyways. Silence followed except for the occasional clatter of spoons on bowls and slurping noises.

"What the fuck is a difference engine?" someone said.

Another voice followed: "Let's build a giant catapult."

Alice shouted, "People! Stand up if you want to talk, or we'll be here all damn day!"

A man stood up and raised his hand. Alice pointed to him, and he said, "I think we should build a big wooden bar. You know, like something nice for the brewery and everything."

Alice nodded and wrote "Bar" in one of the blocks on the board.

Another stood and said, "Giant-ass catapult." Alice wrote it on the board as well.

So the morning went. Lane noticed people always seemed to want their thing to be gigantic or enormous. There was also an odd predilection toward things that could be considered weapons. Lane tried to think of something Alice would appreciate, so he suggested, "What if we built a dock for the lake?"

There were a few laughs, and he heard Max say, "We already tried that last year. It sank. Why don't we ask Cindy if she wants anything done around here?"

Alice nodded and smiled at Max. Cindy shouted from the kitchen, "Just clean up after yourselves, ya damn animals!"

Several people stood and offered to give lectures on various topics. Derrick pulled out his pad and began reading off his ideas about the new manhood, but there was little reaction. Another person wanted to have a group talk on sexual differences. After a while, a cheer went up, and people began stomping their feet while shouting, "Vote! Vote! Vote!"

Lane saw a series of white pieces of paper being handed out, and on each was a black spot. He was handed one himself. People began walking up to the board and placing a dot on the spot of their choosing. After looking at the various choices, Lane decided to put his on the bar. He shuffled away from the board and went over to where he saw Morgan and a few other people chatting.

"Hey there. So do we build whatever one has the most spots?" Lane asked.

Morgan laughed and put his hand on the shoulder of the man next to him. He leaned in fairly intimately toward the man and said, "Just one, he asks! Everyone, this is Lane. The lawyer who helped get that whole mod thing underway. No, what will happen is the top three or so projects will be picked. Whoever suggested them is then put in charge. You can walk around to whatever project you like and work on it. At the end of the day, we sort of…celebrate again, I guess."

"That doesn't seem like a very good way to get anything done," Lane said quizzically.

Morgan shrugged and said, "Probably not. But it beats the hell out of sitting around listening to people ramble about virtual markets. You end up getting to know one another better this way."

CHAPTER 29

They paraded out of the hall in a big mass, jostling one another and shouting as they marched out the main doors. Several groups went underneath the hall, where they found boxes of tools, nails, and other supplies. Others were demanding pads and searching for design specifications for what they wanted to make. The winners were a giant catapult, a bar, and by a slim margin, making the bonfire bigger. All of these things were to be built in the big field near the bonfire. Cindy had told them to stay the hell away from the main area.

Lane tried to ask what he should do, but Alice seemed caught up in making sure the group leaders actually did some leading, and Derrick was hanging back to talk to Cindy. They shooed him out of the hall when he offered to clean up breakfast. Following a group carrying enormous planks, Lane managed to make himself useful by snatching a package of nails that had been precariously set atop the wood. He saw Morgan talking to the same guy from earlier that morning and opted to follow.

"So what do you think you'll build?" Lane asked.

Morgan said, "Oh, the bar, I guess. I like the idea of it anyways. I doubt any of us know how to build one. Does anyone have a leveler? We need to make sure that part is right. I know that much."

Most of the men headed straight for the catapult-building group, while the second-largest chunk went for the bonfire. It ended up being Lane, Morgan, and a few stragglers who were too hungover to know where they were going. "It says here we should just make a series of frames, and then connect them together," called out the man who had proposed the bar. He was chubby and hairy. To Lane he looked like one of the people who had skipped showering.

Morgan and his friend began clearing out a space on the ground and checking it with a leveling program with their pad. The man in charge, whose name was Doug, pointed Lane toward the pile of wooden beams. Lane picked one up while Doug grabbed the other end before staggering toward the starting point. Lane had never held a piece of wood quite like this one before, and it soon slipped from his grip. When he dropped it, he realized he had picked up a splinter. He paused to pluck at it with his fingers. Doug waited on him, looking a little exasperated, before walking over and picking another plank up in the middle and carrying it himself. Lane finally managed to catch the splinter with his teeth.

Eventually they had enough planks lined up to begin nailing them together. Doug showed everyone what the pad indicated and demonstrated by nailing two pieces together. Lane eagerly picked up a hammer and nail, but when he tried to get the nail into position, his hand kept instinctively jerking away at the last moment. When he finally did manage to get it to connect, the nail went in crooked. He yanked the nail back out with the claw side of the hammer, put it back into position, took a deep breath, and brought it down as hard as he could while forcing his hand to stay in place.

The hammer hit the edge of his thumb. "Ow! Goddamnit Ow! Shit, shit, shit!" He began sucking his thumb and looked down to realize the nail had still gone in crooked. An exasperated Doug walked over and took the hammer from him.

"Just hold the wood up while I nail it, all right?" Doug said.

Lane nodded, but after a few moments, his arms began to shake under the weight. Doug could get the nail hammered properly, but now the board was crooked. Lane could tell Doug was not trying to be rude; there was a certain degree of compassion about him, and he spoke in a calm tone. But after the third nail had to be yanked out, Lane was too embarrassed to keep going. He said he wanted to go see how the other groups were doing as several people walked up to see what they could do for the bar.

Lane thought of the culture grid and reminded himself that he did not fit in here. It was OK; this was not his reality. But it was hard to block out everything around him. He didn't know anything about construction. The man back at the bar had clearly been trying to help, but Lane was just unaccustomed to being around this many men period. Alice was nowhere around, and Lane considered going to find her as he made his way to the catapult.

He could immediately see why everyone had begun deserting the project. What they had put together looked more like an elaborate seesaw than any sort of catapult. Instead of taking orders, Lane hung back and checked his pad to see how one went about building one. It was all about the weight and countering it with a sufficient beam. What they needed was a space for the beam to swing through so it could lever farther through and throw more weight.

Lane listened to the group arguing with one another about the catapult and quickly realized they understood the problem, they just couldn't agree on how to resolve it. You could technically just add more weight and not worry about lever space, but nobody seemed interested in finding that many rocks. Making the catapult taller, on the other hand, meant another trip to the woodpile and then figuring out how to keep it all together.

After a while Lane voiced a nervous "Perhaps we could…" but nobody noticed. One man had started asking when they would be serving beer again, and another wondered about lunch. They began to sit down, poking at their pads or walking away from the project to go check on a different one. A glance over at the bar showed it was taking off without Lane.

He took a deep breath, admonished himself for being so silly around a bunch of guys, and marched up to the catapult site. Using shovel, he started to dig out a large hole. Most of them watched in silence, curious to see what he would do next. Once the hole was deep enough, Lane took the longest plank he could find and rammed it all the way down. Then he filled in the loose dirt. Several people jumped up with an excited shout and took another wooden plank to measure out a distance between them.

"I see! So now the weight will just swing?" one asked.

"Yeah, make sure that's wide enough. We'll want it even wider than that. It's just a big circular motion," Lane said.

One man clapped him on the shoulder and blamed the beer from last night for making them all so dense. They set to work hammering the structure together. After a while, lunch was rolled out in the form of buckets of protein bars, fruit, snacks, and more kegs of beer. A few people began grumbling about promises of meat and a roasted pig, but they were quickly shushed before the talk spread. Lane smelled it more than he noticed it. The smell of freshly cooked meat was not unfamiliar to him, but the stuff was completely non-Standard. He could not remember the last time he had eaten animal protein.

Lane took a tentative sip of the beer but was happy to see it was a much lighter lager for drinking on a sunny day. The kegs were housed in ice, and people were pouring them into every container they could find. Cups, bottles, bowls, anything else that worked. By the time he made his way back over to the catapult, he had finished a drink off, and a second was being poured for him.

"All right, where are we at?" he asked.

There were shrugs and the slight sound of beer being slurped up. "OK, a few pairs need to go out and bring some rocks to act as a weight. We'll also need some sort of sack to hold the missile or whatever it is we plan to launch with this thing. We can worry about aiming it later," Lane said.

The hours ticked by as Lane barked out orders and suggestions while they set up the catapult. The going was slow, as they all kept drinking and getting steadily more intoxicated. By the time it started to grow dark, they had finally gotten the lever to swing fully without crashing into the weight.

Lane heard the sound of a bell right as the first croaking of frogs reached his ears. He paused and took stock of how the other projects were doing. The bar was, shockingly, almost complete. It was mostly a roofed platform with a table nailed to one end, but Doug had never seemed too concerned with redefining the concept of a bar. They had hauled a keg into it and were pretending to be ordering drinks. The bonfire had evolved into some kind of elaborate castle. Multiple towers sprawled in every direction. Lane was not sure what kept gravity at bay to support its intricate structures, but he was almost sad that it would have to burn. It wouldn't be able to hold up longer than a few hours anyways, he supposed.

The bell rang again, while behind him the catapult team dropped the weight again. Another clean toss, slinging the empty sack high into the air. "I'll bet you could launch a canonball with this thing," someone said.

There was a cheer, and someone suggested they use one of the empty kegs instead. A whooshing noise followed that, and there was a fit of laughter. Even Lane giggled a bit at the idea of a big keg flying through the air.

"About time to see if we really get to eat that hog," Morgan said as he walked past. He looked sweaty and tired, but he had a beer in his hand and a smile on his face. "After we eat, we can come back here and see how well your contraption works."

Lane walked by the lake and toward the Great Hall. It was empty when he reached the top of the stairs, but the sound of people shouting and footsteps told him the group was back toward Cindy's house. He walked along the path and felt a tinge of pride at the work he had done with the catapult. It was a good machine, and he understood why the GDK ran their conference this way now. The bar hadn't been a good fit for him. But he had been useful for the catapult project. Maybe the culture grid was not so accurate after all.

As he got closer to Cindy's house, he was a little nervous to see a group of guys standing around his rental car. They had set several cups on top of it and were peering into the windows. He heard one ask if it belonged to Cindy, and another snorted in laughter. "What rich twit do you think actually drove a car to the GDK Con?" another said.

They laughed at this, and Lane hurried past. He had the impression that Alice and Derrick had a bit more clout to tell them off if they tried to mock them for the luxury.

In the backyard was a great black steel cylinder with a red glow emitting from its every opening. On top was the source of the smell Lane had been detecting all afternoon: an enormous pig. More kegs of beer were floating in tubs all around. A quick glance around showed the same raucous group resuming their ways from last night, but slightly subdued around Cindy as she sat in a small chair near the pig, fanning herself. As Lane went to go pour himself a beer, a man tripped and fell. Cindy immediately shouted at him to drink a water and take a walk. Everyone clapped and laughed, the man sheepishly obeying when no one else shared his sense of outrage.

As Lane poured the beer, he felt a pat on the shoulder and turned to see Alice. "Congratulations! I hear you actually managed to pull the catapult project together. You know half the time they never even make anything. One of the girls was just telling me the bar almost fell apart before someone who had actually built a house spoke up."

Lane found himself giving off a glowing grin without having any clue what to say or do except to shrug and act as if it were nothing.

He nervously jumped when he realized Alice was holding out her cup and looking at him expectantly. He took it and began pouring a beer for her. "So, how are the women doing? I know you were worried about the men last night and everyone getting along," he asked.

Alice shrugged and gestured. The female GDK were still all huddled together in a group, but several men had infiltrated now. One woman jokingly pushed another man and laughed loudly when he did a mock impression of someone hammering his finger and yelping.

"Doing a project together does a lot for people, particularly if you let them jump around and pick what feels right for them," Alice explained.

Soon the pig was cut, and great heaping plates were passed around the crowd. It had a vinegar-and-apple taste to Lane, with a bit of pepper and smoke mixed in. The animal's fat had boiled throughout and given it an incredible tenderness he had never tasted before. He was told it was fresh, grown on a nearby farm and bought with GDK funds. The money made from the wars and trading in *Tyrant* along with other games made real in feast. It was delicious.

After he had eaten a second helping, he was handed a stick. It took him a moment to realize it was a torch. There was a strip of cloth wrapped around one end and a chemical smell coming from it. A person appeared with a lit torch, and Lane realized it was Derrick. Alice was standing beside him. The crowd grew silent as Derrick's torch touched the tip of Alice's. Everyone was silent as Alice quietly walked to a nearby person and lit his torch. Slowly, the flame spread to everyone around. Lane leaned over to ask someone what was happening, but he was quietly shushed. The rustle of flames was the only noise except for the occasional frog off by the lake.

In a quiet voice Alice finally said, "Let us go and see our works."

CHAPTER 30

They walked slowly back to the lake, past the cabins, and into the field where they had built the day's projects. No one spoke. As they came to the bonfire pile, Lane realized the people who had been involved in its construction were breaking off and standing around it. He half expected them to light it but realized that would not be until later. The group who had built the bar also broke off, and Lane followed his group toward the catapult.

Off in the distance, he could see Alice and Derrick talking with Doug and the other people who had stuck around building the bar. They were showing it off, the sturdiness of the structure and its supports. Lane began checking the catapult over to make sure it would work. He whispered to one of the others, "Did we ever test it? To see if it would even launch anything?"

The man looked around and whispered back, "No, not really. I mean, we swung it with some sticks, but never like a rock or anything."

Lane idly fidgeted with the torch and wondered if he should try it. He supposed it could hit someone, so they wouldn't want anything too big or dangerous. Maybe a small rock would do it. He began searching the ground, kicking up stones and dirt. He wanted the catapult to work for Alice. He wanted her to be impressed.

Lane finally found one that was small enough that he was sure it would not pose much risk to anyone. He looked back and saw that Alice and Derrick were inside the bar now, so no one over there would be able to see them. "Let's give it one test before they get over here, OK?" The group who had helped him build the catapult were quiet at first. Then one man said, "Fuck it, why not?"

Lane dropped the rock into the bag for the missile and put his weight on top of it to bring that end of the catapult down. He took a deep breath and quickly looked over his shoulder. They were still inside the bar. He hopped out of the way, and there was a quiet rattle and whooshing noise as the long catapult flew up and released the rock into the air.

"Heh, whoooooosh," someone said.

Lane was just about to give a halfhearted attempt at making the noise himself when he heard an odd clunking noise. He looked back at the bar and saw that they were still inside. Then he heard the sound again, followed by another, then another, and then an incredible cacophony of wood collapsing into wood. There was shouting, and Lane turned to see the torches over by the bonfire were scattering. Even in the pale light they gave off, he could tell that the giant wooden bonfire castle was collapsing.

"Holy shit, I think you just…uh oh, man," one of the helpers said.

Lane could see several of the torches were heading in his direction. After a few moments, he realized Max was one of the people approaching, his face twisted into rage.

"Who did it? Who smashed the bonfire?" Max roared.

Lane looked around and saw that the others were slowly backing away from him. His face must have given him away because Max stormed up to him, torch still in hand. "You? The fucking lawyer? The little twerp who couldn't even bring himself to ride in the bus with everyone else because he's too high and mighty for that?" Max shoved a finger into Lane's chest, and it stung. The torch waved close enough to his face that he felt its heat.

Suddenly, instinctively, Lane found himself sizing up Max. Max was smaller than he was. He was about Lane's height but lacked the muscle. Lane made this assessment coldly and with little emotion. He dimly realized it was the same feeling of calmness that he felt when Koff or Kayla was screaming at him. Except instead of thinking of a comeback, he was judging how hard it would be to gouge out Max's eyes with his hands.

"Get that torch out of my face," Lane said while looking Max in the eyes.

"Or you'll what? Smash my bonfire? You fucking rich prick! Why? Why did you do it?" Max demanded.

"It was an accident. I wanted to see if the catapult would work," Lane answered.

In response Max waved the torch in Lane's face again. Lane caught it in the middle and twisted the handle against Max's grip, but he wouldn't let go. Without thinking, Lane's hand lashed out and struck Max in the face.

Max cried out. "Both of you stop it this instant!" Alice shouted. Lane felt arms wrap around him and begin dragging him away. His focus slowly came back, and he realized there was an enormous circle around them. Someone had grabbed Max as well.

"What the hell is wrong with you two? Max, it's a bonfire. We were going to burn it down no matter what. Being in a giant pile is not a big deal. And Lane, I expected better from you." Alice spoke toward the crowd more than either of them.

"Why did you knock it down, huh? Drive up here in your own personal car. Did the Tyrant pay for that? Did she? Big fancy lawyer has to come and knock over my own project with his stupid catapult!" Max shouted.

Alice looked at Lane with a look of disgust. "Is that true? Did you knock it down with the catapult?" she asked.

Lane felt a horrible sinking feeling as she stared at him. "It was an accident. I just wanted to make sure it…it was going to work. I didn't aim, I couldn't even aim the thing or see where it was going to go," Lane tried to explain.

A look of outrage crossed her face, and she said, "Look, maybe you should go."

Lane's mouth dropped open. Alice turned her back to him and shouted, "All right, everyone, nothing to see here." She began marching toward the pile that had once been the bonfire.

Everyone began to follow her, a few laughing or muttering, but most were silent. The ones who had helped him build the catapult tried to not make eye contact as they walked by. He felt the arms loosen their grip around him and turned to see that it was Derrick who held him. He looked at Lane and shook his head. "You have to understand, you destroyed someone's work. In real life. Just…you really should get out of here." And then he began walking after Alice as well.

Lane's mouth trembled as the members of the GDK slowly made their way to the bonfire pile. They began throwing torches onto it, and the enormous stacks burst into flames. He felt his emotions pulling him in every direction at once. He was angry at Alice for not understanding, but he didn't want to be angry at Alice. He was hurt that Derrick had turned on him too, but Derrick was weird, and who cared what he thought? He hated Max for being such a child about everything, but he couldn't stop feeling angry at himself for putting that rock in the catapult in the first place. No one had even stopped to look at his work.

Applause began to go up as the fire got brighter and bigger. The light from it began to spread out in an enormous circle, and Lane could see the edge of the light give way to darkness. He stepped back a little and then several times over to stay out of the light. He considered waiting until some time went by before approaching the group. Instead he finally found the point where the light from the fire stopped and sat outside of it. The circle of firelight spread so far that he was almost in the trees at this point. He sat down against a tree, gave one enormous sigh, and then let go. He began to cry.

And then the moment passed. Lane accepted that no one was going to come out and see if he was OK. No one was going to invite him back to the circle. He looked out at the crowd and watched. They had been getting deep into the beer again, and there was shouting and cheering as people danced and roared around the fire. He could see Derrick darting around groups, chatting and toasting them with his cup. He could just make out Alice as she talked to Max. She would go to other people and talk for a while, only to return to Max and put her hand on his shoulder.

As the crowd got rowdier, Lane noticed more people going over to his catapult and poking around. Someone decided to launch another rock at the bonfire, and it landed with a splash of sparks and cinders. There was a roar of laughter, and then more rocks were launched. Eventually they realized Lane's design allowed them to fire the catapult in the opposite direction. A test volley launched the rock toward the bar, where it bonked on the roof with a loud thunk. It occurred to Lane that it really had been a bad idea to build the catapult right in between two projects. He hadn't picked the work site, but he hadn't moved it or aimed the catapult away either.

After another rock launched into the bonfire, and this time the sparks launched into the huge crowd around it. More yelps, and Lane was happy to see Max go storming toward the catapult with a kindled torch. He tried touching it to various parts of the catapult, but it was not lighting. Finally he just lit the bag where the rocks were being loaded, but the group that had gathered around the catapult began shouting at him. Another dragged down the weight and launched the catapult while it was still on fire. The bag broke free from the swing and flew into the air. It landed on the roof of the bar.

Lane snickered at this turn of events. There was more shouting, and people began pointing fingers at Max. It made Lane happy to see him shout back, the sniveling twit. The fire began to spread around the bar, and soon the whole roof was on fire. Lane could see Doug now, the one who had taken charge of building the bar, walking out with a beer in his hand. After a few moments of staring at the flames, he began to laugh roaringly. He threw his empty beer cup at Max and walked back to the bonfire.

No one was yelling at Max or the other people who had been fooling with the catapult. Lane could see that Max was still angry about the whole thing. Alice again walked over to him and put her arm on his shoulder. He shouted angrily and began to storm off. He was heading in Lane's direction. As he drew closer, Lane got up and began slipping further back into the woods. His eyes had adjusted to the dark by now, and he moved easily.

Lane's heart skipped a beat as he realized Alice was chasing after Max. Neither of them seemed to have noticed Lane, and they could not see him from his new spot deep in the woods. Alice called out for Max, and he stopped and turned, his back to Lane. She wore an odd, pleading expression on her face. She walked up to Max slowly and wrapped her arms around him.

Lane's heart stopped as Max embraced Alice, and they began to kiss. He could see Alice's hands resting on top of his back and slowly stroking downward towards his pants and shirt. Lane felt too tired for the feelings that were coming over him, but they came anyways. His lip trembled again as he heard a soft moan come from Max, and then he was taking off his shirt. Alice followed suit, but Lane could not see much because Max blocking his view. Then they were on the ground, rolling in the grass, and Lane took a careful step back. He tried not to look, but he had to walk so slowly to get away undetected that there was no helping it.

He took one last, half-accidental and half-intentional look in their direction. He could just make out the shadowy figure of Alice naked and on top of Max. Her arms were on the ground as her arched back moved up and down and she softly groaned with each pulse. He could see her breasts; they were larger than Lane expected, and they heaved in rhythm with the motion. Lane heard Max gasp, and suddenly Alice began to go faster, faster, and then she leaned back and began lifting herself with her thighs. As she began to moan more loudly, Lane forced himself to turn away. He felt the beginnings of an erection and was ashamed.

Using the light of the fire as a guide, Lane moved around the perimeter of the circle. He saw that the bar was almost completely aflame now. After he had put enough distance between him and where he guessed Alice was off in the darkness, Lane reentered the circle of light. It had grown considerably smaller. Many of the people who had been there originally had gone to bed, exhausted from the day's work and the previous night of drinking. It was getting late, Lane guessed. He slowly approached the kegs and drew little notice from the few quiet clusters. He walked to a keg, but no beer came out when he pressed the pump. The second one floated in the water as well, but the third had enough in it for a cup. He sipped on it as he watched the flames burn, and his emotions flickered and kindled like the dying flames before him.

"Hey, has anybody seen the patriarch?" someone asked the group.

"Yeah, she's off in the woods fucking Max," Lane said loudly. He spat in the bonfire and walked back into the darkness.

CHAPTER 31

Lane awoke to the sound of snoring, but it had not kept him up this time. It was sunny out. He rose quietly before anyone else in the cabin and headed to the bathroom. By the time he was washing his hands and splashing water on his face, he had already made up his mind to leave. He grabbed his things and headed toward the car.

Even the frogs were quiet. Lane came down the road and realized his car had attracted some unwanted attention over the night. It was covered in toilet paper and some sort of white film that Lane hoped was soap. He threw his things into the back of the car, pulled out a Standard shirt, and wiped off the windshield. He sat in the front seat, plugged in his pad, and started the car up. He felt used up, like charred wood that had been consumed and gone cold. As he tried to start the car, his pad warned him that it would not drive until he cleaned the external sensors off.

He got out of the car again with the shirt and wiped the little black panels on each side of the car. He looked out over the field, the lake, and the winding road up the hill and debated whether he really should leave. He still didn't have Tally's address in Montana. Lane had gotten the impression it would take more than a car rental to get out there. No one had seemed to have any idea about her location except that she was "out there" now. He decided to just leave and work on it later.

Lane got back into the car and got underway. He only had to press a button instructing it to return to the rental agency. The car did a scan of the area and almost jerked Lane's head as it reversed and then ground gravel as it launched out of the driveway. As the car continued down the dirt road, a great sense of relief washed over him at not having to be there anymore. Lane tried to think of nothing in particular, but as the minutes inched by, he found himself reflecting on the conference. The image of Alice and Max kept repeating in his mind—her arching back—as did the anger at the unfairness of it all. Max had actually burned a place down, but no one tried to kick him out. Then the rejection hit him, and suddenly he was wishing he could have fit in somehow.

By the time the car got back onto the paved road, Lane was angry all over again. He gritted his teeth over every petty insult from Max. He thought about losing Alice and heard her telling him to leave again and again and saw look Derrick had given him before just shaking his head as if he were a child.

Lane brought up his pad and opened a new message to Eve. He told her he wanted to meet as soon as he was back in Charleston. He wanted to follow up on her offer.

Lane then began to change his filter. As he spotted articles that he had included because of the GDK, he tabbed them and removed them. One was about a man's right to an appeal after rape charges had been filed. A recent campaign to increase unemployment benefits and rights for space miners had received a sudden cash donation. Men's roller derby was making a comeback. Lane removed these stories and their sources out with the flick of a thumb.

He checked his messages. There was a response from Tricia finally, but it only said that they needed to meet in person to talk. No reply from Eve yet. Lane sat his pad down and stared out the window as the forest passed by. He found himself missing the miner litigation. Those were real problems. People trying to make sure they would be compensated for physical damage for things that had been beyond their control. It wasn't a virtual world out in space. You didn't file a petition with the designer to demand something be changed. It was bigger than that. Lane didn't want to deal with virtual problems anymore.

He finally began to doze off. The car switched automatically into sleep mode, which meant it traveled at a reduced speed and would brake at the slightest movement. Lane dreamed of empty fields and running through them. At first he was being chased, but then he began to recognize that he was dreaming. The contours of the dream world became apparent to his mind, and the dream altered. He began to chase something. He could not make it out; his heart both lusted for it and was repulsed by it. He was just barely able to discern its form when he awoke to a tapping sound. It was the woman from the car rental agency. Lane rubbed his eyes for a moment and opened the door.

"I have to warn you, this was not included in your rental plan. Cleaning the car will be extra. Is that…tell me this is soap," she said as she ran a finger along the hood. She held it up to her nose to smell and gave a look of disgust. "Like beer and soap and…ugh, just go. I don't even want to hear it."

Lane didn't even try to explain anything. He felt no responsibility, and he had no explanation for why the GDK had done it. The woman held out her hand for Lane's pad and then plugged in her own. A few taps later, and every trace of the car software was gone.

He took his luggage and made the short walk over to the train station. A glance at the times showed him he would be able to catch an early train. Lane checked his messages again, but there was still no response from Eve. The image of Alice's back arching and Max's groans came to his head, but he shoved them away. He wished he could delete it.

The train finally arrived, and Lane sat down in one of an empty pair of seats. He stared out the window as the trees turned back into the endless rows of crops and tall machines harvesting from them. He suddenly wondered what it would be like to work there. It would be good work, the kind where you didn't have to think. Plowing and tilling the land, making the food that everyone ate, and generally keeping the population from starving.

Lane suddenly wanted to know if he could do it, how any of it functioned. He did a quick search and saw percentages and stats roll by, and the long list of credentials required to be a farmer came up. You had to have training in robotics, farm cultivation, chemistry, and geological science. Lane shuddered as he remembered the years of philosophy, computer programming, and information theory he had dragged himself through to become a lawyer. He had been obsessed with getting out of the dorms then. Becoming a space lawyer was just another fantasy now, he thought with disgust, like all the ritual and pomp of the GDK. He would have to go back and tell Koff he had resolved nothing except costing the firm extra for the rental car.

The train worked its way back to Charleston with little disturbance, and Lane was happy to see he had arrived back by early afternoon. Eve had still not sent a response, so he sent another message letting her know he was back in town and knew the location of the GDK base. He had one final parting gift for the group. He went home, ate a protein bar, and showered himself clean. By the time he stepped out, there was a message on his pad from Eve. It said to come by her house.

Lane wasted no time hopping on the bus to downtown Charleston. It crossed onto King and began nosing its way down the peninsula. Lane began to ponder how exactly he was supposed to even do this exchange. When he had sent the message, he was only thinking about getting back at Max. Was he supposed to withhold the location of the GDK fleet until Eve had sex with him? Would she know what to do, or was this new to her as well?

As the bus finally came to the stop closest to Eve's home, Lane's nervousness kept growing. It reminded him of the anonymous sex program. Strange women wanting to know his dick size and how far away his apartment was and could he not link with them on their profile? He could reach down and turn on the sex program and go for a walk. The odds were good that someone would ping him, and she would ask nothing in return. Eve wanted something from him this time, and that made it feel different somehow.

He knocked on the door and heard a distant "Come in!" Lane stepped inside and looked around the house. It was still immaculate and lavishly furnished, the capitalist sensibilities of excess and accumulation scattered around more conservative furnishings—a house for a virtual queen whose wealth spilled into the real world, and Lane was about to make her richer.

Lane did not see anyone and sat himself down. When Eve finally appeared, he was a little surprised at how plain she looked. She wore only a long green skirt and T-shirt. He had expected her to do something more to entice him. She looked distracted and remained standing as she sipped on a glass of water. She did not offer Lane anything.

"So you know where their fleet is?" Eve asked.

Lane nodded. "Heard one of them mention it at the conference."

Eve studied his face for a moment before nodding and sitting down. "I don't have a lot of time left. I'm guessing they are still sluggish from the conference, or else they would have made a move by now. The designers are going to do a retcon soon and pull the mod. Whole world is practically dead; no one is playing until it goes back to normal. With that location, it would be a huge blow against them."

Lane said nothing. He could tell she was as nervous about this as he was. He suddenly stared at the floor and tried to swallow.

"You can't brag about this online, you know that, right? I have too many men working for me. It would mess with the whole dynamic in their head," Eve said quietly.

Lane nodded and answered, "Oh, of course not. I never brag about sex. I'm very private about it," Another image of Alice entered his mind, but he shoved it aside.

They were both silent. The ice in Eve's glass clinked, and she took another sip. "It's funny; I figured sex wouldn't have much value to someone like you. Money maybe, or something else?" she said.

Lane looked at her and smiled sheepishly. "I have lived off Standard goods for a while. I don't mind it. If that's OK, I mean, what I'd like is—"

Eve looked surprised and then began to laugh. "Oh my God, you are completely freaked out by this!"

"What? No I'm not! OK, it is weird. I'm giving you something for sex. Except it's this fantasy exchange. I'm giving you the location of a secret base in a virtual world where your virtual enemies are living. But it equals a lot of money. And it's important to you, and it's definitely important to the GDK. Which is the main reason I'm even here—because all those people care, and I want them to."

Eve stood up and walked over to the bar with a slow pace. "Drink?" she asked.

"No, I'm all right. You know things didn't go well at the conference for me. I didn't—it wasn't a good fit. Totally different cultures. I don't know what I was thinking, really. They were just such…assholes. Or something, I can't tot—" Lane hadn't been paying attention as he spoke, and he was interrupted as Eve stepped in front of him. He looked up and craned his neck a little; she loomed tall. Her breasts suddenly seemed large in the loose green T-shirt, and she had her drink angled just so that it touched the side of her chest. She had a familiar look on her face as she studied him, one he had seen when she was playing *Tyrant*. Without warning, she sat down on his lap.

"Were they mean to you, Lane?" Eve asked. She had sat on his hand while it was still in his lap, and he twisted it awkwardly to get it free.

"I don't know. There was this one guy who had it out for me. And we…" Lane said as Eve leaned against him. She carefully took a sip from her drink before setting it down. Shifting her position put his hand again underneath her. He extended his fingers and pulled his hand along her side, and she gave a gasp and a smile. Lane felt an erection surge as Eve shifted again on his lap, and he knew she felt it too. He ran his hand up her backside as she leaned in, their lips running together before her tongue met his.

Eve's legs were still facing away from Lane, and his other hand began to pull at them. He wanted her to turn, to open herself to him, but she resisted. His hand began to move along her legs before it crossed over her underwear. Eve pulled back and suddenly reached for Lane's pants. She pulled herself up just long enough to unbuckle his belt and sat back down. Without hesitating, Lane lifted himself enough to pull down his pants while his other hand grabbed Eve's thigh. She gasped again and seemed to pull away, but he held her. Lane couldn't resist. He pulled her dress up and yanked her underwear down.

He entered her at an awkward angle, his hands shaking as she gasped and lowered herself so that he entered her fully. She finally turned her legs, raising one over his head and twisting herself while he was still inside. Then with both knees, she raised herself and grabbed his head in a grip far more powerful than he would have expected her to have.

"The base?" she said.

"It's in the Gibson Cloud," he said. She reached behind her, still holding herself above his erect shaft, and typed something into a pad that she had set by the table. As she was setting the pad back down, Lane grabbed her roughly and thrust himself back inside her. "Lane, oh!" she said in surprise. His arms were locked around her now, his hips thrusting as she sat on his lap. His erection felt like stone, impossible to feel at the angle he was at, and so Lane shoved her onto the floor. "Lane," she said again, but he barely heard her.

Blood pumped through him, and a silent anger that been brewing inside him the entire weekend drove him. Longer even, for months, years, maybe his entire life. He thrust into Eve blindly and without any awareness of her. He ground his cock into her walls as he gripped her head in his arms. Her hair had splayed out on the floor, and he clutched bits of it in his hands tightly. He was so hard and numb that he tried to angle her body against his cock so he could orgasm by lifting her up.

Like a tiny glimmer, he could feel just the beginnings of sense in the head of his penis. Harder and faster he went as he felt it, chased it inside of her, through her, and throughout. He was panting now, and he was dimly aware that she was as well. When it finally came, when Lane finally found it, he groaned and shut his eyes for the explosion of pleasure. When it passed, he gave a few half-hearted thrusts before toppling beside Eve on the floor. He was panting for breath and staring at the ceiling. Eve said nothing.

He looked around and realized that in the moment he had torn off Eve's dress and underwear. He couldn't remember doing that. Lane could think of nothing else to say but "I'm sorry."

Eve replied, "Can you fuck me like that again?"

CHAPTER 32

Tom bounded down the halls of the mining ship *Black Swan* with ease. The low gravity provided by the ship's rotating outer ring gave just enough weight to keep the cargo in place and make sure you put enough weight on your bones to keep them from decaying on a long trip. The dim, flickering lights of the craft were the only indication that it was the night shift, a term that had little meaning to the portion of the crew on duty at this hour. They had just left the Gateway Port and had been in visual range of the Earth for several hours.

Tom paused outside a door with a large red cross on the side. There had been six accidents on this trip. One fatal, two critical, and three serious. He flexed his hand and felt the tinge of pain that the ship's doctor said would be with him for the rest of his life. While decompression wouldn't kill you immediately, spending days in a space suit waiting for the lifeboat to slingshot around the asteroid field took its toll. A glance inside the window showed that there had been no change in his friends.

Tom paused as he saw Herbert and tried to make eye contact. They had been talking for a while, but Herbert had been seeing Colson on this trip. Screwing another miner's partner was a hazardous hobby. Colson hadn't made it off the rock, and Tom was wondering how Herbert was taking it. Probably not well. "Hell," Tom thought bitterly, "I'm not taking it well." When the oxygen meter calculated how much longer they had with twelve guys, six in suits outside the mining unit and six in partial atmosphere around the core, they had drawn straws. Afterward, Herbert and Colson talked for a while alone. Then Colson filled out some forms on his pad and gave it to Herbert. Then he said good-bye.

They were at full capacity from this trip—250 million tons of mixed asteroid iron, give or take a few thousand tons of regolith dust. When they took this thing to dock near the moon, it would be shuttled out and melted down into refineries before transportation back into the solar system. Tom once again did the calculations in his head for value, counting taxes, and counted out his share from the haul at 1.2 million. It took him a moment to realize there was an error in his math because the injured would get a larger share for lost limbs, and the dead would get no share at all. He came up with roughly one million instead.

Tom swung around the pole and came out onto the view deck. Out the window was a blanket of stars and a small blue sphere. His weight settled as he stared at it. That was Earth. The place he had been born. The place that would be consuming most of the iron they had mined out. And all Tom could think about was how much he hated the place.

He hated the way women stared at him whenever he walked into an expensive restaurant. The way a waitress would say, "This area is for paying customers." He hated that he couldn't get drunk without some cop asking him if he was OK and following him back home to make sure he didn't accidentally rape anyone. Everything was safe. Everyone had their Standard share they could hide behind and retreat to.

The only thing that disgusted him more were the men on that wet rock. Most of them thought they were too good for Tom. Would sniff their nose at his money and drink their Standard liquor. Half of them would ignore you when they found out you were buying drinks. The other half couldn't think about anything else but your money. Before you even blew your load, they were wanting this or that. Most of them had never been to space. None of them could really understand it when Tom tried to talk about what it was like on a trip.

He hated the pads. He hated the virtual goods. The pretend markets and the pretend people who inhabited them. He hated people waving these idiotic grids at him and telling him they were having a reality disagreement. "No," he would say, "you're a fucking moron who doesn't know what they're talking about and should shut up!"

Tom froze as he realized that he had accidentally said that last part out loud. He looked around nervously, but no one else was there. The moment was disturbed when his comm signal chimed. "Tom, where are you?"

"View Port Seventeen Bridge. Go ahead," Tom answered.

"I've got a…blue cloud thing that just appeared near there. Are you seeing this? It just appeared, and then the ship passed through it," the voice said. Tom looked out the window but saw nothing. He began moving over to the far end of the viewing area to see if he could spot something from a different angle.

"Negative, Bridge, I'm not seeing—wait, OK. I just saw some…blue sparks outside the port. Looks like some kind of electric…woah!" Tom jumped back as a surge of voltage erupted inside the room. It arced past him, leaving the hair on his head standing. "Bridge, it's inside the ship!" Tom shouted. He waited for a response, but none came. Tom suddenly felt the effects of weightlessness creep over him, and he began to slowly lift off the floor. His stomach turned at the sudden shift, and he gritted his teeth.

He slowly began to spin, unable to control his motion with the lack of gravity. As he turned, he realized there was an enormous steel wall behind him. It did not register on his brain at first because seconds before, this had been an empty room. The crew would come here and drink or talk. Sometimes you could get an alone moment with another of the boys.

His mind began to recognize that it was not actually a wall, but a ship's hull. He could tell by the signs of solar damage and the scratches that only space dust traveling at hundreds of miles a second could do. As he continued to rotate, he realized the hull was not just in front of him but in the entire room. It filled it, went all the way down to the end. He could not even see the hallway anymore.

He panicked. His arms flailed, his legs kicked, but he was weightless and unable to get close to anything to push off. Then he began to hear the slow hiss of air. It was coming from all around him. And the most awful grinding noise of metal on metal. Tom panicked as the sound began to fade until all the air to carry the vibrations to his ears was gone. By the time he had completely spun around and was facing the view port again, the *Black Swan* had sheared apart.

Tom's final thought, as the cold filled his eyes and ears and the air sucked out of him completely, was to wish he were back on Earth.

CHAPTER 33

Eve was quiet as he got up from her bed and dressed. It seemed like the thing to do. She didn't pretend to be asleep or ask him to leave. She simply woke up and watched him. He mumbled something about having to get to work, which was true, but he had no reason to rush. She said nothing as he exited her house, and Lane briefly wondered if any of this had been a good idea.

Lane stepped outside quietly as morning set in over Charleston. There was just the slightest hint of a chill in the air, and he shivered slightly. Even the metal gate of twisting vines was cold to the touch. The closest Charleston ever got to winter was the early mornings before the sun returned things to their normal tropical temperature. He began walking toward Calhoun and was reaching for his pad when he barely had time to stop himself from running into a patrol woman.

She was tall and stout, and her clothes fit tightly to show her broad shoulders and muscle. On one hand was a black glove that Lane immediately recognized as the weapon of choice for a patrol officer. An array of electronic circuits meshed with complex fabric that would allow it to become as hard as steel, pass a current that could drop a gorilla, or project enough force to break a person's arm with ease. She clapped her gloved hand on his shoulder.

"Good morning sir, did you just exit that residence?" she asked. She was looking at Eve's home.

Lane followed her look and nervously stammered, "Yes, yes, I did."

The hand tightened ever so slightly. "Sir, we have no record of you being given permission to enter that residence, nor has the owner registered a male entering her domicile. Your last status update placed you on a bus to Lower King," the officer explained.

Lane stared at her in horror. He had only done a handful of criminal cases, but he immediately recognized the implication of the officer's statement.

"I was invited! She just—there is a certain amount of discretion involved here, and I was respecting her privacy. Please! Look, you can go ask her, I'll call on my pad," Lane said. As he reached into his pocket, his vision blurred as a mild shock passed through his body. The glove's taser feature had activated with no warning.

"Sir! Keep your hands where I can see them!"

The world spun for a moment, and he was suddenly on the ground with an arm pinned behind him.

"Based on the failure to provide a status update while inside the residence of a single female who has also not provided a permissive update, there is probable cause for your detention until we can determine the safety of the female," the officer intoned.

Lane's head was pounding from the current, and he shouted, "You're outside her house. Just knock on the door!"

"At which point the subject resisted and attempted to disrupt the arrest," the officer finished. Suddenly a car pulled up, and Lane recognized the police markings on it. The officer lifted Lane bodily with the gloved arm while she kept an iron grip around his wrist. A door opened on the car, and he realized someone was behind the wheel. The officer pulled Lane's pad from his pocket and then thrust him into the backseat. She walked around to the front and handed the pad to the driver.

"Wait, goddamnit! How do you even have a car this quickly if this isn't all plan—planned," Lane finished as he was bodily thrown inside the vehicle. There was no need to restrain him. Once the door closed, there was nothing to grab onto or anything he could do inside the reinforced interior of the vehicle. "Look, I don't know what this is about. I'm an apprentice lawyer. I know my rights, OK? It will save us all a lot of hassle if we just wait a minute and check a few things out before everyone starts jumping to conclusions," Lane said.

The officer did not respond; instead she punched in a destination to the car's controls.

For a single, horrible moment, he wondered if Eve had been the one to call the patrol woman down on him, but it soon passed. What would be the point? If she wanted to deny having sex with him, her fans and staff would believe her over him. Their entire reality demanded it. Any explanation he gave would assume a form compatible to them, which meant implying he was lying. Lane gloomily realized this would be true for most women's realities as well. Not many people included rape sympathy in their news feed.

A loud ping sounded from the driver's pad, but the officer tapped a finger over it to silence the device. Another ping interrupted, and the officer again tried to silence the device. Suddenly the car's loudspeaker crackled, "Warning: emergency deactivation procedures have been initiated. Please prepare for the vehicle to stop."

The officer loudly swore and picked up the pad and began furiously typing into it. "Authorization override acknowledged. Manual driving initiated."

Lane rocked back in his seat as the car suddenly accelerated. The driver's hands were on the wheel, and she was speeding up. "Look, I don't know what's going on, but can you please just wait until someone talks to Eve about this?" Lane pleaded.

There was again silence as the car sped down the streets of Charleston. When the patrol car pulled around a bend, a bus came into view. The officer jerked the brakes and turned right off the main road. Lane was thrown across his seat and yelped when he bounced off the wall of the car. He reached for his seatbelt and was fumbling with the lock when the car's brakes squealed loudly. Lane was flung to the other side of the car.

He moaned and gently touched the already-forming knot on his head. He could feel swelling and heat underneath his hair. Lane looked up and saw a woman standing in the middle of the road. She was dressed the exact same way as the women he had seen following Eve: black suit, sunglasses, and this time wearing a black glove like the patrol officer's. It seemed to have a series of crisscrossing blue circuits along it, but Lane noticed this only because her hand was held up in a stop gesture.

The officer slammed the horn on her car, but the woman out front did not budge. Swearing again, she unplugged the pad from the car and opened the door. "Are you deaf? Get out of the way! Official police business!"

Lane had to strain to hear the other woman's reply. "You were given a direct order to halt your vehicle, Officer."

The two women paused, and Lane nervously wondered if things were about to get nasty. He wasn't sure what would happen if two of those gloves ran into each other. Patrol officers rarely used excessive force, but broken arms and ribs were not unheard of.

"My orders are to get the suspect back to the station for further evaluation," the officer said coldly. Her gloved hand was clenched, and she held the car door between herself and the other woman.

"Check them again," the black suit said. She took a step toward the officer. Seconds ticked by as the patrol officer stared at her, unmoving. Lane was almost positive she was about to attack. Then the moment passed, and the officer checked her pad. She looked up almost immediately.

"Who are you?"

"An interested party. Please release the man," the suit replied. The officer tapped another button on the pad, and the doors popped open on either side of Lane. He shakily stepped outside. His head still throbbed from the bump he had received. "Return to your vehicle. I think you'll find this data won't be reflected in your records. Please give me his pad as well. No further trouble will be required on your part. And thank your commanding officer for me," the suit said.

The officer got back in the car, flipped the pad at the black suit, who caught it with one gloved hand, and then drove away. Lane looked around to get his bearings and briefly wondered if the past few moments had even really happened.

The woman in the suit walked up to Lane and looked him up and down carefully. She reached into a pocket and pulled out a small blue cloth, crunched it up in her hand, and handed it to him. It was ice cold to the touch. "For your head," she said.

Lane placed it over the knot and took a quick breath as the chill sent a shudder through him.

"What's going on? That wasn't any normal arrest. What did those cops want? What do you want?" Lane demanded.

The suit stared at him. "As I said, we are an interested party. And your situation has become a lot more complex, Lane," she finally replied. She handed Lane his pad. "It's best you find out the rest through primary sources. Go to work, Lane. You have a lot ahead of you."

CHAPTER 34

Lane took a few moments to check his pad and realized he was several blocks away from the nearest bus stop. Rows of pink houses and whitewashed homes were on either side of him in one of the nicer Charleston neighborhoods. The pad did a time comparison and suggested he walk. A brief ping, and he saw a message from Eve saying she hoped he had a nice day. Had anyone even spoken to her? Why had the woman in black rescued him?

A double ping rang from his pad as he walked to work, and Lane checked to see who would want a video chat. It was Tricia. When he accepted the transmission, he saw her face was red and bleary eyed. "Lane! Answer your fucking meeting requests! God, can you believe it?"

He stared at the pad blankly, unsure what it was saying.

"You can't be serious," she said. "Have you not checked your news feed yet?"

Lane glanced briefly at the icon, noticed the flashing alert button, and mumbled, "I got arrested. Give me a second." He tapped it, and the news began to appear. "Possible Gate accident leads to loss of millions in iron. All-male crew decimated by rampaging ship owned by Gateway; they deny responsibility."

Lane wrinkled his nose at that and recognized it at as another GDK filter. "So what? Two ships rammed into each other? It's not that common, but it happens." Lane said.

"For fuck's sake, what reality are you filtering? Here, follow this link!" Tricia snarled.

Lane was shocked that Tricia of all people would resort to criticizing a reality. The link popped up through the video chat and was entitled, "Gateway ship mysteriously 'appears' inside mining vessel: Travel technology disaster?" Lane stared at the title, his mind sensing what Tricia was trying to tell him but still not yet making the connection.

"It's…the mod…it's real?" he said quietly. He had stopped walking. He looked away from his pad. He saw the name of the street he was on, knew where it went and what would happen if he followed it. There was a little dip on one of the corners you had to watch out for. A little park with a lake was down the corner where ducks would appear sometimes.

"It's a PR campaign. I wanted you to meet me in person to make sure you understood it all, but now…Lane, it's the biggest meme-planting job I've ever seen. After I did some tracing on the accounts Gateway was using for that mod, I realized they have been funding hundreds of projects across multiple realities. I don't even understand half of it. Boosting the appeal of genetic modification in movies, some women's literature getting sponsored for a production grant, everything you can think of. If the *Tyrant* thing wasn't so obvious, I don't think I would have even made the connection. That one stood out with the appeal, and now it all makes sense," Tricia said.

"How is it real? It can't be an ad; the mod is a disaster there. Everything has gone crazy in *Tyrant*. The game's economy is crashing, and people are hoarding ships. All they did was show that the whole thing will be a mess," Lane said.

"Lane, you don't plant an idea in someone's head by walking up to them and telling them what to think. There are a thousand other ideas coexisting with it that connect and influence it. This is like that time there was a food shortage back when we were kids, and the government had that big media campaign to make everyone not hoard food. Remember? All sorts of posters, plays, shows, and all that stuff. It's just this is much bigger," Tricia replied.

Lane had started walking again toward work. "What do we do with this?" he asked.

Tricia shrugged and said, "I have been freaking out all morning since I saw the news. There's a woman outside my apartment who followed me to work the other day. I don't know where she is now, and I was at work freaking out, and my boss sent me home, and Lane, do you think the ship was a part of the meme? Like the accident itself? What is Gateway doing?" There was panic in Tricia's voice now.

He felt tense and irritable, unsure of what to do or say, let alone to Tricia. "I'll report all of this to Koff and see what she says. She might not believe me, I didn't even find the mod owner like I was supposed to. The whole North Carolina thing was a bit of a mess. I'll be in touch, OK? Just send me all your reports and data. Drinks later tonight? Koff will sort it out; don't worry," Lane said.

Tricia nodded and blew her nose before turning the video off.

When he arrived at work, everyone was silent. People were staring at their pads while they stood around the office. The death tolls were starting to come in. Almost the entire crew of at least one ship had been killed. The feed asked him if he would consent to seeing gory and disturbing footage, and after Lane agreed, gruesome images appeared. Arms that had been perfectly sliced off, bits of face and blood in zero gravity. The missing limbs were at strange angles, as if someone had just drawn a line down the ship and everything on one side vanished.

Lane numbly walked by Derrick's desk and saw that it was empty. Sally was staring at her pad, and Grace didn't even look up from her desk. She wasn't looking at anything at all. Lane headed straight to Koff's office. His stomach was beginning to feel upside down, as if by seeing the images, the situation felt close somehow. For a moment he felt as if he had to explain to himself who he was again.

The door to Koff's office was closed. As Lane reached for the handle, he heard a man's voice muffled, and then Koff barked something back at him. Lane knocked on the door. He heard Koff shout, "Can it wait?" and Lane pushed the door open. He had expected to see someone sitting on the couch, but instead he saw Koff looking at a large monitor connected to a pad. A man's face was on the screen, and Lane realized Koff was video chatting with him.

"Lane, this is not the time. I got your message. You didn't get the release signed. Figure out how to find wherever it is she went. Now get—" Koff paused speaking as Lane sat down on the couch and leaned forward.

"It's Gateway. They knew this would happen. They…the mod was some kind of ad. Or branding or something. The point is they knew about the accident."

Koff stared at Lane with no expression except for her mouth slightly hanging open. He noticed out of the corner of his eye that the man on the screen seemed to have a similar expression. "Mother, can you turn the camera a little bit so I can see who is talking?" he asked.

Lane suddenly felt very uncomfortable. Koff tilted her pad and with the other hand opened a drawer at her desk. Within moments, a candy was in her hand and expertly unwrapped before she popped it in her mouth. She began chewing immediately.

"Evidence?" Koff said.

"I had a friend trace the account funding the mod. She took it back to the company using the account and then followed some other money trails it was producing. It all goes to funding various shows, legislation, and virtual stuff to create a giant meme for…this thing. The ship teleporting into the other one," Lane said. It was beginning to dawn on him how bizarre all of this sounded. "I don't think Gateway did it on purpose. Or maybe they did, I don't know. I think they were trying to plant some kind of idea in people's heads about the space travel thing before actually announcing that it was real."

"Because?" Koff asked. She reached for another candy and popped it into her mouth. She crushed the wrapper in her fingers and placed it neatly in the desk next to the other one.

Lane tried to think of an answer but realized he hadn't really thought about motivation yet. Tricia had seemed so certain about the whole thing, but she had also been crying.

"Does the why of it really matter?" the man on the screen said. "If this isn't a gate travel accident, then there is potential liability. Almost all of the iron on that ship was destroyed, not counting the recovery fees for the people who died. You, young man, what did you say your name was?"

"Lane. I'm an apprentice here. Who are you?"

"My name is Jacob. I am a space lawyer for McAngus & Lee, Orbital Branch. It looks like you know my mother already," the man said.

Lane could see the resemblance immediately. A shot of adrenaline passed through him as he realized he had gotten the attention of another male space lawyer. This could be his chance.

"Yes, yes, so there's a bit of nepotism. Do you think you can work with this? It all sounds crazy to me," Koff asked Jacob.

"That depends. How good is the data on this, Lane?"

"I can forward you the same report Tricia sent me. And the article from her feed—she follows some realities that I don't. It started with an appeal filed for a mod and…it's a bit complex," Lane explained.

Jacob replied, "Try me."

It took longer than Lane expected. Koff would give him an irritated look or Jacob would begin to fidget with something, but Lane was never sure what part to take out. All of the things that happened in *Tyrant* were both relevant and not really at all. As he kept talking, his mouth went dry. Koff tapped on her pad, and a few moments later there was a knock on the door. Kayla walked in with a glass of water. She headed for Koff's desk, but Koff waved her away. The look of pure venom she shot at Lane as she served him was exhilarating. He took a sip and kept explaining. This really was his chance at getting out of his apprenticeship.

"So, they made the mod real?" Jacob asked.

Lane nodded enthusiastically, but Koff snorted irritably. "No, obviously they invented the technology and then started this whole campaign to plant the meme in people's heads. What the meme is, exactly, I don't know. Your friend Tricia has linked this to everything from fem porn and flash comedies to virtual reality fundraisers. Jacob, there is a lot of speculation here. I don't like it," she said.

"How do you plant an idea across the entire grid?" Jacob said. "Is that even possible? Every single reality is going to absorb it differently. Every woman and man will take it in a scattered manner. No one is going to believe that the entire population can be manipulated when all you have to do is go look it up to see what's going on."

"I agree," Lane said. "They probably just wanted to make sure they had complete control over it when it came to market. Half of the things in the report involve legislation to change tax burdens around or change how the benefits work for a particular group. They just wanted the public to have a favorable reaction to the whole idea."

"Which certainly isn't going to happen now that they have killed a ship full of iron and men," Jacob said. "Who gives a damn what they were up to? We have enough to file a claim for total liability and bypass an AI judgment for immunity with this. A bit of tweaking and some finesse, and we can get this shifted to the popular vote. I'll put in a bid for the company. Since we'll be the only ones even trying to offer them a shot at getting their money back, we should get it, no problem."

Koff looked from the monitor to Lane and drummed her fingers on her desk. "Godamnit, you two are already pairing off into a little boy's club. Fine, let's do it. Oh, and Lane, time to start brushing up on your space law."

CHAPTER 35

As he walked back to his desk, Lane could not help sticking his head in Kayla's office. She was sitting in her chair, with one hand on her belly and another holding an earpiece to her head. "Kayla, I just got put on a space law assignment. I know that's an area you tend to cover. If you could forward me some sample media for popular votes, that would be awesome."

She glared at him before giving a single stiff nod.

Lane sat down at his desk and began to plan. The goal was to make a demand for complete compensation for the loss of the ship and crew. Space law granted someone immunity for collisions that occurred when the ships collided in a gate path. Because the decision was purely one of probabilities and legal application, it had to go to an AI.

Of course, in reality, the law had rarely ever been used because most people had the sense to stay out of the gate paths. The odds of two ships otherwise colliding with each other unintentionally were so astronomically unlikely that it had happened only once or twice. The AI would be operating with almost no heuristic variation, no meaning space, and no examples of application in the rule. It would be a straight shot, and the claimant was almost guaranteed to lose. But if Tricia's idea was correct and this was a freak accident involving some kind of new technology, the laws would not apply. It would go to the popular vote. And there, they had a chance.

Jacob and Koff had decided that the best course of action was to make sure the mod in *Tyrant* stayed active. Since it was an enormous virtual economy and the mod had caused so much chaos, they could use it to support any move for a public vote against Gateway. Media was Lane's job. Jacob was going to get his telemetry team to start calculating the odds of whether or not this was an actual gate accident. Koff had little interest in either, announcing instead that she would handle the bidding for the claim.

As far as Gateway's interest in the mod lawsuit or the CEO calling, things had suddenly gotten quiet. Lane had neglected to tell either of them that he had burned a few bridges over the weekend with the GDK but assured them they still had a good repertoire with the Tyrant herself. Even if they hated Lane, Derrick would still have pull with the Gay Death Knights.

Lane had decided to make no mention of the arrest or the woman in black. While he admitted to knowing the Tyrant fairly well, he didn't want to have Koff breathing down his neck about screwing the witnesses. Nor did he want to admit that he had almost been accused of raping a woman.

Lane sent a quick message to Eve about having an offer for her and another to Derrick asking him when he would be available. After a moment, he added a message to Tricia thanking her again and forwarding her payment for the work. Don't forget about drinks later, he added. After a moment Lane decided to send a text to Morgan and Dale as well to see if they had any ideas about marketing to a virtual community. Then he checked the news about the accident again.

There was a live video feed being taken by a ship in nearby orbit. The tugs had attached to both of the ships, and when they began pulling the two ships, they slid apart with almost no friction. It was unnerving to watch, and the news feed kept repeating the image. A huge web of twisted metal halls and steel meshes on the outside pulled apart to reveal two totally separate wholes.

Lane was a little surprised to see the commenters on the business reality feed getting angry with one another. Several of them did not participate in this reality but had changed their filters because of the accident. They were protesting the violation of men's rights and posted links to their own versions of the event. Lane flagged the comments for filtering and checked his feed for other stories.

A few articles had cropped up talking about how Gateway's explanation made little sense because of the physics involved. In Lane's reality none of them accused Gateway of using any sort of new transport technology. Instead, some hypothesized a micro wormhole had formed, while other suggested it was alien beings tampering with the gate system. Lane typed in a comment suggesting people check out the mod for *Tyrant* and suggested it was all a meme scheme by Gateway. It got no response.

A ping from Eve had a short message: "Mod is still active. GDK have scattered after base attack. Info was good. Need mod to go down now."

Lane frowned and tried to think of what to say back. He finally typed, "Mod part of PR campaign for Gateway. May prove they were using new travel technology, caused accident. Need it to be in game and not old news."

There was no response, but Eve sent him a link to the *Tyrant* economy feed.

The value of the game world was still nose-diving. The labor values involved in operating ships and transporting materials had almost completely collapsed. Large amounts of the game's capital had returned to unclaimed status. Which was a polite way of saying that nobody knew what the capital was anymore. The few players who had held onto value by investing in ships found these depreciating because the weapon systems involved in the game now performed completely differently. Some players had adopted new business models that preyed on those still relying on how the game had played before the mod, but this wasn't generating new capital. It was just eating what was left. Production had become infinite in the game, and the value of scarcity had followed course, becoming nothing.

Lane wondered if this was what would happen in the real world as well. Gateway employed millions of people. Entire industries involved the manufacture and development of goods to be used for space travel. If it suddenly became possible for ships to just travel instantly to any destination, all of those jobs would become meaningless. Most of them were held by men.

He typed in response to Eve, "This is bigger than the game. Can discuss payment options."

The response came back immediately, "Would not be cheap. Will have to find a way for players to support it. Probably need GDK too."

Lane stared at the message for a while and felt a sinking sensation in his stomach. Derrick hadn't responded to him or come into work yet. His invitation to Morgan and Dale had been accepted though. Maybe he could ask them for some advice when they met at the Tohickon. Lane felt a presence hovering over him, and he turned around to see Kayla watching him with her pad in hand.

"Not playing games this time, I see," she said.

Lane gave her a smile before rotating his chair so that his back was to her. He wanted to savor this moment. She coughed finally, and he turned back around. "Oh! Those examples on space law. I forgot all about it while I was checking out the public reaction. Folks are calling it the biggest space accident in history. Should be a good case."

Kayla punched a few keys on her pad, and Lane was asked if he accepted the file. He looked down, and his eyes landed on her belly, which was already noticeably larger. "How is the baby coming along?" Lane asked.

"It's all right. I've had dozens of offers to help mother the child. Some of them are pure wack jobs. Some of them seem like they'd do a better job at it than me. My Mom didn't believe in having Other Mothers," Kayla said.

Lane nodded. "I had a couple. They would swing into the dorms sometimes and give us nice food."

Kayla nodded and glanced at the monitor Lane's pad was linked to. "So the mod thing worked out after all? I remember it was tied to Gateway somehow, but it has something to do with this gate accident as well?"

Lane nodded and realized there was a touch of emotion in her voice. He knew she would have wanted the file, but it hadn't crossed his mind that she would care about the reason he had gotten it. He realized she wanted to know it was because of the mod and not because he was somehow better than she was. Or maybe, as Lane noticed her hand again going nervously to her stomach, it was about Koff's disapproval of her pregnancy. A moment of vileness passed in which Lane considered telling her that he had been handpicked for the job before he decided he didn't have the heart for it.

"It's the mod thing. Turns out those video games paid off after all," Lane said quietly.

Kayla nodded, reassuring herself of some invisible bit of logic Lane could only begin to sense, before heading back to her office. It occurred to him that it was the most civil exchange they had ever had.

Lane checked the file Kayla had sent him and realized it was a random assortment of videos and notes on the subject of space law. He scanned it briefly but did not see much new information. Space law was generally trickier because it would affect a larger portion of the populace. Cultural variations and reality spectrums had huge degrees of separation, both spatially and temporally. You didn't just say what you wanted, you had to approach it from numerous perspectives and angles.

As Lane opened the file on jurisdiction for orbital laws, he recalled that this morning he had expected to be fired from his job. He wondered now what exactly he had gotten himself into instead.

CHAPTER 36

Lane stepped outside the office and checked his profile for the seventh time. True to the woman in the black suit's word, there was no trace of the arrest. Lane spent the rest of the day trying to access the GDK forums, but his profile had been revoked. The public ones were quiet or filled with speculation on the gate incident. Some people complained that nobody was playing the game because they were too busy talking about the accident.

Jacob had gotten permission from the mining company to represent them in the case, and a claim had been filed by Koff just before Lane left. Jacob sent Lane an e-mail warning that the mod had to stay active in *Tyrant*. The bigger the disaster in the game's world, the better. He asked Lane to not do anything stupid and wait until they put together a plan for their meme campaign.

The Tohickon was more full than usual when Lane walked in. Even if many of the patrons were still glued to their pads as the news unfolded, people seemed to be talking to one another more than usual. Lane was surprised to see an overhead monitor broadcasting an expert who was proposing that it may have even been an attack on the mining ship, that the Gateway markings were a ruse by pirates and it was all some sort of conspiracy. Lane found it strange that the owners of the Tohickon were going to make anyone listen to a particular reality feed. Lane ordered a beer, non-Standard, and finished it quickly before sitting down.

Morgan arrived with Dale in tow, the latter sitting down with Lane while Morgan ordered them both a drink. "I just can't believe it," Dale said. "When I first read about it, I thought the whole thing was some kind of bizarre joke. Like one of those video things where they act like it's real? Then it just kept cropping up in my feed, and it started to hit me!" He was dressed like a woman again, but without the makeup. It looked like a comfortable dress.

"Did Tricia tell you about the mod yet? She called me this morning. Apparently Gateway has been putting together a meme for this thing for a while now. The mod was just one of hundreds of different things they were putting together to plant an idea in everyone's head," Lane said.

Dale looked shocked while smoothly accepting his drink from Morgan.

"They've certainly ruined their public perception, then. I haven't seen people this frothing in the forums since that food shortage years ago," Morgan said. He took a sip from his drink and eyed Lane curiously. "You mentioned needing to know something about GDK in your invite?"

"Yeah, I'm locked out now. We're starting to put together a media campaign for a case against Gateway. I know the mod is still active in *Tyrant*. What is going on with the GDK?" Lane asked.

"Their main fleet was hit," Morgan said. "The Tyrant figured out where it was hidden, and stole every ship she couldn't blow up while the patriarch and captains were all hung over. The economy is bottoming out, and a lot of members are pushing to just move to a new game. Alice is… well, there's talk of splitting right now. Between the attack and finding out about her and Max during your little blowup, she has lost a lot of core support." Morgan seemed dismissive; a touch of disdain was in his voice as he paused to take a drink.

"Bunch of hetero nonsense," Morgan said. "Apparently most of the men who voted her in had crushes on her and thought they were the special ones. After they realized she was screwing Max, all that goodwill dried up. She still has the women's support and a lot of the old patriarch's anti-culture crowd, but that's not enough. Shame, they were good customers."

"I didn't know it would be that big of a problem," Lane said. A pang of guilt hit him as he realized this was his fault. He had been so angry with her, and it had just come out of him in front of the fire.

Morgan must have seen the look on his face because he patted Lane's hand sympathetically. "Don't blame yourself too much. A lot of them never liked her to begin with. Others thought you got a rough deal at the con and were bitching about it the next day. After they found out she slept with Max and was playing favorites, it made for a nice little conspiracy to use against her. Losing their fleet and most of their assets sent it all tumbling," Morgan said.

"How on Earth can you two talk about some silly virtual world at a time like this? This is real! People are dead!" Dale said as he slammed down his drink.

"Miners are killed all the time out there," Lane angrily replied. "Nobody gave a damn about it then. I know because I've done the cases. Missing arms, shattered lungs. You'll understand if my reality is just a bit more used to this kind of thing." He guessed Morgan didn't know he had revealed the GDK's location to Eve.

"Gentlemen, I think we are having a difference of…maybe not reality exactly. This accident is far outside the scope of anyone's reality," Morgan said.

Dale was still upset, and Lane found himself even angrier as Dale began to ramp up the drama. "To just sit and worry about some stupid mod while you try to blame this on Gateway. Like anyone could be so crazy as to advertise, or plant an idea about something that doesn't even exist yet. You're ignoring what has happened to these people for the sake of your stupid lawsuit," Dale said. He began to fidget and seemed about to cry.

Morgan glanced at Lane and silently mouthed the word "apologize."

"For what? A difference in reality? I'm not apologizing for anything. People have differences in reality every day, thousands of times a day. The whole point is you don't have to apologize. You certainly don't go crying about it either." Lane was still angry, but the sight of Dale beginning to cry was making him feel worse. He sighed and handed Dale a napkin. It was soon sticky and wet as Dale wiped his face and blew his nose.

"I guess you're right," Dale said. "It's not just you. Bobbin and Turk are having a fight about this as well. Bobbin was being insensitive about the whole thing, and Turk took up for all the miners."

"Who?" Lane asked.

"Oh, must be outside your reality. It's a mancom. Gay couple that goes out and gets involved in weird stuff every week. The actors are dating in real life as well. Turk used to be a miner, so he's worked up about the whole thing, and Bobbin is just a celebrity from some fashion votes. Turk is furious with Bobbin right now," Dale explained.

"They're already writing this stuff into the show?" Lane asked.

Dale shook his head. "No, the actors are mad at each other in reality. In the show, they play as a farm boy and a street cleaner. You know, very country bumpkin type of thing. I don't think they have mentioned it yet."

Morgan waved his hand to get their attention and pointed to the monitor that was broadcasting into the bar. "They are making an official announcement concerning this incident. It's broadcasting on all reality spectrums. I repeat, Gateway is making an official announcement on all reality spectrums. Going now," the monitor said.

A tall, brown-haired woman walked into view. She was pretty, with a thin face and large eyes that never seemed to be looking in one spot. She had on a sleek white suit. A title appeared underneath her that announced that she was the CEO of Gateway, Incorporated. She stood at a podium, and behind her was an enormous window into space.

"Good evening, ladies and gentlemen. This morning a tragedy that has shaken the world took place. A fully crewed mining vessel with her cargo was completely destroyed when it collided with another vessel bearing Gateway markings. Due to rampant speculation and distorted filtering across the culture grid, we at Gateway have decided to address each issue in turn.

"First, it was not a freak quantum incident with the gate system. They are still perfectly safe and guaranteed for all of our clients. The ship responsible for the collision was a prototype using a new device we like to call the Infinity Drive. It allows a ship, for a moderate amount of energy, to travel to another location in space, effectively accomplished instantaneously.

"This technology is very new and, unfortunately, still being tested. The incident with the *Black Swan* was a tragic accident where unforeseen variables interfered with the intended destination of the ship. Our engineers, although the best in the world, could not have predicted this outcome.

"As we continue to work with this new technology and introduce it to humanity, we at Gateway want to remind people that despite this setback, this is still an incredible breakthrough for humanity. No longer must the stars be a great, insurmountable distance for us. No longer must we wait until a gate has been established before traveling there is possible.

"The Infinity Drive is not just about travel. It's about freedom. The stars are wanted now. Limitless resources are now a possibility. Earthlike planets are now within our grasp. Your grasp. In your lifetime you could relocate to another world and set up a new home for our species. Discover new resources and enable even greater technological discoveries. As we move beyond this tragedy, together we can see this as a beginning instead of an end."

The video cut off, and the commenters on the feed looked genuinely shocked. The moment did not last, and they soon erupted into chatter. Everyone in the Tohickon did the same as people began arguing about Gateway's revelation. Lane could not help himself; he gave Dale a smug smile and leaned back with satisfaction. "How is that going down with your reality, then?" he asked.

Dale frowned and shook his head, checking his pad before setting it down. "I'm not convinced of anything. What if they're just covering up a flaw in the system? Their entire business revolves people feeling safe when they travel those gates. For all we know, that collision happened in the ring system, and they just towed it miles away. You're just…this is just…I'm not wrong. We're just having a reality difference here."

Lane stared at Dale incredulously. "A reality difference? She just said the damn thing was a faster-than-light drive!"

Morgan chuckled and said, "Actually, they're calling it the Infinity Drive, I believe. Looks like they have changed the playing field on you."

Lane turned to Morgan and snapped, "Yes, they walked right into mine! They admitted the whole thing is true. The whole incident was that Infinity travel nonsense. Everyone will see now that they should be…that they're…" Lane trailed off as he began to realize just what exactly Morgan was saying.

"You are going to have a tough time winning a popular vote on a conspiracy theory when they just admitted the conspiracy. Infinity Drive. What an idiotic name. They'll shorten it to I.D. engine, I imagine. Start putting forum plants to get the lingo going. Wipe out every trace of this incident being a negative across the whole culture grid. That company has always been clever with their advertising, but this on such a bigger scale," Morgan said.

Lane pulled out his pad and began furiously marking down notes. "We can't let them change the name. We need it to be Faster Than Light, or FTL. That's the name of the mod in the game. We have to get this linked back to *Tyrant* and get people concerned about this. The impact on the mining industry, on all the jobs, and the economies…" Lane trailed off as he rapidly typed out a list of forums to begin checking and cataloging for metrics and word use.

"You're *still* talking about the damn game?" Dale said incredulously.

Lane was too engrossed to pay attention.

"He is talking about a media war," Morgan replied.

CHAPTER 37

Lane ordered a second drink as Morgan began to fill him in on all of his ideas for planting a meme against Gateway across the culture grid. They all seemed to involve shows he would put together for Lane for a reasonable fee. Lane sent a quick message to Koff and Jacob asking them what they thought but got no reply. When it got to the point where Morgan began pushing for Lane to start signing guarantees on payment, he said he would forward along the requests and headed for the door. He did not escape without promising Dale a role in anything he sponsored.

Lane stepped outside and thumbed a message to Tricia. As he walked down the block, he was surprised to see his pad vibrate: Tricia had left a voice message for him. He held it up to his ear and listened. "Lane, I can't go out. There's another woman in black outside. She's just sitting there now. Can you please come over here and just…I don't know what. I don't want to do this over text. Harder to track the data if it's voice."

Lane stopped and debated his options. He almost instinctively began texting Tricia that there was nothing to worry about and that the woman might be there to help, but it would take too long to type it all out. He turned around to begin walking toward the bus stop that would take him to Tricia's when he almost ran into a police officer.

She was shorter than Lane and had on a blue-and-orange uniform to make it easier to see her. A gloved hand was immediately between them as Lane jumped back. She had her pad out and did a scan of Lane. "Sir, you have been drinking. You have consumed three drinks in a one-point-forty-seven-hour period. Are you intoxicated?" she said.

Lane froze, unsure if this was to be a repeat of the morning's events.

"Sir, the bus to your residence is in the opposite direction. Would you like me to escort you there?" the officer asked.

"No, I'm fine. I was going to visit a friend. She's nervous about some stuff, and…you know," Lane said.

The officer raised an eyebrow at him. She checked her pad and punched a few keys. "Based on your direction and the recent voice message, I'm guessing you're heading toward Mount Pleasant? You're not going over to the West End, at least? Crowds have been gathering there. Demonstrations about this Gateway thing. Male groups. All officers are intercepting potential rioters and discouraging them," the officer explained. She held up her pad, and Lane saw a map of the city. There were various red and blue dots moving about, with one highlighted red dot being right where he was standing at that moment.

"You predicted I might be about to riot because I had a few drinks? What are they even protesting?" Lane asked. He found himself feeling safe around this woman for some reason. At least she was explaining why she might arrest him.

"We don't know. They didn't post it, and no one is updating their feeds. Been getting alerts ever since the space accident this morning. Steer clear of any large groups of men and lay off the booze," the officer said.

Lane hurriedly began walking toward the bus stop. He could tell by the slow footsteps of the officer behind him that she was watching him go.

When Lane finally got to the bus, he was surprised to see a large crowd milling around. Some of them were weighed down with shopping bags. Others seemed to be drinking beer. Lane realized several were clearly drunk and talking loudly.

"They're gonna take the whole thing over. I'm telling ya. No more space. No more mining for us. It's over now. Not a goddamn thing left for us!" a man shouted. His friend was trying to calm him down but having little luck. "What use are we now? Huh? What's a bunch of old space miners gonna do now?" he said miserably.

The people waiting began to edge away from the man. Lane noticed that some had shopping bags filled with protein bars and other Standard items. They must have cashed in all their rations ahead of schedule.

When the bus arrived, he moved toward the back and kept his head down. He heard the occasional whisper, but many people were still glued to their pads. The feed was filled with chatter about Gateway's announcement. Would they be colonizing new planets? When? Who would go? Lane's feed was filled with articles speculating about the impact of the new technology and how long it would take to bring it into circulation. Several posters complained that they would not be able to maintain their virtual accounts in space or on another planet because of connection issues.

True to Morgan's prediction, Lane noticed that a handful of users began shortening it to I.D. Then ID. Then id. A user posted an image of the two letters randomly appearing around a picture. If you pressed the letters they would hold in place, but the moment you let go, they were popping off again. Lane was a little happy to see one made out of rainbows in another forum. Most people chided these images as too soon. Lane wondered if they were already the product of some kind of Gateway campaign, but he had no way of telling. Even if it wasn't a party directly working for Gateway, the person producing the images could have gotten the idea from the meme.

The bus came to a halt, and Lane stepped outside near Tricia's dormitory. She lived in a residential co-op with several other women. Lane had visited a few times years ago when they were sleeping together but had not been back since. The paint was a bit more cracked, and he noticed a few more potted plants. It was otherwise the same. He looked around nervously for anyone standing outside or acting suspicious, but he couldn't see anyone.

Lane pinged Tricia's pad to let her know he was outside and then remembered she had an intercom system on the doorway. He buzzed her apartment, and she let him in without responding.

Three women were in the courtyard chatting in hushed tones while sitting around a table. "My cousin does the metrics for the gate passages outside Venus. He's already worried about his job now. I try to tell him being on the Standards is a cakewalk, but he is old-fashioned like that," one said.

Lane knocked on Tricia's door, and she called out that it was open. He stepped inside and wrinkled his nose at the smell of old food and stale air. Dishes were piled up in the sink, and there was a bag of garbage in the hallway. Tricia had always been messy, but this was excessive even by her standards. Like Lane, having a salary allowed her the luxury of living alone, but the apartment was still small.

Tricia sat at the table with her pad plugged into a keyboard in front of her. She had a beer next to her, but it looked forgotten as she stared unblinking at the monitor. She tapped a few keys before glancing at Lane and nodding to him.

"What…what did you want exactly?" Lane asked.

Tricia looked at him with a puzzled expression.

"You asked me to come over here? Because of a woman in black? I looked around outside and didn't see anyone. What are you looking at?" Lane said.

Tricia rotated the monitor in his direction and then hopped up to look out her window. "After I got sent home, I couldn't stop thinking about this whole thing, so I started putting together programs to track all the public data. User comments, phrasing trends, meme distributions. I already had the algorithms to gauge the heuristics. It's an incredible opportunity to watch a complete culture shift happen in real time. Here, watch this," Tricia said. As she walked back over, she pressed few keys on the keyboard. "I set the Gateway meme ideas to blue in the system and bolded it."

An image of the culture grid appeared on the monitor, zoomed out to the maximum value possible while still within Condorcet limits. A clock in the upper corner set the date to prior to the accident. Tricia tapped another key, and the timer began moving. The culture spheres moved about the various hardlined grids of permanent values at the usual pace. There were tiny blue dots here and there throughout the grid that were also floating about or vanishing.

Suddenly a big blue circle appeared, touching nearly everything on the grid. "That's the event," Tricia explained. It quickly began to dissolve or vanish, breaking up into oddly shaped chunks as the various realities contacted absorbed it. Or seemed to—the information flow caused many of the circles to begin rapidly shifting location. Lane thought that many were visibly shaking, and he saw several that seemed to divide into two or three circles.

"What is that? How does a culture grid split like that?" Lane asked. Tricia tapped the circles that had divided, and their basic properties came up. Mining rights, men's authority, patriarchal history, group therapy, digital therapy. "Those are male cultures. What is happening to them?" Lane asked.

"You tell me," Tricia said. She grabbed the beer next to the monitor and smelled it. She walked to the sink, poured it out, and reached for a new one in the refrigerator. "There hasn't been a cultural event this big in decades. Even something like a government announcement doesn't have this big an impact. You would have to go back to…I don't know, the debt riots from a century ago or the World Trade Center attack in the North Eastern Union. A disaster experienced completely virtually by the majority of the population. Just a ship accident wouldn't be enough, and just a major tech breakthrough wouldn't either, but combined and with this much impact… that blue sphere? That's not the news of the *Black Swan* getting torn apart by a Gateway ship. That's the announcement from Gateway about what happened."

Lane felt a numbing chill run down his spine, his hand pressing the keyboard and replaying the sequence again. They were silent for a while before Lane finally spoke. "I just came by to tell you that I don't think the women in black mean any harm."

Tricia took a long swig from her beer. "If they're so harmless, why are they following me around? Sorry for being so emotional earlier. I popped a tranq med and had a few beers. Doing *much* better now. I'm, uh—" she suddenly tripped and caught herself on the counter. "I'm pretty fucked up," she said quietly, staring at the floor.

As Lane rewatched the video and the culture spheres begin moving rapidly across the grid, he noticed the system seemed to have tiny visual glitches. Bits of culture sphere would remain in their old positions or become ensnared in other visualizations. The male realities eventually began connecting with the female ones and distorting them. "I've never seen the culture grid do this before. It looks like…like a virtual world grid," he said.

Lane suddenly realized what the image was reminding him of. "It looks like anticulture," he murmured.

He glanced over at Tricia and realized she was slumping against the counter precariously. He went to her and managed to catch her just before she flopped onto the floor. Her arms went around his neck, and she landed against Lane's chest.

"What's anticulture?" Tricia asked hazily.

Lane put his arms around her and lifted her up. He sighed and began walking her toward the bedroom. "It's the notion that a part of me would not mind staying the night, while another part of me knows you're clearly drunk and that it would be wrong. And another part of me is freaked out because this very morning I was arrested for rape. And now I'm suddenly aware of all these things going on in my head. And I don't know what it means anymore," Lane said.

"That's kinda scary. Lane? I'm scared. Of everything right now. Are you scared?" Tricia asked.

He laid her down in the bed and pulled a blanket over her.

"Yeah. I'm scared too."

CHAPTER 38

Lane woke up the next morning in his own bed a few minutes before his alarm. He immediately grabbed his pad and checked the feed. On the bus ride home, he had tweaked it to as wide a filter as possible while highlighting all stories related to Gateway. There were thousands of posts on the subject.

He kept coming back to the pad as he went through his morning rituals, trying to find a way to efficiently screen the information that wasn't just glossing it over. A lot of people were complaining about people not being respectful of each other's realities. There were at least fifty columns from mining authorities claiming that attempts to make the Infinity Drive anything but a business issue were patently absurd. The Women's Space Union, on the other hand, argued it would finally begin to pave the way for more people to go into space and be afforded opportunities on the free market. Commenters debated across realities, claiming to invalidate the other side while oblivious to any arguments against themselves.

By the time Lane was on the bus, he had set the filter to removing opinion articles and personality columns to focus solely on objective pieces. There were numerous speculation articles on whether or not the Infinity Drive would have a huge impact on the space economy or how many new jobs it would create. Simulation games for the impact this would have on the system were created overnight and discussed by the players.

Lane opened the most popular simulation game to see what reality it was broadcasting. You could invest, store, or distribute resources in a simplified space economy. It was designed to be short and simple, and to allow players to realize there was a way to profit from the new Infinity Drive if you just invested in the right industries. Lane "proved" the new technology would be a boon to society on his second try.

As the bus came to his stop, Lane typed out a brief comment criticizing the game. He complained that the options were simplistic and it cut off after a ten-year period. After playing through a round, it was obvious there was little depth to the system and not nearly enough complexity to match what was going on in *Tyrant*. He posted a link to the economics of that game and explained the parallels of the real world to it.

By the time Lane had walked to the office, he had thirteen responses logged. His own comment had been downvoted into the negative. The most upvoted comment told him he had barely played the game and clearly had not experimented with it enough to be making judgments. The next agreed and suggested Lane try to win the simulation with less resources. What had impressed the next user was how well someone who didn't have a lot of money could expand his or her capital with a few wise moves. Lane stopped reading after that.

Lane continued to try to argue with various articles and posts spreading the idea that the new Infinity Drive was a great thing. There was little to no commentary on any actual litigation. Few articles were so bold as to undermine the tragedy of the *Black Swan*, but a few suggested that this should be treated the same as any other Gateway accident. It was a cost of operating in the free market, and people knew Gateway had immunity.

If Lane argued the miners should be given full compensation for their losses, he didn't get much of a reaction or only a few lukewarm agreements. If he criticized Gateway for the accident, users asked him if he had a better idea how to test out something like the Infinity Drive. A few times Lane made halfhearted attempts at arguing the Infinity Drive itself might be bad for the space economy, but this was met with heated rejection and anger. If he mentioned *Tyrant*, people dismissed the claim as crazy and clearly not the same thing. After an hour of trying, Lane leaned back in his chair and tried to remember what he was even arguing about anymore. Was he against the technology? Was this only about helping this one individual ship?

Lane saw Derrick walk into the office and sit down at his desk. Before he'd even plugged in his pad, Lane walked up to him. "Derrick, good morning! We've got a huge case handling the Gateway accident. The PR is going to be a nightmare. We need the GDK and some anticulture to get it done."

"That sounds awesome, Lane. And I'd be really intrigued if there was a GDK left to salvage. But between the Tyrant somehow miraculously realizing that our fleet was hidden in the Gibson Cloud and a pretty nasty rumor that the patriarch was playing favorites when she kicked you out of the conference, I'd say there isn't going to be much consensus from them. On anything."

"It's that bad? I figured it would be a setback, but it's not like…it's not like anyone died, right?" Lane asked.

"No, but a lot of permanent characters were wiped out. As well as resources. I spent most of yesterday rallying what was left, and it's barely enough to bother with since the economy is crashing. No money means we lose the players who were sticking around because we were rich. Alice and Max cost us the ones who were there on principal. Or had a crush on Alice," Derrick explained.

"Why? What is the big deal?" Lane asked. He had known it was going to be bad from Morgan, but hearing Derrick's matter-of-fact tone and seeing the look on his face made it somehow worse.

"I don't expect something like slut shaming to show up on your reality, Lane. Or anyone's, really. You have to get pretty far into male culture to find it anymore. But that's the stuff the GDK is built out of," Derrick said. He rubbed his forehead, and Lane realized that he looked as if he had not slept in days.

A ping from Koff popped up on his pad: "Where are you? We have a meeting."

He had forgotten to check his notices. Lane dashed up the stairs and opened Koff's door without knocking.

"As you can see," Koff was saying, "under at least eight different quantifications of the poll data and the metrics we're getting right now, a popular vote is coming out about seventeen percent short on Gateway. People are big fans of the technology. Of the idea behind it."

As Lane sat down, Koff shot him a venomous glance. On the monitor were two male faces. One was Jacob, and the other Lane didn't recognize.

"Ah, Mr. Weber, this is Lane. He's the attorney who first brought our attention to the possibility of the media campaign underway by Gateway. Of course, now it's in full force, but there are a lot of indicators it has been going on for at least a month. So, you'll see from the data here that an AI decision does have some possibility due to the newness of the situation. Going over graph twenty-four no—"

"What if they did it on purpose?" Lane said abruptly.

Koff's glare returned, and Jacob looked shocked.

"The public announcement they made about the accident touched every single culture sphere on the grid," Lane said. "Between people who care about miners, the loss of human life, and the possibility of new technology, every single person listened to one coherent message from Gateway. No reality filters, no opinion columns: they were the one source in a system that is designed to let people only hear what they want to hear.

"Let me show you on the culture grid." Lane offered access to Tricia's new video to Koff and Jacob. Silence followed. Jacob was fumbling with his pad and typing something rapidly. Koff's expression softened as she looked at her pad and watched the video. Weber only stared at Lane.

"How did you come to this conclusion?" she asked.

"The same woman who picked up on the Gateway marketing plan put it together. She normally works in data archives, and she knew what to look for. I'm sure she could explain it all much better than I could. The point is we can't let up on this thing. What we need is to start pushing back in the media and start planting our own meme. We've got to connect it back to the *Tyrant* virtual world so that people will start considering the idea that maybe this whole invention is a bad idea. We have to convince them that they don't want this, so that when it comes up for a popular vote on the mining ship, people vote to punish Gateway," Lane said.

"I'm sorry, but are you saying that the Infinity Drive or Super Jump thing or whatever we're calling it…we're saying this is a bad thing now?" Jacob asked incredulously.

"From our perspective, how is it not? The entire mining industry is going to be upended by this. All of your clients in space make their money from the shipping and processing of asteroid minerals. Our client here, Weber, is in the exact same boat. His entire business model is going to collapse once this technology becomes available," Lane said.

"Lane, how on earth are you going to convince anyone from other realities that this is a problem? Why would a person with no free market license care about this or someone working a government farm?" Koff asked.

"Because all this is really going to do is eliminate more jobs. More than half the population is unemployed right now, and someone has just invented a way to make that number even higher. And the ones who are going to be hit the hardest are men. No more space mining, no more deep-space operations. Those are the jobs getting axed here. And that's all going to come to an end now. Every guy in this room knows what it was like to grow up dreaming about space. About getting out and doing something noble for society. Something with a purpose where you can feel useful," Lane said. There was anger in his voice. Outrage at a threatened dream that had been Lane's for almost as long as he could remember. This was his chance.

"What exactly are you proposing? You can't uninvent something. Scientific progress is linear," Jacob said.

Lane found himself annoyed at his dismissive tone. Of course Jacob didn't care about the threat to the space industry. He was already a space lawyer. He couldn't understand what it was like to be stuck.

"More importantly, Lane, how does this technology not enable more people to get off the planet? To open up new worlds for everyone?" Koff asked. She was probing the idea, pushing the frame and seeing where it would lead. "Think, don't react. There might be something to this," she added.

"You can't be serious, Mother," Jacob scoffed.

"I believe I'd like to hear from the lawyer who has an idea besides giving up on reclaiming my billion in damages, please," Weber said. It was the first time he had spoken since Lane had sat down.

"Look," Lane said, "we can probably find support from the Luddites. There are a lot of feminists and other groups that are protesting the way technology replaces people's labor in the workforce. That's clearly what this is going to do. And not slowly or in any sort of gentle way. The moment they start distributing those things, huge amounts of infrastructure are going to become obsolete. The men's rights groups won't even blink at rallying behind this. I already heard last night that there were protests forming here. Maybe there are others."

"So we are proposing that perhaps we should not pursue a technological innovation of this magnitude?" Koff pressed again.

"No. It sounds wrong if you say it that way. Not enough heuristic space. We need to do a better job of making Gateway the villain here. We need a flame war. We need celebrities talking about this. We're not trying to stop the development of the Infinity Drive, we're trying to make sure the FTL technology gets developed appropriately and in a way that benefits everyone. Which includes finding suitable work for the population instead of just adding another couple million to the unemployment line. This is about…people wanting to work," Lane said.

"And my money," Weber added dryly.

"So, we build this meme up in the culture grid, take the case to public vote on whether or not Gateway should be responsible for my damages, and hopefully win. Then…we get to be the people who said the Infinity Drive was a bad idea?" Jacob asked.

"No, we're the people who said that Faster Than Light travel is going to have some consequences," Lane said.

CHAPTER 39

The issue with the Infinity Drive, Lane was rapidly realizing, was not having something to say, it was getting people to listen. Koff and Jacob had tentatively agreed to see what Lane could put together. Yet no matter how Lane phrased it or how many images he tried to tag inside the post, it was either downvoted or ignored entirely. He couldn't understand it.

He tried switching to other realities, and then random ones, and then he became so frustrated that he began posting the comments without even reading the posts he was placing them on. Which only made it worse because that got him even more downvotes, and it gave his overall profile a lower culture score. The lower his score, the more his comments became invisible to people.

Koff called him back into the office after an hour to see what phrases and ideas were striking a chord and did not seem the least bit surprised when Lane reported that none were working.

"First," she said, "they've already been planting the idea that Faster Than Light travel is a great idea and we're all going to be better off with it. Second, and I really wish you'd appreciate this point more than you seem to, it probably IS a good thing that Gateway has done this. God knows how people are going to handle this information without any sort of preparation. There are going to be more resources, more planets, the whole galaxy at our disposal. It just sounds too good, like there's going to be lots of opportunity and all that."

Lane protested. "But it's not that simple. There are all sorts of pro—"

"I know. I got that. Back when you promised our client you could win an untested lawsuit with no background data. But this is going to be a bit bigger than you sitting around posting comments on data feeds. We are talking about manipulating public opinion on a grand scale. You need a group of people who are good at recruiting behind the scenes where Gateway's marketing isn't going to be there to bicker with you on the forums. Or frankly, more likely their converts are bickering. You need people susceptible to this message," Koff said.

Lane took a deep breath and felt adrenaline pass through him. He was losing his grip on the situation. Jacob had seemed annoyed with him when their conversation ended, and Koff was pressing him for results when he had only been at it for an hour. If he screwed this up, they would submit the case to an AI, and that would be the end of his chances at proving himself. His shot at leaping to space lawyer status would be gone along with his free market license. "I know where to find them. Can you get Derrick in here?" Lane asked.

Koff shrugged. "I suppose so. Why?"

"Because he's the former leader of the GDK, and they'd be perfect for this," Lane said.

"So? Ask him to help. Or ask whoever the current leader is," Koff said.

"That's the problem. I may have…caused them to get destroyed in the game. And slut shamed their leader. Actually I didn't shame anyone, but I sort of yelled about her having sex with someone, and people got angry about it," Lane explained weakly.

Koff rolled her eyes and typed a message into her pad. A few moments later, there was a knock at the door, and Koff told Derrick to come in. He scowled as soon as he saw Lane.

"So, you're the former leader of a cult? And you always seemed like such a nice married guy," Koff said. She was already reaching for the candy bag. As she pulled it out, she swiveled her chair and brought up her newsfeed on the monitor. Derrick began to protest, but Koff held up her hand. "Just sort this shit out. I've already got my son fussing because this isn't the way space lawyers do things. You two are both heterosexual men who still live on Earth. Surely you have some common ground left."

Derrick awkwardly drummed his hands on his kneecaps. Lane felt an impulse to imitate the gesture but resisted it. He wondered how old Derrick was. He didn't seem to be that different an age from Lane; they looked about the same, but that didn't help much once a person reached adulthood. Derrick could have had a kid almost anytime, depending on his wife.

"What would it take to put Alice back on top in *Tyrant*?" Lane asked.

"It was you who gave up the location, wasn't it? I figured, and Max and Alice have probably guessed too. I warned her about that, but she didn't see why you would bother to help the Tyrant out. What did she offer? A couple hundred bucks?" Derrick snapped.

"Derrick, if you would please answer the question," Koff interrupted.

"She captured the vast majority of our ships. Just rolled up with enough boarding crews on hand to take an entire fleet. So we can start by having those returned. A cease-fire long enough for us to rebuild some infrastructure. Nobody can get a damn thing done with the FTL mod," Derrick said. He pulled out his pad and flipped through a few documents. "And for what it's worth, you need to put up a video apologizing for what you said and say it's not true."

"No. I won't lie to smooth things over because people are pissed that she fucked Max. She *did* play favorites with him over me. That was wrong of her back at the con, and you know it," Lane snapped back irritably. The old anger and that empty feeling boiled up in him suddenly as the memory of having to watch her with Max came back—that she had chosen him over Lane.

"Lane, considering everything Derrick is asking for is free or completely virtual, I'm not totally following what your hang-up is on the apology part," Koff said. Lane began to protest, and Koff swung around, candy in mid-pass to her mouth. "Look, if it's any consolation, I agree that fucking your employees is a bad idea. Why don't we just see if this Tyrant girl will agree to the other parts? Derrick, can you get your other Tyrant person on the line and do the same?"

"In exchange for what?" Derrick asked.

"We need to create a lot of memes that will get out to a lot more obscure groups on the grid without getting downvoted by Gateway's plants. The information about what's going to happen when this technology goes public and the impact it's going to have. We need GDK's infrastructure and all those rainbow comics and videos coming out and supporting us," Lane explained.

"You do understand those people aren't working for no reason, right? I don't just walk up and order them to do something. They have to give a damn," Derrick said.

"I watched a bunch of guys build a bar, a bonfire, and a catapult for no other reason than to have the patriarch compliment them on it," Lane replied.

"Will you two PLEASE just contact the two women you keep speaking for?" Koff asked wearily.

After a few minutes of typing and pings going back and forth Derrick said, "She wants to talk to the Tyrant herself."

Lane glanced at Eve's reply to his messages and said, "She says she has a few demands of her own. But mainly she wants money," Lane said. He typed a brief response back. "She says she'll talk to anyone we like if we can point her to a bank account with assets in excess of a million. Just to make sure we're not wasting her time. And she wants to meet in person."

Koff stared at Lane.

"Hey, you're the one who said you wanted a capitalist around," he said. She tapped a few keys and sent him a bank account for the firm. It had increased considerably, courtesy of their new client, he thought with a touch of satisfaction.

After the bank account number was sent, there were more pings and tapping keypads as a meeting location was arranged. Eve had set the location to Market Street near the vendor booths.

Lane decided to leave early while Koff and Derrick were collecting themselves. It would have been an awkward exchange. As he hurried down the block, he noticed a faint chill in the air as summer was coming to an end in Charleston.

Lane followed his pad's directions to a series of empty stalls near the back of the market. Rows of people in Standard clothes were selling spices, grass baskets, grits, junk trinkets, old clothes, and other Southeastern eccentricities. Most vendors were unlicensed and just making a few dollars on the side. The structure was still built from the original brick and cracking concrete; only the paint and wood had been replaced over the centuries.

Lane saw Eve, who waved and gave him a brief hug when he drew close. She was dressed in a light jacket and long pants, business wear for a formal setting. She looked beautiful to Lane anyways. "Funny place for a meeting. They used to sell slaves here, you know. That's why it's called the Market," Lane said.

Eve shook her head. "You should adjust your filter. They wouldn't have sold slaves here back when that was allowed. People considered it vulgar so it happened outside the City. They hid the slaves and the slave markets from themselves."

"Oh," Lane murmured.

Derrick and Koff came through one of the stalls as a crowd of Standard-dressed women walked by.

"Eve. Resident Tyrant. To whom am I speaking?" Eve asked.

Koff and Derrick introduced themselves, Derrick doing so more stiffly than Lane had expected. It occurred to him that this was the first time he had ever spoken to a person he had been fighting for years with the GDK. As they exchanged greetings Alice came up behind Derrick. Compared to Eve she seemed disheveled. She had on no makeup, and there were bags under her eyes. A twist of hair was sticking out.

"Hi. Alice. Patriarch of the GDK, despite what some might be claiming. I don't know who any of the other women here are or what you want, but I was told I might be able to get my fleet back," the patriarch of the GDK said curtly.

Eve raised an eyebrow but made no response. The sound of pings from stranger's pads and light chatter filled the silence.

"Well, my name is Koff, and I run the Charleston Branch of an interplanetary law firm. Which normally sounds more impressive when I'm not around you virtual people. We are trying to have a lawsuit go to the popular vote over the Gateway accident for the *Black Swan*, and right now all our projections are indicating we're going to lose. So we need to start turning the culture grid against the Infinity Drive and Gateway. We believe we have information that can do this. We just can't get a foothold in the culture grid without being downvoted or ignored. Which is where you folks come in."

"What sort of information?" Alice asked.

"Enough to do the job in the right hands," Koff replied.

"All right. We want the fleet back. We want the Tyrant to lay off our bases and refineries. And Lane there has to post a video that he made it all up about me and Max," Alice said with a touch of disgust toward the end.

"The ships you can have. Stripped of the FTL mod and major tactical weapons. None of it is worth anything with the economy the way it is anyways. How long of a cease-fire are we talking about here?" Eve replied coolly.

"One month. And we keep major tacticals. You're not the only person who wants us dead. The matriarchs are putting together an alliance," Alice said.

"Three months, and the cease-fire goes both ways. I don't want your ships in my space. No more FTL strikes, especially not on *Sojourner Truth*. I'm still paying for the repairs on her. And that includes halting all propaganda and that awful rainbow business. What is this about a post with Lane?" Eve asked.

Alice and Derrick were quiet to that.

"At the GDK con I might have mentioned seeing Alice and another member having sex. She wants me to say it was a lie," Lane said.

Eve snorted and began laughing. Derrick blanched and glared at Lane. Alice said nothing.

"Oh dear, you don't screw the help when you're in charge of a bunch of men. Otherwise you're going to have to spread your legs for all of them," Eve said, cackling.

"I didn't know I was being stalked at the time. Or that half of them would end up being jealous. Or that the other half would start taking what I do with my body as some kind of personal insult. What do you know about being called a whore anyways?" Alice snapped back.

"Maybe the weekly harassing e-mails from GDK members with pictures of rainbows coming out of my vagina? Or constantly claiming that every single guy I have working for me has slept with me? Say what you want about the matriarchs, at least they just call me a bitch on their private forums and leave it at that," Eve replied calmly.

Alice said nothing, an expression of shock and surrender coming over her. Lane suddenly realized just how tired she looked.

"Right," Koff said. "That sounds like we have had a basic meeting of the minds. Alice, I'm going to talk about money with Eve here. I don't think you need to know about that conversation. We'll work out the basics of the exchange once we've agreed upon a sum we'll pay her and then a method for you to start getting our info into the right hands."

"Fine. Just give it to Derrick when you're ready. It's not like they'll need much convincing anyways," Alice said.

"Why is that?" Lane asked.

"Because most of the men in the GDK already hate the Infinity Drive," she answered.

CHAPTER 40

Time seemed to move quickly when spent in the virtual forums and metric charts. The backlash against the Infinity Drive was, as Alice predicted, well underway before Koff's arrangement with the GDK and Eve. People protesting began to fill the news feeds with a paranoid rage that surpassed anything he could have conceived on his own.

Lane felt more as if he were selling weapons to some rebellious faction as he passed out Tricia's graphs and data interpretations. Derrick would send him an alert about a forum argument the GDK had started, and Lane would read the exchange and then provide links and articles that would only feed the wrath of the commenters. An endless barrage of jokes and downvotes greeted anyone arguing in favor of the Infinity Drive.

Lane had failed to make much of an impression with his criticism of Gateway's simulation games; the GDK were very thorough in their work. They immediately found exploits that made the game unplayable in multiplayer and employed them so often that other players were forced to copy the strategies, which made the game awful to play. Lane was not even sure these players cared about the Infinity Drive or Alice's requests; they were just there for fun.

"Do you suppose that the *Black Swan* was a kind of anticulture?" Lane asked Derrick. They were sitting at a round table in a corner office, apart from everyone else at McAngus. Koff had told them they were working exclusively on the Gateway case until it was resolved.

"Not really. This isn't a virtual system. There isn't a fourth wall that we are all sitting behind aware of the unreality of the whole thing. It's just competing cultures," Derrick replied.

"But it's not real yet. The FTL or Infinity Drive or whatever. Gateway is posting all these planets they plan to visit and giving updates on how much better the technology is becoming. We're posting articles about how there will be even fewer jobs, fewer people able to participate in the space market, and all the damage it's doing to the culture grid," Lane said. Derrick pushed his pad away and leaned back in his chair.

"Wouldn't we be the anticulture then? We're the ones claiming that this progress will cause more damage than good. We're reframing the public narrative to make it look as if technological innovations have always damaged society. At the same time, there's no way for someone to not recognize what we're saying is absurd. We're saying that the ability to travel beyond our own planet is bad. The only person who could possibly agree with that has to be aware that the value is being tinkered with. But they're agreeing because deep down inside they don't want the FTL," Derrick replied.

A ping from his pad told him that Weber was contacting him asking for another update. Lane groaned. The old man always wanted to do things by video chat. Lane smiled over his instinctive flinch at the sight of the old space lawyer. A long tube ran up his nose and seemed at home around his gray, lined skin. The combination of artificial light and the slow shifts in his metabolism due to zero gravity gave him a sickly pale color. His breathing was audible.

"Lane. How goes it?" Weber asked.

"Most of the realities with significant overlap in economics, capitalism, or space markets are now polling in our favor. We have several gendered realities, particularly men but several female subsections as well. It's…proving a challenge to inspire much interest from the more conservative female realities. Most of them view capitalism as outdated and view the FTL as a way to undermine it," Lane said.

"You said as much during my last call. What—" Weber was interrupted by a wave of raspy coughing. A clawed hand came up and wiped his mouth before he continued. "What we need is something that will reach farther across the culture grid. Quit fooling with your public narrative nonsense and get on this. Weber out."

The video screen closed and Lane replied, "Worthless old bastard!" He began typing out a message to Morgan, who had been promising to have something that would appeal outside their reality for days now. A second was to Eve. Lane typed out the message, reread it, and then changed certain portions because he worried about the tone. He asked how she was doing and whether could they meet sometime. He also asked whether she had any interest in reaching out to gendered realities. Neither responded immediately.

"How do you even reach other realities? I'm looking at the metrics, and half of these groups have totally different media variables. It doesn't matter how compelling the frame or how tight the heuristic space if they aren't watching us," Lane complained.

"In *Tyrant* we always had to deal with apathetic players," Derrick said. "The old patriarch always said organized people who have their minds made up are the rarity. You have to get them working on something together. We used to paint GDK on ships, do big flashy raids that weren't worth the cost, or just have big meetings in public. People would put in a lot of time getting it setup and then care about it by default."

A ping from Eve interrupted the exchange. "I'm already seeing you all over my feeds and reality. PR isn't my thing."

Lane frowned and asked her if she had any advice for getting better leverage with female realities.

There was a pause before Eve responded. "You understand I am not magically appealing to women, right? I made a career out of appealing to men by killing them in a virtual world. Not a lot of people relate to that, much less women. I do badly on the votes with my own gender. I'll broadcast whatever to my followers, but I draw the line after that. This is your problem."

Lane worried he had said something wrong. He'd just wanted some advice on what to do. Or more likely, had just been hunting for an excuse to message her. They had not spoken since the meeting when Koff had dismissed him so that they could have "girl talk" about the payment. He typed back, "Sorry! Just looking for ideas."

"Oh. It's OK. You wouldn't know about it. Why don't you have some sort of public protest? Something that isn't virtual," she sent soon afterward.

Lane thanked her again.

"Do people in gendered realities like doing outdoor events? Like parades and stuff?" Lane asked.

Derrick shrugged and said, "I'm a heterosexual man in a monogamous marriage. I barely even register on the culture grid anymore. Just check their metrics."

Lane brought up the culture grid and began scrolling with his finger. He took several strokes to get outside any circle or square that did not impact him. He tapped a greenish circle, and a label appeared that said, "Luddite Thespians." The proportions of gender were mostly female, but not 100 percent. He zoomed in on the circle and with his finger on the center, drifted out to the edges. Articles, images, comments, and videos whirled by to represent the proximate meaning and activity of the group based on their digital conduct. After a moment, he decided to go ahead and add them to a list of possibly sympathetic realities. They would go outdoors anyways, maybe organize some kind of cookout like the GDK con.

Lane gave the pad's screen a long tug and sent it wandering into another set of realities he had never heard of. There was a group of people who dedicated their time to pretending they were colonial settlers. Rather than do this in a virtual setting, they would organize places and pool money to build sets. This took quite a bit of work and organization, so much so that the community seemed to revolve more around the planning than the actual events. Lane added it to the list.

The core frames of the various groups were equally surprising to Lane. There were several circles that organized themselves primarily around sex. When he ran his finger through the abstraction, it was all pornography. Lane added them. Another revolved around pet sharing. Lane included those as well. Lane was surprised at several enormous culture circles that were primarily devoted to childcare, the surprise being that many of the people in the feeds had no children of their own.

"That reminds me. I prepared your statement about Alice and Max. If you could thumb and confirm?" Derrick asked. He held out his pad and showed Lane a brief message stating that he had made the story up on orders from Eve. Lane reluctantly pressed his thumb onto the pad and allowed it to confirm the message on his own profile. Neither spoke for a time.

A ping on his pad interrupted Lane as he was digging through the culture grid. "I was thinking about staging a play. Maybe do a spoof on *The Wizard of Oz* and the whole silver standard thing. Here's a link; it was a good movie," Morgan said.

"Can we do it outdoors?" Lane asked.

CHAPTER 41

Lane was sitting on the side of the plaintiff's table of the Interstellar Courthouse with Derrick as he watched Koff and Jacob take their seats. Before them was a panel of three judges, old women with plain black robes hanging at their sides. The structure was built of asteroid iron and white paneling, the lights reflected off the dual surface in a glare.

Koff laid her bag of candy out of sight while at the defense table sat several space lawyers representing Gateway. They were all female, most of them as old as Koff, but one seemed fairly young. There was a camera on Lane and Derrick as well, but Koff had been adamant that they were not to speak unless she or Jacob asked. Koff began by asking why Gateway's attorneys didn't think a popular vote could resolve the matter.

"I understand that from a formalist perspective, the system was intended for the Gateways. But the spirit of the law, the reason the last popular vote granted us immunity, was that unforeseeable risks can't be blamed on Gateway. No one wanted that accident to happen. Something we are not making a big deal out of, for obvious reasons, is that Gateway lost a ship as well. Billions in privately funded research was destroyed. The Infinity Drive represents an incredible opportunity for the entire species," Gateway's head attorney explained. Lane thought her name was Olivia, but he wasn't sure. She had only said it once in a curt exchange before both sides began referring to themselves as their clients. None of them had public profiles to check.

Lane watched as Koff's hand slowly began to inch toward her candy bag. She dipped past the camera, making as if she was reading some sort of document, before plucking one into her mouth. Her face was stone again, the candy undetectable to the eye, and she responded. "Dear, if you want to win the 'who lost the most in the tragic space accident' contest, be my guest. Our point is that the Gateway System and the FTL drive are not the same thing. And the reason why is predictability. It is, to the public, an acceptable possibility that a ship traveling through a gateway can collide with another. What is not an acceptable possibility, to the public, is that a ship might collide with them just because. Could I wake up tomorrow with a ship in my house? Is it because the pilot made an error? Is it because I shouldn't have been in my house that day? What we are saying is that declaring you should be totally immune 'just because' is unacceptable. You foot the bill for these accidents until you can convince society that they are safe."

For a single second, Lane could see the shift of the candy in Koff's jaw. Gateway's attorneys looked annoyed as they glanced at their pads, reviewing some note or image that would help them along. There was a cough and silence on their end as they were given time to prepare a response.

"I can't answer your questions because Gateway doesn't know itself. We barely understand how or why the Infinity Drive even works. It was a test that went horribly wrong. We don't know how to guarantee that it won't happen again without further testing. Which, if another accident happens, could be even more costly than this one. Without disclosing any industry secrets, a lot changes with the size and mass of the vessel being moved. We did not fully appreciate this fact until after the test. Nor can we understand without more tests," Gateway's lawyer explained.

"Can't you just do the tests someplace far away?" Jacob asked.

"I assure you, the ship was already well beyond known space when we were performing the test," she replied. She pressed on her pad a few times, and a large map of the galaxy appeared. One tiny dot labeled "Accident Site" was located on a large spiral of stars and gas, while the other was entitled "Projected Jump Site." It was not even inside the Milky Way Galaxy.

"Why is it called the projected location?" Jacob asked.

"Because we aren't even really sure where it ended up the first time. The ship had no crew. The entire thing was on autopilot. After losing contact, we assumed it was gone for good. Jumped into a star or planet," she replied.

The piece of candy shifted in Koff's mouth. "You had an unpiloted ship that could appear anywhere programmed to return back to our solar system? Which you lost? How can you argue that something like this is unpredictable?" Koff asked.

"From what we have salvaged of the ship's computer backups, it thought it was going into a gas nebula as a part of its reconnaissance of a neighboring galaxy," she replied.

The red light came up, and the plaintiff's time was up. They immediately began typing into their pads. The youngest, another woman whose name Lane couldn't remember, was the first to speak.

"What do you expect to accomplish with a public vote?" she asked.

Koff tapped a key on her pad, out of sight from the cameras, which signaled Jacob to take this question.

"We want compensation for our client. An AI vote will lead to an automatic loss," Jacob said.

"And after the public vote? If you win?" she asked.

"That would conclude the matter as far as we're concerned," Jacob answered.

"You wouldn't be filing any more cases for compensation? This is a hardcoded rule you would be creating with this vote. All Infinity Drive incidents would be someone's responsibility. Is that a result you and your client would like to see?" she asked.

Lane saw Koff tap the pad, but Jacob ignored her. "We believe people have a right to work in the market safely without fear that spaceships are going to appear from nowhere. And if that right gets violated, someone should be responsible," Jacob replied.

"People have a right to work in the market safely. That's an interesting word to use, safety. Very large heuristic space in that word. Almost all realities have an applicable meaning for it. They vary, naturally, particularly when it involves someone outside your culture. Would you say that a safe market is a…stable one?" she asked.

Lane now understood why Koff was furiously pressing the pad. He could tell Jacob was annoyed, and the flickering on his pad must have only been aggravating him more. "He is walking right into a trap," Lane thought. "She is going to corner him into saying he wants the market to be stable and that it never changes. That his company and way of doing business stays that way forever."

"Stable in the sense that you don't have to go aro—" Jacob began. Koff started to speak but suddenly she emitted a cough instead. A gag reflex, and she was bending over. Lane realized with horror that she was choking on a piece of candy. Jacob was frozen, and Derrick was rising from his chair with a glass of water.

"What he means to say," Lane said loudly, "is that we believe the free market, or the invisible hand, or whatever capitalist lingo you want to use, can involve a lot of creative destruction. Which, as we witnessed with your FTL drive, can even kill. Not everyone is so fortunate to have a free market license as your company."

The young female attorney shot him a glance and looked back at Jacob. "What effect does the Infinity Drive have on the people on Earth if it's for space travel?" She was hoping he would feel cut off. He didn't get the chance before Koff finally spat out a candy onto Derrick's shirt.

"A curious question from someone who is claiming this technology is going to benefit all humanity," Koff choked out. Derrick seemed unfazed by the candy-colored stain on his shirt.

The young lawyer opened her mouth, but one of the older women interrupted. "There is a certain point where the merits of this technology, once safely applied, are clearly objective. In all realities. Judges, you have our data," she said. A green light appeared under the monitor to indicate the judges concurred with the request to close the hearing. They would send out their answer in a few days.

The elder space lawyer for Gateway approached them, looking uncertainly between Koff and Lane as to whom she should be speaking. Koff stepped forward hastily. "Can I help you?" she asked.

"Gateway wants this settled. We're willing to talk a substantial compensation in order to avoid the case going to a public vote," she explained.

Koff laughed and said, "We'll get more than just compensation if we win this one dear. My client has given us strict orders to not settle the case. We go all the way."

Outside on the courthouse steps, Koff angrily turned to the trio of men following her. "Godamnit, Jacob! When I press the interrupt button, it's not because I want to hear you start rambling about your right to profits and lawsuits. It wouldn't have been half so bad if it hadn't been such an obvious framing trap!" Koff exploded.

"I had it under control! This lawsuit is about money, Mother. The people voting are going to know it, and there's no point in sitting around pretending otherwise," Jacob snarled back.

As Koff began launching into a rant about not telling her how to frame a financial dispute, Derrick leaned over to Lane and whispered, "I counted at least seven narrative frames, if you include reality conflicts. What about you?"

"Four. There are only four. But definitely all four," Lane whispered back.

They continued down the court steps as mother and son continued to argue.

"Bah, a classicist. There are realities enough for more than four narrative frames," Derrick replied.

Lane glanced at Koff. She was still arguing with Jacob, and he was beginning to look uncertain. "Mother, I am the space lawyer in this case! Weber gave me final authority, not you! I am not a child, and I don't work for you anymore. You can't tell me what to do whenever you like!" Jacob yelled.

Koff began launching into a retort.

"Maybe," Lane said. "But this is a capitalist lawsuit. There's only four. Maybe just the one frame in capitalism: winners and losers."

Koff glanced at the two of them, and Lane realized it was time to go.

CHAPTER 42

Kayla opened the door to the conference room Derrick and Lane were working in, with Morgan walking behind her. Morgan looked uncomfortable, a condition that Lane did not think was common for him. He pulled his pad out and tapped at it loudly after sitting.

"Never been in an office like this before," muttered Morgan.

Lane snorted at the comment. The idea that an influential broker of virtual stocks and goods had never been in a real office was funny to him.

Morgan seemed offended. "Laugh all you want. My clients are not the type to be farting around a desk."

Lane noticed that Kayla was still in the room, staring at the three men. He realized it might be the first time that three men were alone in a room at McAngus in years. Lately she had been looking more disheveled at work and out of sorts. Lane wondered if she wanted him to ask her for something or give her something to do.

Derrick spoke up finally. "We're working on the PR for the lawsuit still and trying to figure out something that will generate some news in the feeds that aren't paying attention to the FTL media. Any thoughts on a reality we can work on?"

"I saw your list of realities to try to affect. A lot of those groups don't interact with one another. Some of them have very strong anticapitalist core values. Others do not like men. I don't mean like boys need to be taught better or we should rehabilitate them more. I mean like believes we should terminate the entire gender. What was the parameter when you made the list?" Kayla asked.

"Likes outdoor events," Lane said.

"That's it? Are there even realities where people say they don't like being outside?" she asked.

"Well, it's all for a show that none of the realities dislike, *Wizard of Oz*. So, theater," Lane said.

"It's that movie where they throw the ring in a volcano before the eye eats them," Derrick said helpfully.

Lane turned and said, "I thought it was about blowing up that space ship. With the laser sword people."

"What? Do either of you even watch full-length films? It's not a movie if it's a five-minute summary," Morgan said, exasperated.

"I don't have a clue what any of those things are, and I'm involved with a lot of the realities on your list. Be careful," Kayla said. Then she walked out, closing the door behind her.

"Great pep talks around here," Morgan said.

"She's pregnant, and our boss does not approve," Derrick replied.

"Koff? What would she have against a pregnant woman? She had a kid herself," Lane said.

"Maybe it's because she's carrying it to term instead of in a tube. Maybe it's something totally off grid. Anyways, things have been dicey between them ever since the baby shower," Derrick said.

"Sounds like a bunch of stuff that doesn't involve our reality," Morgan said.

Lane nodded, and Derrick shrugged.

Morgan laid down his pad and showed them the forums he had links to that day. There were some clever graphics and images being voted on announcing Morgan's next big show. A beautiful woman in red slippers and a blue dress stood at center while what looked like a man dressed as robot, a homeless person, and a lion stood around her. They were voting reasonably well in the various feeds, not at the top and not at the bottom of the votes.

"Now my reality extends a bit outside the hetero limits of you two. Technically you're both a bit more entrenched with women, but the ones I do know are not in your neck of the woods. Getting the performance to appear in those other reality feeds was not an issue. But now that they are checking it out, they seem to be disagreeing on how the whole thing is being run," Morgan said.

He tapped up the first forum discussion, and Lane followed him on his own pad. At a glance, the posters seemed to be arguing over whether or not they liked the lead female's outfit. Several others wanted to know why she was hanging out with a homeless man who might rape her. There was also a surprising amount of protest at having the robot be gendered like a man. Everyone liked the lion, though.

"Well, just have a vote or something. That's what we do in the GDK when people start getting pissy," Derrick said. Morgan gave him an exasperated look and scrolled to another forum. In this one they were discussing the plot of the story. Some people thought it would make more sense if the girl made friends with the witches and overthrew the wizard instead of taking these strange men with her. Others couldn't believe anyone would be able to overcome a woman with an army of flying monkeys.

"They're complaining about all of it! You can't have a vote about the whole story!" Morgan said.

"Look, you start bossing them around, they're going to leave. Clearly they're interested in this *Wizard* thing. That's good. Harness it, ask them to vote on how they think the play should go. What does it matter so long as we're getting them to work together and care about an anti-Gateway event?" Derrick said.

"That's just the thing. No one thinks that part makes any sense. I had to rewrite the entire play to make it all about why Dorothy can't just teleport home. Everyone thinks it's silly! Half of them don't care about capitalism, and the other half don't care about FTL," Morgan said.

"What's important is that they're here and debating something. It doesn't matter what so long as they know it's against the Infinity Drive. Set up the polls. You're tracking the metrics on this, right? I'll send them over to Tricia and see what she can figure out from it," Lane said. He stood up and closed the forum window.

"Where are you going?" Derrick asked.

Lane glanced at the two of them and debated saying he was meeting Eve for drinks. He doubted either of them would keep it secret very long. "Taking care of some things. See you tomorrow," he said.

As he walked out, Lane glanced at Kayla's office. The door was closed, but in the window, he could see her putting earbuds in. He wondered what she was listening to for a moment and then kept walking. A quick message to Tricia asking her how she was doing and another job request for her out before he was out the door.

As Lane stepped outside, he realized it was already getting dark. He was starting to walk toward the bus stop when he spotted a man across the street watching him. He was wearing a pair of black Standards and watching Lane. Without thinking, Lane jogged across the street and waved him down. He recognized him from the GDK con, the ones who had been standing around the keg.

"Hey! Hey there. I don't think I ever got your name. I don't know what this is about or what the GDK thinks they're doing, but stop harassing my friends. Did you have anything to do with that arrest the other day? Did Alice send you?" he asked.

The man smiled at Lane and said, "Whoosh little man. We don't work for women anymore. Maybe we should have you arrested again for us selling us out to your slut boss."

Lane felt a hot rush come over him and he pulled out his pad. He brought up the alert program and held it up where the man could see. "If I hold down this button, cops will be all over the place in seconds. I'll file a complaint against you. Because I'm a lawyer, I know how to allege it so your Standard rations get frozen. I'll have you logged into permanent observation for months. Even if I lose, even if your GDK friends beat me, the next few months of your life will be miserable. No matter what," Lane said.

"I could beat the shit out of you," the man replied. He squared off menacingly at Lane.

"Then it will be permanent. And I'll recommend hormone therapy for that violence problem. And if you do touch me, you had better believe I'll win," Lane answered. The man blinked and stared at Lane. After a few more uncertain moments, he began to walk away.

Lane waited until he was gone, took a deep breath, and headed toward the bus station for his date. On the whole ride he felt a surging pride that he suddenly could not get enough of.

Eve had arranged a nice place, far more elegant than the usual diners and cafes Lane frequented. Ancient brick and wood matched luxurious asteroid paneling and stenciled black rock art. The panels depicted scenes of marsh grass and live oak trees in a chromatic silver and onyx. Eve had said to meet her upstairs. The downstairs area had a few men sitting around tables and a lot of women. Most were wearing Standards, and Lane saw a few checking their meal plans on their pads. The stairs going up had a red cord across them, and a broad-shouldered woman was standing next to it. He walked up and began reaching for the cord.

"Excuse me, the upstairs is for paying customers only," she said.

Lane realized she was assuming he wouldn't have enough money for the place. "No, no, I'm meeting someone here," he said.

The woman looked unconvinced. She pulled out a pad and asked for his name. A few taps and a double-take on Lane's face gave way to a smile as she set the cord aside. He walked upstairs and saw a handful of empty tables. Around one was a cluster of women, drinks in hand, chatting softly. He saw Eve over in a far corner and made his way to her.

When she saw him she smiled, stood up, and gave him a hug. He was a little surprised at first but then hugged her back. She had on just a hint of perfume. Her dress was beautiful as well, tight fitting and made of a strange material that was soft to the touch.

"I'm glad you asked to see me again, Lane. I wanted to thank you for all your help. Things have been so exciting ever since I met you. Not to mention profitable. Do you mind if I order the wine?" Eve said as she handed him the menu.

Lane glanced briefly and panicked at the prices. The woman downstairs had been right to question him.

"Relax! This is my treat. You paid for it, along with the dress and some other new gifts I bought myself. I'm even thinking about retiring as Tyrant. Maybe get a show started or design a new fashion line," Eve said. She seemed happy, gushing almost.

"Don't quit too soon now, we still have to finish the deal. Keep the mod going so that people can see what a mess *Tyrant* is becoming because of FTL," Lane reminded her. Eve frowned and was about to speak when the waitress interrupted. Eve ordered the second most expensive bottle on the menu.

"About that. I didn't want to bring this up exactly, but some people are figuring out how to survive. Don't get me wrong, the game is still a mess, and the developers are practically begging for another vote to have the mod removed. But it got voted in, so they're not going to remove it arbitrarily. It's just the virtual economy is…maybe not the disaster you're hoping for," Eve said.

"I suppose as long as it was a big enough disaster at first, that won't be a problem. It was a big problem, right? I know the GDK were complaining about it," Lane said.

Eve shrugged. "I was ready for it. Anyways, you haven't logged on in ages, so it's not like it's a big concern to you. Let's talk about something else. How is your lawsuit going? Think you'll be getting a bit of change yourself soon, Mr. Space Lawyer?" Eve asked.

Lane felt the little flicker of attraction in him dwindle as Eve's question made him think of Weber and the tubes running up his nose.

"We haven't won that yet either. We still have to impact all the realities who don't really care about any of this. Any one of them could be picked up for the popular vote," Lane explained.

"Oh, and what do you have planned?" Eve asked.

"We're going to give them a show," Lane said.

CHAPTER 43

The sex wasn't as good this time around. Lane felt an anxiety that hadn't been there before. He found himself wondering how Eve felt about it, which made it worse. He was too hard, and after he realized he wouldn't be able to finish, he asked her if she was done. She said yes. They lay in her bed, her hands running over his chest hair while her feet occasionally rubbed alongside his. The sheets were smooth and silky.

"I'm glad you're not mad at me," Lane said.

She was curling her fingers around his chest slowly. "Why would I be mad at you?" she asked.

"Earlier today, when I was asking you about those other realities, you seemed annoyed," Lane said.

The fingers stopped and slowly spread into a palm. It seemed to be gently pressing on Lane. "It's all right. A difference of reality," Eve said.

"Tell me," Lane said quietly. He was beginning to drift off into sleep.

"When I was little, I always wanted to go to outer space. I took all the courses I could find online, studied for my exams, and got as many certifications as I could. It's a pretty sexist business, though. Back then a mining ship was either all men or all women. It's easier to balance oxygen, fuel, and equipment if you're just dealing with one gender. That's what they claimed anyways," Eve said.

"Some ships still do that. I think it's just tradition now," Lane said sleepily.

"So I got an internship at an office full of women. And it was awful. Always whispering when you walk into the room. Anytime I ate too much, someone would have to comment on it. It's hard to explain. One time one of them decided she wanted to have a child, so she went off the hormone inhibitors, and it was like working with a crazy person. She would flip out at you and then never even feel guilty. Never apologize," Eve said.

"Oh, I'm sorry. I've never run into that before. In my office there was only one or two bad apples. Maybe that's why Kayla was so cruel—a hormone thing. It's outside my reality really," Lane said.

"Who?" Eve asked.

"This woman at work I used to fight with all the time. Stupid stuff. My boss put her in charge of me, and she was always finding problems with my work without ever being much help," Lane said.

"For me, the worst thing about it was how jealous they would get over appearance. Who had lost the most weight, whose dress was better, whose hair was better that day. We didn't even have men around, but whenever one did come by, suddenly they would all be in a competition to see who could get them. One day I just got fed up with it and vowed to never work with women again," Eve said.

"I think I'm the opposite. I've never worked around very many men before. The law business on Earth is mostly women now. The guys have to go where the clients are, which means space. As a kid I wanted to go to space too. It never occurred to me that men went there because they had to," Lane said.

"What makes you think they have to go? You can do anything you want if you just take the classes and study," Eve asked.

"It's…hard to sit still like that as a boy. On your own. Most men don't have anyone to make them. Most of my Other Mothers didn't know what to do with me. I didn't like being on dorm very much, things happened that never sat well with me. So I studied obsessively just so I could leave. Most guys I know got past their Standard requirements and never picked up another course," Lane said.

"Oh. I never had any trouble with online school. It was like the looks thing, grades were one of the ways girls competed. Most of the men I know compete over their virtual assets. How powerful they are in a game or how much skill they have. *Tyrant* was a breeze after working in that office of women. Half of them wanted to sleep with me, and the other half only cared about the virtual stuff. They didn't know what to do when I started fighting rough," Eve said. There was a touch of satisfaction in her voice.

"Be careful," Lane murmured before letting out a slight yawn. He vaguely thought he heard her ask why before sleep overtook him.

When Lane awoke the next morning, Eve was sitting in a pair of pajamas, hunched over her large Canvas unit. She had plugs in her ears and seemed to be concentrating over what looked like *Tyrant*. Lane sat up and waved to her. She waved back and smiled at him. There was an awkward moment as they looked at each other, Lane uncertain of what to say or do. Usually he had been kicked out by this point in the date. She seemed strange to him in the morning, as if she were a different person even though she was doing all of the things he associated with her. Lane got up and dressed.

"So, ah, thank you again. For everything. It's good to see you," Lane said.

"Oh no, it's fine. I'm glad you came," Eve said. She was still sitting, and Lane was still standing. "Sorry, this is a bit unusual for me. I don't normally, you know," Eve said.

"It's all right. Let's get together again soon, OK?" Lane said. He was tense as he said it, unsure of what it would imply.

"OK. Yes. Let me know about the show thing. I'll post it in my feeds," she said.

"Definitely. Can you…do you think you could walk me to the door?" Lane asked.

Eve looked at him curiously and shrugged. She followed him to the door and looked both ways before giving him a thumbs-up. They said good-bye again, and Lane leaned in for a hug, and Eve, unsure what he was doing, got out of his way. The moment passed, and he stepped outside quickly.

While he was in the shower back at his apartment, a ping rang out on Lane's pad. He stepped out to check it and saw it was from Koff. "Public vote approved" was all it said. She didn't have to remind Lane that it meant they needed to work that much more for the event. The specific day and time would not be given to the parties involved, instead selected by a computer. Then a random sample of people would review all of the information and briefings of each party and vote.

They would need to prepare a video. And they would need to keep trying to reach people and help them make up their minds before they watched it.

Lane stepped inside the conference room and saw Derrick activating the large monitor. A culture grid popped up with several dozen circles shifting across at a rapid speed. Rule squares were being pushed and pulled by invisible hands inside it as well. Then the screen would flicker, and the entire image would be rearranged again.

"What is it?" Lane asked.

"Our theater show has become a culture," Derrick said.

Lane looked at him in surprise.

"After you left, Morgan and I set up those polls, and he warned about this happening. It's funny. All you need for a culture system to form is to just ask how to resolve a conflict. Nothing has been stable, but it's interesting to watch. Some of them want to get rid of all the men in the show. Another group wants to rewrite the whole story. Now I think they're bargaining among one another about who gets to have what," Derrick said.

"Derrick, did all the members of the GDK come back?" Lane asked.

"No, a lot did but the ones who always hated Alice are still gone. Why?" Derrick replied

"Ran into one of them yesterday. Have you checked on *Tyrant* lately? How is the game doing?" Lane asked.

"Why?" Derrick asked.

"Oh, you know, just making sure it will be convincing. We want everyone to believe that's a good example of how the actual FTL drive will work. It's our biggest link between Gateway and this whole disaster being premeditated," Lane hastily explained. He didn't want him to know about Eve.

"Most of the new players have no chance of starting their own corporations or getting their own ship now. They have to start hauling for the Tyrant or a matriarch. We're just starting to get our infrastructure back together, and then we'll be doing the same thing," Derrick said.

"Has the value gone down in the economy? Is everyone losing money?" Lane said.

"Not exactly. The wealth is concentrating. Which is kinda the same thing, depending on who you are. After Gateway made their announcement and we started making all these posts and jokes in the forums, people got interested and flooded back into the game. So the numbers are up, but the change was so radical that the rest of the game hasn't really adapted to it yet. The designers are sitting tight because they are making even more money than before, and we're all just getting by," Derrick explained.

Lane wasn't sure if he had answered him or not. "So it's better or worse than before?" Lane asked again.

"It is unpredictable," Derrick said.

The two sat quietly as they watched the rules and cultures of their *Wizard of Oz* show shift and twist in real time. The bending and warping of people's wills, abstracted out into a visual explanation that was supposed to summarize every click, word, image, and sound a person made within the virtual forums. On the screen was a consensus to be summarized visually, the consent given by participation alone. Lane had often looked at culture grids he had participated in and had little feeling for what they reflected. He wondered if these users would feel the same way, the disconnect from circles and squares to meaning so vast as to render the process only important to outsiders.

"What are they disagreeing over so much?" Lane asked.

"Whether the show should be real or a game," Derrick said.

CHAPTER 44

The lights of the Tohickon were red and yellow. Lane sat at the bar alongside Dale, who was dressed as a man tonight, and Tricia. They were all staring directly ahead and away from one another. Lane was getting drunk. Dale was upset because he had been voted out of *The Wizard of Oz*. And neither was excited to see Tricia sporting a single silky pink glove. It was a civilian defense model. She had used Lane's latest payment to buy it for protection.

"I thought you would be happy!" Tricia said.

"I don't have any problem with you wanting to defend yourself. It's just that I took care of it for you. Those people following us aren't going to be a problem. You didn't have to go buying that thing," Lane said.

"I meant my report," Tricia said.

"Oh. That," Lane said. Tricia had finished compiling the metrics on the opposing realities. They were in favor of the lawsuit. In fact, they were in favor of banning the technology entirely. The mod as evidence of Gateway's conduct and the impact on the culture spheres had spread across the realities, each one twisting and changing it. Metrics on the masculine realities were giving even more favorable numbers. Despite untold millions in meme planting and aggressive advertising by Gateway, it had barely taken a few grassroots movements and some tweaking of the public narrative. People across the culture grid were against faster-than-light travel. Their lives were built on certainty and no one could tell them what, exactly, was going to happen with this much change. So they rejected it.

"It's just that there's no way any of us are responsible for that reaction. This was already in the system. It's depressing that people would automatically be against something so revolutionary," Lane said.

"What's depressing is that those bitches have turned the *Wizard of Oz* into a complete farce. The only man left is the straw man! It's not even really a show anymore. Everyone is just dressing up in these costumes and going out to show off. Morgan keeps bragging about how they interpreted the silver standard message into the whole thing with those stupid tokens, but what does it matter? It's not a show if everyone is in it," Dale said miserably.

"Hey, I'm running it. You can dress up as Dorothy or Toto or whatever you like. I still have some authority in it, right?" Lane said. He patted Dale on the shoulder.

"I don't understand why you have such a problem with the glove," Tricia said. "Does it threaten you? I would never use it on you, Lane, and I'm very careful with it. The power charge is on the lowest setting."

"No, it's not that. I guess I was proud of myself for marching up to this guy and demanding they leave us alone," Lane said.

"God, that again," Dale said with exasperation. "Do you really believe a group of ex-GDK is actually following you two around? For what? All your info is being sent out on the pad anyways. What are they trying to do, scare you? It's just some kooks with bad taste."

"Hey, I never said I thought they were ex-GDK. I'm the one who put together Gateway's scheme, my money is that it's them. And Lane here is... Lane has been doing a lot of..." Tricia trailed off as she tried to think of what she wanted to say. "Lane here is a very good networker. And I think that's important for something this big," Tricia said finally.

Dale laughed and Lane frowned, even more annoyed now.

"A networker? I've been the driving force behind this whole lawsuit! I'm the one who stuck my neck out to get Koff to give me more time. I'm the one who salvaged the first hearing after Jacob messed everything up. I went to that GDK conference and figured this whole mess out," Lane said sperately.

Tricia rolled her eyes. "It wasn't an insult, Lane. But technically I'm the one who figured out what Gateway was up to. And Eve and the GDK decided to push the mod vote forward. It's just when I was comparing all this data and all the conflicting realities, I noticed that you're the bridge between all of them. Before this I had never even heard of *Tyrant,* much less the Gay Death Knights. Yet you put my research into their hands. Gateway can't keep up with how fast their memes are spreading now," Tricia said.

"Oh, I love that one with the rainbow hitting the miner in the face. The little image of him smiling, and then pop! Rainbows and ships," Dale said, laughing.

"For me it's the picture of this businesswoman. It's so funny to see all the money falling out of her," Tricia said, laughing with him.

Lane chuckled with them. "I've seen both of those, actually," he said.

"See! That's my point. You got both those jokes from your feed. Here, hand me your pad," Tricia said. Lane handed it to her, and she brought up his feed stats. She flashed them to Dale, who stared at them for a minute before bursting out laughing again.

"What even is this?" Tricia exclaimed. "Business, law, economics, feminism, space, space unions, God you have dozens on here. Where's the humor? Where's the culture filters? You hardly have any frames ticked off!"

Lane snatched the pad away from her and sheepishly closed the stats. He had been experimenting ever since Derrick suggested he branch out a bit more with his reality feeds.

"Have you done any metrics on this *Wizard of Oz* game?" Lane asked.

Tricia gave him a toothy grin, but she seemed willing to let him change the subject. She reached for her own pad and pressed a few buttons.

"I'd mention the bridge thing again, but honestly, you don't have anything in common with these people, period," Trish said. "And they don't really have much in common with one another. They all hate Gateway, though. And capitalism. And going faster than light. They all agree that Gateway is capable of staging an elaborate accident for the sake of spreading capitalism and mining interests. Did we ever figure out if that was true or not? Some of them think men are secretly behind it, some think capitalism is capable of corrupting anyone. I think it's a bad idea to get all of these people together. Particularly in real life."

Lane groaned and banged his head against the bar slowly.

"Oh, there, there, we're all going to come together to unite against whatever it is we're uniting against," Dale said as he rubbed Lane's shoulder. "I'll be coming. Tricia, you're going, right?"

"Maybe. There aren't a lot of women who line up with my reality preferences, but maybe I'll get lucky," Tricia said.

"You're still dating women?" Lane asked.

"Ever since I started doing these side projects for you, I've had to go through mountains of male-centric data," Tricia said. "Forums, reality subsets, just so much testosterone and bizarre patriarchy crap. It's just all so one note. Either they are radically for everything Gateway is proposing and it's our duty to colonize the stars as a species, or they think it's going to kill all of us. There's no shortage of reasons why it's going to kill all of us, but that's the consistent theme. I'm just sick of it. Sick of the whole tired notion that this is how we do things, so this is how it's done and we're doing it, so shut up. Just…change, you know?"

"I don't think it's a bad thing," Dale said.

"What?" Tricia said.

"Not wanting to change," Dale said.

Lane glanced at him. "Dale, you're wearing men's clothes for the first time in weeks."

"Yeah, but you haven't asked me why," Dale said.

"Oh. I don't know, I figured you had some sort of reason for it. What does it matter?" Lane asked.

"That's exactly my point," Dale said. "It didn't even register on you. Tricia here has sent me two messages about it. So have most of my other friends. But you're just sitting here complaining away or badgering me about the stuff you're fixated on. I think that's nice. It's something I appreciate about men."

"I don't think flirting with Lane really explains anything," Tricia snapped.

"Outside your reality, dear. And I thought you didn't talk about other people's realities that way." Dale said.

"I don't know what is with everyone and reality courtesies, but I swear if I did a metric, the increase of incivility and people accusing one another of being wrong must be at an all-time high. Everyone is on edge these days," Tricia said.

"It's because we're all talking about the same thing," Lane said.

"But we're not," Tricia said. "That's the whole thing about acknowledging everyone else's right to a reality. I see things differently. What's normal to you is offensive to me. Let's acknowledge it."

"But it has never really been about something important. Not like having enough food to eat or a place to sleep. The public vote takes care of all that. It even takes care of us if we get too drunk or too fat. It lets us know by tracking our metrics and gets us back on track. An entire pricing market based on people's decisions that's more efficient than the free market itself. It's easy to not care what another person is thinking when you can safely sit in your own universe. The FTL thing is just too big. No one really knows what's going to happen next. If it's right or wrong, or if we can even agree what to do with it," Lane said. He took a swig from his drink and ordered another. He wondered if another policewoman would appear to badger him about going home.

"I wish people had a better word for it than big," Tricia said. "Or complex. That's all anyone says about it. I was watching *The Mothers* this morning, and all they talked about was how strange and big the whole thing is. We'll have access to more planets, easier shipping, colonization, and all the new things waiting to be discovered out there. How did we get to a point where all that opportunity seems like a problem?"

"Speak for yourself," Lane said. "I still like the idea of getting rich and being able to buy whatever I want. If this works out, I'll still get my free market license and become a space lawyer."

"Buy what? A big house so you can sit by yourself? Fancy food? Good booze?" Dale said. He wagged a finger at Lane and shook his drink. "I think you're both wrong. The Infinity FTL whatever is not an issue of everyone talking. It's that we're all being asked the same question."

"Oh, come on, you're reciting Gateway memes now! Space rangers, space pirates, and space lawyers. It's the new meme," Tricia said. Lane looked at the two of them in surprise. "You haven't been following the Gateway stuff? It's on all the main feeds."

"A little. That was more Derrick and the GDK's area. How is it feeding?" Lane asked.

"Oh, for me it's lots of attractive men telling me about all the wonderful things that will happen when men can go make their own man planet and throw off the shackles of matriarchy and blah blah blah. The lack of sophistication is appalling," Dale said.

"It's totally different in mine," Tricia said, "It's all being downplayed, like it won't affect anything. Earth will be Earth, and space will continue to be space. Things will stay safe is the big frame they keep using."

"You heard about their new game, at least?" Dale asked Lane, who shook his head.

"Just came out. It's one of those personal ones where people walk around and tag locations, take pictures of themselves, build a big data matrices together," Dale said.

Lane stared at him for a moment before hastily pulling out his own pad. He checked the polls for the *Wizard of Oz* event location.

"Where do they have people going?" Lane asked.

"All over the peninsula, but mostly upper Charleston. Marion Square is the end point. Why?" Dale asked.

Lane held up his pad. The location for the *Wizard of Oz* game was Marion Square.

CHAPTER 45

Lane pinged Derrick a message on his way back to the office about the Gateway game but only got a brief "On it" in reply. Lane did his best to sign up for the game himself as he rode the bus but soon realized it was invite only. He could guess the basic features, though. Locations would be selected by the designers and kept secret from the players. Whenever a player entered the area he or she would be notified and asked to perform some kind of task with your pad recording. Run a lap around the park, ask a store for something, or just take a picture.

You could use it to build a kind of image—a democratic impression of a place built out of all the videos, photographs, and comments. The activity gave meaning to the space, and the times and variables of people gave it resonance, the connection made of both the physical and the digital. A painting you had stepped in and heard. Sometimes people would compile all of their comments and select the adjective chosen most often. Others would just rate their feelings and graft the metrics onto a photograph. One of Lane's favorites had been an entire grid of moods and thoughts during a sunset overlooking the Ashley River.

And they were going to do it during the *Wizard of Oz* show.

A bemused Koff was standing in the conference room as Lane tried to explain the gravity of the situation. "Boys, if they are already in our favor based on the forums, what does it matter about the actual show?" she said wearily. "We've got a shot at winning this thing when it goes to the popular vote. Jacob has his best specialists putting together the hearing videos. We even lined up a man to do the narration, the one who does the angry cat cartoon, which has appeal across both genders."

"I understand, but these people have barely absorbed anything out of us," Lane said. "Out of the endless amounts of cash Gateway could use to influence this decision, this is what they're choosing? Metric art? We have to assume there is more going on than just this."

"Clearly you have not seen just how terrible Gateway's PR on this has been," Koff said irritably. "They have a video of two people talking about how we should be grateful that someone went to the trouble of inventing the FTL drive. It's appalling."

Lane blinked and stared at her. He hadn't expected someone like Koff to resent the idea of FTL as well.

"It really is obnoxious," Derrick said. "My wife was telling me about this creepy one advertising that we could move the whole family to this big jungle planet. Why on Earth would anyone want to do such a thing? I agree with Koff, Lane. I think this metric thing is just a desperate attempt by a company that cannot spend its way into winning."

"Do you have an invite to play? Does anyone on the GDK?" Lane asked.

Derrick shook his head. "No, not even the alts. We have had to expose ourselves a lot for this media campaign, and a lot of our anonymous accounts are tagged."

"What is it that is bothering you so much, Lane?" Koff asked.

He fidgeted awkwardly and looked away for a moment. "I think…I believe it's…well, this was supposed to be just about the lawsuit. About getting the damages for the one ship. And now we've maybe convinced everyone that the whole thing should be done away with. What if Gateway is right? What if they can't develop this technology without some kind of immunity? Maybe we should settle."

"Oh good God," Koff snapped. "Settling is not an option. Do you honestly believe a bunch of sexual imagery with rainbows and crude videos convinced people that having a spaceship appear in your house is a bad thing? It's common sense. All those realities were already inclined to believe it. We just gave them a way of expressing it." She began moving toward the door but stopped as she was making ready to leave.

"Would you have any interest in going space lawyer on some distant planet?" she asked Lane.

He shrugged and nodded, silently answering yes to something he had wanted almost his entire life.

"Just curious. Might be good to have a lawyer out there," Koff said as she exited.

"Seriously?" Derrick asked.

"I have nothing here to make me stay. Anyways, what else is going on with the case? We have three days until the *Wizard of Oz* event. What have they voted on?" Lane asked.

Derrick changed the screen and brought up the culture grid for their big event. The squares were unmoving, although there were many more, while various culture spheres shifted around the grid. Below, Derrick had linked up a stream of text and images that would highlight locations of interaction. A discussion of advanced weaponry flashed by, another on food stocks, rape culture, an image of a cat eating a rainbow, on and on as the debates and actions of hundreds of people was represented on the screen.

"Is there always this much noise? I still can't tell anything about what's going on," Lane said.

Derrick froze the grid and passed his pad over to Lane. He placed a finger on it, and an image of a blue rose appeared. He tapped his finger on it to see the specific moment. Two people were arguing about what sort of flowers they thought Dorothy should be given by the Munchkins. This would be for the third tier of the play, which only the elected actors would get to do. She was showing her favorite sort of flower. After a few more random checks on the grid, he noticed that Derrick was fixated on his pad. When he glanced over to see what he was doing, Lane realized he was playing *Tyrant*.

"There's not a lot left to do at this point," Derrick said. "We just received a load of our ships back, and I'm getting things set up for Alice. She wants to have a raid ready to go by tonight, and I told her I could get them outfitted in time."

Lane decided he wanted to go see Marion Square for himself and check on how progress was going. Down the street were shops and stores filled with goods from licensed free market shops. The clothing was of various prices, some of it cheap and others carefully crafted out of scarce materials. Up the street was the Public Commons building, where you could get the Standard clothes, food rations, or medical supplies that everyone who was under the Standards received. Marion Square wasn't quite in the center, but it was the first place on King Street that really indicated you were somewhere else.

The Square was a large field with two rows of trees. Two sidewalks crossed it to form a giant X in the center. There were crowds of women sunbathing in skimpy outfits or clear suits that would absorb the sunlight without exposing themselves. A few men here and there gawked, wearing Standard shorts and playing sports nearby to attract their attention. The place was otherwise empty; Morgan would not begin construction for another day.

On the far end was an ancient statue of John C. Calhoun. Lane walked down the X and crossed the grass. He searched for the name under the public narrative and saw a long list of flags and reality triggers. Lane flicked his filter off and checked the pure data. He was a famous politician from the 1800s. A strange photograph appeared of a grey-haired man who seemed to be scowling at him. Lane's eyes skimmed over his various honors and accomplishments. He had been a slave owner who argued in favor of keeping slavery in the South. He had been vice president and a senator. A link to a speech that he had given in the Senate was highlighted. Lane clicked it, and a scratchy, male voice began to speak.

I may say with truth, that in few countries so much is left to the share of the laborer, and so little exacted from him, or where there is more kind attention paid to him in sickness or infirmities of age. Compare his condition with the tenants of the poor houses in the more civilized portions of Europe—look at the sick, and the old and infirm slave, on one hand, in the midst of his family and friends, under the kind superintending care of his master and mistress, and compare it with the forlorn and wretched condition of the pauper in the poorhouse...I hold then, that there never has yet existed a wealthy and civilized society in which one portion of the community did not, in point of fact, live on the labor of the other.

Lane sat down on the concrete stairs of the statue as he wondered what Calhoun had meant. It was thoroughly outside his reality. Life before the austerity measures, before the food programs and housing organizations, differentiating a person based on physical appearance instead of metrics, and allowing wealth to divide a people so much that one had no choice but to serve the other. Whatever reality Calhoun was talking about was long gone in Lane's world, and there was little between them to connect the two. But the phrase that kept ringing out in his head over and over was "the labor of the other."

He kept repeating it to himself, like a mantra or totem against all the feelings and confusion. Like one of those music jokes where people would only play one line from a video until it took on an independent meaning from its context. Like the GDK's whooshing noise. The words were a naturally occurring event turned into a symbol whose meaning changed constantly.

Lane looked out over the square, the women and men enjoying the sun, and found himself wondering what any of these people thought about the FTL. He had been angry at Gateway at first, shocked by the *Black Swan*, but he hadn't expected people to actually agree with him. Wasn't anyone curious about what was beyond their own planet? He had never done this well with a popular vote, and Lane could not shake Koff's idea that people had already been predisposed to believe this. It made him feel as if he hadn't earned it.

A rumbling in his stomach made Lane reach for the Standard bar he had pocketed for dinner. It was beginning to get dark, and there was a red hue in the sky. The labor of the other, he said to himself again. Lane stood and began walking toward the bus stop. Who was his other doing all the work? Lane supposed you could say it was the people who worked for money. People worked, whether it be real or virtual, because they wanted something. Raw materials still needed to be harvested for construction and there was still necessity, but it was far away. The other labor was out there in space where the miners and last great capitalist corporations operated. That was the only other labor Lane knew of. He again wondered if this lawsuit was such a good idea.

CHAPTER 46

It was the day before the big event, and Lane was in the conference room with Derrick minting tokens. Each one would represent a single credit, backed by McAngus and redeemable by the serial code on the back. The ka-chink of metal being crushed into a new form interrupted the space of the room at regular intervals. There was a box full of them by each man's side.

A ping on Lane's pad broke the rhythm, and he saw it was Weber calling him. "Lane, I've just gotten the reports back from Koff. Outstanding work! Congratulations! With these metrics, we'll have the popular vote won without a hitch," he rasped across the speakers. Behind him Lane could see a window and the moon. Weber appeared to be floating in zero gravity so that the tubes in his nose came up over his face at an awkward angle.

"Ah, thank you, sir. I don't know how much credit I can take for the whole thi—" Lane stammered.

"Don't be modest. This was all your idea, boy. We'll make a space lawyer out of you yet!" Weber said. A fit of coughing came over him, ringing out over the silence except for the continued ka-chink of Derrick printing money for the *Wizard of Oz* game.

"What is that noise?" Weber asked.

"Tokens for tomorrow. We've got people coming from all over the region to participate. All the hostels are reserved, and dorms are renting out all their extra space. The whole city is packed," Lane explained.

"Eh? I thought you were putting on a show," Weber said.

"Oh, the people participating decided to change it. So now we have these stations for various parts of the story. There is a Munchkin Town section and an Emerald City section. Then the person arranging it all, Morgan, has set up actors to give out quests while reciting scenes from the play. They get tokens for doing all this," Lane was saying as he realized Weber did not understand a word of it. "It's a show with tokens, yes," Lane said.

"Whatever. Just don't let that Gateway nonsense get you down. If they want to have thousands of people photographing it, then let them. What matters is the numbers, and we already have them. All you have to do is hold on!" Weber said.

Lane wondered if this was meant to be some sort pep talk because the only effect it was having was making him feel terrified.

"All right, will do, thanks, good-bye, got to get back to making money, thanks, good-bye," Lane said before closing the video chat.

Ka-chink, another coin tumbled into the box. Derrick looked at Lane and shook his head before chuckling again.

"What now?" Lane asked.

"Just marveling at how out-of-touch that guy is. I'm sitting here essentially printing his own money into a token currency, and all that registers is a bunch of metrics from an AI," Derrick said. He reached into the box and took out a token. "Hundreds of these tokens are going to be spreading to the entire Southeastern region, with Weber's company promising to back each one up as a credit. He's practically in business with each one of these token owners. Yet the only thing that registers is winning his lawsuit. So much for the free market license guaranteeing a rational actor."

"You would be any different? That ship had billions in equipment, staff, and raw ore. With the crew dead, the entire profit goes to the company," Lane said. Ka-chink.

"The whole lawsuit could hardcode a rule to make Gateway have to pay for any accidents with the FTL," Derrick said. "And if the people running that company are anything like Weber, that might be enough to make them abandon the whole project. It just seems crazy to limit this whole thing to money. It's not a virtual world, you know. There are no fixes."

"You'd feel more comfortable in a virtual world?" Lane asked.

Derrick pressed and ka-chinked another coin into the box. "I know what's going on there, at least. We got back our entire fleet in *Tyrant*, and Alice is back in control with most of the GDK. We have even launched a whole new campaign that has all of the members rallied," Derrick said.

"Oh? What are you up to?" Lane asked.

"You understand if I don't exactly give you any more secrets," Derrick said.

"Oh! Right, sorry. I mean, sorry about that whole thing. Glad it's working out," Lane said. So much had happened since the GDK conference that Lane had little feeling about it. He thought of Alice briefly, he saw her face in his mind and replayed the image of her and Max out at the fire. There was only a brief sensation of dread.

"Yes, these things seem to have a way of working out," Derrick said. Another ka-chink followed, but silence came afterward. "All right, that's it."

"That's it? We're not making any more tokens?" Lane asked. While the box easily contained several thousand tokens, the projections for the event had far more people showing up.

"That's all the money we have left to allocate. Everything else is tied up in costumes. Morgan is having the big X in Marion Square painted yellow for the Yellow Brick Road. Plus the huge set pieces. That's our whole PR budget. The whole point was to convert their realities by voting on how to run the show. The job is done Lane. Relax. Have you seen the setup yet?" Derrick tapped on his pad, and a file became available on Lane's pad.

"No, I was ignoring the whole thing hoping it would just resolve itself." Lane said sarcastically.

"You can't miss this, Lane. What if something goes wrong?" Derrick said earnestly.

"I was kidding. I thought you said the job was done," Lane said, a little annoyed.

"Oh, well, you still don't want any bad press to come out for the unconverted," Derrick said. He pulled out his pad and turned on *Tyrant*. The silence in the room was now only broken by the random taps of Derrick's fingers as he pushed and prodded the virtual system. Lane wondered if he should mention something to Eve but decided against it. He picked up the box of tokens and left the office for Marion Square.

The nature of the entire park had changed. The space was gone, and in its place were multicolored houses and prop buildings. Wooden roofs over circular huts were at one end of the park, while at the other, tiny square green buildings were propped up to make them appear much bigger than they were. People were everywhere. Lane walked alongside the grass, a bright string and wooden stake warning him to stay off the paved path until the paint was dry.

He saw a crowd reciting lines while reading from their pads and heard Morgan shouting instructions over the group: "Louder! You're going to have to imagine there are dozens of people standing around shouting and demanding things from you. Speak up! You can worry about characterization only if the people really ask for it."

There was some grumbling from the group before one woman complained, "Why did you write me all of this backstory if you wanted me to just shout out the quest part? Who's going to hear it if I don't complain about the Witch?"

"They can look it up on their pads!" Morgan explained. "You all should have recorded your quest monologues already. If people want to hear it, they can access it from their pads. If they want to see you do it, fine, we'll make sure to alternate. But I have done these kinds of things before, and I promise you, people will love you just the same if you get to point."

"What's to keep people from skipping us and just going straight to kill the Wizard?" asked a young boy.

Morgan rolled his eyes and spotted Lane. He waved at him and gestured for him to bring the box.

"Because they won't get as many tokens if they do it that way! Everyone, this is Lane. He is our little benefactor for this show. Everyone say hi," Morgan said without looking at Lane.

There was a deadpan hello from the group before they went back to their pads and reciting their lines in a wave of emotional information.

Morgan snatched the box of tokens and popped it open. "Is this all of it?"

"Yeah, I know. Apparently that's all the money we had left. Each one of those has to be exchangeable for credit," Lane said sheepishly.

Morgan ran his hand over the coins and then sniffed it. "Ugh, it's that metallic grime smell. I hate it," he said as he set the box down. "Lane, each person here is expecting to get a token for completing a quest. That was the whole arrangement, voted and hard coded. With this many tokens, we'll run out before the show is even getting started."

"They're just tokens, right? We'll just give them more through their pads or something," Lane said.

"No good. The physicality is the whole point of this thing. People walk around, collect tokens, and exchange them right next to the quest site. That way they can feel the pleasure of having all their work get turned into money. The tokens have real value, so people will also have the temptation to just leave with them," Morgan said.

"But that doesn't really have anything to do with the lawsuit. Or FTL. Or make sense," Lane said.

"Well, Lane, that's probably why I told you and Derrick that crowd-sourcing a play was going to be a disaster. It doesn't matter what the game is about because nobody reads the backstory stuff. All that matters is that they think it's about bashing Gateway and showing up and capitalism and…" Morgan checked his pad, "reliving the burden of patriarchal economies. I don't even know what that is. I'm just reading the top-voted meanings from the grid."

"People realize this is about the public vote, right?" Lane said angrily. The acute sense of fear was beginning to swell in him as he realized that he had been ignoring a very important part of his job for Weber. He had been so busy focusing on forums and tweaking the public narrative that his own event was spiraling out of control. This was supposed to have been Derrick's thing.

"We'll put up some signs, make sure people are transmitting locative flyers, relax. I've already got it figured out. We're just gonna inflate this currency system. That'll make the whole thing drag out until people go home," Morgan said.

"What does that even mean?" Lane snapped.

"Lane. Lane. Relax. Obviously you have not played in a virtual world that uses currency. It just means printing more money to stretch out the value of the tokens. Handy trick when you have too many new players in a game and only a few veterans. All you have to do is go make some tokens, maybe brown or green or something, and we'll set up an exchange. Five green ones equals one silver one. See? I just quintupled our tokens."

Lane groaned as he thought about walking back to the office and the endless monotony of ka-chinks.

"Wait. If it takes that many tokens to get a silver one, doesn't that mean people are just going to do the same thing over and over?" Lane asked.

Morgan reached into his pocket and pulled out a box of marijuana cigarettes.

"It's making fun of capitalism, Lane. So yes," Morgan said.

CHAPTER 48

Lane lurched awake as a stranger gently shook his shoulder. It was an old woman who had a worried expression on her face. "Young man, are you all right?" she asked. Lane looked around in a panic, scared he had missed his stop. He had been up late into the night printing green tokens and had barely gotten any sleep. Derrick had helped some but went home to see his family. The bus was idling quietly, and several passengers were looking around, wondering what the holdup was. His pad alert had been beeping.

"Is it his stop?" the driver asked.

The old woman looked at Lane worriedly again. She probably thought he was drunk and had passed out.

"Yes, thank you. Sorry! I've just been up late. I'll get off here, thank you," he said. Lane stood and lifted the enormous box of jangling metal. The old woman nodded and sat back down in her seat. The other passengers looked back into their pads. Lane lifted a hand to her as he exited, and she raised hers back.

He carried the box across the finished set of *The Wizard of Oz* in what had once been the parade grounds of Marion Square. Everyone seemed to have a costume. Some were wearing crisp green suits that had clearly cost a great deal of money, and others wore Standard outfits dyed green and older clothes that would have been sold for cheap or given away. He saw several witches in elaborate ball gowns or people wearing green makeup in all-black costumes. One man had a green face with a green suit, and it looked as if someone was arguing with him about the costume being fair.

Lane walked over to Morgan, who was lecturing several people wearing elaborate straw dresses, and set the box down next to him. Morgan glanced at Lane and nodded toward the box. A woman in a blue dress with red shoes was standing next to Morgan silently, and when she saw Lane, she walked over to him.

"Well, he's no fun like this. Want to go get a coffee with me?" Dale asked Lane. It took Lane a moment to recognize him. Dale's makeup was done perfectly, and the wig made his face seem much slimmer.

"Dale! I didn't recognize you. It looks good. Are you one of the witches?" Lane asked.

"I'm a Dorothy. You think I look pretty?" Dale asked.

Lane raised an eyebrow, not sure if the question was asking Lane if he passed for a pretty woman or if Dale as a woman looked pretty. He decided to just say yes.

Dale reached into Lane's box and pulled out a handful of green tokens. "We can use these at the refreshment stands over there. Walk with me," Dale said.

Lane followed and worriedly looked over at the box of tokens just sitting out in the open.

"Won't somebody take them?" Lane said. "They're valuable, right? We don't really have a way to track who has what token."

Dale placed a hand on his arm and tugged him away. "It would be nice if someone did. This printed money nonsense makes me feel so inferior. It's so literal, I have a bunch of these tokens, and you do not. The sooner it's all handed out to everyone, the better."

The refreshment booth was just being set up, and a young girl was tending the counter. She stared at the green tokens for a minute, more curiosity than questioning their validity, before pouring two cups of coffee for Lane and Dale. She pointed at the bin over to the side for them to drop the cups off when they were done. It was non-Standard brew.

They sat on a bench and watched the people trickle in. Lane was too tired to talk, and Dale was too busy checking out the other outfits. There were a lot of Dorothys, Lane realized, and like the players, their costumes were of varying quality. Some had glittering red slippers, and others had cheaply painted Standard shoes. A few shoes were silver colored, though whether that was a mistake or part of some weird backstory Lane didn't know. A few people wore lion costumes, which almost all seemed to be universally cheap and half-assed. There were a lot of women in metal armor suits, which Dale clucked over and said they were probably all the same group. Apparently one of the realities had decided to represent themselves as cyberwomen by not displaying any gender at all. That group had collected a few pockets of men following them around in a listless fashion.

After they finished their coffee, Dale got up to find Morgan. Lane decided to walk around and see the game unfolding. He had never been to a festival like this. People seemed to be generally having a good time as they walked to the various events and waited in line. After a brief speech from one of the actors, they would walk to another part of the square, where various people in the group seemed to act out some lines they read off their pads. A few green tokens would be handed over, and then they moved along to the next site. Certain characters had to be present for certain events, but that looked like the gist of it. There was a lot of straw man swapping because there were not enough to go around.

Lane also began to notice people who were not dressed as any particular character at all. They had their pads out and were constantly staring at people in costume. Lane saw several women in Standards strike up a conversation with a Dorothy, who pointed them toward Munchkinville. They walked over and began to wait in line.

The event began to feel organic in its flows and rhythms. Everyone was moving with purpose all around, each one walking with a goal and the validation of a green token. The scattered signs about miners' rights and stopping Gateway had no part in these feelings, but rather made a background noise to them.

Lane began to feel better about his chances at becoming a space lawyer. He pulled out his pad and tapped a careful message to Eve. The event was going great; would she like to join him?

More and more people were arriving, with and without costumes, and each minding his or her own particular objective. Lane saw several plainly dressed people snapping pictures with their pads or recording the actors talking out various scenes from the show. He guessed they were a part of the metric art. Maybe Gateway had made a miscalculation with their whole plan. Maybe all they would do is film the event being a huge success and boost his case with the positive associations.

A ping sounded on Lane's pad, and he saw Eve's reply. "Can't. Under attack in *Tyrant*. Something big," it read.

Lane sat down on the concrete steps leading up to the Calhoun statute and was beginning to type a response when he felt someone standing over him. He looked up and saw a tin woodsman costume that included a mask and helmet. The sun reflected off the surface and into his eyes, making him squint as he looked up at the person.

"Hello, Lane," said a familiar voice. The woodsman took the mask off, and a flood of messy red-and-pink hair came tumbling out.

"Hello, Alice," he said. They looked at each other silently for a moment. Lane felt a tiny drop in his stomach and a sense of longing before it fizzled away. Alice had an enormous grin on her face, and she seemed to be enjoying herself.

"Sending your little Tyrant a message?" she asked.

"I figured you were leading some kind of raid against her. Nothing she can't handle, I'm sure," Lane answered. He wanted to stand and move around Alice to keep the sun from glaring into his eyes, but he felt as if it would make him look weak.

Alice sensed his predicament and stepped to his left, blocking out the sun from his view. "I have something I'd like you to see," she said. She handed Lane a pad with what looked like a film of *Tyrant* playing. Enormous ships and fighters were swirling all over the screen as explosions rippled across. Lane recognized one of the ships as *Sojourner Truth*, Eve's flagship. It looked as if it was taking a beating. In the far corner was a radar screen that seemed easier to follow. Lane tapped it, and a zoomed-out picture of the ongoing battle appeared. Red and blue triangles were appearing and disappearing everywhere on the screen, interrupted only by the white flicker to indicate a ship had perished.

"Amazing, isn't it?" Alice said. "The algorithms going on to have a full-blown battle with every ship using an FTL mod are some of the most complex I've ever seen. A couple of the boys claim they put them together in just a week, but I think they're bullshitting me. They have been working on them ever since we got the mod. A person can't even run them; it's all on autopilot. Derrick is just selecting ships to pull out for repairs or to abandon the fight. Can you guess who doesn't have a battle plan for using FTL?" Alice was enjoying herself, the impersonal metal suit around her unable to hide her relaxed posture. She leaned in close and studied Lane's face.

He tried to look away. "She'll figure something out," he muttered.

"Oh, I don't disagree. Half her fleet is on the other end of the galaxy chasing the tracking mods she put inside those ships she gave to us. She might have a few tricks yet. But I think once we take out her precious flagship, she will start losing steam. So I'm here to make you a little offer. A trade-off, one that is going to take place in *Tyrant* and here in the real world."

Alice squatted down and placed a hand on Lane's knee while she slowly pulled the pad away from him. "I want the Tyrant to fully step down and give me the throne. Including ships and facilities. She can keep whatever money she has." Alice reached a hand out to Lane's face and gently ran a finger down his cheek. "Such a shame how things ended up between us. You're cute," she said. She just barely licked her lips before standing back up.

"Even if I could offer it, what are we getting in return?" Lane asked.

"I won't turn this entire PR event into a disaster for Gateway to record," Alice said.

"Bullshit. This is real life you're talking about, not some power play in a virtual setting," Lane snapped. He stood, coming up several inches taller than Alice. He took a step toward her, but she held up a gloved hand whose texture Lane was all too familiar with. She had even painted it silver.

"Oh come on, Lane, is there really a difference anymore? Do you own a fleet of mining ships? Are you a licensed free market corporation operating off-planet? No? Then what does it matter? It all ends up as money, real or virtual," Alice said.

"How could you even turn this into a riot anyways?" Lane demanded.

"You have one hour."

CHAPTER 49

Lane watched Alice saunter into the crowds and decided there would be no point in following. He typed out a quick warning to Koff that read, "We have a crisis. Find Derrick." Another message to Eve: "GDK is going to sabotage event. Need to talk." Lane brought up Derrick's contact information and began typing out a message but deleted it, began typing another, and then deleted that one as well. He pressed the voice message instead.

After a few moments, Derrick answered. "Hello, Lane. I take it Alice has spoken to you?"

"Yes! What the hell is going on? Did you know about this the whole time?" Lane demanded.

"Yes. You can consider this my resignation from the firm, if that's what you're asking," Derrick said.

"Have you…is this…have you lost your mind?"

"It's just a job, Lane. Just money," Derrick replied.

"But why? How can you just trash your reputation with this firm?"

"You really don't give a damn about anything but this space lawyer bullshit, do you? It doesn't faze you that you sold out an all-male organization. I spent years making a safe place for men to talk about their fears and concerns. A place where they could make jokes and be themselves without worrying about some other reality blotting them out. Got them organized, got them to start actually doing the damn virtual lessons, and actually made a group of men something to be reckoned with! And you, YOU, just threw it away. You even had to slut shame our leader on top of it! And for what, Lane? Did the Tyrant pay you? Did she fuck you?"

Lane was shaking with fury as he listened. It was Derrick who had invited him into his stupid reality, and now it was suddenly his fault that he didn't fit in. "None of your damn business. But for the record? Your patriarch is a slut, Derrick. A complete and utter whore," Lane shouted.

"Compared to what? You? Lane, you've fucked half the office. You just work around women instead of men," Derrick snapped.

Lane took a deep breath and looked around him. Throngs of Standards, lions, straw men, Dorothys, and tin people were crossing the yellow path to various destinations. There were enormous lines forming now to the various events. People were clustered in random groups as well, talking and laughing. Tokens were being handed around freely, and many people had drinks and food in their hands. Someone with a camera pad held up glanced at him but had her attention drawn away by a bickering pair of Dorothys.

"How are you going to turn this place into a riot?" Lane asked.

"I'm not going to give it away, Lane."

"If you want me to convince Eve or Koff that I shouldn't just ignore your threats, I suggest giving me something better than that," Lane snapped.

"Well, Lane, everyone at that festival is playing a crowd-sourced game. Now who do we know who is really good at manipulating popular votes and crowd sourcing? A couple of key votes on Gateway's private forums, a couple of fake accounts in our own game, and suddenly we've got the perfect pressure cooker," Derrick said.

"The game? You rigged the entire game to end in a riot? So you could win a virtual throne?"

"Not necessarily a riot. Eve gives up the Tyrant position to us, and we leave it alone. You get your big event, Gateway loses the lawsuit, everybody ends up happy,"

"How am I supposed to convince Eve to give up being Tyrant?"

"The same way you get any of you free market creeps to do something. Offer her money," Derrick said. The voice channel went dead.

Lane looked at his pad again and saw two replies. From Eve it said, "Not my problem." From Koff it said, "He isn't with you?"

Lane began furiously typing out a response before he found himself uncertain about what he should type. There was a flaw in the system, but he had no clue what it was or even why it would result in a riot. There were dozens of different realities playing at *Wizard of Oz*, but none of them seemed on the verge of rioting. He typed, "Flaw in the system, will cause these groups to fight. They're demanding we give them the Tyrant position" and sent it to Eve and Koff simultaneously.

There was no response from Eve. Koff replied, "Figure it out. What is Tyrant position?"

Lane was about to begin typing out an answer when the sound of clanking tokens made him look up. A young girl was carrying a box from the refreshment booth back over to the station where people were lined up to act out a scene and receive their prize. They were recycling the supply of the green ones. Lane grimaced as he realized the easiest way to make a group of people start bickering in a game: take away the rewards.

He raced over to the girl and snatched at the box. She shouted in surprise and tried to pull away, but not before Lane got a peek inside. "It's all right. I'm one of the sponsors. You can ask Morgan. How many of these tokens are silver?" Lane asked. From just the surface it looked as if most of them were green, but that wasn't a problem necessarily.

"Not very many. Why?" the girl asked. Lane swore and began looking around the square. Over to his right was a person dressed in a Standard shirt but nice pants, holding a pad up, recording him for the Gateway metric art.

"No reason. Please find Morgan immediately. No, wait, get these tokens distributed, but tell someone to find Morgan. It's very important," Lane said.

"Ping him on the pad," she snapped as she began marching off toward Munchkinville.

"He doesn't always answer! Just do it!" Lane shouted after her. He pulled out his pad and copied Morgan to all the messages he had already sent. He glanced at the clock on his screen and noticed ten minutes had already gone by. If they were going to attack the money supply, how was it going to happen in one hour?

Lane began walking toward the Emerald City out of the dim hope Morgan would be there. He saw a group of Dorothys arguing with straw men and veered their way to hear what was going on. One was saying, "Your reality clearly doesn't include a basic core of fairness if you think that's a good deal!"

"Oh come on, three green tokens for one silver is fair! You got here hours ago. They stopped giving them out when we got here!" the straw man shouted.

"Offer is ten tokens or you take a hike, little man," the Dorothy replied. The other women standing next to her began pulling on her arm, telling her to ignore him.

"Stupid greedy bitch! Hogging it all to yourself!" the man shouted back as she walked away. Lane noticed two people with pads recording the scene. One was wearing Standards, the other dressed as a lion. Lane realized you didn't even have to be playing a game to want to record something like this. He began jogging a little faster toward the Emerald City.

A ping from Morgan appeared on his pad as he reached the gates. Lane didn't even see the response. He instead shouted to voice message, "It's the silver tokens! They got them all somehow!" Lane heard two people shouting and saw a group of actors shouting at the quest giver.

"We've got plenty of the green tokens! Give us the silver ones!" an irate tin person screamed.

"We want some money!" shouted a straw man.

Lane was desperate now. He ran around a corner and almost crashed into Morgan.

"Lane! Calm down! What are you messaging me about?"

Lane was panting as he explained everything that had just happened.

"Lane, there are easily four times as many green tokens as silver ones. There is nothing going on with the money supply. People are probably just keeping them to themselves as souvenirs."

"All right, then what? How are they going to turn this into a huge, angry mob?" Lane asked. He glanced to his left and saw a well-dressed woman with her pad, turning in a semi-circle as she recorded everything around her.

"I don't know. Maybe the old-fashioned way with a bomb or something. It's the GDK. They don't really do things traditionally. How would a bunch of men led by one angry woman do it?" Morgan said. He was checking his pad and receiving pings at a rapid pace as he spoke. "Well, there's definitely something going on with the silver tokens. I had a few people ask, and the exchange rate is shifting ahead of schedule. The game is certainly going to be a bit wonky soon."

"What does that mean?" Lane demanded.

"The money is starting to concentrate. Always happens in these sorts of things. Players figure out how the system works and start maxing it out. Swap one silver token for eight green tokens, use that to get some shirts or one of those free game passes. Then you flip that for ten to twelve tokens. The things are all used for goods here in the square, and those shops are all redistributing the money back to the quest centers. It's just that since there are a finite number of tokens, it can't…" Morgan froze and looked up, alarmed. His pad pinged. Then again. Then several times over.

"That can't be good," Lane said.

Morgan shook his head and punched something into his pad. "Yeah, OK, everyone is saying they're about to run out of tokens. Not to worry; we'll just get the money flowing again from whoever has bottled it up, and everything will be back under way."

"How are we going to find the tokens?" Lane said as he scanned the crowd.

"Strangest thing, this nice woman in a black suit gave me a couple of silver tokens with transmitters in them this morning. Even had a program to scan for them. Yup, here we go, all five of the marked tokens are by the fountain. Come on," Morgan said. He began walking at a brisk pace to the other side of the square. The fountain was where the Wicked Witch of the West's castle had been built. The steady stream of water made it easy for people to splash the witch and finish the scene.

"So they were going to just dump all the tokens into the wicked witch quest and have everyone get into a fight over the tokens? Seems kind of silly," Lane said.

"It's a PR disaster, Lane, not an actual disaster. You can't get anywhere in this damn square without someone filming you. They have already done a pretty thorough job as it is," Morgan said as he pointed. Nearby, a tin person was slapping a straw man in the face while the straw man shoved him back. Lane couldn't make out what they were shouting, but it sounded like another difference of reality.

They arrived at the witch's castle, and Morgan glanced at his pad before walking around the back of the castle prop. Two tin persons were sitting next to a sack, drinking beers and chatting amicably. They didn't even glance at Lane or Morgan. Lane held back and nervously looked around while Morgan walked up to them.

"Ah, excuse me, but you seem to have collected a lot of the silver tokens for the game here. If you could maybe give those over to me, I'll get them redistributed so everyone can have a good time, all right?" Morgan said sweetly.

The two tin persons blinked at him and then looked at each other.

"We don't know what you're talking about," one said. They both stood and put themselves between Morgan and the bag.

"Oh, but you see, I think you do," Morgan said. "Because that bag has the tokens in it. And I know that because they have a tracking device in them. Now let's not do anything rash that's going to have to get the police involved."

They crossed their arms over their chests.

Lane began backing up around the corner of the castle. Once he was out of sight, he sprinted around, through the line of irate Dorothys and lions, to the other side of the castle and began walking quietly around. He began to tiptoe once he could hear their voices again.

"Look buddy, I don't know what you're talking about, but you're not getting inside our bag. We got these tokens fair and square," one said with a touch of anger.

As Lane came around the corner, he saw that their backs were to him. Lane carefully approached the bag, reached down, and snatched it up just as one of the tin people glanced behind him. Before his big silver hands could catch him, Lane had turned and was sprinting away.

As Lane rounded the corner of the castle, he suddenly felt himself lift into the air as an incredible pain blossomed in his leg. His hands clung tight to the bag, and he landed on his shoulder in the grass. His legs curled up in pain and he groaned aloud. Standing over him was Alice, her helmet off and her silver-gloved hand reaching out to Lane.

"Well, I guess you have changed after all, Lane. Didn't expect you to figure it out and find the tokens so fast. Doesn't stop a thing, though," Alice said.

A silver hand locked into his shoulder and began to squeeze. Pain shot through Lane and he groaned again, his grip on the bag loosening despite his will to keep it tight.

Alice reached down and picked up the bag.

"All right. All of you. That's enough. Put down the bag, miss," a female voice said.

Lane glanced over to the source and saw a woman in a black suit. Her hands were at her side, gloved in black.

"Who the fuck are you?" Alice said.

"Gateway Security, miss. Now hand over the bag."

CHAPTER 50

"You're not getting this bag except from my cold, dead ha—"

The woman in black struck Alice. She moved almost faster than Lane could follow, one second standing almost five feet away, and the next driving her fist into Alice's side. Alice flew backward, but her gloved hand kept its grip on the bag. There was an odd ringing noise in the air, and Lane realized it was Alice's tin suit.

"This, is not, tin," Alice said as she was gasping for air. The agent nodded and pulled one arm back into a fighting position. Alice got to her feet and looked down at her suit. There was an enormous dent in one side. As she collected herself, Alice began to carefully circle the agent, slowly taking one step and then another as she began to work her way to one side. She still had the bag of tokens in her hand.

The agent mirrored the motion. After a few moments, one of the men who had been arguing with Morgan leaped at the agent. Her hand shot across his throat. There was a sound like a hand slapping on wood, and the man crumpled to the ground.

"Miss, I strongly suggest you put down the bag of tokens. I've increased the power to my glove. Your armor won't stop the blow next time, and I won't be able to control how much damage it does," the agent said.

Lane got back to his feet and got a better look around. Morgan was staring at them a few feet away. The remaining man from before was staring at his friend crumpled on the ground and clearly thinking twice about making any moves. Alice had stopped trying to maneuver around the agent. She nodded to the GDK goon and then flung the bag high into the air toward him. The agent reached for it, but Alice charged straight into her and tackled her.

The goon rushed forward and caught the bag while Alice and the agent rolled on the ground. Alice screamed in fury, but the agent made no sound as she fought. No one had been paying attention to Lane because the GDK man ran straight by him, tokens in hand. Lane's leg shot out, and he let out another groan as the man's legs rammed exactly the same spot Alice had struck. The goon toppled over with the bag, and it flew from his hands straight into the crowd. When it landed, there was the sound of clanking tokens and shouts following. The bag had opened, and the tokens had scattered on the ground.

Lane saw that the agent had gotten on top of Alice, and a silver hand locked with a black glove as Alice struggled. After the agent managed to push the arm out of the way, she head butted Alice. Blood was coming from her lip and cheek now. Seizing the opening, the agent flung Alice's arm aside and punched her across the jaw. The crack was audible.

There was more shouting as people began to throng around where the bag had fallen. Lane saw that the Gateway players were still filming everything. "Get out of the way, you big bully! Share, damnit!" a woman shouted. A lion tackled Dorothy and flung her aside. "Brutes! Savages! Fucking animals!" a straw man began.

Lane limped over to Morgan, who was now staring at the mob forming around the bag of tokens. People were on the ground clawing the pieces up while others jostled for a chance to get close.

"Should we do something to stop them?" Lane asked.

"Like what? With all that scarcity, the stupid things are overvalued. You're liable to get hurt," Morgan said.

Just then a tin person emphasized the point by kicking a lion in the stomach and snatching a silver token out of his hand.

"You're going to tell them that it's a part of the game's message," a woman said behind them.

Both men turned and saw another agent, different from the one who had struck Alice but similar looking. "Gateway Security," she said in reply to the questioning look on their faces.

"Gateway? Shouldn't you be happy about all this?" Lane asked.

"Who are you to tell us what to say or do?" Morgan snapped irritably.

The woman tapped her glove on the wrist twice and then beckoned them to follow her. The agent who had been fighting with Alice had secured Alice's arms behind her back. There were two others on top of the men as well. A large black van was pulled up on the corner. The agent lifted Alice with one arm and placed her inside the back of the van.

"It's easier to show you than to explain it here. You, Morgan, stay here. Act as if everything is all right and that this is all part of the plan. Tell people to use the tokens, and there will be another random event at the end of the game," she said.

"What? What event? We haven't got anything planned," he protested.

"Think of something, or we'll think of it for you. It doesn't matter. Lane, follow me," she said. Another black car pulled up and she got inside, leaving the door open behind her.

"Lane, what is going on?" Morgan demanded. Lane shrugged and looked back at the mob. It was already dispersing as people had gathered all of the tokens. People seemed to be complaining at the various quest centers, but the lines had dissipated in all the confusion.

"I don't know. Stay here, get everything smoothed over. All these Gateway players are still watching us. I'm going to see what this is all about," Lane said. He got in the car.

The interior was black and made of a material that felt like real leather. There were two other women in the car along with Lane and the agent. The vehicle was arranged with a rear seat and two on either side. Without saying a word, the woman sitting next to Lane reached down to his pant leg and began pulling it up. He hissed from the pain. She placed a black-gloved hand over the spot where he had been struck, and it felt icy cold.

"Relax. This will help with the swelling," she said. After a moment his leg began to feel numb. Lane had never seen a glove that could be used as a cold compress. The numbing sensation began to spread, and Lane realized there was some sort of current passing through the glove.

"Who…I don't actually know where to start. Why have you been following me? Or my friends? I thought you would be the ones who would want to sabotage this whole thing."

The women looked at one another.

"Our job is to protect the unknown variables in this lawsuit," one woman said.

"Or you could say we protect people from information that would be unhealthy for them to know," another said.

"OK, so it's a bit hard to explain, but maybe the easiest explanation is that we deal with things that occur off grid or that will involve things off the grid. The problem is that it's stuff that no one is really conscious of or can be conscious of, so even we aren't completely informed about it," the one holding Lane's leg offered.

"Oh, you mean anticulture," Lane said.

"That's a nice term for it, but the culture grid has absorbed it already. That renders it inaccurate. Your friends in the back over there, the woman in the metal armor and her guy pals? They were about to inadvertently set off an enormous anticulture bomb," an agent explained.

Lane was not sure which had spoken; they all looked similar and spoke in the same lilting tone. "They were going to make a bunch of people aware that they were playing a *Wizard of Oz* game?" Lane asked.

"No, they were going to make a bunch of people perceive their own realities in transition," another explained.

The car pulled around a corner and began crossing into the old shipping ports. Lane glanced outside and nervously wondered just who exactly he had gotten in a car with.

"I still don't follow. Alice was going to set off a bomb of existentialism?" Lane asked.

"No, that was extortion. The PR disaster itself was going to cause another massive value shift in the culture grid," one said.

"Crashing your *Wizard of Oz* show as Gateway's metric art turns it into an even bigger media event, would eventually ripple out into ninety-nine percent of the culture grid," the agent with the cold hands explained. She pulled her hand away from Lane's leg. It felt completely numb now.

As Lane tried to look as if he understood what they were saying, he noticed that the car was actually accelerating toward the water of the Ashley River. "Ah, you know we should probably—" he said as he braced for impact.

The moment passed, and Lane realized they were hovering over the water and zipping across the river. Lane had not been aware that hovering cars existed up until this moment.

"Where are we going?" Lane asked.

"Fort Sumter," the driver said. Which would have bothered Lane more if they were still on land because Fort Sumter was on an island in the middle of the river.

"It really is hard to put it into words. Whatever we say about anticulture your consciousness will assimilate into its reality. It takes a lot of sustained information noise, a lot of things you don't believe suddenly becoming true simultaneously, but even saying that makes it a bit quantified," one offered. "Look, I've read your data. You know that when Gateway made that public announcement, it affected every reality on the grid, right?"

"Yes. I thought it looked like anticulture, but it can't actually happen in reality, though. It only works in virtual settings because we're all…you know you're not really in a game, so you are consciously caring and not caring. There's no way to separate yourself from the real world to perceive it," Lane offered.

"Not really true anymore, if it ever was. And anticulture does a lot more than just disrupt virtual economies when it gets into reality," she said.

The car landed back on the ground with a thump and a brief shake. Fort Sumter was a tall structure of imposing black asteroid and steel. Centuries ago it had been the place where the opening shots of the Civil War were fired. It had been converted into a tracking station for incoming convoys from outer space. The car slowed, and Lane saw they were approaching a gate. Above it, in large lettering was the Gateway logo and the phrase, "Keeping the Truth True."

CHAPTER 51

Lane stepped out of the car as the other agents began to exit. They were inside a large hangar with other vehicles. The other car pulled up, and the doors opened to reveal more agents as they hauled out a bandaged Alice and her two GDK accomplices. Alice looked angry and had gotten a decent amount of blood on her suit. She kicked out at one of the agents as they dragged her inside.

They formed an entourage of black suits, a limping Lane, two scared men, and an angry tin woman. The procession went across the hangar and into a large elevator that looked as if it could contain several loading vehicles. They began to descend.

"Aren't we going below sea level?" Lane asked.

"It's all asteroid. Whole facility is air- and watertight," an agent explained. Lane briefly tried to figure out which agent she was but was at a loss. They were all dressed the same, spoke the same way, and vaguely resembled one another. The Gateway Security agents did not differentiate on the outside.

"How did you manage to build this entire place with no one noticing? I can't believe we're under Fort Sumter," Lane said.

Alice tried to talk but immediately cried out in pain. Her hand went to her jaw, and she shot Lane a look that seemed to both contain a plea and a glare. The other agents ignored her.

The elevator came to a halt, and waiting to meet them was yet another agent dressed in black with a vaguely ominous black glove on either hand. Next to her was a tall woman in a white suit. She had bony cheeks and was wearing makeup. She seemed familiar to Lane. On each ear was a glittering black diamond. Lane recognized this as a rare kind found only on asteroids where little to no light reached them. It was one of the tokens of an accomplished space lawyer.

"Hello. Lane, I presume?" the agent said. "This is the CEO of Gateway, Incorporated. Her name is…" The CEO's hand shot up. "Ah, apologies. You understand a person who desires a little privacy, I'm sure."

Alice began to laugh, or what would have been laughter had she not once again grimaced in pain. Lane could only guess how much damage a direct punch from a power glove would do to a person's jaw.

"It's a pleasure to meet you. My counsel told me about you, and I've read a great deal of your metrics ever since. Security has been telling me about your unique, ah, capacities," the CEO said.

Lane looked around, confused, but he could not read anything from the blank expressions of the other agents.

"I don't know what that means," Lane said flatly.

"Oh, well, perhaps it would be better to show you," the CEO said. She gestured toward a huge monitor behind them, where Lane saw a map of Marion Square. There were hundreds of dots around it, with bits of text and photographs or video icons appearing over the top.

"That's your metric art, isn't it? Is this live?" Lane asked. The CEO tapped a few buttons on a very small pad she was wearing on her wrist. Lane had never seen a pad model like that before and couldn't tell what she was actually touching or how it worked. A video icon blinked and then expanded onto the screen. It was Morgan, holding a crying Dale still dressed as Dorothy though looking a little disheveled.

"It's just what the FTL will be like." Morgan said. "Someone totally outside the system putting an unvoted, unauthorized action out there. Dumping all those coins out and causing that mob. That's why you need to vote against Gateway and bring back miner's rights. They should be held accountable when these kinds of things happen!"

The video zoomed back out. A view tracker underneath it indicated it was already crossing into the hundreds of thousands. "Your capacity for getting the right people involved with the right things at the right time," the CEO explained.

"Oh, the nexus thing," Lane said. "My friend Tricia, the one who put together a lot of the data on this, she mentioned that too. I was sort of hoping to be the hero and save…something, but I guess it's nice to connect people."

"He already knows about the arrhythmia dispersal, but he calls it anticulture," one of the agents said.

"Impressive. I'm guessing your Gay Death Knight friends told you about it?" the CEO said. Lane nodded, and Alice grunted. "Yet you were going to knowingly set loose an enormous impact event of the stuff in the real world?"

"I was told it didn't work in the real world. I don't think I even knew you could describe it as "stuff". And anyways, that's all their doing," Lane said as he gestured at Alice. "Look, can someone please tell me what this is all about? With all due respect to the CEO here, what is it any of you want?"

The CEO looked around and then glanced down at her wrist pad. Several of the agents turned and busied themselves with various tasks in the facility, plugging their pads into the larger servers, sitting and checking information, or heading back toward the elevator.

"The point, Lane, is that the Infinity Drive is going to cause a Condorcet fault thanks to your little anticulture movement. Which means everyone in the culture grid is going to vote against it because the majority is voting against it," the CEO said.

"If you mean vote against you for killing a ship full of miners, yes, the aggregate is rapidly moving against you," Lane replied.

"I appreciate your insistence on short-term goals in this matter. But it is important to me that you understand this goes far beyond just a cash settlement in your client's favor. Your profile indicates you should be able to grasp this," the CEO said.

"Yeah," Lane said softly.

"The Condorect line will not just hard code against the Infinity Drive," the CEO said. "It will permanently destabilize the culture grid.

The anticulture is already breaking apart the barriers and balances between everyone's realities. Respect for other people's worldview is completely degrading. Eventually culture diversity is going to plummet and the larger cultures will start absorbing the smaller ones. And then it's going to get violent when the big ones start to clash. This is the first physical assault a Gateway Security has performed in the line of duty in years." To indicate her point, she brought out a feed that began to list off disruptions on a global level. Everything from protesting marches to bitter forum arguments was on the rise.

"So what?" Lane said. "The biggest breakthrough in space travel was announced by the biggest disaster in space travel. People are upset."

"I'm inclined to agree with you, Lane," the CEO said. "We have not, as a civilization, had a technological breakthrough in a very long time. The pads everyone uses and takes to work are similar to the ones people were using centuries ago. This particular breakthrough will render obsolete millions of jobs and leave the majority of the male population in space unemployed. Most of them maintain one or two realities at best. Where do you think those men are going to go if the market does not expand to create new jobs?"

"Everyone is aware, everyone participates," an agent added. "That's how the culture grid works. The system can't sustain that large of a single male reality coming back to the Standards on Earth. The anticulture has done too much damage to handle it. The system will deteriorate into a monoculture. Everything will be jeopardized."

"So what happened in *Tyrant's* economy is going to happen in real life?" Alice croaked. Her hand was gripping her jaw, and she grimaced when she finished speaking.

"Actually the outcome of the mod in *Tyrant* was considered optimal by our metrics," the CEO said. "Unrealistic since there are only a few hundred realities operating in that space, but still optimal. Wealth concentrations are unfavorably high, but we have not yet projected an outcome where that doesn't occur. It's just not possible with this much change."

Alice made an attempt at a grin, but her teeth were still red. The effect was disturbing.

"Our primary goal was just to make the introduction of the technology go as smoothly and comport with people's worldviews as much as possible. It would not be an earthshaking event, and instead impact them little more than another piece of software. Thus our meme campaign. Unfortunately we did not factor in the possibility of the *Black Swan*. Even after it happened, we did not factor in your being be able to make this much progress with your counter-campaign. Which has resulted in a massive exposure of anticulture into the entire grid right when our boys are coming home," the CEO said.

"If it has already happened, then what do you need me for? Or her?" Lane said as he gestured at Alice.

She was tugging at the wires on her jaw and grimacing through the pain.

"Because as we said back in the car, reality absorbs everything. And with your help, it will absorb this."

CHAPTER 52

It did not take long before the CEO, the agents, and Alice with a freshly wired jaw and a dose of painkillers began planning a way to stop the spread of anticulture and work out a way to integrate the event into the existing culture grid. Lane quickly felt left out of their camaraderie as a set of alliances formed and shifted between the women.

"I had no idea how much of a problem this whole thing would be. In *Tyrant* they just retcon the game when things mess up. I would have never taken these sorts of risks if I had known," Alice insisted.

"I understand completely," the CEO said. "There is so much going on in this case that we didn't realize what was happening until that man, Weber I think it is, announced his next bold plan for taking us down. Insufferable idiot. There are thousands of metrics to track, and your group did such an amazing job of staying off grid that we never caught it. We were following the Tyrant around and Lane's data expert instead of the real parties involved."

Alice mustered what looked like a smile but still looked ghastly with the wiring on her jaw.

"Wait, that was you following them around? But what about the rape arrest? What about the guy outside my office?" Lane asked.

"Oh that was us Lane," Alice said. "And I know what you mean about tracking all this. It has not been easy leading the GDK, but they have really come around. Especially when you realize how many of them are men."

Lane raised an eyebrow at her, thinking of the slut shaming fiasco, and debated mentioning the fact that Derrick had been the one to turn the GDK into the organization they were today.

"Yes, you are very remarkable with that demographic," the CEO said. "Which brings me to the issue of what sort of groundwork we can start doing to assimilate the Infinity Drive into cultures that dislike us. Gateway, capitalism, the drive, all of it. How are we going to get people who hate these things to accept it?"

"As the only man here, I think I might have some insight on this issue," Lane said.

Alice shot him a look, but the CEO turned and nodded to him.

"It's about certainty," Lane said. "Not the actual existence of it, but just the idea. People are threatened by the FTL—or I guess we have to start calling it the Infinity Drive now—but people are only upset by it because they don't know how it will affect them. It's just they don't want to admit it. That's the conundrum: they want to stay here on Earth with their Standards and virtual lives, but they don't want to admit it. They still know progress is a good thing."

"People would prefer playing video games and living on Standards as opposed to the hope of a better future?" the CEO asked.

"Excuse me, but I think you are outside your reality spectrum," Alice said.

Lane wondered if the alliances had again shifted between the two women. The CEO's expression did not change, and she gave a warm smile.

"My apologies, I was not thinking. In space we are very blunt about our belief in work ethics and the value of good labor," the CEO said. "Please, Lane, continue."

"All you need to do is make not going into space seem appealing. Make it so they don't have to confront the realities of it, make it someone else's problem. We need to make them comfortable with it," Lane said.

"The frame is solid to me. You think men will agree with this?" the agent asked.

Lane shrugged. Alice nodded.

"All right, we have a frame. Now for the real problem: What shall be the message?" the CEO asked.

Alice jumped in before Lane could say anything. "I'll start talking with the GDK about it immediately. We're just a little preoccupied at the moment with some business in *Tyrant*." She made another attempt at a wired smile.

"I would talk to Morgan. He's the one who put together the *Wizard of Oz* event, and that seems to have gone over well," Lane said. "I can send him a message if you like."

"Please," the CEO said.

Lane pulled out his pad and typed a hasty message to Eve asking her how things were going. He typed another one to Morgan, telling him to wrap things up and be ready for another project.

The agent tapped her glove and slid her finger in a strange motion. "Why don't we just have him brought here?" she said.

"All right, I'll just ping him with the event," Lane said wearily. He was suddenly tired, and his leg was beginning to ache. "If you'll excuse me, this has all been a lot."

Everyone nodded, and Alice began talking about her ideas for a rainbow meme hitting spaceships as they landed on new planets.

Lane brought up Eve's profile again and sent her another message. He brought up the *Tyrant* newsfeeds, but there was not much information there. It took Lane a moment before he realized nobody would have time for reading or typing if there really was a huge battle going on. He glanced at Alice. She was nodding her head as the CEO and agents talked. He checked the video options for *Tyrant* and saw there was one with thousands of viewers.

He opened the link. The screen slowed for a moment under the weight of how much information it was processing and then picked back up. On his pad there were thousands of ships, firing weapons and blinking around the battlefield. Scattered around were wrecked ships, bits of debris and fire floating in waves, the signification of incalculable amounts of violence diluted into a virtual field of zero consequences. It was beautiful.

Lane brought up a list of ships in the area and immediately zoomed in on *Sojourner Truth*. It was still firing the weapons that functioned, but the ship was starting to roll badly. The GDK fighters were relentless in their chipping away at the enormous ship. A few weak shots, blink, the FTL kicking back in, and then another volley of shots. Lane realized they must have been at this for hours.

A ping on his pad from Eve said, "Don't think they would take my surrender at this point."

Lane typed a message telling her he was watching the live feed, wishing he could be there with her at that moment. Everything he had known about Eve had been wrapped up in being Tyrant. Every purpose she had shared with him and every task she had asked was related to this world. And her place in it was dying. *Sojourner Truth* shuddered as an enormous missile crashed into her hull, the shockwaves rippling out and incinerating a few GDK fighters that were too close. The weapon systems went down completely.

Lane sent a voice call to Eve's pad. It rang a few times with no response. Lane held his breath, but Eve answered finally.

She didn't say anything at first. He could hear her breathing, ragged and just on the brink of sobs, which Lane gave their space before speaking.

"Looks like you have had a long day," he said.

Eve sobbed and let out a long sniffling sigh. "It's the FTL attack they're using. I can't organize into a defensive position or get my guns to bear before they've already moved around. They tried it with bigger ships at first, but *Sojourner Truth* is equipped for that. I should have built her to fight smaller ships. Now look at her, getting chipped apart by these idiots in fighters and cruisers. Oh…Lane, just look at what a mess they have made of her."

"Eve, I'm so sorry. You going to let them board her? She's the most powerful ship in *Tyrant*."

"Oh, you knew? I could never tell how much you learned about my world," Eve said. She sounded distant now, the tenses to talk about her life in *Tyrant* were shifting between past and present.

"Things are wrapping up, I think. I'm talking to the CEO of Gateway and some other folks about getting this case settled. All of it, virtual and real."

"Oh, that's wonderful. Glad at least one of us is going to have a job," Eve said.

"The ship, Eve. They are going to take it soon," Lane said.

Almost in reply, a dizzying red-and-blue explosion erupted from *Sojourner Truth*. It expanded out of the video feed and consumed almost the entire sector in an inferno of plasma and digital death. When the wave passed, every ship in the area had been destroyed.

"No, they are not," Eve said. She took another long breath, and Lane heard her hold back a sob. "Hey, I'm going to wrap up some loose ends. Let's get together later, OK?" Eve said.

"I'd like that," Lane said.

She turned the voice chat off.

An agent had walked up behind him unnoticed. She extended a pad out with a list of terms for discussion. "We are about at a point where you can start contacting your client and the other lawyers at McAngus. It would help us if you could be…persuasive in the importance of resolving this dispute beyond the financial concerns," she said.

"We have strict orders to not settle the case," Lane asked as he checked the list. "It would be a lot easier to persuade them if I had something to offer."

"We are still willing to offer a massive settlement in this matter," the agent said.

CHAPTER 53

"Stop. Go back. No, no, too far, forward just a little bit. OK, freeze," Morgan said. He was barking orders from behind Lane, who was controlling the stream of images appearing on a large monitor in front of them. Morgan had been brought to Fort Sumter in a matter of minutes after Lane's suggestion. During that time Lane had been trying to get Koff and Weber on the voice chat but with little luck. Weber was on space time and probably asleep; Koff just didn't answer her pad sometimes.

On the screen was a short green man with large black eyes and pointy teeth. Lane had no idea what it was or what it even meant.

"It's certainly alien. Primal, I guess. Am I supposed to be scared of it? Aroused?" Lane said, referring to the green man.

"I'm not sure about the sex thing," Morgan said. "To me it's just different. Like I should probably be bashing its head in with a rock. It's all the things I don't want to be or see in someone else. Short, tiny teeth like an animal, those big eyes, and that green skin make it look sick. I've seen similar stuff, but I am not sure where. Threatening yet human too. Can you identify the origins?"

Lane double-tapped on the image. It was the cover of an ancient book that had been scanned into the image archives. Variations appeared over the decades before the potential heuristic space of the image gave out. It was absorbed into other graphics, the traits it took on having different meanings and foreign cultural contexts.

"I find it fairly disturbing as well," the CEO said. Both men turned and looked at her. "What do you propose we repurpose it as?"

"When we searched the culture grid for Infinity Drive, we got a lot of hits," Lane said. "So, if I understand this correctly, that means people have already culturally absorbed it. Since mining has already been around for a while, the only other thing that wouldn't be fully absorbed into the grid would be moving to another planet."

"But you would have unlimited potential. New lands, resources, even the possibility of discovering new civilizations. There's no real limit," the CEO said.

"Yeah, we need to start producing some horror movies about that," Morgan said. "Anyways, what our little friend here is going to do is be our new mascot for moving to another planet."

"So, for example, Tau Ceti Four is the closest habitable planet for our species," Lane said. "So what we do is announce there are all sorts of gravity problems and gas issues, maybe a virus or the air isn't breathable, and we have to create these new genetically modified people to inhabit it for us. If people want to modify themselves or their kids, there may be procedures available at a future date. Then we flash this image up there as a computer projection of what it might look like. We'll have some movies, a few pop albums, maybe some video games about trying to survive on a planet as one of them. Make it really unpleasant."

"And lots of dying. And monsters eating them," Morgan said.

"You'll forgive me if I am still struggling with the concept, but are you saying we have to create an underclass of people who will be sent to foreign planets? Instead of us?" the CEO asked.

"Yes, a new manhood, maybe. Completely repurpose the concept," Morgan said. "That phrase alone will make it light up the culture grids. The more I look at the thing, the more it bothers me. If that's what progress is going to look like, you can count me out."

"I see. And you think that will get people to accept the Infinity Drive?" the CEO said.

"Technically, I think we're trying to get them to be okay with it. Not excited or upset, but just to develop a healthy amount of disinterest for a while. Maybe a very long while," Lane said.

"You must do quite well as a space lawyer at McAngus," the CEO said.

"Ah, actually I'm not a licensed space lawyer. Still an apprentice," Lane said sheepishly. He knew she had to know that already. The pretended lack of knowledge was a courtesy.

"Interesting. Have you had any luck reaching your boss or client?" the CEO asked.

Lane shook his head and stood up to try again. He decided to try video chat this time. There was still no answer from Koff. He tried Weber and got an answer after a few chimes.

"All right, all right. I saw your message. What is it?" Weber snapped. He inhaled deeply from the oxygen tank and glared at Lane.

"It's about the lawsuit," Lane said. "I think I've found a way to settle it. I can get you your damages fully compensated in exchange for some agreements about broadcasting. Some nondisclosures, full compliance with a new PR campaign, and some other minor things."

Weber looked at Lane as if he were speaking a foreign language. "Settle? Why would I want to settle? That damn FTL is going to put me and every miner out of business, you idiot. The whole point was to get that law hard coded! Buy us all some time to bury Gateway in so many lawsuits they'll never want to test the technology again. This isn't just about my ship anymore, son. It's about the shipyards that manufacture the freighters. The training academies. The millions of men working those mining ships and all those orbital platforms. What are they supposed to do? I thought you had the makings of a space lawyer, but now I don't know. You can't even comprehend something so, so basic as…" Weber's rant came to a halt as another spasm of coughing racked his body.

Lane's own face had hardened into something blank, expressionless. He looked around the room while he waited for Weber to regain his composure. Morgan was working the pad to check for other possible images. The CEO was talking to an agent. Alice was over in a corner, typing into her pad.

"And another thing, what are you even doing talking to Gateway like this?" Weber shouted. "How much did you tell them about our case? Some damn woman threatens you with a power glove, and suddenly you're spilling the Standards to settle the most important lawsuit you will ever see in your idiotic career. Wait, *were* seeing. You are officially off this case. Where is Koff? I want Koff now, damnit!"

Lane's eyes glanced at the disconnect button. "I'll let her know your views on the matter," he said.

Weber was about to launch into another tirade when Lane ended the conversation. He sighed and wondered briefly how he could manage to have mixed feelings about even this. He felt dread at what he would say to Koff. And fear. And anger. With women he had always felt the urge to shout back or resist in some way. Listening to the old man talk, Lane had simply wanted to turn it off.

"It did not go well?" the CEO asked.

"He does not have a very good grasp of realities beyond his own," Lane said flatly. His pad emitted a ping. He didn't have to look to know it was Koff. He wasn't even sure why he wanted to be a space lawyer anymore if it meant ending up like Weber. There had to be a way for Lane to make space lawyer have a new meaning.

"Not quite the mentality we need right now," the CEO said. "Do you have any ideas?"

"Maybe. Weber has decided that in his reality, I am not much of a space lawyer, which in my reality means I am very likely out of a job right now, which is making it hard to think," Lane said.

"I'll make you a space lawyer today, assuming you can resolve this," the CEO said. Lane smiled and began walking toward Morgan. "Why? What are you planning?"

"I'm wondering if there might be a way to short circuit their case," Lane said. He picked up a pad and began tapping into the screen. "Can this Gateway Security access find a person who's off grid?"

An agent nodded, and Lane punched in a few more keys.

Morgan continued to make tiny adjustments to the green man. A compression of the shoulder bones and a widening of the hips to obscure the gender. He made the eyes softer, much softer, and the blackness luminous. The sharp teeth remained, but he removed the claws from the ends . A final few touches gave one the impression of a child more than a monster.

"Broadening it out for women's realities?" the CEO asked.

"I figure making it into a little monster might be a bit much. Now it just looks pitiful," Morgan explained.

"Found her!" Lane said excitedly. "The mod owner. She really was in Montana. She was completely off grid, but all the information she was dumping still kept a marker on a few of the people she ran into."

"The evidence link?" the CEO asked. "You think if you can get the mod owner to release the appeal, there won't be any plausible connection between Gateway and the accident being willful?"

"There never really was much of a plausible connection," Lane said. "We just put so many crazy conspiracy theories out there that eventually some of them had to stick. This will just give us some fodder for showing Weber is just trying to make a buck off a tragedy." He was staring at the pad, searching for something different now.

"It really was an accident, you know," the CEO said.

Lane looked at her, and for the first time felt a raw determination, rendered real by its tantalizing closeness.

"You really can make me a space lawyer, right? Not sitting around an office somewhere but actually out in space?" Lane asked.

The CEO nodded. "Sure. Space lawyer can mean whatever you want it to mean. You can work for me, or I can simply arrange for your free market license. Our work with the Infinity Drive is just beginning. New ports are already being constructed. The decommission of the space gates and the production of new ships is underway. Thousands of jobs have been rendered obsolete, and a thousand more must be created in their wake. The technicalities, the details, the world building will be immense. Your work here has been excellent, but if you work for me, it is only just getting started."

"I've never had a female boss compliment me before. It's nice," Lane said.

"I appreciate your need for purpose and validation." the CEO said.

"Thanks. Can you pay for my ticket out to Montana?" Lane asked.

CHAPTER 54

The elk pranced nervously from tree to tree, its head swishing this way and that to test the air. It eyed the patch of huckleberries hungrily but held back. A drift of snow fell onto its eyes and made the creature blink. The wind shifted and gave it a scent of the hill that it could not quite see. Or what could be hiding there.

Tally once again found herself questioning the wisdom of refusing to use electronics. She could attach a pad to her rifle sight, calculate the range, synchronize her GPS position with the elk, and not even bother to aim anymore. The pad would just tell her when to shoot. But then it wouldn't be her shot, she reminded herself, and tried to force her breath to lessen even more. The animal was getting suspicious that it was being watched.

A few tentative steps toward the huckleberries, a glance back toward the hill with that smelly bush, a few steps closer. It was so hungry. Off in the distance, there was the faintest sound of snow scraping and grinding. As it grew the louder, the elk froze, looked, and ran. It did not understand what was coming, but it knew that strange things almost inevitably meant danger.

Tally stared as the elk turned and ran, wondering what she had done wrong this time and what she could have done differently. She was hungry for meat, and it had once again run away. Then she heard it too and immediately recognized the sound of a snowmobile. Cursing, she rose and saw the red machine and its rider still some distance away. They were heading directly toward her.

Being dressed in camouflage, carrying no electronic devices, and spending the past two months in total isolation skirting the border between Montana and the Western Alliance, Tally panicked that someone had still been able to find her. She was totally alone. She had no way to call for help. She gripped the rifle and crawled up the large rock she had been sitting next to. As the snowmobile drew closer, fear turned to anger. By the time the rider arrived, Tally found herself furious.

"How far does a person have to go before they can finally be left alone?" she shouted.

The rider got off the snowmobile and rubbed his arms rapidly. She could not make out a face or gender; the person was covered in snow masks and gear to protect against the cold.

"S-s-sorry," a distinctly male voice said.

Tally gripped the rifle a little tighter. The last man she had run into had also not seen another human being in a long time. He had had some nasty ideas about what two people alone in Montana ought to be doing. He'd apologized too, but that was after Tally had clipped him with a bullet.

"How did you find me?" she asked.

The man recovered and reached over to the snowmobile. He held up a pad so Tally could see, and she could make out some sort of tracking program. He had apparently been following her trail with it.

"You didn't follow me all the way from Charleston with that thing," she said.

He laughed and stomped his feet a few times to get the blood flowing. "Gateway sent me. I'm a space lawyer. Remember *Tyrant*? Your mod has caused…well, I guess it didn't cause anything. In the game it did, but you see, with the Infinity Drive event that's causing a lot of overlap in the culture grid. The anticulture levels are getting out of control, and Gateway is defusing the situation by paying off the opposing side. They were anyways; the miners are trying to bide time in the free market." The man sucked in an enormous breath after the long speech. He was definitely not from here; the elevation was making him winded and confusing.

"Gateway promised me I'd be left alone if I stopped interfering with the meme," Tally said. She loosened her grip on the rifle. Men with bad intentions did not talk very much. They mostly asked questions.

"You really have been totally off grid, haven't you? No news, no reality checks, nothing real?" the man said.

"You just scared off my dinner. That's pretty real," Tally said irritably. "I haven't had protein in a while, and I'm tired of eating oatmeal. Winter is here, and I'm starting to realize maybe I should have planned this out better."

The man reached into a pack attached to the snowmobile. After some rummaging, he pulled out a package of jerky and tossed it to Tally. She caught it with one hand and stared at it. She sighed, tore it open with her teeth, and began to chew on a chunk. It was elk meat.

"Your mod for *Tyrant* is causing my boss some trouble. It would mean a lot to us if you would sign off on an agreement, authenticated with an eye scan, thumb print, and voice recording, disavowing any connection between Gateway, Incorporated and the FTL," the man explained.

Tally chewed and considered the request. The man didn't seem to know that she hadn't just made the mod for *Tyrant*, she had made the technology itself. It had been her idea to introduce it to the game as a test run and her parting revenge to tie Gateway to it with an AI appeal. And now, somehow, they had found her.

"Gateway is not a part of my reality anymore," Tally said.

"Then it won't be a problem to say specifically that it was not Gateway behind the mod," the man said.

"A lie?" Tally asked.

"Been a while since I heard that. Consider it a difference in perspective," the man said. He pressed a few keys on the pad. "It is not really being asserted for the truth of the matter anyways. It is mostly about creating another perspective that people will be more comfortable with as…other issues develop."

"That's the nice thing about being out here. Something can be true again. Or a lie," Tally said.

"I can arrange for you to have all the meat you could ever want. Or a mansion, any sort you want and anywhere you want. Guns, clothes, food, whatever. Money even, if that's your thing," he replied.

Tally stood up and pocketed the packet of jerky. She glanced back toward where the elk had gone and wondered if the huckleberry bush would be a good lure for something larger. A bear, perhaps, or maybe a herd of goats. She thought about the man's offer for a while. It would be nice to have unlimited credit. Maybe indulge in a scope for her rifle. A better jacket or a nice thermal unit for her campsite. Why even keep it a campsite? She could demand a cabin appear wherever she liked.

Yet she knew it would just start tumbling back into the old ways. She'd keep wanting things, and every one of those needs would be met. She could already have them met now, but from the sound of it, the man was proposing there would be even more. Less time spent getting things, less energy spent preparing things, until she would never have any reason to even leave her great big Montana mansion. And inevitably, she would turn back to people. And that was something Tally never wanted to do again.

"Can you make it so no one can ever find me again?" Tally asked.

"Probably. It was not easy this time, if that makes you feel any better," the man said.

"See if you can make it a little harder. I'll take the rest of your jerky and a promise that you'll get out of here as soon as it's done," she said.

The man nodded and extended the pad to her. First she pressed her thumb onto a long, typed-out statement that she did not care to read. The feel of the electronics was familiar and strange at the same time. She suddenly wanted to ask him what was going on, what people were talking about these days, and who had won the Roller Derby Nationals?

Next he held up the pad, and it scanned her eye. She blinked as the beam pierced her cornea, a pinprick of the senses that had no pain and left no mark. She would not have even dwelled on it if she didn't find herself again wondering what the statement was confirming. But she dreaded the endless waves of nonsense that would come with it. The space of information, the heuristic debates, and the ceaseless echoing of every action into reaction and reflection. Until finally there was nothing left to do but admit there were realities other than yours, contradicting every decision and action infinitely.

"Do you want to read the statement aloud?" the man asked.

"No, I'll just confirm it," she replied. She spoke her name and said the time and date, reading them from the pad, and then claimed that she had just done a retinal scan and thumbprint. Everything in the statement was true. He pulled the pad away and tucked it into his jacket.

"Sure you don't want anything? The place I rented this from said they remembered you coming through town occasionally. Why don't I just set up a line of credit there? In case of emergencies at least," he asked.

She sighed and looked back toward the Elk. There was a lot of risk in going after it. She might not be able to get back to her campsite. Even if she killed it, getting the meat back would mean dragging it by sled. She might get sick, or she might run out of food. She had made arrangements for supplies, but she didn't know how long it would last.

"All right," she said faintly. "Just a line of credit."

SUGGESTED READING

Somethingawful.com
Fark.com
Reddit.com
Neogaf.com
Facebook.com
EVE Online
Infotopia by Cass R. Sunstein
Playing by the Rules by Frederick Schauer
Legal Language by Peter M. Tiersma
Play Money by Julian Dibbell
The Poetics of Space by Gaston Bachelard
Experiencing Architecture by Steen Eiler Rasmussen
The Black Swan by Nassim Nicholas Taleb
The Complete Essential Zizek by Slavoj Zizek
How to Read Lacan by Slavoj Zizek
Play Between Worlds by T.L. Taylor
Architecture and Disjunction by Bernard Tschumi
The End of Men: And the Rise of Women by Hanna Rosin
Synthetic Worlds by Edward Castranova
Newsgames by Ian Bogost, Simon Ferari, and Bobby Schweizer
Procedural Rhetoric by Ian Bogost
How to Do Things with Video Games by Ian Bogost
Parchment, Paper, Pixels by Peter Tiersma
I is an Other by James Geary

The Information: A History, A Theroy, A Flood by James Gleick
Decoding Advertisements by Judith Williamson
Thinking in Systems by Donella H. Meadows
Basic Economics by Thomas Sowell
Virtual Justice: The New Law of Online Worlds by Greg Lastowka
Complexity Management Theory by Peterson JB, Flanders JL (SSRN paper)
Legal Complexity: Some Causes, Consequences, and Cures by Peter H. Schuck (SSRN paper)

Made in the USA
Middletown, DE
26 May 2018